THORUNN

ESTHER T. JONES

STARREN ISLE
PRESS

THORUNN

Published in the United States by Starren Isle Press
www.starrenislepress.com

The author's official website is:
www.etjwrites.com

ISBN-13: 978-1-7331506-1-3
ISBN-10: 1-7331506-1-3

PRINTED IN THE UNITED STATES OF AMERICA

THREAT RISING

Bo came up on Kenton's left, shifted back, fangs bared. "You've gone whiter than normal. I take it the humans aren't here to hold hands and sing with us?"

"They killed a hinnom tree. Just like that. When they could have tapped the one right next to it."

Bo handed Kenton's quirn back to him. "This is the part where you tell me they didn't know any better and we should give them another chance?" His furiously lashing tail told Kenton what he thought of that opinion.

"No. They plan to ravage the forest. They plan to murder us all."

Also by Esther T. Jones:

Tedenbarr of Have Lath

A young man struggling to get home, a brewing
civil war threatening to tear a kingdom apart . . .

"Quite the adventure, filled with . . . action . . . danger, and
laughs." —*Authors LT Anderson*

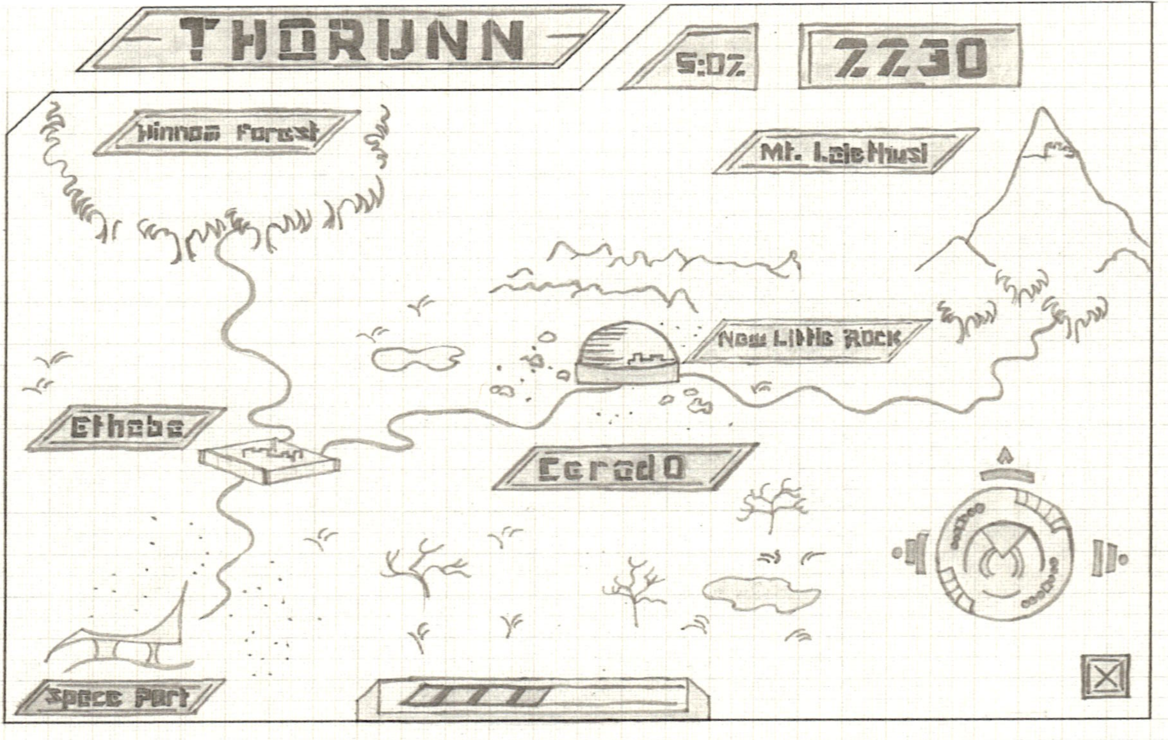

THORUNN
5:02
2230
Winnom Forest
Mt. Leie Nhusl
New Little Rock
Ethebe
Ceredo
Space Port

THORUNN

It began as it always did, in the middle of the night.

Kenton jerked awake at the screams that came from outside and shaded his eyes against the flashes of light filtering through the shuttered windows.

"Ken?" a sleep-soft voice called. "Are the bad men here again?"

Kenton nodded and slipped out of bed, glancing towards the bedroom his parents shared. A light was on, visible through the curtains hanging across the doorway, but he didn't see shadows moving or hear their voices.

"Come," he whispered, taking his sister's hand. "Let's get to the cellar."

Annie padded quietly alongside her older brother to the kitchen, where the siblings opened the larder and lifted boxes to reveal a well-worn trapdoor.

"In you go." Kenton handed Annie a solar-powered emergency light once she reached the bottom of the ladder. He slipped in after her, using a rope attached under the boxes to pull them back over the trapdoor once it fell shut. "Can I have the lamp?"

Annie passed it to Kenton's waiting hands. A click sounded, and light filled the tiny room.

Kenton coughed. He hoped they wouldn't have to

stay down here too long. He missed his bed and stuffed animals already. The cellar wasn't really more than a hole in the ground that fit four people and some boxes of food. The solar lamp provided some light, but there was little ventilation, and Kenton's parents had been adamant about the dangers of staying in the cramped space for too long without them.

Tonight, only Kenton and Annie had squeezed themselves into the musty cellar. Umama and Pa hadn't come down yet, and Kenton wondered if they were trying to talk to the soldiers again, pleading with them to see reason. Speaking with them had worked so far, but Kenton didn't understand why the soldiers kept coming and hurting them—hurting the whole town of Ethaba—when the only thing they'd done was befriend the forest people, but Pa had said that sometimes the only right way is the hard way, and the hard way doesn't pay much, and refused to speak more on the matter.

Kenton shivered and hugged Annie closer. They dared not speak, lest their voices carry above. After the lamp started to dim, Kenton switched it off to save power, and they sat in the darkness, waiting for their parents to come and get them.

They waited so long that Annie fell asleep, drool collecting on Kenton's shoulder. He drifted off as well, awakening later to find his arm trapped under Annie's. Manoeuvring around her was awkward, but Kenton managed and flicked on the solar lamp to check the time.

Five hours had passed—almost the whole night!

Umama and Pa had never taken so long to fetch them before. Kenton shook Annie awake.

"It's daytime now. Keep hiding while I look for Umama and Pa, okay?"

Annie nodded, words lost in a wide yawn. Kenton wrapped their blankets more snugly around her and tugged on the rope to move the boxes atop the trap-door so he could scramble out.

Upstairs was quiet. Too quiet, and a bad tingling began to churn in Kenton's tummy. Early morning sunlight filtered in from the still-shuttered windows, and he frowned. Usually they'd been thrown open already. If only the clasps weren't so high he could have unlatched them himself, but he had to let them be, moving on into the sitting room, which had his and Annie's beds tucked in the corner.

Mister Lion still sat on his pillow, and Kenton gave him a brief hug. Mister Lion surely was scared after hearing the solfire and yelling all night. Kenton clutched the worn softie to his chest and pushed aside the curtains leading to Umama and Pa's room.

He called for them, jumping onto the bed when they didn't answer. But his now taller vantage point offered no further clues to their whereabouts. Kenton ran back to the kitchen and ducked into the short cor-ridor leading to the front. He hadn't noticed before, intent on finding his parents, but the door was ajar, creaking as the breeze turned it this way and that. He crept to the opening and peered out.

He couldn't really be seeing what he was seeing.

Maybe he was still asleep with Annie down in the

cellar, or else he'd accidentally started watching a grown-up movie on Pa's clip. But no dream could be so realistic, no film could truly capture the awful details of the bodies that lined the rubble-strewn streets, some still smoking where solfire had sliced them through, all lying in puddles of blood and other things too foul for Kenton to put a proper name to.

Like their own, some houses were untouched, but most had disappeared as if they'd never been, torched completely to the ground. Chickens and baby anlo wandered the smoke-wreathed town, followed closely behind by scaly scavenger skreets. Grown-ups and large anlo lay in scattered pieces surrounded by hordes of buzzing flies.

Kenton took one disbelieving step after another, hardly aware of his feet moving him forward with a leaden numbness, or of Mister Lion slipping through his fingers, and before he quite knew it, he stood in the middle of the street, barely registering the stench that rose from the bloated carcasses. A flash of light caught his attention, and he gasped. Umama's necklace lay broken in the muck. She would be so upset to see the pearls Pa had saved for, trodden so carelessly into the ground.

Kenton dug around to gather up the pieces, but the string was broken, and they slipped between his little fingers over and over again. A few of the pearls made their way into his nightclothes' pocket, but still more rolled away down the road, and he chased them without thought, stopping short when a shadow crossed his path.

The morning sun shone bright in his eyes, and when his vision cleared, Kenton found himself staring at a regiment of well-equipped, grimacing soldiers. Their leader bent down, reaching with a blood-stained glove for the pearl in front of Kenton.

"You can't have that!" Kenton said. "That's Umama's."

The man picked up the grimy sphere anyway and wiped off the filth onto Kenton's shirt.

"A real, genuine pearl—is that right? Where'd a poor farmer like your mother get something like that?"

"Pa gave 'em to her." Kenton's voice shook no matter how hard he tried not to cry. He fisted the others still in his pocket, and the soldier's expression turned greedy.

"Actually, they belong to the Hexagon now."

"No. These are Umama's. You can't have them."

The soldier laughed, a nasty, frightening sound. Kenton backed away as the man leaned down again.

"I can, seeing as she doesn't want them anymore."

"Liar! These are her favourite." She never took them off. Not ever. They looked so pretty with whatever dress she wore, and Pa always grinned his biggest when she touched a hand to them whenever she laughed.

"Traitors don't get to have favourites. 'Specially not dead ones."

"Liar!" Kenton repeated. They weren't traitors, they simply weren't.

Yes, maybe some people in Ethaba didn't like that

Pa was friendly with the leopard-like forest people, but being friends with someone wasn't a crime. Pa and Umama had sat him and Annie down just the other day and explained that it was very important—in fact the most important—to make friends with people that appeared different from them. Kenton guessed the soldiers hadn't been taught that by their umamas and pas. In any event, he wouldn't let them have Umama's favourite jewellery—she'd need it when she returned from wherever she'd gone.

Kenton took off down the street, running home as fast as he could, heedless of the solfire zipping past his head and leaving smoking holes in the walls he dashed past. He slammed the front door shut when he made it inside, fumbling with the locks and jumping in fright at the small tap to his shoulder.

"Oh, Annie," he gasped, "it's only you. Run back to the cellar. I'll be right there."

But when he turned around, those lying soldiers stood in his house, some in the kitchen, others spilling out into the corridor, all poking around, pocketing whatever they pleased.

"Get out! Get out of my house!" Kenton screamed. They ignored him, not concerned with two children barely knee-high.

Smooth silicone touched his palm, and he turned round eyes on Annie. Where had she found Pa's sol? Kenton brandished the weapon at the soldiers. Maybe now they'd take him seriously.

"I said get out!" Tears blurred his eyes, and he

wished with all his heart that Umama and Pa would step into the kitchen and make the rude, loud thugs leave them alone.

"Trying to be a hero?" The same soldier who'd eyed the pearls with such interest outside plucked the sol from Kenton's hands before he could react. "Guess someone has to, since dearest mommy and daddy are too dead to bother with such nonsense any longer."

Kenton began crying in earnest as Annie's sweet, small voice asked, "What's dead?"

"Glad you asked, child. Since your brother doesn't seem to grasp the concept, how would you like to give him a demonstration?"

"No!"

But it was too late.

The soldier ripped Annie from Kenton's arms and pressed the end of his sol against her temple. A brilliant flash lit the room, and between one heartbeat and the non-existent next, Annie's limp body fell to the floor. Kenton started to scream and scream and scream.

The soldier sneered.

"Shut him up."

The next instant Kenton's head exploded with blinding pain, and he flopped to the ground alongside Annie, giant black boots the last image he saw, the swift crunch of them against the blood-spattered floor the last thing he heard.

2

———— ● ————

Finally, Laine was off that stupid spaceship. The long flight was over, and he could begin his new life. Though how "new" and "his" it was, was up for debate, seeing as it hadn't been his bright idea to abandon Earth. But he was on Thorunn now, and his first priority? Grabbing snacks. Laine slung his travel bag over his shoulder and headed for the spaceport's vending machines.

"Laine Alexander Riven!"

Yeah. He probably should've stuck around to give Mom and Dad a hand with their things. Maybe if they hadn't forced him on this trip he'd be a little more eager to assist them. He snagged a chocolate bar and dragged himself back to his parents.

"Give that here, and go help your mother with the luggage."

Laine looked his dad in the eyes and deliberately unwrapped the bar before popping the whole thing in his mouth. Dad's jaw tightened.

"Laine, so help me—" he began, but stopped when Mom laid a hand on his arm, her long black hair tumbling free from the loose bun she'd pinned it into for the last leg of the voyage.

"Jack, darling, Gordon awaits us. We need to meet him and arrange for the rest of our things to be shipped to the house. Laine will keep 'til we reach his place."

Dad calmed immediately. "Yes, of course, dear." He patted her hand before turning back to Laine. "Don't think that because we aren't on Earth anymore you can still give me attitude. You're not eighteen yet, and this planet is too dangerous for you to chance it on your own. Am I clear?"

"As ice," Laine muttered. Of course he wasn't so stupid as to run away. If that hadn't worked on Earth, it definitely wouldn't work on Thorunn. He wasn't keen on being dragged back home by bounty hunters who cared little if all his limbs were still attached when they dumped him on his parents' doorstep. He readjusted the straps of his bag and followed sullenly after Mom and Dad to meet Gordon outside the spaceport.

Stepping into the bright sunlight was an adjustment. The spaceport had grav controls to compensate for Thorunn's slightly increased gravity, but they extended no further than the doors. Mom wilted under the sudden pressure, and Dad rushed to steady her, not faring much better himself. Laine kept his feet just barely as they made their way over to the man projecting the "Riven Family" sign from his clip and squinted hard at the unfamiliar, empty scrubland shimmering with heat-induced mirages.

"Laine," Gordon said by way of acknowledgement. He was about Dad's height, strapped into a thick riding jacket, a sol holstered at his side, his helmet tucked under one arm.

"Uncle." Laine hadn't seen him since Gordon had left for Thorunn—when Laine was just starting grade school—but from the little he remembered, he hadn't changed much, still sporting dark scruff in contrast to Dad's smooth-shaven appearance. They could have been twins otherwise. "Or Gordon if you'd prefer—I'm not picky. It's been a long time, but if you're cool with not getting in my face about rules and stuff, we'll get along fine."

Laine extended his hand, but Gordon ignored him, turning to Mom and Dad instead.

"I see what you mean about his cheek. Couple months here should clear that right up." Gordon chuckled and took Mom's bags, motioning for them to follow him. "Though I can't help wondering why y'didn't leave him on Earth 'til he straightened himself out."

Laine scowled. Leaving him behind would have been the kindest thing his parents could have done. He'd certainly fought with them enough about it. Maybe spent a night or two in the space shuttle's engine room when he couldn't stand Dad yelling at him any longer. As amazing as Thorunn was touted to be, it was still the place where the Apollo XXII colony had disappeared without a trace, a place where he had no friends, no network to get whatever he wanted at a moment's notice.

"I couldn't dump him on Alanna's family like

that," Dad said. "He's my son, my responsibility. I'm with you in hoping a change in environment will effect a change in heart."

"Sweet!" Laine said, spotting Gordon's vercycle and pushing past his relatives to get to the gleaming machine. It hovered gently above the dusty red ground, all sleek lines and humming power. "You have the new Blackline VS?"

At least, it had been new four months ago when they'd left Earth, but he hadn't gotten the opportunity to try one back then. They were reputed to handle very, very well. Laine was inches away from touching the smooth black paint when Gordon caught his wrist in a tight grip.

"You're not so familiar with me that you get to touch my things."

"No exceptions for your favourite nephew?"

"No exceptions for ungrateful teens who can't be bothered to address their betters with respect."

"C'mon, man, I call loads of people by their first name. No big."

Gordon tossed the suitcases into the back compartment of the attached sidecar. "Maybe not now, but I'm not so stupid as to let you trample all over me even in something this small. You don't touch or you can walk."

That was a dumb ultimatum if Laine ever heard one. Ethaba was a good thirty miles away. Mom and Dad weren't going to agree with letting him wander through an unfamiliar landscape all on his own. Their plan to "reform" him and other such nonsense would surely be spoiled if some wild creature plucked him off the road mere hours into their first day on Thorunn.

Gordon was still eyeing him suspiciously, so Laine made a big show of climbing into the attached sidecar without laying so much as a finger on the body. Mom got in beside him, and Dad took the seat behind his uncle. Gordon fired the thrusters, and they began to speed smoothly over the dusty, winding road. Confident that all his uncle's attention was on keeping the powerful machine from upending its passengers, Laine let his fingers skim over the vibrating fender. Let Gordon try to make him walk now.

No way.

He had not just been kicked out and left behind.

Laine stared morosely at the fading trail of reddish dust. Maybe they'd come back for him if he waited long enough? From the way Gordon had ignored Mom's pleas when he'd tossed him out after their abrupt stop, Laine very much doubted it. Given that Gordon was older, had a fully charged sol, and controlled their transportation, he'd probably convince Dad it was for the best, even if Mom could get his father to see reason.

Laine hated this stupid planet. Giving people stupid ideas.

But if they weren't coming back for him, he might as well amble on 'til he reached Ethaba. Laine shouldered his pack and touched his ear to activate the map projection stored on his clip. Gordon's house wasn't specified on it, but he could always ask around after he arrived. Laine kicked at the dirt. He had an eight-hour trip ahead of him, and the wilderness of Thorunn suddenly looked far more foreboding.

His clip registered the temperature at a good ninety degrees—and climbing—with a high air pressure falling as rapidly as the humidity shot up. And yet, an odd chill lingered in the air. The in-flight guides to Thorunn hadn't mentioned just how miserable the planet's atmosphere was. Not even the intriguing sight of Thorunn's twin moons hanging almost full in the daytime sky was enough to keep Laine's mind from his current predicament.

But it wasn't like he'd never been on his own before. He simply had to stick to the path, keep walking, and maybe he'd reach the compound by midnight. It sucked he'd have to arrange his new room so late, but Gordon and Mom and Dad could just deal with the noise. They'd brought it upon themselves by leaving him in the scrubby wilderness with who knew what ready to snatch him away.

Laine trudged on. The red dust he kicked up stuck to sweaty skin. The humidity grew worse as the hours wore on, and he didn't much like the look of the sky behind him. The "Official Guide to Thorunn" he'd downloaded during the interstellar trip assured him no rain would fall until frix season, but that didn't make the sparking mass of low hanging clouds any less unnerving.

A rumble like thunder began in the distance,

accompanied by a high-pitched whine marking it as belonging to a vercycle. So Gordon had changed his mind after all? Laine immediately stopped walking and plopped into the dust, trying for all the world to look like he'd been lounging there without care. But as soon as the vercycle flashed into view, he realised his ears had misled him and the machine sped towards Ethaba from the spaceport, not the other way around.

Laine scrambled up and raced after the quickly vanishing transport, shouting himself hoarse over the roar of its engine. The rider looked back and slowed to a stop.

"You're crazy t'be walking out here in this heat!"

Laine shrugged as he eyed the rider who'd forgone a helmet—a teen about his age, dark hair set above pale features. Irish, from his accent.

"My family's just come from Earth, but there wasn't enough room for all of us and our things on our rented vercycle, so I offered to stay behind 'til they unloaded enough to come get me."

"An' y'had the bright idea to chance it in this weather 'stead of hanging out at the spaceport?"

Admittedly that would be quite the flaw in logic. Laine was a little mad he hadn't thought of going back and renting a vercycle of his own.

"I wasn't aware it was a crime to enjoy long walks in nature on Thorunn."

The teen threw back his head and laughed, before gesturing for Laine to join him on the vercycle.

"Name's Andy. Best be getting on 'fore both our

parents come haring after us."

"Laine. You're the best, dude."

Andy grinned and handed Laine his unused helmet. No other riders were ahead of them on the road, and the miles flew by, Ethaba's gates looming large not twenty minutes later.

Andy scanned his palm at the door, disengaging a complicated series of heavy locks, and the massive steel doors slid partly open. Once inside, Laine thanked Andy again, who waved him off, saying he was sure he'd see him around sometime. Laine looked forward to it. Not even an hour in and he'd already gained an ally? Thorunn was shaping up to be more advantageous than he'd thought.

He found Gordon's house easily due to Andy's helpful directions. It sat close to the large research building-slash-hospital that was the centre of the outpost town. Before he could touch his clip to ping his parents, the front doors slid apart.

"Told you he'd find his way here," Laine heard Gordon say from inside. Laine kicked off his shoes at the entrance and headed in the direction of the voices. Mom rose to greet him, but Gordon got in her way.

"So? Learn anything?"

"You're a cruel, heartless jerk."

"Laine!" Mom shot him a disapproving look.

Laine stuck his hands in his pockets. He wasn't going to apologise for the truth. If Andy hadn't come upon him while running errands, anything could've happened to him out there.

"You're about to hate me more." Gordon turned to Dad. "D'ya want to do the honours, or should I?"

Dad didn't look up from the chess set he was focused on, muttering, "Please, by all means."

"Tch. You merely want me out of the room so's you can mess with my pieces."

"That's my obligation as your little brother."

Gordon snickered and pushed past Laine, then dragged him through to the kitchen. He indicated the curtain hanging before a narrow entrance. "This goes down to the basement. I've been using it for storage, but I figure it'll accommodate you just fine."

Gordon seriously needed to double-check the definition of "accommodate." A bed, cabinet, and chest all crammed together with little room for Laine's stuff was pretty much the opposite of the word.

"You can't expect me to sleep in this dump. There's not even a door."

"Get used to it. You could have been sleeping in the literal hole in the ground this was before I did a complete overhaul of the place. Alanna made food—it's upstairs once you're settled in."

Gordon left, taking the stairs two at a time, light briefly penetrating the dim space as he swept the curtain aside. Once the fabric resettled, Laine sprawled out on his new bed. He'd walked for a considerable time before hitching a ride, and his feet and legs hurt. To top it off, Dad hadn't even been able to drag his eyes away from chess—of all things—to greet him, or wonder how he'd made a trip that should have taken him eight hours by foot in a quarter of that time, and Gordon had stolen away his reunion with Mom, the only person who'd been happy to see him.

But as much as he wanted to stay in bed and sulk, hunger and thirst prompted Laine to creep up to the kitchen. The food Mom had made smelled appetising, but the display on the fridge listed some rather appealing choices indeed.

"Whoa, whoa, whoa! You're too young for that." Gordon plucked the glass bottle Laine had grabbed out of his hand. Laine rolled his eyes, but Gordon simply crossed his arms and stared Laine down. "This is my house, and until Jack scrounges up enough money to move y'all out, you comply with my rules. Got it?"

Laine nodded and settled for water instead, gritting his teeth to keep from contradicting his uncle aloud. His house, his rules, huh? Not the first time Laine had heard that.

"Pass me the eggs will you, dear?" Dad said. He and Mom were the only ones seeming to enjoy their "Riven family reunion" meal. "Goodness, this imitation coffee is strong, Gord!"

The man in question grimaced, and Laine took a small delight in his uncle's irritation at the nickname Dad used.

"Better than the swill they serve at the Centre, Jackie."

Dad hummed noncommittally, the nickname not seeming to bother him, and tried a second sip, his lips turning down after swallowing the bitter liquid. "Speaking of, I've an appointment there in about a half hour. I was hoping you could direct me to the lab I'm s'posed to report at?"

"Sure thing. And while we're there we can pick you up a sol and get Laine registered for school Monday."

"But that's tomorrow!" Laine burst out, looking from Mom to Dad and Gordon. He had nothing—he wasn't ready. He hadn't even recovered from the space-lag. No way could he sit through a full day of classes. He crossed his arms and tipped his chair back. "I ain't doing it."

"Laine, sweetheart, school's been in session here for almost two weeks already. If you don't go tomorrow, I'm afraid you'll drop behind."

Mom didn't say it aloud, but the implications couldn't be clearer. With all the suspensions he'd gotten his freshman and sophomore years, it was a wonder he had enough credits to start on Thorunn as a junior. Someone had to have pulled a lot of strings. It sucked, but if he didn't go tomorrow, he risked having to repeat the year, and that wasn't the first impression he wanted to make on everyone at Ethaba High. He'd never, *never* gain his lost respect back.

"Surprised he hasn't already, from the records y'all sent ahead."

Mom dropped her head into her hands at Gordon's admission. Dad pecked her hair and left, mumbling about getting ready while Laine glared daggers at his retreating back. Those records were private, thank you very much.

As if sensing his thoughts, Mom attempted to diffuse the situation.

"Don't be angry with your father, Laine. We made the decision together."

Great, now he was mad at Mom. Not a good feeling.

"Wouldn't be very responsible if they sprang you upon the staff unsuspecting." Gordon patted Laine's head condescendingly as he collected the dishes. "I'd rather think they'd like to be informed that an idiot delinquent walks their halls."

The not-good feeling caught fire, and Laine sprang out of his seat, aiming a fist in Gordon's direction. Gordon put him on the ground before he could blink, ignoring Mom's little cry of shock. Laine tried to scramble up, but Gordon's foot on his chest kept him pinned, and Laine coughed at the lack of air.

"Let me up, and fight me like a man."

Gordon laughed and crouched down to Laine's level. "Much as I'd love to, I'd rather not get written up for nepoticide." He flicked his dish towel at Laine in an almost playful manner. "I suppose I could claim self-defence—you did come at me first."

"Gordon," Mom said and rose from her seat. "Stop behaving like a child. I am grateful for your hospitality, but I will not continue to tolerate your callous mistreatment of my son."

Gordon grumbled but stepped back and resumed cleaning up, leaving it to Mom to fuss over the bruises Laine could already feel forming. Presently

Dad called for her, wanting some help with his tie, and then Laine and Gordon were alone in the kitchen.

"Get changed and meet me and your dad outside. I wish it weren't so, but in-person ID registrations are still required here in Ethaba."

Laine crossed his arms, ignoring the throbbing the motion prompted in his chest. He'd already decided to play along, if only to establish his reputation at Ethaba High, but that didn't mean he wasn't going to sulk and complain every step of the way. Gordon didn't seem to care, only giving him a light shove towards the curtain before heading up the second-floor stairs.

Laine rifled through his duffle bag and pulled on a red pair of athletic pants and a grey hoodie before joining Dad and Gordon outside. He cast a longing glance at the locked garage where Gordon's Blackline must be stored, but the Centre was within walking distance, so they stuck to the mostly intact sidewalk.

"That the best you could do?" Gordon said, indicating Laine's clothes. Behind him, Dad's face grew pinched as he took in the decidedly informal outfit. Both men were scientists, it only made sense that their button-downs, ties, and other work clothes made up the bulk of their wardrobes. Laine's nice things were still at the bottom of his duffle. Maybe if he'd had more than a few hours to unpack, he could have thrown something a bit nicer together.

"Thought you'd want to look a bit more respectable on the day you get your picture ID."

Wait, what? Pictures?

"No help for it now." Gordon grabbed Laine's wrist and kept him moving towards the Centre at a fast clip. Laine twisted, but couldn't dislodge him. Dad looked off to the side, trusting his older brother to administer a level of physical control he hadn't tried on Laine in a long time.

Laine kept glancing around, hoping no one saw him being marched through the streets like so much trash. Sixteen years old, but because he lacked the muscle and height of Gordon, the man treated him like a child.

Laine didn't manage to break free of the bruising grip until they arrived at the *Ethaba Scientific Research Centre,* according to the giant lettering adorning the front of the ostentatious building. And then he was herded off to a set of rooms sharing space between the Centre and the attached *Ethaba General Medical Institute.* The examination rooms were cold. The graphically detailed anatomical diagrams projected onto the walls didn't lend the atmosphere any sort of welcoming presence.

Laine hissed as the attending nurse poked at his bare chest.

"First day in and already picking fights?"

Laine decided he didn't like the man. Nurses in general weren't very kind people, but he especially hated the ones who liked to comment. They were there to do their job, not make snarky remarks over the state of his body.

"If you must know, my uncle's a brute who likes to

hit kids."

"Mm. You'll excuse me if I take the word of the esteemed Doctor Riven over that of his purportedly rebellious nephew. Now stick out your tongue, and say 'Ah'."

Laine complied as slowly as he could. Everywhere had an identical story. He could complain to the cops, nurses, and doctors all he liked, but they always took the side of his parents, teachers, or whatever juvenile probation officer had been assigned to his case that month.

Thorunn it seemed, wasn't any different.

Laine slipped his shirt back on after the physical, opting to leave his hoodie off for the picture. With the assumptions these people had already made about him, it wouldn't do to add to their biased preconceptions by looking like a bum on his permanent ID. His dad and uncle had already gotten to the medical staff—he still had a chance to present the best side of himself at school, even if it meant he'd spend all night digging out his most stylish outfits from the bottom of his duffle.

<hr>

"Morning, Mom!" Laine called to Alanna upon entering the kitchen for breakfast before his first day at Ethaba High.

They'd been on Thorunn for all of two days, and she still didn't know what to make of the place. Laine seemed to have settled in fine—insomuch as he'd found someone to antagonise; Alanna just wished it hadn't been the person providing a roof over their heads—and Jack by all reports was getting on well with the botany team at the ESReC.

Gordon's house spoke to his long days at the lab—well kept but lacking a personal touch. Alanna looked forward to seeing what flowers she could grow in his garden's mineral rich soil. She missed being home, really home, among the trees and shrubs that grew alongside the Pamunkey River.

California had thrown many wonderful opportunities Jack's way, but she wondered if Laine would have grown up quite so truculent if they'd stayed in Virginia on the ancestral land of her people. Her family had thought her mad to go out West with Jack—madder still to leave Earth and traverse the stars to a planet named for its chaotic lightning storms.

But Laine was the most important person in her life—had been ever since she'd seen the first fluttering ultrasound, heard those first, steady heartbeats. If starting a new life on Thorunn was what it took to bring him back from whatever dark path he'd flung himself upon, then she could accept that it might be months, decades even, before a trip back to Earth was a possibility.

"Morning to you too, darling," Alanna said. "I made your favourite—bacon and eggs with a side of sweet potatoes."

Laine plopped himself down, though not without casting a searching eye around the room. Seeing that Gordon and Jack were quite gone for the day, he relaxed and started to practically inhale his breakfast.

"Where'd y'get sweet potatoes?" Only because she was his mother did Alanna understand the garbled sentence coming from Laine's stuffed mouth. "Synth'siser ain't good enough t'whip this up. Swear this was the real thing, spices an'all!"

"It's the real thing."

A piece of food dropped, ungainly, from her son's open mouth into his cup of orange juice.

Alanna winked at him and held a finger to her lips. What the spaceport officials didn't know wouldn't hurt them, and the delight writ full across Laine's face was a joy to behold after his grumpiness the last few weeks, grown excessive since meeting Gordon. "Something special for your first day at Ethaba High."

"Ugh, don't remind me." He devoured the rest of his breakfast and pushed back from the table. "I know if I don't go I risk not graduating on time, but does that even matter? This is a colony planet. 'M not gonna need calculus to make it here."

Alanna put her arms around Laine, squeezing him in a hug, which he allowed despite the eye rolling doubtless going on where she couldn't see.

"Indulge your mom, sweetheart. One year." She shrugged and touched the heavy beaded necklace resting on her collarbones. "If you still hate it, then we'll see about a different path for you. But you have to try. Give it your all for least a year. For me?"

Laine hugged her back, resting his chin on her shoulder. He'd grown on the trip. Not quite yet as tall as Jack or her brother-in-law, but she had to stand on tiptoe to look him in the eyes anymore. She missed the days when those brown eyes focused only on her, when a playful tickle was all it took to set him off in peals of laughter. But he was sixteen, not six, and she had to let that image of her sweet little boy go.

"I'll try. Gordon threw a map at me last night—a hand drawn paper map—and said the school wasn't far. Knowing him, that probably means if I don't leave now, I'll be stupid late. Would suck to get written up my first day."

It wasn't exactly the attitude Alanna was hoping for, but he'd said he was going, so she'd take it. No one ever said reforming a teenage boy would be easy.

Laine broke out of her arms and grabbed his backpack. "See y'later, I guess."

"Remember!" Alanna called as he disappeared from the kitchen, "This is a new place. We're starting over here. You can choose a different path."

How could he not, when surrounded by all that Thorunn had to offer? So much of the planet was yet unexplored—even if Laine eschewed school in a year's time, he could make his living in some other way.

But Alanna wanted so much more for him. Laine was too smart to spend his life as a bounty hunter, living vivaciously and burning out before reaching his prime. Until the day she drew her last breath, she wouldn't stop fighting for him to understand that.

———————— ● ————————

"Whoever said I wanted to start over?" Laine muttered as he navigated the dusty streets of Thorunn towards Ethaba High. The sun—nicknamed Sól if he remembered the in-flight guide correctly—had just risen, casting the town in hazy sepia tones. "Everything was fine until this stupid move."

At least, it was going to be, but with how quickly they'd fled Earth, Laine hadn't had time to settle his debts. He'd never be able to show his face out West again.

It still stung, the way his parents had bundled him into the car when he'd gotten home from school one day, driving for hours and refusing to answer questions about where they were going until the Nevada Interstellar Spaceport had loomed into view. By then it'd been too late to make good on his threats about jumping out, and they'd packed all his belongings into the back of the car anyway.

He wouldn't be surprised to learn that Gordon had actually engineered that plan, since his parents' usual method of attack was to try talking first. Mom he could stand to hear out for a few minutes, but Dad had a way of going on that got under Laine's skin, nagging and digging at him 'til he had to blast the music on his clip at max volume and bang up the stairs to his room.

The door never quite shut anymore, not after he'd slammed it one too many times, cracking the supporting plaster and dislodging the hinges. That had been a real shame. But at least he'd had a door.

Ethaba High emerged from Thorunn's orange-rust

haze, gleaming white. Despite only being a little past eight o'clock, the iron-gated grounds were quiet. He'd ended up late on his first day after all, disappointing himself, Mom, his new teachers. But if he was already going to be in trouble, and everyone else was already occupied with class, why shouldn't he take advantage of the stillness and scope out the place and especially whatever passed for a computer lab? It never hurt to know how to get into school records.

So it was that Laine stepped foot into his homeroom class a full thirty minutes late on his first day.

"I got lost," he said in response to the raised eyebrow of the teacher, who welcomed him to Ethaba High before presenting Laine to the rest of the class. He pointed Laine to his seat, and with a muttered, "thanks," Laine made his way over and slid behind his new desk. The chair's hard plastic dug uncomfortably into his legs, a testament to where the money in Ethaba wasn't going.

The teacher—a Mister Kim, going by the name neatly written on the board under the word "homeroom" continued to ramble on and Laine's classmates were creepily hushed. It was first period, for goodness' sake! A little rowdiness was expected. Good thing really, that he'd come in late. He didn't know how he'd have survived a whole forty minutes of mind-numbing quietude his first day in.

The bell rang, and Mister Kim gathered his things and left, upon which chaos erupted. The sudden change baffled Laine, but he began to pack his things, ready to move to his next class.

"Yo, where'ya off to?" The kid on his right was sandy-haired, with gapped teeth that a round or two of braces could surely fix.

"My next class?"

The teen shook his head. "Nah, we don't do things the traditional American way. Principal Kim set up the classrooms how he remembered from when he was a kid, and it's worked pretty well, so the board allows it. You've gotta stick here 'til the next teacher comes in."

"All day?"

The teen nodded.

"We're here in this room all day?" Laine stressed the last two words, brows scrunching together as he failed to hold back his disapproval. One at a time, he took his things back out of his bag and placed them with slow, sullen movements on his desk. He'd hoped to run into Andy at some point, but he wasn't in the class. A class Laine was stuck in until school let out. With a very chatty neighbour between periods.

"Yup! We got math next, in about ten minutes. Name's Dustin, by the way."

"Laine." He shook the proffered hand. "Case you didn't catch it earlier." When he'd been introduced by *Principal* Kim. The long, searching look the man had given him now made a lot of sense. No way he was going home without being written up. Mom was going to be *so* disappointed. "Why was our principal teaching homeroom anyway? Normal teacher out sick?"

Dustin chuckled and leant back in his chair, propping his feet up on his desk. He unwrapped a lollipop he'd pulled out of his bag and pointed it at Laine.

"It was a special day today."

"Which I kinda messed up by being late, huh?"

"You got it!" Dustin popped the sucker into his mouth and dug in his bag for another, which he offered to Laine. "But y'couldn't help it if you were 'lost'," he said, with a wink, "so I wouldn't worry about getting in trouble or nothing. Long as you're on time tomorrow."

The next teacher entered before Laine could answer or accept the candy, and Dustin scooted his chair back into place, the second lollipop joining the first, sticks bitten off so as not to alert the scattered looking woman who seemed more suited to teaching English. She made Laine stand to identify himself, but other than that nothing exciting happened, and his other classes followed suit.

"What kinda meat is this?" Laine asked, prodding at the dark, thick cut slab as he sat in the cafeteria with Dustin, trying to work up the appetite to try the strange new foods Thorunn had to offer.

"Anlo," Dustin replied through a mouthful of what looked like mashed potatoes. If mashed potatoes oozed russet red on the inside. They probably weren't potatoes at all—good thing he hadn't picked them up on his way through the lunch line. "It's pretty good."

"I don't remember anlo featuring on the in-flight guide?" Laine cut off the smallest bit and tasted it. It was slightly smoky, a little beefy, and quite salty. There was also a sweetness to the flavour, and it wasn't bad, all things considered.

"Rumour has it the lost colony tamed quite a few, but when the lokians got them, the anlo vanished as well. We've only recently rediscovered them out on the plains of the Cerado." Dustin gesticulated widely with his fork. "Think rhinoceros, but with longer legs, better eyesight, and three horns triceratops-like. Here, let me access your clip, and I'll send you our school's Thorunn handbook. It's way more up to date than anything you could have downloaded on the flight over."

"How long is the handbook? Can I listen to it?"

Dustin stared at Laine, half-chewed meat falling from his open mouth. "You don't read?" he whispered. "Reading is the most amazing thing in the world. Listening to a piece of literature, even one as dry as the school handbook, isn't the same."

Before Laine could respond, Dustin went off about the importance of reading to Laine, who had never been more glad to be called back to class after lunch.

The day ground on, but after his last period, Laine was presented with the exciting choice of picking a club. Dustin informed him in no uncertain terms that opting-in was mandatory, and he was captain of the chess club, the "best club in Ethaba High" according to him. Laine promptly picked the most opposite extracurricular he could find on the list, though he didn't say as much when Dustin pestered him about his choice of lacrosse.

"It's a popular sport back on Earth. Plus, given I'm part Native American and all, it'll make Mom happy I picked something with Native roots."

"This is where we split then. Gym's that way. I gotta sweep and set up before our members arrive."

Dustin trundled off to an empty classroom and started tidying it. Laine watched for a moment, scoffing at his classmate's enthusiasm for orderliness.

The gym was just down the hall, and Laine easily navigated to the locker room, where a uniform and lacrosse stick were thrust at him by none other than Andy.

"Jacques mentioned the new kid had signed up fer lacrosse, an' I knew it had to be you—looking forward to seeing how you play with the team."

"I take it you're team captain?"

Andy was already in full gear, grinning at Laine from behind his blue and silver helmet, thickly gloved hands twirling his stick in a non-stop blur.

"Aye, had to fight an' claw my way into the position, but it means all the more to me 'cause of that. An' the guys respect me since I earned it fair an' square." There was a challenge in those words that Laine took a step back from, instead finding a bench to sit at and strap on his boots.

"Don't think I'm competing for your title anytime soon," he said. "I can barely stand as it is. Hoping this club'll help."

Andy nodded and banged his stick twice against his chest. "I'm living proof of that, moved here at ten an' could hardly walk down the street without having to rest every few metres—Yoon Ah says I looked like a newborn fawn 'til I took up lacrosse."

"Yoon Ah?"

A bright grin broke out on Andy's face. "Principal Kim's daughter. My girl. We've been friends ever since I tripped over my own two feet on the way home when we were kids, an' last year we made it official. We're taking it slow, but we have something real."

One of Andy's teammates, a black teen with a thick French accent, passed by and clipped Andy on the shoulder. "Don't let 'im talk your ear off about 'is chérie—we'll never get on the field!"

"Ah, Jacques, you'll be the same when Mariola accepts your Fall Formal proposal, just you wait!"

Jacques grinned and pushed Andy towards the door, Laine following after, still fumbling to lace up his uniform. The green of the lacrosse field was a welcome contrast to the stuffy, sweaty air of the locker room. Various boys were spread out across the pitch, doing pushups or throwing small rubber balls back and forth in lazy arcs. Laine counted twelve teens including himself.

"Listen up, Ospreys! This here's Laine, our newest member." The rest of the team waved at Laine as Andy threw an arm around his shoulders. "Get started running drills while I show newbie here the basics an' we'll jump into a scrimmage soon as he's trained up."

Andy pulled Jacques and Laine off to the side, and began demonstrating his movements as he talked, gesturing for Laine to imitate him.

"First lesson, always keep your stick, called a crosse, rotating—like that, good. No matter what, keep it moving. That constant swinging back an' forth is important 'cause once you catch the ball"—Andy tossed the ball sitting in his net into the air, caught it again and weaved his stick around, up, down, and sideways—"the centripetal force that's generated'll keep the ball in your stick's net when you're running around. That's called cradling.

"Second, keep your hands spaced apart when catching, but shift them down an' close the gap when throwing, like this." Andy flicked his ball to Jacques, who snagged it neatly out of the air and returned it just as swiftly. "Third, think of the crosse as an extension of your arm. Got it?"

Laine nodded and went through the range of techniques Andy had explained. After a few dropped passes he started to get the hang of it, and Andy declared him ready to play, assuring him he'd pick up the rules along the way.

Loud whoops burst forth from the team when their captain announced the start of the scrimmage, and a multitude of crosses thrust into the air with a ferocity that made Laine's pulse jump in excitement. He had half a mind to smear the eye black on his face until it emulated war paint.

The game was quick but intense, lasting no more than half an hour, with breaks at ten-minute intervals for water and lytorade, but Laine could barely move his legs at the end of practice, never mind lifting the lacrosse stick high enough to throw the ball.

"My lungs!" he wheezed, hanging onto Andy for support, "They're on fire."

"Eh, might've overdone it a touch, but you're decent fer a beginner."

Andy launched into a long list of things Laine had either done right or could stand to improve on, concluding his lecture by clapping Laine on his injured back—he'd been hit a lot during the game—and saying, "While the equipment does belong to Ethaba High, y'can borrow it so long as you fill out a release form an' hand it in to Principal Kim."

"I'm to practice outside of school hours?"

Laine grimaced a little. Lacrosse club had sounded causal enough, but Andy and the others played like they were doing battle. Laine wasn't sure he'd survive another few days of it, let alone the rest of the semester. Apparently they ran the seasons concurrent to the school year, so he only had a few months to prepare for the most important game of the season. Andy saw his questioning expression and poked him hard in the cheek.

"Don't you dare quit. You owe me fer that ride to town the other day."

And there was the crux of the matter. Backing out now wouldn't do his reputation any favours, so Laine offered Andy his best grin.

"Aye, captain."

"That's the spirit!" Andy whooped and thumped Laine across the chest, which hurt, before steering him back to the locker room. The place was bustling with teens high-fiving and ribbing each other about their plays and passes, many a mock wrestling match breaking out as they stripped off their gear and freshened up. Different members of the team stopped to welcome Laine to the Ospreys as he tugged off his cleats and shoulder pads.

Once he had most everything stowed away in his new locker, Laine hit the showers, the warm water soothing his aching muscles, though it did little to reduce the bruising—he'd have to ask Mom for some sports paste to smear on the afflicted areas. Before that though he had to visit the principal's office so he could sign out his stick and a couple balls and get practising.

———————— • ————————

"What's our kid doing now?" Jack asked upon arriving home and catching sight of Laine tossing a ball up and down in Gordon's back yard. Alanna gave the soup on the stove another stir while adding in some herbs and spices.

"He went and joined the lacrosse team at Ethaba High. Came home all bruised up but wanting to run drills straight away. Apparently he did all of his homework at school, which excuses him being out there for hours." Alanna couldn't quite help the exasperation that slipped into her voice.

Jack pressed a quick kiss to her lips before tugging off his tie. His aching feet were probably glad to be off the floor as he sank into one of Gordon's tall wooden chairs.

"As long as he's doing well—heck, long as he's actively interested in going to school, he could take up painting for all I care."

Alanna picked up her husband's jacket from where he'd flung it on the table, and gave Jack a small look of disapproval as she shook out the creases and folded it neatly. Jack offered her a sheepish smile that promised he'd take better care where he put the offending garment in the future.

"He's always wanted to belong somewhere," she said. "And absent that awful Orquídeas gang, I suppose he figured a sports team was the next best choice." Alanna set the soup to simmer and pulled out the chair next to Jack. "All those nights we spent agonising about whether moving here was our best option or the worst mistake of our lives—seems our decision is already bearing fruit."

"And I've been hearing I'm going to be eligible for a pay increase before Christmas!" Jack grasped both her hands in his, pressing a little too hard in his excitement, but Alanna couldn't help but be swept along by his enthusiasm, so the little pinch was easy enough to ignore. "We can get our own place by the new year—you can have your own garden and stop trying to bring Gordon's back to life."

"Yes," Alanna agreed, a soft smile stealing over her face, "how wonderful! I think this truly may be the start of a happy new beginning for all of us."

Laine shattered the moment when he banged into the kitchen, stripping off his sweaty clothes and leaving them in a haphazard pile in front of the curtain leading to his room. Laine kicked off his shoes and was heading in the direction of the shower when Alanna made him go back and stash them in the corridor. He grumbled, as expected, but had been so long practising outside that he had little energy left to put his heart into it and acquiesced quickly. His socks got stuffed into his shoes, and Alanna recoiled once she caught a whiff of their stench. She tapped her clip, adding scent-cancelling spray to the grocery list for the next time she made a trip to the corner mart down the street.

"What's for dinner?" Laine asked once he'd returned, dark brown hair still damp from his brief shower. He looked around much as he had that morning, his tense shoulders relaxing when he noted his uncle wasn't home. Alanna would have to have a word with her son. The suspicion Laine held for the man wasn't healthy. Bad enough he could barely speak two civil sentences to his father—he didn't need to add Gordon to the list.

"Leave some for your uncle," Jack said, eyeing the alarming rate at which Laine consumed the soup Alanna had dished out.

"Gordon ain't here. Why does he get to enjoy Mom's hard work?"

Jack put down his spoon.

"You will refer to him as *Uncle* Gordon."

Alanna pressed her fingers against her eyes. Was it too much to ask for just one family meal without the two men she loved getting into it?

"As long as we're staying here, we will take every

opportunity to repay his hospitality," Jack said. "Do I make myself clear?"

Alanna reached across the table and touched Laine's hand lightly, giving him a significant look. He nodded almost imperceptibly at his father, but Jack seemed happy with that small response and continued to eat, even as Laine sullenly drank the rest of his dinner and bounded off downstairs.

"Why can't I get it right?" Jack let his spoon drop into his half-finished bowl. "Why are you the only one out of the two of us he'll give an audience to? It can't still be because of what happened back then, can it?"

"That's the one thing I guarantee will get a door shut in my face if I try to bring it up," Alanna said and rose to clear away the dishes.

"No doors now." Jack inclined his head pointedly towards the curtain Laine had disappeared behind.

"And yet he seems further away than ever." Quiet descended upon the small space once more, underscored by the running water and the slow classical music Alanna had put on earlier that day.

"Ah, well, best be getting to bed myself—we're out on expedition tomorrow—Gordon assures me it'll be perfectly safe, but with the history of this place, I can't help being anxious."

Jack came up behind Alanna, kissing her again. He felt unusually hot against her; hopefully he wasn't working himself too hard at his new job and forgetting to eat.

"If Gordon says it'll be fine, I believe him."

The in-flight guide had been very clear on the fact that nary a lokian had been sighted near Ethaba in the last five years, so Jack really didn't have anything to worry about. He left with one last parting kiss, and Alanna went on with her work. All things considered, Laine's first day couldn't have been better. She didn't even get a note of any sort from the school!

A wave of warmth washed over Alanna, and she stumbled, nearly dropping the soapy mug in her hand. The space lag must still be catching up to her; she'd never been so tired after a trip before. After she finished the washing, she was joining Jack in bed and hoping she felt better in the morning.

Whatever ailed her likely wasn't anything a good night's rest couldn't fix.

3

The night air was cool by the Laika River, and Kenton stopped for a brief drink, letting the fresh tasting water wash away the lingering traces of the nightmares that had driven him out so late. The current rippled slightly, and he jumped back, narrowly avoiding the dark shape that burst up out of the shadows, snapping at empty air.

Kenton slipped his quirn into his hand and activated it, counting on its low hum to dissuade the sharp-toothed aquatic creature. The beast hissed at him a few times but eventually subsided, slipping back under the rushing river in search of easier prey.

Danger averted, Kenton thumbed off his quirn and retreated deeper into the forest. A thin path had been cut through the thick undergrowth, and he stepped lightly along the spongy trail, navigating by what little moonlight seeped down through the thick canopy. A dark imprint caught his eye, and he knelt to inspect it.

Vana'byss tracks.

He touched his fingers to the impressions, which were still wet and seemed to head towards the kitterstone deposits. Kenton straightened, melting farther into the shadows. The path ahead would widen in a few metres, the twin moons casting the trail into brilliant sepia tones. He'd have to take the long way around if he wanted to remain undetected.

Kenton doubled back about a hundred paces and swung up into the trees, moving quiet as any klia'an across wide, twisting branches. When he dropped down on the other side of the deposits, the creature he tracked crouched in plain sight, drinking from one of the shallow pools in the smooth rock clearing.

A midnight bird screeched, and the vana'byss flickered out of sight.

Kenton stilled, not daring even to breathe until its four black-coated limbs began to materialise into view once more. He crept forward, close as he dared, closer than was probably safe, but the vana'byss was intently focused on the various stagnant pools that might serve as spawning areas for its young come frix season. Kenton was sorry to have to dispatch the bony animal, but he couldn't let it take up residence in the tribe's main kitterstone mine, much less let it become comfortable enough to lay several clutches of poisonous eggs. He levelled his quirn at it.

At the last moment, it scented him—snapping its head up—and lunged, powerful hind legs disappearing mid-spring.

Kenton kept his fingers wrapped around the shaft of his weapon and breathed out slow, so slow, eyes as wide as he could open them, and there! A shimmer in the air gave away the invisible beast's position and he squeezed hard, a stunning bolt of frix shooting out and aborting its lunge. Sparking energy lit along every bone in the vana'byss' writhing body, and it dropped like a stone to the ground mere paces from Kenton.

He sprang forward and quickly ended its suffering, wary of its twitching limbs and jerking shiny, black head. A quick slash of Kenton's still-dripping hunting knife turned some nearby vines into sturdy ropes, and he strapped the vana'byss to his quirn before heaving the hefty mass onto his back.

Sunrise lit his path home, the cacophonic clamour of early morning birdsong a startling contrast to the steady humming of the nighttime forest. The light revealed some berry trees that Kenton had missed, and he popped handfuls of their fruit into his mouth, glad of the refreshment after his restless night.

Lanae still lingered in the sky by the time Kenton arrived back at the village, though the sun did its best to outshine the second moon, having already banished Lanaekim to the realm of darkness. Kits of varying sizes scampered about, some shifting and watching him with wonderment, all clearing a path for him as Kenton strode towards home, the vana'byss carcass thumping against his back with every step.

Climbing the Tree of Elders proved difficult with the added weight—if not for the abundant vines twined about the massive chishish trunk, he might have fallen to the ground many times over. Kenton barely remembered to bow after he tumbled through the spinner-floss curtains of the loft's main entrance.

"Greetings, Innah."

"Greetings to you, child. Sit down." Her tone

lacked the warmth it usually carried, and Kenton found no comfort from the padded cushions he settled upon.

"I had a nightmare," he blurted.

"Seri mentioned. She worries; I worry. Hunting alone—especially after sundown, is not done until you've passed Igis. And it's certainly not done night after night as a way to flee your problems."

"I can't stop seeing them. At least when I'm out there, the darkness drowns out their screams."

The Innah took a long puff of her pipe, focusing her honey-coloured eyes on Kenton. The vana'byss was still strapped to his back, starting to stain the cushions around him with an odd-smelling fluid, its weight pressing down upon him like the guilt stirred up by the Innah's calm gaze.

"It's been almost ten years! I shouldn't, the dreams shouldn't still come. Shouldn't my heart have healed by now?" Kenton sat back, feeling his cheeks flush in embarrassment at the force of his outburst. "Forgive me. I'm not feeling myself."

The Innah leant forward and cupped Kenton's face in her warm hands. The soft touch did more to comfort Kenton's aching heart than the exhilaration that still filled him from his nighttime excursion.

"Ever since we snatched you from the jaws of death that day, we've tried everything to help you forget. But maybe I've failed you in this. Mayhaps I should have had you confront that awful night."

The Innah's ears drooped, a rare showing of grief from her. "You were so young, and I thought not speaking of it would help. And then I could never find the right time or words. Forcing you to turn to this"—she gestured at the dripping creature—"hunting and slaying one of the most dangerous creatures in the Hinnom Forest—not to mention your eyes are much limited after sunset. You have every disadvantage working against you out there, and losing you, my only son—!"

She trailed off, but Kenton could fill in the rest of her intimation. Leader of the tribe she might be, but in his heart of hearts he called her "Mother." He imagined the void she'd attempted to fill after the deaths of Umama and Pa and Annie would only grow to consume him if something ever happened to her. It wasn't hard to imagine she felt the same about him and his adopted sister, Seri. He grasped her wrists gently.

"Dearest Innah, I promise I'll be more careful."

She nodded, the soft purr that filled the room a sign she accepted his words and forgave him. Kenton arose, taking the stained cushion with him, and strung up the vana'byss in the back room.

As he rinsed off its stink in the washroom he stared at his reflection. The blue of his eyes seemed dulled, the whites laced through with red. When had he last seen them looking normal?

The nightmares had come and gone over the years, but the most recent ones were especially, painfully persistent. Without proper sleep, passing Igis would be a struggle, and that stung to admit, since less than half a year ago he'd had every confidence that the trials would come easily to him.

Kenton ran a wooden comb over his shoulder-length hair until he was satisfied no bits of vana'byss remained in it. No matter that the whole of Tribe Osinan knew he wandered at night—it wouldn't do to appear dishevelled at morning meal and cast dishonour upon the Innah.

He stepped out to the ledge, rhythmic drumming catching his ear as he drifted to his seat and took it mere moments before the Innah rose to address the village. All except the littlest of kits subsided into respectful silence as she spoke, though once she'd resumed her seat the chatter broke out again, accompanied by the passing of dishes and water pitchers.

"I can see why you took so long washing up!" Seri, seated on Kenton's left, wrinkled her nose. She broke her bread and smeared it with issa flower nectar. "Vana'byss really do stink when they die, don't they?"

"Your nose is too sensitive; I washed every little bit off me."

"Sure, sure. Next thing, you'll be showing up with face paint like the other Igis hopefuls."

"So that pot of paste in the washroom isn't yours?" Kenton raised an eyebrow as he took the jar of nectar from his adopted sister. Seri popped a second piece of bread into her mouth to avoid answering the question, and Kenton grinned. Everyone prepared for Igis in their own ways.

One nap and a second meal later found Kenton

headed out to join the rest of the tribe at frix-proofing the newest loft canopy covers, clothes, and whatever else might be vulnerable come storm season.

Klia'an claws could grip and propel them above the understorey with ease, but not even Kenton's hinnom bark gloves could replicate the same, so he had to resort to liana swinging. One misplaced hand or a singular failure to avoid a large, thorny, or moss-slick branch and Kenton could easily become just a broken body on the distant forest floor.

Despite those dangers, or because of them, blurring through the forest on long trailing vines was Kenton's preferred mode of daytime travel. He never felt more alive than the moments he twisted to avoid an oncoming sapling, instinct long born of experience propelling him forward with unerring accuracy.

The trees thinned abruptly—no new liana to grab onto—and Kenton flailed, almost launching himself into the air five metres above a hard drop onto unforgiving kitterstone.

"Here's the last of our Igis Chosen!" Supervisor Irja called out as Kenton slid down his vine and loped over. The middle aged klia'an tossed Kenton a bundle of hinnom leaves and directed him to his work group for the day. To Kenton's delight, he spotted the grinning face of his best friend among them.

"Yes! We're paired together today!" Bo said, upon seeing Kenton approaching his team. "Seri doesn't get to hoard you all to herself. But tell me, did you really fell a vana'byss earlier?"

"Third one to be brought back to the village this

month."

Kenton stretched his bundle over a rounded dome and quickly laced the sides together before pouring molten hinnom sap over the thick leaves. He stepped back while everything cooled.

"It's those cursed humans—no offence—over at the settlement. They're up to no good, and it's messing up everything in the forest."

"A couple vana'byss more than we're accustomed to is hardly 'everything'."

The black-furred youth lashed his tail, hissed words more S'hinoian than Klia'an. "Maybe not now, but after what they did to my father and your family, I don't trust none of 'em. We can't watch 'em closely enough."

"Different people live there now."

"And how many have tried to talk to us? Ken, your dad was the only one who attempted to bring us together, and look what that got him."

Each word Bo spoke jarred Kenton, but he gritted his teeth and forced himself to listen. The Innah had been right—how could he move on if he couldn't confront the terrible events of his past?

"I'm not saying we should trust all humans unconditionally, but we're not all bad."

Bo continued to protest, but Kenton spoke right over him. "Look, why don't we head to the forest outskirts after we're finished here and observe for ourselves what the scouts were reporting back?

"I can tell you right now what we'll find. Nothing good."

"See for yourself first before you make that determination."

Bo rolled his eyes but nodded, and they returned to the task of making frix-proof loft covers.

The work was intense but passed quickly—troops of eager young klia'ans ferrying buckets of hinnom sap back and forth, whilst others transported the dried covers and articles of clothing back to the village—and it wasn't more than an hour past midday when Kenton and Bo found themselves dismissed, free to do what they wished with the rest of their afternoon.

Dappled sunlight cast intricate shadows across Bo's dark fur—the young klia'an having elected to shift to all fours, his lithe, jaguar-like form padding silently next to Kenton through the muffled outer forest. The quiet was unnerving in a place usually filled with so much sound, the deceptive calm pointing to the intrusion of outsiders, and before long, the chop, chop, chop of steel machetes assaulted Kenton's and Bo's ears.

Bo pressed himself farther into the undergrowth, a shadow amongst the wide trunks and leafy fronds hiding them from the searching eyes just beyond. The muttering chatter and singing of swinging steel grew louder and closer, forcing Bo and Kenton to take to the trees lest they be discovered. They peered down at the party stopping to set up camp directly below them.

"A research team, right?" Bo growled in rough S'hinoian, ears flicking back at Kenton's answering nod.

"Wait here." Kenton unslung his quirn and tucked it into the pack strapped to Bo's back before dropping almost to the ground and creeping as close as he dared.

Ever mindful of the glowing sols at the hips of the soldiers standing around the perimeter of the destroyed forest foliage, Kenton focused all his senses on observing the men in expedition clothing—cream and tan khakis, multi-pocketed vest jackets, sturdy hiking boots, and the like—all measuring things and taking notes on holoscreens. A quick *snick* of Kenton's hunting knife provided him with a makeshift leaf amplifier, and snippets of conversation in a language Kenton had rarely spoken in near a decade reached his straining ears.

"Yes, boss! Buckets coming right up!" The portly speaker—his face hidden beneath the brim of his hard hat—produced two large containers, which he handed off before fetching more from the vercycle floating at the mouth of the trail that ostensibly led to the scrublands between the Hinnom Forest and Ethaba.

Kenton tilted his head, confused. The scientific party was nowhere near the Laika River—what immediate need had they of such large buckets? He leant closer, hoping to infer the answer from their rapid-fire conversations.

"But, Gordon," one of the scientists began, hurrying after a tall man who strode from tree to tree, "I thought we were here to study the local flora and fauna, so we can better thrive during, what was it you called it, frix season?"

Gordon stopped, putting a hand on the man's shoulders. "That's exactly why we're here, little brother. Let me show you something." Gordon pressed a bucket into his brother's hand before ushering him a little deeper into the forest.

Kenton followed the pair, keeping flush to the branch he watched from. Again he raised the leaf funnel to his ear, parting the leaves below him in time to see Gordon strike at a young hinnom tree and catch the fast-flowing sap in his bucket.

Kenton clenched his fist. That tree would die; it hadn't matured enough to be tapped.

"This, this is why we're here." Gordon pointed at the bucket with his knife. "Our records show the natives called this hinnom sap, and rumour has it it's more resistant than rubber, as flexible as spandex, and harder than steel when dried."

"And if you crack the secret to it, you'll make a fortune. Explorers could fly safely across the sea."

Gordon smirked at his brother. "Beautiful, isn't it? Liquid gold." A rapt expression seized his face before he snapped back to business. "That's where you and the rest of the team come in, Jack. If your initial analyses prove fruitful, we get the funding from Skytown to continue our work. Imagine the possibilities. All contained in this vast rainforest, ours for the taking."

It was not. Not theirs.

Kenton gripped the amplifier so hard it fell to

pieces in his hand, and he had to fashion a new one, catching the last snatches of Jack and Gordon's conversation as they took the now filled bucket back to their camp, the violated hinnom tree weeping its life onto the forest floor behind them.

"What about those lokian creatures I heard live here? Surely we'll encounter some resistance?" Jack asked, huffing from the weight of the bucket.

"Key word, creatures. They can hardly take advantage of Thorunn's gifts, so we might as well. And any trouble we do run into, well. No one can argue with a bit of retribution for the lost colony."

Jack shrugged, a little helpless gesture that betrayed a certain measure of doubt, but his answer didn't reach Kenton, the two men having re-entered the camp.

Bo came up on Kenton's left, shifted back, fangs bared. "You've gone whiter than normal. I take it the humans aren't here to hold hands and sing with us?"

"They killed a hinnom tree. Just like that. When they could have tapped the one right next to it."

Bo handed Kenton's quirn back to him. "This is the part where you tell me they didn't know any better and we should give them another chance?" His furiously lashing tail told Kenton what he thought of that opinion.

"No. They plan to ravage the forest. They plan to murder us all."

———————————— ● ————————————

The Innah looked up sharply as her human son

came tumbling through the spinner-floss curtains of the council room. To his credit he rolled into a bow, forehead touching the floor, before he jumped up, eyes burning with a brightness the Innah had thought lost to him.

"We're all going to die."

A collective gasp rose from the seated council members, and the Innah struggled not to lash her tail in annoyance at Kenton's theatrics. But he wouldn't make such a dire statement without reason, so she folded her arms in her sleeves, took a long pull of her pipe, and tipped her head at him to continue.

"Apologies, Innah, council, but it's true. Maybe not next week, or next month, or until after first frix, but by year's end, the men of Ethaba are going to come and kill the hinnom trees and slaughter us. Bo and I overheard them at the outskirts today. Somehow they know what hinnom sap can do, and they're more than eager to destroy everything in their lust to possess it."

Kenton paused, and the Innah bid him sit beside her, giving his trembling legs a break.

"Their suspicion of us blinds them to the fact that they could but ask, and we would be willing to trade knowledge with them." She let the weight of her words settle upon the room. "Instead they take and take, like they took your father from you, dear child, when his only crime was befriending me. This time it does not seem they will be content to leave until they have accomplished our complete annihilation, just as they destroyed our brethren who lived on Mount

Lalethusl."

She turned to address the council. "What do you propose we should do?"

Immediately, a loud commotion broke out as the members of the council argued furiously with each other, ears pinned back and snarling fangs exposed as they hissed and growled and generally failed to come to a consensus.

"And what about Igis?" Irja called out during a momentary lull in the heated discussions. "We simply can't resolve this issue and hold the trials at the same time."

Kenton tensed, and the Innah's stomach tightened. To not hold Igis—to deny the young of their tribe their opportunity to be recognised as fully-fledged adults? From the crestfallen expression on his face, she knew that Kenton hadn't even considered that possibility during his mad dash to the council room. He and Seri and all their friends were supposed to pass the ordeal before first frix. Another thing the men from Ethaba were about to steal away.

"What if we can?" Kenton said, jumping to his feet. "Igis is all about stealth, cunning, surviving on our own to prove we're worthy. We could do that and keep the forest safe."

The Innah took her pipe from her mouth and caught her son's eye challengingly, waiting to hear what madcap scheme he'd devised.

Kenton met her gaze without flinching before doing the same of every council member in the room. A few looked away under the weight of it, and the Innah made a note to speak with them later—if they couldn't hold the gaze of an Igis hopeful with far less wisdom and experience than they, their time on the council might be drawing to a close.

"We divert the scientists' attention away from the forest and onto their own settlements and outposts," Kenton said, his words drawing a collective gasp from the room. The Innah arched a brow, flicking her right ear as Irja addressed the proposition.

"You expect to carry this out without retribution? Kenton, any move we make against the humans gives them all the pretext they need to finish what they started back then."

"Not if they don't know it's us behind it. Any strikes we make would have to one, appear as if they're perpetuated by other humans, by two, looking as though they come from the northeast, and three, destroy only the scientific equipment centres without any loss of human life. That would slow them down, give us time to formulate a better plan of action. We can accomplish all that by first frix. I know it."

In the space it took Kenton to breathe, the clamour redoubled, dissenting opinions rising almost to shrieks and the Innah wanted to clap her hands over her ears.

"Enough!" she bellowed. "Are you not so far from Igis yourselves that you would come to screaming over this matter?" After the room settled, the shame-faced council members not daring to lift their eyes from the floor, she continued, "My son has the right of it. We must act, and yet we cannot deny our children their adulthood. Kenton's plan is solid—we can work out the logistics of it later, but it is the best, most immediate hope we have of protecting ourselves and maintaining our revered traditions."

If they threw away all their ancient customs and order at the first sign of danger, they threw the heart of themselves into disarray. And if they had acted sooner at that time, Kenton's parents might still be alive. The Innah couldn't help but allow him to rectify the wrongs of the past. That much she owed him.

"It is settled. Now, whom do you nominate to lead the Igis Chosen?"

"Kenton is the obvious choice, is he not?" Praha said, twisting the tips of her ears in that nervous habit she had. "For any missions along the way that might involve being seen; he is human, the other humans might not notice aught amiss until too late."

Irja purred in solemn agreement. "'Twill lend credence to Kenton's idea that the humans think other humans are the culprits. I too, nominate the boy."

One by one, all the other members gave their assent until only the Innah was left. She motioned for Kenton to kneel.

"Kenton Wishings. We, the governing council of Tribe Osinan, do hereby appoint you to lead the Igis Chosen through the ordeal. Furthermore, we solemnly task you to take appropriate action against the human settlements and outposts, as benefits us and destroys their incursions on our home, without the loss of a single life, klia'an or human."

Kenton touched his forehead to the floor. He trembled, and there was an odd scent about him—not fear exactly—something closer to horror-filled anticipation, and not for the first time the Innah wished she could reach into his mind and pluck out the innermost thread of his thoughts.

How ever was she to know what path to set him on? How to direct him away from the road that would lead to his ruin after she'd tried so hard to steer him from the darkness that haunted him? But larger things were at stake, and she needed him.

"I am honoured to be burdened with this task, Innah. I am your quirn and shield."

———————— ● ————————

"How much of that did you hear?" Kenton asked upon spying Seri lounging in his hammock. She shrugged.

"Enough."

Kenton plopped onto the hammock and buried his head in his hands. "Seri, I don't think I can do this. I can't even sleep through the night—how am I supposed to lead a, a, a campaign!?"

"Sending one of the elders with us would defeat the purpose of Igis. You fancy redoing the trials?"

"Don't tell me you actually want me to do this?"

Seri got up and started to pack. "Not as such," she called from her room, "but I don't want to live in fear of the humans attacking our village, and I really want to be looked at as more than a kit."

She poked her head through the curtains and held

up two different garments. "Grey or brown for the Cerado, do you think?"

Kenton rolled out of the hammock and began gathering his things as well. The earlier they could leave for the foothills the better. No matter how much he didn't want to lead a group of bright-eyed Igis hopefuls—ears still rounded like their younger brothers and sisters, the eye-dark of their adult colouration not gown in yet—every moment they dallied was a moment longer the Ethabites came closer to realising their plans of devastation.

Seri had a point. This was his time to prove himself. To be counted a full-blooded member of Tribe Osinan. To—was Seri packing her softie?

"Lady Lanaekim isn't going to help us out there."

Seri stroked the little cat figure gently before setting it back down.

"Time to trade in my toys for weapons, huh?"

"Only through Igis."

One more change of clothing and Kenton was packed.

Seri followed him to the kitchen where they gathered some provisions before descending the Tree of Elders. Word had spread quickly, and a group of around fourteen travel-ready klia'ans milled loosely about, some shifted to s'hinoian form, packs snugly attached to hinnom-sap-hardened harnesses.

Bo bounded up to Kenton and Seri, a question on his lips. Kenton clapped twice for silence, hoping he looked more commanding than he felt.

"Tribe Osinan is under threat, our lives here compromised. I've been appointed to lead us through Igis, an Igis like we've never known it. The ordeal is no longer about surviving on our own but about protecting the tribe. No chance to retake the trials will be ours if we fail." Kenton hefted his pack, the smooth hinnom wood of his quirn a comforting weight where it was strapped into its familiar place across his back. "I'll let you know the plan on the march."

What plan that was Kenton didn't quite know. The outline he'd given the elders was no more than that. But he did know the first step was acquiring flying transports if they wanted to return before first frix. Kenton unrolled his map as he started to walk through the forest, the others following two at a time. His hands shook so much he could hardly make out the villages and outposts he planned to attack.

"Having second thoughts?"

Kenton, to his credit, did not shriek at the sudden appearance of Bo on his left.

"I just keep thinking, if I hadn't proposed this mad idea, what would the council have elected to do? What if you'd told them what we heard?"

"They'd probably still ha' picked you on account of my 'bloodthirsty tendencies'," Bo said, scrunching up his nose. "Were up to me, I'd wipe 'em all out."

"Bo!"

The young klia'an was unapologetic. "What's better, clipping a weed, or pulling it out by the root?"

"I almost agree with you," Seri said, taking the map and perusing it. "But we can't be the first to spill blood, and until they make a move, we are obligated to conduct ourselves with honour."

"Honour?" Bo spat on the ground. "Honour has only ever gotten good klia'ans dead."

Kenton gripped Bo, stopping him in his tracks. The other Igis Chosen kept going, parting silently around them, following Seri as she took to the trees.

"You don't think I want revenge against the men who took both our fathers from us? Who slaughtered my sister? I think about my family every day. But I can't let that hurt turn me into a murderer. You can't let that hurt jeopardise the mission. Please, Bo, be satisfied with the mayhem I do intend us to cause."

Bo shook off Kenton's hand, golden eyes narrowed into tiny slits. "Fine. But I can't promise I'll be happy." He crossed his arms, staring Kenton down.

"No one should, faced with what we're about to do."

Bo rolled his eyes and leapt into the trees, shifting mid-air and scrabbling at hinnom boughs with newly sharpened claws, leaving Kenton to stare forlornly at the sullen six-foot long mass bounding away. The men of Ethaba were always a sore spot with Bo, and Kenton hoped they wouldn't argue every time the subject came up during their mission.

Kenton looked back down the trail. He could still see the giant chishish tree that had been his home for years, and something deep in his core resisted the idea of leaving it behind. Was it because something whispered he might not survive to return with the others? Kenton shook off the thought and swung up into the canopy, moving quickly to catch up with the others.

They made camp that evening on the outskirts of the Hinnom Forest, not far from the clearing the scientists had left. There were no signs of them so late, though doubtless they'd be back early the next morning; Kenton planned to be well past Ethaba by then. He himself stayed up most of the night, only allowing himself a few hours' rest before Seri came to shake him awake, a sympathetic look on her face at his bloodshot eyes. But a headache that would fade by midday seemed a reasonable trade for letting the others sleep uninterrupted—it wouldn't do to frighten them with his screams before they'd even left the forest.

Kenton and Seri gathered the Igis Chosen as pre-dawn birds began to cackle.

"Just there, beyond those trees," Kenton said to the assembled group. "The Cerado. Dry, hot, and exposed. Until we're past Ethaba, stay shifted to your s'hinoian forms for better camouflage. We mustn't risk attracting the attention of patrolling soldiers or a vyss'ngryr mated pair."

The young klia'ans nodded, harnesses reflowing to adapt to their feloid shifted shapes, clothes shrinking into their belts with the press of a button, and in a matter of moments, Kenton was the only one left standing on two feet. Like this, surrounded by little over a dozen of his friends in the cool forest undergrowth, he could pretend this was how Igis was supposed to start. That the elders watched them from hidden stands in the tallest trees, monitoring their progress, noting at which trials they excelled and which ones they failed.

But today they hunted not the poisonous vana'byss or the krytas birds with their bright plumage and stabbing beaks. They weren't struggling to build shelters to protect themselves against the fury of the frix storms, or carving out new weapons for threats their teeth and claws were ineffective against.

Today they hunted man, and Kenton had to somehow get them home alive.

4

Laine couldn't help his grin when he caught sight of the video playing on repeat on Ethaba High's bulletin board. Less than a month and he already occupied the spot of honour reserved for outstanding students. Mom was happy with the good grades he'd been bringing home—a necessary sacrifice to achieve success in the one thing at the school that actually mattered.

"Admiring your handiwork?" Yoon Ah said as she came up beside him.

"You know it!" He watched himself score the winning goal against the rival team he and the Ospreys had crushed last week. Then he watched it again. And again.

"Andy complains about how much he has to wrangle you guys, but if Dad is putting the team on display so early in the school year, he's doing something right."

"Doesn't hurt to have such a cute cheerleader in the stands."

Yoon Ah blushed, her long hair—aqua this week, she rotated through colours faster than outfits—falling in front of her face when Laine winked at her.

"Hitting on my girl again, Laine? You're really angling fer a week of fetching lytorade an' towels fer us ain'tcha?"

"Come on. You wouldn't bench your star player when I'm only acknowledging a universal truth."

Andy slung his arm around Yoon Ah and levelled a mock glare at Laine. "I'm certainly not gonna deny that Yoon Ah's the prettiest girl on all of Thorunn, but I don't need to hear you say it."

"Oi, Laine!" Dustin called as he rushed past, arms full of books, "Class's in two minutes, and I need your answer by the end of the week!"

"Ugh, that stupid mathletes event. It's technically right before the last match of the season, so I don't really have a way to get out of it, but guys, I hate hanging out with Dustin."

Yoon Ah and Andy exchanged matching expressions of concern.

"Surely a little trigonometry talk is hardly a burden when he practically worships you."

"No, but he follows me around at all hours of the day, constantly badgering me to join chess club and astronomy club and engineering club just because I happen to have the second-best math grade in class, and it's honestly exhausting at this point."

He'd petitioned Principal Kim to let him switch seats, but after an awkward talk wherein Laine had to explain that no, he was not being bullied—the opposite in fact, his classmate was too helpful—his request had been denied, and Dustin continued to pester him with lollipops from his seemingly bottomless bag.

"You could be a little nicer after all Dustin's done to make you feel welcome," Andy said.

Laine shrugged. He'd been nice, the first week or so, and Dustin had taken the inch, and gone several light-years, so Laine had had to lay down some ground rules, and it was nobody's fault but Dustin's if Laine avoided him outside of school. If he kept up the pestering, he'd soon find himself ignored during classes as well.

"Maybe, if he'd just shut up about the 'intricate beauty of numbers.' Anyway, your house after school since we're taking a day off from practice, right?"

Andy nodded, and Laine fist bumped both his friends before dashing into class where Dustin was making increasingly worried signals at the approach of their English teacher, a man prone to giving pop quizzes on his favourite subject: great writers of the late twenty-first century.

After suffering through that and history class, re-visiting the tragedy of the Apollo XXII colony for what had to be the fourteenth time—seriously Professor Grennal had a sick fascination with showing the slides of the ghost town the soldiers had found—Laine grabbed his things and met Andy and Yoon Ah on the front steps of Ethaba High.

Twenty minutes later found the teens lounging in Andy's room at the Frenally residence. Yoon Ah lay on her back on Andy's bed, feet pointed towards the headboard, legs crossed and reading a book while Laine and Andy sat on the floor playing an old racing video game and surrounded by various snacks and soft drinks.

"Hey!" Yoon Ah said suddenly, snapping her book shut. "Didn't you say your dad's been acting really weird about the basement lately?"

"Come to think of it—take that, Laine!—I think, yeah. But basement's locked with encryption even I can't crack, so 'less you know how to bypass government level security, his secrets stay his."

Andy proceeded to trash Laine, crowing at his success as Laine gripped his controller, shock and betrayal welling up in him. He swore and threw the device down, ignoring Andy's shout of "Careful!" as the projection flickered and disappeared.

"I'm done. Dunno why I agreed to play this stupid game in the first place."

"We can do something different, mate, no need for destruction of property."

"Locked. Basement," Yoon Ah said, bouncing over to the door before catching Laine's eye. "I know you take shop on Fridays. Can't you get us in?"

"Babe, y'can't ask Laine to break into a room my dad expressly keeps locked."

"Not like we'll take nothing." Laine joined Yoon Ah at the door. "Aren't you curious about what your dad doesn't think you're mature enough to handle?"

"Fine." Andy took his time putting the game away. "But if we get in, we don't touch a single thing."

He led Yoon Ah and Laine downstairs, past the expansive collection of family portraits on the walls. Yoon Ah paused to gush over the newest one, ostensibly from Christmas, given the ugly sweaters everyone but Mrs. Frenally looked desperate to remove.

The entrance to the basement turned out to be under the stairs, behind a simple wooden door that required an old-fashioned key to open. A screwdriver borrowed from the kitchen made short work of it, and the door creaked open to reveal a second set of sealed doors, a glowing palm scanner set into the wall next to them.

"No way they teach you how t'disable one of those at shop," Andy said as Laine stepped forward to inspect the scanner.

"Can you imagine?" Laine slid his fingers behind the top casing. "But growing up in L.A.'s good for a couple things." The scanner flashed red, then green, and the hydraulics on the door disengaged, locks clicking and whirring as the steel panels parted and slid into the wall on either side.

"Still got it!" Laine gestured to Yoon Ah. "After you, if the lady doth please."

"I mean it about that towel an' lytorade duty, mate. You're on thin ice."

Shaking his head in exasperation, Andy flipped on the lights, forcing each teen to shield their eyes against the sudden bright neon onslaught that faded to a sickly blue black-light glow.

At the bottom of the stairs, a lab like something out of a bad sci-fi flick greeted them. Apart from the whirring of machinery, it was oddly quiet, lights blinking from all manner of electronics. Screens and monitors lined one wall, their computers lying under long tables piled atop with all manner of boxes and wires. A neatly arranged tray of tools balanced halfway off a polished desk.

"Did you hear that?" Yoon Ah gripped Andy's sleeve.

They froze, but Laine's ears detected only the low humming of the UV lamps clustered at the back of the room. Andy's dark hair ate a hole in the space, a weird void next to the bright green-blue of Yoon Ah's hair.

"I'm serious. Something's down here with us."

A tap turned on, the rushing water a shocking sound in the eerie space. Laine jerked towards the sink to turn it off—only, there was no sink.

The rushing, *hissing*, grew until it filled the room, emanating from a single point, a squarish object flung over by a black cloth, the edges of which seeped green light.

"We woke it up," Yoon Ah whispered, clutching wide-eyed at Andy, who'd edged past Laine back to the foot of the stairs. "It sounds . . ."

"Told you this was a bad idea." Andy tugged at Laine, almost succeeding at getting him up the steps, but Laine pulled away, never appreciative of having hands on his person, and fell forward, colliding with the cloth-covered object.

The resulting ache in his foot told him he'd struck metal, and before he could recover his common sense, he swept off the covers, immediately scrambling away in horror at the pale green monstrosity he'd uncovered. It had only black where eye sockets should be, long fingers reaching insidiously towards him, gnashing maw inches from gouging his cheeks.

"Laine!" Yoon Ah screamed, rushing towards him.

This time Laine didn't pull away at the hands dragging him back, unable to speak with what little breath he could gasp. The hissing turned furious, metal jangling and scraping as the creature shook the cage that confined it, that kept it at bay, because of course, Andy's dad wasn't so foolish as to leave a savage beast unrestrained in his illegal terror basement lab.

"That's a—" Once Laine saw the creature was contained behind thick, crisscrossing metal bars, his initial fright faded, and he crept closer, mindful to keep out of range of that stabbing beak. "A pterosaur?"

If pterosaurs glowed green under UV lights, had multiple, sunken in eyes, and shimmered in a way that made it hard to see more than one part of it at a time. "That wasn't in the in-flight 'Guide to Thorunn'."

"S'not in the school handbook or on the edda-net either," Yoon Ah said, finger to her ear, snapping photos with her clip. "Babe, I hate to say it, but this is pretty big for your dad to be keeping from us."

The leathery winged creature continued to hiss at them, wicked looking claws scrabbling through gaps in the metal, and the rusty, nail scraping sound emanating through rows of sharp teeth made Laine very glad Yoon Ah had yanked him out of harm's way.

"Maybe he's discovered a new species an' doesn't want his peers taking the credit—happens incredibly often in the world of science."

"You don't think it's shady he's keeping an extinct,

on Earth anyway, animal locked in his basement—behind a heavy layer of security, I might add?"

"For our safety, Laine. Can you imagine if that thing got out?"

Laine threw the cover back over the cage. Yoon Ah had her pictures, and he was getting a headache from trying to look at the creature that never quite solidified, its wings, legs, and belly shimmering in and out of view, like a chameleon blending in with its surroundings.

"We'd be safer if we all knew these things existed, instead of the truth being literally covered up!"

"You're right, it doesn't look good. But he's my dad. I trust him. There's a perfectly logical reason he's been keeping this under wraps—not the least that he works fer the government an' is contractually obligated"—Andy stressed the last two words, his brogue growing thicker as he grew more passionate—"not t'talk about top secret projects!"

"Adults always lie," Laine shot back. Andy just couldn't see reason and it was infuriating. "Always tell you it's for the greater good, but when has it ever been? All their half-truths just benefit them and never us. Isn't that right, Miss my-mom-ran-off-in-the-middle-of-the-night-and-no-one's-seen-her-since?"

Sudden silence descended on the basement, broken only by the slap of Yoon Ah's palm striking Laine's face. The slight girl rushed past him up the steps, soft sobbing drifting down to him and Andy.

Laine dodged the first fist Andy threw his way, but stumbled on the stairs, nowhere to go, no way to avoid the furious punch that cracked against his jaw, disorienting him as he scrambled to get away.

"Make ma girl cry, will ye?" Andy spat out, pouncing onto Laine, striking harder and faster.

Laine kicked out at him, arms up to cover his face. On Earth, he could've taken Andy, no sweat, but even after the last few weeks of nonstop lacrosse, he still hadn't adjusted to Thorunn's higher gravitational pull, and the more he exerted himself, the quicker he tired. Plus, Andy had jumped him without warning, pinning him on the hard concrete, granite steps digging painfully into his spine.

Yoon Ah's mom had left, that was a fact. She needed to grow up and not run away crying whenever someone brought it up. But though in the moment Laine had wanted to hurt Andy by hurting Yoon Ah, each blow Andy now delivered made Laine sorely regret his impulsive decision.

Laine's left arm dropped, and Andy landed another punch to his face. The pressure came first, then the pain, and Laine swore he could feel his eyeball trying to leak out through his bones. Andy had definitely fractured his cheekbone, if not shattered it altogether, which was probably much, much worse than getting a chunk of flesh stripped out by the softly sibilating creature in the cage.

"Andy," he tried, getting another punch in the face for his efforts.

"No, you shut up!" Andy was breathing hard now, punches coming slower, giving Laine time to defend himself and land a few hits of his own. "So what if I trust ma dad? So what if he's been keeping secrets? Good or bad, that's fer me to decide, an' don't you dare bring Yoon Ah into your pathetic, delusional paranoia!"

He stepped off Laine and hauled him out of the basement, each step leaving another black and blue bruise on Laine's back. He twisted and scrabbled, but Andy's grip was relentless, and despite his struggles, Laine found himself on Andy's doorstep—schoolbag thrust into his arms—before he could quite get his vision to clear. His face throbbed, pain radiating out from his teeth into his skull. Andy's apoplectic face swam before his eyes, and Laine blinked rapidly to clear the black spots dancing in his vision.

"Get out. Star player or not, I'd better not see you at lacrosse club anytime soon."

Strength was not Laine's friend as he rose trembling to his feet. He staggered over to the doorframe, clutching at it to keep his swaying body upright. He jerked back as Andy slammed the front door shut, almost catching Laine's numb fingers, the harsh Thorunn sun blinding after the darkness of Doctor Frenally's nightmare-inducing basement.

Laine had just the presence of mind to hail a vercycle idling across the street before his legs gave out, and he tumbled into the dust. It was probably too much to hope that whoever stepped off it wouldn't call his parents. Mom was going to be *so* disappointed.

———————————— ● ————————————

Alanna pressed her hands against the crinkly sheets of the bed in the small examination room at Ethaba General. She tried not to bite her lip—it hurt enough as it was—but each moment the doctor delayed returning ratcheted up the tension holding her body rigid. She closed her eyes and breathed, trying to dispel the doubts and fears that had plagued her since she'd first discovered the bruises.

She'd tried to brush them off as nothing, but when the accompanying headaches wouldn't cease and the tiredness lingered no matter how long she slept, she'd had to admit something was wrong. Still, she'd kept her fears to herself, not wanting to visit Ethaba General and deplete their alarmingly dwindling budget, but Jack had come home early one day and found her in bed with all the lights off and fresh bruises mottling her arms, and insisted she go, no matter how it ate into their finances.

The door opened, and a tall, bespectacled man stepped through. His impassive face gave nothing away, but that in of itself was a tell. If nothing were wrong, he'd be smiling, wouldn't he?

"Mrs. Riven?" He took a seat beside her and pulled out his holoscreen, adjusting his glasses as he flicked through the data. "How much detail would you like to know about your condition?"

Alanna gripped the white paper until it tore off the bed. "Leave nothing out."

"You have early on-set Bowman's. We're still not sure how you contracted it, but this isn't a disease we've figured out how to counteract. You have months at best."

"Will it hurt?" Her voice came out smaller than she meant it to, as she thought of Jack, pacing worriedly in the hall outside. Of Laine, off at a friend's house. All the dreams she'd had of their new life—they were all washing away downstream, no place to be stopped up.

The doctor sighed, deep and long. "I won't lie to you. The end is never pleasant. But we'll do everything in our power to keep you comfortable until then."

"And when"—Alanna's voice trembled—"when will I get really sick?"

The doctor flicked through his notes. "Given the early stage of the disease, and assuming no outside stressors, we might not have to admit you until Christmas, at which point things will deteriorate quite rapidly." He glanced through the tiny window at Jack's silhouette. "You should make plans as soon as possible."

"You won't tell him, will you?"

"I'm bound by oath to keep anything we discuss private. But I urge you to inform your husband, Mrs. Riven. Sooner rather than later."

Alanna bit her lip. She couldn't. Jack was settling in so well—the news would throw him off-kilter—no, it would destroy him. Not to mention, Laine could always tell when Jack was holding something back. If he found out about her illness before she could properly prepare him, there was no telling how he'd react.

If she still had until Christmas, she'd wait until the

day after to break the news. They'd have one last perfect holiday together before the end. By then both Jack and Laine would be established enough to carry on.

But oh, she'd never see her home again, never close her eyes while she lifted her face to Earth's sun or hear the late-summer cicadas and crickets in the woods where she'd played as a little girl.

The doctor handed Alanna a box of tissues, and she was startled to discover she'd been crying, hot wetness splashing down her cheeks. The man looked at her with the softest, kindest expression she'd ever seen on a medical professional.

"Take all the time you need," he told her gently, placing a warm hand atop her arm. "I'll write a 'script to help with the pain meantime."

He remained in the room, quietly unobtrusive while Alanna collected herself. After she'd downloaded his prescription to her clip, she wiped away the last of her tears and freshened up at the small sink near the door. She thanked the doctor for his time, not quite looking at him, not wanting the reminder of how little time she had left.

"What's the verdict, then?" Jack asked anxiously, gripping her hand as soon as she stepped through the door. Her attempt to hide her wince didn't go unnoticed, and Jack let her hand fall, looking as nervous as she felt.

"As I suspected, just terrible headaches brought on by Thorunn's higher gravity. I still haven't adjusted yet."

"You sure? What about the bruising? My colleagues—"

"It all goes together. The doctor knows what he's talking about," Alanna interrupted, struggling not to cry. She'd never kept anything from Jack before. Would he forgive her after she was gone? "We just need to stop by the pharmacy on our way out. I should be pain free in no time."

Jack took her hand again—much more gently—and gave it a soft squeeze.

"I'm glad to hear it. You don't know how worried I've been." The relieved grin he gave her stabbed her like near-molten knives. "Since I already clocked out for the day, what should we do with the rest of this fine evening?"

Alanna smiled, trying to tamp down the feelings of guilt pulsing in time to her ever-present headache. "Well, there is that little *Grille d'Anlo* place I've been wanting to try."

—————— ● ——————

"If I press here, does it hurt?"

Laine yelped and glared at the man through his one good eye.

He seemed familiar, despite the leather jacket he still wore even inside—though he'd switched his stiff riding gloves for soft, white ones and was apparently unmindful of the blood dripping onto him from Laine's swollen nose and knuckles.

"First your uncle, allegedly, now Andy—you really have a knack for picking the wrong people to tick off."

Laine finally placed him. The nurse who had given him his physical his first day on Thorunn. Average height, dark hair cut just below his ears, and attractive features that resembled Principal Kim too much to be coincidental.

"Now, Yoon Ah assured me you won't mention this little incident to Dad and subsequently get Andy kicked off lacrosse club for fighting if I don't take you to Ethaba General?"

Telling on Andy was a tempting prospect given the damage he'd done to Laine's face, but a stint at Ethaba General could damage Laine's reputation at school and destroy any remaining trust between him and Mom—not to mention the bits of independence he'd gained by staying mostly trouble-free on Thorunn.

"Yeah," he slurred through his teeth, lingering pain keeping his jaw shut. He'd been assured the local anaesthetic smeared across his face would take effect any minute now, and he was still waiting on it. "I take it you're Yoon Ah's brother?"

"Peter Kim, really wishing I hadn't taken the Nightingale Pledge right about now. Yoon Ah told me what happened, and there's precious little holding me back from finishing what Andy started."

Despite his harsh words, Peter's hands were steady as they cleaned Laine's wounds, daubed on iodine and guided his face into the medical grade nano-diffuser set up in the spare room of the Kim family residence. The insides of the machine glowed a soft yellow when Peter turned it on, though Laine felt little more than a cool, almost wet sensation as the nanites worked at knitting his flesh and bone back together, the anaesthesia finally delivering on its promised pain relief.

Close to a half hour later, Peter switched off the nano-diffuser and turned Laine's head this way and that to inspect his handiwork.

"Looks good," he pronounced.

"What about my bruises?" Laine demanded, irritability slipping into his words as pain crept back into his jaw and a low-level throbbing danced along the bottom of his eye. "And I still can't quite see right."

Peter shook his head as he swept about the room, making sure every little item was in its proper place. "Regulations prohibit the use of nano-diffusers for more than twenty minutes a day on anyone under eighteen. Same reason I can only use it on half power. It's up to nature at this point. Maybe some painkillers. But you'll need a prescription for anything stronger than what we have in our medicine cabinet."

And Laine wasn't about to step foot in Ethaba General anytime soon, so he'd have to suffer through with whatever he could find in Gordon's kitchen. At least his recovery time had been reduced from months to weeks—the marvel of modern medicine.

A knock sounded on the door, followed by Yoon Ah herself popping into the room.

"You're the last person I thought would wanna see me," Laine said.

"Don't get it twisted, I'm still hurt by what you

said, but Andy shouldn't have beat you like that. Not because of me. We're ah"—she looked at the floor—"we're taking a break while he gets himself under control."

"What?"

Andy was the best guy at Ethaba High. Adored by all, good student, MVP. Laine had never seen him angry before, and he certainly hadn't thought Yoon Ah would put the brakes on their relationship because of his reaction to Laine's provocation.

The left side of Laine's face spasmed, wringing a tear from his eye. It felt about the same as the guilt that set in and just as difficult to shove aside.

"I pushed him to it—"

"And like I said, I'm still upset over that—"

"But he was only defending you. I'd do the same thing in his shoes."

"I hope not! Both of you need to grow up, starting with your apology to me."

She wanted him to apologise for the truth? It made little sense, but perhaps Andy would let him back onto the team if he could work up enough sincerity.

"I'm sorry your mom left and never came back?"

Peter's whole body tensed like he wanted to hit Laine, and he very visibly breathed deep and held himself back. "Try again."

"I'm sorry your feelings were hurt?"

Both Peter and Yoon Ah crossed their arms, expressions going completely flat.

"I can let you limp back home without any pain relief, if that's what you're angling for," Peter said.

Nothing on his face indicated he was joking, and Laine ran through a dozen different variations of "I'm sorries" before he came up with one that should be acceptable, though even the thought of speaking it tasted like rancid lemons.

Putting on a face that felt contrite, he said, "I'm sorry I said unkind things on purpose to make you feel bad."

Peter's eyebrows climbed so high they were apt to win the Piolet d'Or. Yoon Ah seemed slightly more mollified.

"Okay," she said, nodding. "I'll see you around, then."

"I'd be happy to see you again never," Peter said after she'd left the room. "Here's your meds. Have a nice day, and I mean that as sincerely as you meant your apology just now."

With that he ushered Laine to the front door, shutting it only slightly less hard than Andy had. Thankfully, the Kim residence was closer to Gordon's house than the Frenallys', and Laine didn't have to suffer overlong in the early evening heat before the two-story building came into view.

"That's one heckuva shiner," Gordon said, a smirk highlighting his features when Laine stumbled through the door. "What'd you do, insult somebody's girl?"

"Shove off, Gordon," Laine rasped out, prompting resounding laughter from his uncle.

"Of all the pathetically idiotic teenaged things to do!" A tear or two escaped Gordon's eyes, and his deep, mocking voice followed Laine on his slow limp to his room, floating down through the thin curtain. Unfortunately Laine's face hurt too much to drown out the noise with a pillow over his head.

Andy hit hard, and despite Peter's help, Laine still felt like he'd been kicked by a horse. It hurt more than the falls he'd had in parkour stunts gone wrong back in L.A., and it was debatable whether his eye would be better by the time Andy allowed him back on the team.

But he could play through a lack of depth perception—heck, he'd play blindfolded if he had to. No way was he losing the cred he'd built up the last few weeks. Not over a stupid fight. If Andy couldn't see that his dad was all kinds of shady, that was his problem; meddling further in the matter wouldn't help get Laine back into lacrosse club any sooner.

Laine attempted a little homework as the evening wore on, but the mounting pain soon forced him into a fetal position on his bed, the newly healed bones and skin still tender and aching with the weeks' worth of rejuvenation he'd undergone in such a short time. For all he swallowed, the pills from Peter felt lodged halfway down his throat, providing little relief against the agonising burning beneath his skin.

Laine stayed in his room even when he heard his parents return from wherever they'd been off at, only sneaking upstairs to the kitchen to rummage in the medicine tray when his left eye started leaking tears and refused to quit.

"Acetaminophen, ibuprofen, acetylsalicylic—oh,

hello?"

The tiny bottle stashed at the very back of the tray hadn't been in the cabinet before. Laine could barely make out the bright blue lettering through his watering eyes, but he was sure that tell tale font meant only one thing—an opioid-based painkiller. Very effective, very hard to get. On Earth at least; it seemed things were different on Thorunn.

"Narprolepscene. Let's see just how well you work," Laine murmured, prying off the top with shaking hands.

A bit of water washed two pills down, and he sank into one of the kitchen chairs, clutching at the table as the pain spiked and lessened in waves. During a moment of clarity, a sudden flicker of light and agitated muttering from upstairs caught his attention, and he crept over to the steps leading to Gordon's room-slash-labs on the second floor. The stairs swam unsettlingly before him as he whispered his way up, but finally Laine reached the top, bumbled his way across the short landing, and pressed his ear to the seam of Gordon's door.

"And when did you say you noticed the breach?"

"Around five. I came home to a distraught Andy after a fight with his girl. Which I don't understand, they've been inseparable since primary school, but after running around the bush with him on why, I decided my time'd be better spent doin' somethin' productive in the lab. After a couple minutes, I noticed a few things out of place. Nothing obviously taken, but enough to make me think someone got in."

"Anything incriminating on the footage?"

"I only record when workin'; I wasn't expectin' someone t'get past Hexagon level security."

The unwitting praise felt good. Laine, one. Doctor Frenally, zero. Laine cupped his hand around one ear, the words coming more clearly as the narprolepscene kicked in and the throbbing in his cheek subsided.

"Any idea who?"

A bitter laugh came over the line. "How about, I dunno, everyone? This is delicate work, Riven, an' we're on the verge of a breakthrough. This project—if I can get it t'work—it'll completely revolutionise stealth tech, an' who wouldn't want to get their hands on that?"

"The Cabal *has* been causing more trouble in Skytown recently," Gordon said, voice reflective. His chair squeaked, no doubt in protest to him leaning back against it. "Could be they've started sending out spies. I'd suggest reporting this to the Consul and tripling security. I'm close to a breakthrough of my own in the forest and can't afford any setbacks."

"Already done, just wanted t'give ye a heads up. Anyway, I've gotta sign off, Ira's home an' we can finally eat that dinner I've been keepin' warm for us."

Gordon's farewell was lost as Laine pulled away from the door and crept, noiseless, back to his room. But not before pocketing another few pills. Full as the bottle was, they wouldn't be missed.

Laine stared up at the walls of Ethaba High. They seemed to have grown twenty feet since yesterday, and he was never gladder he and Andy didn't share any classes. A light breeze washed over Laine, making him wish he'd brought his jacket. The Thorunn he'd experienced so far had never been cold, never would be, according to the school handbook Dustin had overenthusiastically read to him, but a metallic taste hung in the air, oxidised pennies left out in the rain too long, threading an ever-present chill into Ethaba's bones.

Laine rubbed at his arms one more time and headed inside. Dustin shot him a worried look when Laine slouched into homeroom, making no attempt to cover the bruising on his face. Dustin wilted under Laine's glare after a weak attempt at conversation and very timidly slid over the details of the mathletes competition. Only the arrival of their homeroom teacher saved the handwritten card from being shredded into a million tiny scraps.

Despite the clock on the wall marking the time in an inexorable crawl forwards, Laine could swear it stopped—and in fact marched backward—for how long homeroom dragged out.

Math was no better, and Laine drifted off more than once, regaining consciousness long enough to growl at Dustin whenever his classmate nudged him. He'd humiliated Laine enough by answering for him when their teacher had taken attendance; Laine certainly didn't need his help staying awake. He hadn't napped during the day since age five, and he wasn't about to start, no matter how the throbbing pain in his entire left side battered at him.

But as the morning wore on, Laine's back and left arm started to go numb, and by fourth period the pen he clutched might as well have been a block of wood for all the good it was doing him. It was study period anyway, so Laine ducked out of his seat when the supervising teacher was helping another student.

He paused at the bulletin board. Surprisingly, his winning play still cycled on it. Yoon Ah's doing no doubt—Andy most certainly would have hacked into the school's edda-net and pulled the footage if not convinced he'd get in trouble for doing so.

Andy's blind trust in his dad was a little scary. Even Yoon Ah had been willing to admit that Doctor Frenally's super secret basement lab, with the radio-active monster hidden in a cage, was super shady.

Laine turned to go and almost collided with Andy himself. He glared at Laine with red-rimmed eyes and made to shove past him, but Laine caught Andy's arm, wincing in pain and suddenly very aware of the circular narprolepscene tablets sitting against the lining of his jeans' pockets.

"Unhand me if y'don't fancy a matching black eye."

Laine held out his hands, wobbling a little when he released Andy. "I ain't here to fight. But Andy, man, you gotta listen. Your dad, my uncle—I heard them talking last night. Your dad is convinced whatever he's working on is both valuable and sensitive enough for somebody to try and break in and steal it—he's got no idea it was us—and he's reported it to the Consul. The Consul, Andy! And my uncle was going on about lokians and some group called the Cabal."

"Mum always tells me the smartest people have no common sense. I'm starting to see what she means." Andy looked at Laine like one might a very small child. "Let me make this as clear as possible. One, both your uncle an' my father—an' your father too, for that matter—work fer the government on highly classified projects. Two, the Cabal is a terrorist organisation that's been plaguing Skytown for the last few years, an' has made it their aim to see anything regarding the Consul torn down."

Andy took a step closer to Laine. "Connect the dots. Course my father's worried, worried a terrorist group might have gotten their hands on sensitive, confidential information that could be used to destroy his work, disrupt our lives, and realise the Cabal's dream of blowing Skytown sky-high. Now leave this an' me an' Yoon Ah alone 'fore you get us all accused of conspiring with known terrorists an' evil creatures like the lokians."

The older teen shook his head and headed off to class.

"Can't say I didn't warn you," Laine said under his breath. Deciding against taking his illicit pain relief right there in the hallway, he limped down the hall to the bathrooms but changed direction when he spotted a nearby service door. A set of stairs on the other side led to the roof, and Laine laboured his way up and flopped onto the little bench installed by the garden club.

Only one other student was on the roof, and they gave Laine a cheerful thumbs-up before returning to their weeding. The little rooftop garden was peaceful, a feeder at one corner attracting all sorts of sweetly singing birds, and an assortment of different sized pots held many fragrant flowers.

Laine worked up enough spit to wash down a couple pills and stared at the sky while he waited for them to kick in.

Frix season—whatever that was—was supposed to be a couple months away, and it was terrifying, or wonderful, but definitely intense, depending on who Laine talked to, the sky too black to make out Sól, let alone Frey or Freja. But no clouds marred the deep blue Laine gazed at. It wasn't the blue of Earth— Thorunn's sky resembled an artificially coloured pool. Night was never as black either, the whole planet bathed in a weird purple haze. If he hadn't been forced to come to Thorunn, Laine might even like the place.

He blinked, and the sun shone right in his eyes. The rooftop was quiet, and when he finally got his floppy neck to raise his head he discovered he was alone. The ground blurred in and out, and he lay back down quickly, holding his eyelids open, because suddenly his muscles refused to do their one job.

"Man, I feel weird," Laine mumbled.

Was it normal for his mouth to be so dry? Opening and closing his jaw didn't seem to be helping. Instead he could feel his breakfast stuck fast at the back of his throat. He swallowed. That helped.

No it didn't. Cold washed over his skin, the numbness from before taking hold of his fingers. He went to activate his clip and missed three times, almost jabbing himself in his one good eye before a projection of the current time flickered into the air.

"I missed fifth and sixth period?" More goosebumps broke out across Laine's bare arms, and he gagged again, wiping away spit with cold hands leached of colour.

But his cheeks—he patted his face. His face was too hot by far, and the edges of the world started to dim like someone turning down a light.

"Laine! Oh my—Andy! Grab him!"

What was Yoon Ah up here for? Laine tried to go to her, and the ground slid out from underneath him, concrete spinning up to crack against his head. His stomach heaved one final time, its spewing contents choking him as he jerked back and forth, clogging his nostrils, and he couldn't breathe,

couldn't breat—

———————— ● ————————

The living room door banged open, and Jack rushed in, an absolutely wild look on his face.

"Alanna, come quick!" he shouted. "It's Laine!"

Alanna jumped up, shoes already half on as her stomach dropped, pulse ratcheting higher as she struggled to find her keys—she knew that tone all too well, the sight of wire-rimmed glasses dangling askew off her husband's nose distressingly familiar. He still wore his lab coat, white material stained from whatever aborted experiment he'd been conducting in the upstairs lab.

"Grab a helmet," he said, snatching Gordon's vercycle keys off the ring by the door.

The ride was short, frantic, Jack almost running others off the road in his rush to reach the hospital. Alanna didn't wait for him to stop or even depower the engine after they reached the ER doors, instead taking off running into Ethaba General while the vercycle growled and spluttered at Jack's efforts to quiet it. The entrance sat beneath an overhang, but finding a better place to charge the solar powered vehicle while inside was the least of Alanna's concerns.

"Back already, Mrs. Riven?" the nurse at the front desk asked. Alanna shook her head, clutching too hard at the counter.

"My son," she gasped, "my husband, we got a call."

The nurse—Kathryn, according to her name tag—flicked through several different displays on her holoscreen, unable to hide the "O" of surprise her lips formed when she pulled up the right information. Jack came up next to Alanna, one arm encircling her waist. She twisted her hands anxiously while Kathryn paged over another nurse.

"Peter'll take you to him," she said, pressing a few more buttons and typing furiously. "Here's the file." She passed over a preloaded holoscreen, and Peter took it while gesturing for Jack and Alanna to "Come right this way."

As they hurried after the young man, Alanna recalled the last time she'd been in the building. How did yesterday feel so far away already? The tapping of their feet against linoleum and the smell of antiseptic was already so foreign despite the hours they'd spent testing her, only to tell her something too awful to quite comprehend.

Alanna shook the thoughts away, trying to focus on Peter's voice.

"—found him just in time. Five minutes later and you'd have been going to the morgue. He's still unconscious but breathing on his own, and we've got a team monitoring him in case that changes."

Peter turned a corner and led Alanna and Jack into a windowless, single-occupancy room filled with various medical professionals. Some were studying the monitors clustered around the head of the bed, others Consulted quietly with each other, looking over their shoulders every few moments, while still more adjusted IV lines and catheters and scribbled messy notes onto their holoscreens—and in the middle of it all lay Laine, so pale he looked half gone already.

Alanna had only seen him so once before, when he'd fallen from a second-storey window and cracked open his skull at only eight years old. From the way Jack shook beside her, he was remembering it too. Before she could stop herself, Alanna reached out and touched her fingertips to Laine's bruised cheek. It was cold and she wondered where the ugly mottling had come from. He looked like he'd been punched in the face repeatedly.

A dreadful thought occurred to her, and her legs gave out, every head in the room snapping towards her when she crumpled to the floor, weeping with a force she could not restrain.

"Alanna? Alanna, what's wrong?" Jack sank down next to her and dabbed at her face with a handkerchief he pulled from his pocket.

She only shook her head, eyes blurry and throat tight. How could she explain that Laine was in the hospital because of her? Because he'd obviously been in a fight and upon looking for something to ease the pain had stumbled across the bottle of narprolepscene she'd taken home yesterday and tucked away where Jack wouldn't think to look? Her husband had only seen the headache medications the nurses had given her and not the opioid-based painkillers they'd pressed surreptitiously into her hands, respecting her decision to keep her diagnosis between her and the hospital.

How could she explain to Jack why she had a prescription that strong?

She opened her mouth to try and tell him, but only choking sobs came out. From Peter's words it was clear Laine had almost died from an accidental overdose, and that had frightened Jack badly enough; she couldn't add to his consternation, she just couldn't!

Alanna sobbed until her tears ran dry, after which she accepted a hand from Peter and pulled herself, shaking, to her feet. The sympathetic look in his eyes told her that he knew why she wept so.

"Mom?"

Her baby was awake! Tears forgotten, she rushed back to Laine's side, peppering his face with kisses as slow-blinking confusion, wide-eyed recognition, and then abject terror swept across his face.

"I didn't mean to!" he stammered, shrinking back further when he spotted Jack hovering over her shoulder. Alanna couldn't see her husband's face, but she knew it must have fallen, a few more lines of regret etching themselves onto his brow.

"Laine," she whispered. "You have nothing to fear. Your father and I love you very much. We know this was an accident—"

"We do?"

"Hush." Alanna stopped Jack from advancing with a splayed hand on his chest.

"I know moving here wasn't easy on you, but you've done well in school, made friends, stayed mostly out of trouble, and we won't punish you"— Jack tried to say something again, but she silenced him with a look, reminding him wordlessly that she came from a tribe with a long history of women chieftains—"for this mistake, but you will rectify whatever situation caused you to end up here.

"You will make peace with whomever you need to make peace, and you will not put yourself in danger like this ever again. We came to Thorunn because we didn't want to bury you under the steel and concrete of Los Angeles. I will not see you buried here."

Laine gulped and nodded. He had tested her time and time again, and Alanna's heart hurt that it took something so serious for him to finally listen. Perhaps it was too much to hope he'd stop rebelling altogether, but this incident might grant her and Jack a few months' reprieve at least.

"How long until he can come home?" Alanna asked Peter.

"A couple hours more at most. We want to make sure the toxins are flushed from his system, but then you're free to go. The doctor will probably want him to stay under observation for the next few days, but that's entirely your decision." He nodded to Jack as well, including him in the conversation. "Sorry you had to upend your day."

"Your frankness has made much of an upsetting situation," Alanna said. "Thank you."

She and Jack lingered the required hours, watching as a young girl claiming Peter as her brother toppled into the room, followed by a worried-looking young man with dark hair and ruddy cheeks, lacrosse gear still strapped to him. The young lady had a chess set in one hand and a bag full of books slung across her shoulder. They must have just come from school.

"Yoon Ah, Andy!?" Laine exclaimed, sitting up straighter on the bed.

That was good. His strength was returning, and colour had started to flush his cheeks, restoring his normal tan complexion. Laine flicked his eyes at Alanna, face reddening further.

"Sorry, guys," he mumbled, and Andy's eyes went wide. He asked Laine to repeat himself, and he did, slowly, grudgingly, but with genuine contrition.

Peter—who had tensed up upon the teens' arrival—relaxed at Laine's words, a smile highlighting his handsome features.

"My sister and her boyfriend were the ones who found Laine, Mrs. Riven," he said. "He owes them a great deal."

No wonder then, that her son had apologised so readily. From their murmured conversation, Alanna discerned it was Andy who had bruised Laine so, and not without cause. But everything that happened after their altercation seemed to have settled the dispute between the three young people, if the smiles beginning to break out were any indication.

Yoon Ah set down her chess board, a beautiful hand-carved magnetic set; she held it upside down to demonstrate once all the pieces were placed, giggling at Laine's surprise, and each teen took turns playing to pass the time.

Satisfied her darling was in good company, Alanna stepped outside, beckoning Jack to follow her.

"There goes our dream of having our own place by Christmas," he said, leaning back against the wall of the corridor and blowing out a sigh through thinned lips. "Between yesterday and today, Ethaba General's coffers will be nicely lined with our credits."

"We'll figure it out." Something inside Alanna twinged as she said the words. Whether from guilt or her actual condition, she didn't know. The end result was the same; she'd be in the hospital soon and haemorrhaging their money away.

Ethaba High was government funded, so Laine's education was one less thing she had to worry about, but Jack was too caught up in his work—every day proclaiming himself on the edge of a breakthrough—to distress him with her news. Alanna had to wait for a better time to tell him. Christmas, she promised herself again, one last Christmas.

Jack would be angry, upset she was leaving him so soon, but she hoped in the end he'd forgive her, find a way to move on and be happy after. If happiness were to be had after losing—as Jack often put it—"the light of my life, heart of my heart."

What would she do if their positions were reversed? Alanna shuddered at the idea of Jack in pain and banished the thought.

"Yes, we will," Jack agreed, eyes shining with excitement. "Gordon and I are so close. I just have to do some more soil testing at the far end of town."

"Where the radiation is?" Alanna frowned. "That doesn't sound safe."

"There's something about the tunnels there that seems . . . out of place. Don't worry, I'm taking the necessary precautions. Once I figure this out, we'll be set for life! I only need a little more time."

Jack turned to look through the slightly open door at the animated—what a lovely word!—sight of their son. ". . . And Laine not getting into any more scrapes." He hung his head. "That's like asking it to snow in the desert, isn't it?"

"Technically, Antarctica is a desert," Alanna pointed out.

Jack waggled a playful finger at her, and it warmed her heart to see him smiling after the scare they'd had.

"Don't you start."

The doctor chose that moment to join them in the hallway. As Peter had predicted, he tried to insist on Laine remaining under observation to make sure he wasn't "a danger to himself and others," but Alanna and Jack stood firm, and a little while later saw them all walking home, Gordon having come by to pick up his vercycle once they'd called and filled him in on the situation. Alanna thought it a shame he hadn't come in, but as Jack had said, theirs was delicate work that couldn't be left alone long.

Her husband disappeared upstairs into Gordon's lab as soon as they got inside, leaving her and Laine alone downstairs. Alanna caught Laine by the arm before he could vanish into his room.

"Today reminded me"—she drew him closer and hugged him briefly but fiercely—"how fragile our lives are. Come, sit with me a while."

She gestured through the corridor to the garden beyond, and Laine followed her outside to sit between the small flowerbeds she'd been trying to revive. The sky was still flush with the sun's amber light, but Thorunn's twin moons had already risen, huge and luminous in the early evening.

"Do you see those stars?" Alanna asked, pointing to them. She rested in a white garden chair while Laine elected to recline on the ground. "I like to imagine that one is ours, visible even from so far away."

"No way," Laine scoffed, picking at the dirt. "Wouldn't be so bright, if that were the case. I think it is possible to see it though, if it gets dark enough. And you have a good 'scope."

"I can ask your dad to borrow one from the ES-ReC. We'll stargaze again like when you were little."

Laine laughed, but a bitter note soured the sound. "Sure, ask him. Whether he'll ever remember is a different case. Especially after today." He blew out a sigh and flopped onto his back.

"Laine, sweetheart, it's been a rough couple months, you know your father's busy and—"

"He's always busy, Mom!" Laine sat up suddenly, ripping out clumps of spiky grass and tossing the flakes in the air. "Yeah, sure, he came today, but to tell me off, I could see it in his eyes. He thinks I'm a failure. I didn't mean—!"

He cut himself off and flung himself back down, staring at the slowly darkening sky above. "How come we have narprolepscene anyway? Isn't it prescription only?"

Alanna closed her eyes. "I've been getting terrible headaches," she said softly. "The medication should ease them, and by the new year, I won't be in pain anymore." There. It was all true. But she knew how Laine would interpret her phrasing. The words being factual didn't make the utterance of them any less a lie.

Laine's frown shifted into a half-smile. "That sucks. I'm glad you'll be okay. I've got enough to worry about, what with trying to convince Andy to let me back on the team."

Alanna reached down to ruffle his hair. The peaceful expression that had eased over Laine's face—that was why she had to keep her diagnosis to herself. She couldn't let Jack and Laine even suspect how ill she was. Not yet. She could carry the burden of her truth a little longer if it meant their smiles wouldn't be extinguished before she slipped away from them.

"Did you know your great-grandfather was a five-time major league lacrosse champion?"

Laine rolled over and propped himself up, eyes gleaming with interest, and Alanna chuckled, ignoring the pain that winced through her. After Laine went to bed she looked forward to swallowing half—no a quarter—of a narprolepscene tablet. After she had hidden them in a new safe spot of course; no sense in Jack coming across them and becoming suspicious.

Alanna shook away the aches and started recounting the story, silently battling the keen weight of Thorunn's oppressive gravity as she soaked up every precious moment with Laine.

Somehow she had to teach him everything she'd ever learned *and* convince him to be on speaking terms with his father in the little time she had left.

It felt almost impossible, but Alanna had never given up on anything before. She wouldn't give up on Laine.

5

Kenton and the Igis Chosen had been traversing the Cerado for a number of days—their path wending east by northeast as they strove to avoid straying into vyss'n hunting grounds, their food and water dwindling down to very little—when their scouts came bounding back with the welcome news that a sizeable water hole had been spotted ahead. Several of the others almost forgot themselves and shifted in their excitement, but a curt word from Kenton held them back. Assuming klia'an form wouldn't be safe until they'd acquired a more human method of travel, and given the strange dome protecting the outpost town nearest them, they couldn't steal transportation until they'd reached the town at the foothills of Mount Lalethusl, still a week's hard travel away.

Kenton updated his maps as they headed for the water, making notes in the margins as to how many trees lined the banks of which rivers, which bluffs hid them and which didn't, and what types of animals they'd encountered—and how to avoid them. Though tedious, the work would greatly aid their return journey. Kenton made sure to review the detailed drawings with the others each night; by the time they finished their mission they'd know every pebble, every speck of dust in the dry, breezeless grasslands.

Preoccupied as he was with noting the position of the water hole, Kenton noticed it too late when the young klia'ans broke rank and sprinted down to the banks of the dark waters where they lapped in relief at the surface that reflected a perfectly clear sky. He shouted after them, but to no avail; thirst held hostage their common sense, only keeping them of a mind to wet their dry throats. One or two actually tumbled in head-over-paws at the very edges in their eagerness.

"You can't drink yet!" Kenton shouted, running to catch up. "Not until we know it's safe!"

"We didn't see or scent anything odd," one scout—Dirnha—responded through a half-yawn, showing off sharp canines.

Indeed, the water hole looked innocuous enough, an inviting expanse set like a precious jewel in the middle of the dusty green and yellow shrubs dotting the Cerado. But Kenton remembered the usual fate of the wildebeests that strayed too close to the edge of many such similar places in South Africa, the country of his birth. His Umama and Pa had taken him on safari quite a few times before Annie came along, letting him take pictures of the bleached skulls he'd discovered in the nearby scrub.

No such bones were visibly apparent, but despite that—and despite the lithe, apex predators klia'ans were when shifted to s'hinoian form—Kenton couldn't help but find wisdom in caution. They were by no means the largest creatures to stalk the Cerado.

He held Dirnha back when the scout made to join the others.

"Don't you see that there are no other animals here? No fresh tracks or a well worn anlo path?" Kenton raised his voice. "Get back from the edges! Your thirst can wait until we can be certain there's no danger here."

Seri joined him in prodding the Igis Chosen up the banks, away from waters swirled with mud and grass. They came, but grudgingly and not without protest, tongues darting out to lick up the droplets clinging to the fur of their chins.

All except Bo.

He had practically his whole face buried in the water, drinking as if he'd never drink again. Kenton called louder, knowing Bo heard him by the way his ears tilted back.

Sighing in frustration, Kenton marched up to his friend and shook his shoulder to get his attention.

"Stop pretending you didn't hear me, and let's get back a bit—we're far too close, and who knows what lurks in those depths?"

"Nothing 'cept some tasty-looking little fish," Bo said, finally dragging himself closer to dry ground where he shook all over, spraying droplets into Kenton's eyes. He smacked Bo's shoulder in playful annoyance.

"We'll draw a sick anlo away from its herd before we leave the Cerado," he promised. "But give me peace of mind, and let's get up from here."

Bo cast a lingering glance at the water, obviously

still thirsty, but followed. Or tried to. One misstep, and suddenly the mud was swallowing him down, a hidden sinkhole just below the surface.

"Ken!" he growled in alarm. A second paw stuck as Bo worked to free himself, scrabbling at the bank with his forelegs.

Kenton leant forward and yelled for Seri, who clamped her jaws around the quirn strapped to his back and planted her paws firmly in the dark earth behind him. Together they hauled Bo out, pulling his hindlegs free with a sucking *pop* and tumbling in a laughing heap onto the edges of the water hole. Bo's tongue darted out to groom the mud away from his coat, and he wrinkled his muzzle at the taste.

"Tchah!" he spat. "Here you are worryin' about vyss'ngryr and the like, and it's the stupid dirt we gotta watch for."

Seri swished her tail at him, flicking her dark-tipped ears as a lazy smirk graced her features. "Next time keep back 'til we've finished scou—BO!"

She screamed as a dark shape blurred out of the water behind Bo, snatching him out of Kenton's hands and dragging him back into the water, disappearing between one heartbeat and the next. Seri shrieked again when Kenton plunged in after Bo, no deliberation, no hesitation.

The dark fathoms of the deceptively deep water settled quickly above his head, but Kenton paid the rapidly receding surface no mind, forcing his eyes open and his body forward, searching for the sinuous monster that had seized his friend. Bo had been right;

there were little fishes in the water, darting away from Kenton's frantic path as he fought against his body's buoyancy to get to Bo before it was too late. Just ahead he could see the dark bottom of the water hole, the monster's retreating form cutting through the murky depths with savage ease.

Kenton pushed himself harder. He couldn't lose Bo. Not when the faces of his dead family still danced through his darkest dreams. Beyond that, none of the young klia'ans would look at him the same, their blind trust in him replaced with a wary suspicion that they might not return from whatever tasks he set them to.

Kenton started to feel light-headed, bubbles escaping the sides of his mouth as he realised he hadn't taken in enough air before diving after Bo. He pressed his lips together further, and there! Bo was thrashing in the monster's grip, blood streaming out from where its teeth punctured his hide. The situation looked dire, but Kenton knew it had to open its mouth to gulp Bo down.

He struck the instant its jaws released and hauled Bo away from the gaping maw, beating back the leviathan with his quirn. He kicked out for the surface as the creature recoiled, its whole body wriggling as it recovered its bearings. Bones and other bits of assorted carcasses peeped out from under heavy-looking rocks—that was why there had been naught around the water hole.

The monster had drowned them all, saving the meat of its victims in a grisly underwater locker.

Bo's head flopped around as Kenton bore them closer to the surface. He didn't dare glance back. The creature was effortlessly fast, and every moment he wasted worrying about how close it was to them was another moment Bo went without air, another moment that Kenton's lungs screamed at him to just open his mouth and replenish them with oxygen. His eyes stung with the filth the churning waters flung into them, and he strained to keep them fixed on the growing path of light that marked the surface, and safety.

Just as the burning became too much to bear, Kenton's head broke through, and he sucked in deep lungfuls of air, sputtering and coughing at the sudden influx. No sooner had a wave of relief rushed over him than he was tugged under again. The monster had latched onto Bo and pulled them back, angry to be denied its prize.

Kenton smacked its head a second time, injuring one of the milky white eyes. Blood and some other gooey substance oozed out, pain distracting the creature long enough for Kenton to make another break for the surface. He somehow had to get to the banks without running out of strength or getting caught in the mud. If that happened, all was lost.

Kenton shifted his grip on the still-unconscious Bo so that he held him solely with his left arm, freeing his right to wield his quirn more effectively. Like the first time it had grabbed Bo, the monster launched itself from the depths,water sluicing off its dark skin, catching the light in a terrifying display of raw strength and speed. In the next instant it would crash down on them, driving Kenton into the bed of the water hole, trapping him in the clinging mud and winning back Bo for good.

Kenton couldn't let that happen.

One arm keeping Bo's head above the waters, Kenton reached with the fingers of the other to hit the button that sent frix crackling up and down the length of his quirn. Between his frantic dive and the terror he felt staring up at the massive bulk above him blocking out the sun, all the breath had been driven from his lungs. His desperate gamble could go wrong, very badly wrong. Frix and water didn't mix at all. Kenton's next breath might well be his last.

But if he didn't fire, it certainly would be.

He squeezed hard. Brilliant white-blue light shot out of his quirn, sending the creature into convulsions, and it dropped like a stone millimetres shy of Kenton, the massive displacement pushing him and Bo towards the shore. It recovered quickly however, not even the loss of its eye dissuading it as it shook off the burning. Burning that travelled straight up Kenton's arm, moulding his weapon to his hand.

He had to get Bo to dry land before the monster tried again—a difficult feat, considering his arm had started to go numb, his legs struggling to propel his leaden body the last few metres to shore. If Bo would just wake up, he'd have an easier time of it.

"Shift, shift!" he yelled directly into the lolling klia'an's ear. Bo's golden eyes were glassy and unfocused, unnaturally open, a result of shock, blood loss, and swallowing far too much water. If Kenton could get him to drop out of s'hinoian form, it might be enough to wake Bo and help Kenton free them both from the leviathan's clutches.

It reared up for another strike, every muscle coiled and ready to spring forth in a death blow. This time would be the last, no more chances if they didn't exit the muddy, reddened waters.

"Shift!" Kenton slapped Bo's face and squeezed the nape of his neck. Even half conscious, the action might trigger an instinctive response. A wild idea came to him, and he levelled his weapon directly at Bo, firing another shot. Bo screamed, coming awake in agony by the way he jerked in Kenton's arms. He turned confused, still-glassy eyes on Kenton, ears pulling back in betrayal.

"Shift," Kenton pleaded. They'd run out of time.

The monster shot forward, intent on snatching its prey. Doubtless it would crush Kenton too for good measure. For so large a creature to exist, it had to have some measure of intelligence, and intelligent predators didn't let a threat go unpunished.

But by some miracle, Bo heard him, and his paws turned into hands, jaguar-like face smoothing into more humanoid features, elbows and knees rearranging, strong haunches losing their mass. Kenton released him not a moment too soon, and the water monster shot through the open space between the two teens, gnashing empty jaws furiously, wicked-looking teeth catching on nothing but water. Kenton fired again and again, ignoring the painful jolts sparking up and down his spine, gritting his teeth against the fire that lit under his skin, arms and legs losing sensation as frix rippled out around him, shimmering waves of electricity energising the water.

Seri had shifted and grabbed Bo as he stumbled forward onto the banks, coughing up water. Thrusting him behind her, she too fired her quirn until the creature finally went still.

A cheer went up from the Igis Chosen assembled a short, safe distance away when Kenton emerged from the waters, bloody and dripping with mud, weeds, and some small, dead fish. He smiled at them, heart going faster and faster, a tightness settling into his chest that wouldn't loosen. The adrenaline that had propelled him wore away, replaced by a bone-deep weariness. He wanted to be glad he'd fought such a terrible monster and survived, that he'd rescued Bo, but nothing even resembling euphoria trickled his way as he stared at the shivering klia'an huddled next to Seri.

Kenton willed his heart to slow as the trio trudged up the banks to settle underneath a small tree. He leant heavily on his quirn the whole way. It still smelled of burning ions though he'd powered it down when assured the creature really was dead.

Seri made Bo lie down on a blanket from her pack and began to apply first aid.

"You too, Ken," she said while stitching and wrapping the worst of Bo's wounds. "You took far too much frix, and you're paler than a human ought to be, I think."

Kenton nodded, heart still jumping, breaths still coming fast, then slow, then fast again, arrhythmic in a way that frightened him.

Was he going to die? He couldn't have survived that awful ordeal only to expire in the middle of the Cerado. Strength seemed to leach from his limbs, and when Seri held the last of her water to his lips he found he could barely lift his head to drink, and she had to massage his throat to help him swallow.

Someone else—Leida, he thought, but his eyes were having trouble focusing, and he couldn't be sure—attached a cool, metal and wood device to his chest, and as the minutes went by Kenton felt something loosen, his pulse returning to normal. Leida—it had to be her, who else would have thought to pack regen-rigs but the daughter of one of the village healers—moved the healing apparatus to Bo and set it to run before helping Seri get Kenton up against the tree and breathing easier.

"We can't stay here long," Kenton said and motioned to the scouts to get their maps and go on ahead. There would be other, safer bodies of water. "The scent of blood'll"—he coughed, lungs feeling like someone was scraping a bed of rusty nails through them—"will attract every scavenger in the Cerado within the hour. We can't"—Kenton leaned over and retched, more water spewing out of him—"risk being here after dark. Not if the chsaa-rhee fly this far afield."

"Dirnha mentioned a stand of trees a little ways on," Seri said. "I'll shift back, and you can ride until we get there and hang the hammocks. Leida can take Bo."

Kenton nodded, too weak to say much else, and after cutting up the fish monster, so at least they'd have some meat, the Igis Chosen left the bloody waters behind.

Kenton blinked awake. He couldn't remember his dreams, if he'd had any. A side effect, he supposed, of the exhausted sleep brought on by his harrowing experience. Recollection of the events after he'd pulled Bo from the jaws of certain death was murky, the memories flitting about just out of reach.

"Ah! Ken, you're awake!" Seri said, stepping into the room, which appeared to be in some sort of cave. Spinner-floss curtains were draped about a doorway to Kenton's right, whilst the walls, hammocks, and floor of the cramped space were lined and heaped about with packs and items that belonged to the other Igis Chosen. An empty bowl sat next to a jug of water on the ground just below Kenton's head.

Seri pointed to his torso. "The others are calling you *Oso Frix*, you know."

Kenton twisted to look at his body. A bright red fractal leaf pattern started at his collar bone and wended its way down his chest and right arm, tinged with blue and purple at the edges. It looked like someone had painted the webbed branches of a many-limbed dead tree into his skin.

"Lightning Touched" indeed. He skimmed his fingers over the scarring across his ribs, unable to hold back a wince.

"How much have I missed?" he asked, rising from the hammock. That simple action alone sapped all his strength from him, and Kenton put a hand against the rough stone wall to steady himself.

"Quite a lot," a voice replied from the doorway. "We've reached the foothills near the smoky village."

Kenton's eyes closed, knees weak in relief, for it was Bo.

The klia'an stepped into the room and tossed himself into Kenton's recently vacated hammock. "Seri's been running things the last few days while I've been hauling your heavy behind around."

Bo's tone turned serious, and he locked eyes with Kenton, tail gone limp in distress. "Which I wouldn't't'a had to do if you hadn't saved me. If I hadn't been so stupid. And now we're both . . . damaged."

Kenton looked over at Seri, who grimaced and came over to sit beside Bo.

"Leida and I, we did the best we could, but liphiz blossoms don't heal these kinds of wounds, and being so far away from proper medical care . . ."

She placed a hand on Kenton's chest, over his heart. No scarring marred that section of his body, as if the frix had realised what a delicate part of his anatomy sat there and passed by in an act of mercy.

"Frankly, I'm amazed you both stayed conscious as long as you did. But your heart is weak, and you'll have to watch how much you exert yourself from here on out. Bo too. His shifting protected him from the worst of it, but Leida advised him against shifting back."

"Until when?" Kenton asked. That had to be upsetting to Bo. He moved between forms easy as breathing, and the forced travel in s'hinoian form had been a constant complaint of his since almost the beginning. Kenton had promised the Igis Chosen could return to klia'an form once they'd acquired transports with dark tinted windows, but it was rather an empty solace to people accustomed to walking on two legs one moment and bounding away on four the next.

Bo flung a hand over his eyes, almost to block out what Seri was about to say, and as she worried at her lip with her front fangs, Kenton read the truth in her golden-green eyes.

"Never, if he doesn't want to risk his heart stopping."

Kenton looked away, struggling to contain the feelings threatening to overwhelm him. He'd hurt them both with his reckless decision in the water, but Bo was alive, and that was the only thing that mattered at the heart of it all.

With Bo and Seri's help, Kenton pulled on a shirt and limped to the outside of the cave, calling the Igis Chosen to attention. He didn't feel strong enough to stand long, let alone lead them on their first mission, but Tribe Osinan's future depended on him pulling it together. He ruffled Bo's and Seri's thick manes, drawing comfort from the soft tufts of fur that soothed his aching fingers.

"Igis Chosen. We're all hungry and tired and eager

to go back home. Back to our families and loved ones, so far away right now. But we can't. Not until we've destroyed the threat the human scientists pose to the Hinnom Forest. The plan is to hit as many research centres as we can before first frix without engaging the resistance they're sure to try and muster. We only fight if forced, though I hope it won't come to that."

"I do," Bo muttered.

Kenton ignored him and carried on.

"Our strikes will cripple them, forcing them to spend time rebuilding and not on retaliation. If we are very careful, we can seed the idea that our attacks come from one of their own, making them turn on each other and buying us the time we need to shore up our defences, or if worst comes to worst, to brave the maelstrom and find a new home across the seas. But remember; if one of us falls, the rest carry on. The mission must come above all."

Kenton paused, surveying each of the faces bright in the firelight before him.

"I need some time to rest, and for the scouts to discern how to liberate transportation from Smoketown. And then we fight.

"Then we save our home."

6

"In breaking news, another attack was carried out late last night at the outpost city of Amahn. Authorities weren't able to respond to Amahn's distress signal before the perpetrators vanished, and there's been no official word on whether this latest vicious assault is connected to the raids that have been plaguing settlements across Thorunn since late September, but it's highly likely that this too is the work of the Outpost Terrorist."

Gordon tapped his clip and cut the broadcast.

"You shouldn't keep watching that, Alanna."

"She doesn't have to, it's all over the edda-net," Laine said, unlacing his cleats. "Every city he gets that much closer to us, and no one's got a clue how to stop him."

"And good riddance to those idea-stealing towns, 'cept now our funding's been cut in half to support military action, which means your dad's paycheck ain't as fat, and I'm stuck with your ungrateful face for another month longer than we'd agreed on."

Gordon levelled an unpleasant look at Mom, who was sipping tea in the sitting room, and Laine moved before he could catch himself, standing between his mother and his uncle as if that would prevent Gordon's malice from reaching her.

Dad—cowardly—shot Gordon an apologetic look accompanied by a long sigh.

"I really thought we'd be out of your hair by now. I know Laine's a lot to deal with—"

"So school was good today," Laine cut in. He wasn't about to sit there and let Dad talk about him like he wasn't even in the room. Ever since his stint in the hospital Dad looked at him different, like Laine was made of some breakable, toxic material, too fragile to leave unattended, but too volatile to get too close. "Got our final match tomorrow, since frix season's supposed to start soon."

Andy had finally allowed him back onto the team a few weeks ago, and Laine had worked himself to the bone to prove he deserved to be playing with the Ospreys again. Course, it didn't hurt that he'd been practising in his every spare moment, checking the limited archives on the edda-net for the best plays and techniques. Andy had been suitably impressed, and Laine had regained his title of star player by the end of his first week back.

Unfortunately his little break also meant he'd had free time after school, and Dustin had practically press-ganged him into signing up for the mathletes competition. At least it'd look good on his transcript.

"If work allows, me and your mother will attend your match," Dad said.

"Your mother and I," Gordon corrected. "And of course you're going—not like we've had any real work around here to keep us busy lately."

"But my testing—"

"Isn't necessary, and furthermore, unapproved. I don't want to see you get in trouble, Jackie, sticking your nose in where it don't belong."

"Don't you mean, sticking my nose in where it *doesn't* belong?" Dad said teasingly. Gordon flicked him in the forehead. It looked playful, but there was a darkness in his eyes Laine didn't much like.

"Come or not, makes no difference to me." Laine hoped Mom would be there though. She'd at least been making an effort. Where Dad had stayed distant, spending all his working hours on research, she'd drawn close, teaching Laine more about their roots and family back in Virginia. If he ever found himself at a powwow he'd be able to jump right in and dance all the steps perfectly. He might even win a contest if he deigned to enter.

It would have been nice if they'd gone over such things back on Earth, where he could actually put his new knowledge to use, but he supposed he'd been too busy running around with the Orquídeas to sit down and appreciate a heritage four time zones and twenty-six hundred miles away.

"You kids are cutting it close with this weather." Gordon had lifted the shades and was peering outside. For the last week, the sky had been darkening, thick grey-black clouds rolling in from the south, occasional sparks of frix lighting up their bulbous forms as they clustered over Ethaba. "Fact, I wouldn't be surprised if the storms started this week."

"Makes it that much better. Racing time, each side trying to score the winning goal before the sky opens up on us?"

Laine could practically feel the energy gathering, and he shivered, a thrill shooting through him, making his fingertips tingle.

"Pressure's on—and not just barometrically," Dad said, winking. Laine groaned, hoping dinner would be ready soon, so he'd stop being subjected to his dad's crappy puns.

"I've got to go." Gordon drained his imitation coffee and moved away from the window. "Our current lack of funding won't stop my bosses from berating me if I've no work to show them when the money does come through. Even if it's theoretical, a model's a model."

"It doesn't have to be!" Dad insisted. He kept rambling even when Gordon closed his eyes and pinched the bridge of his nose. "Just come out to the tunnels with me and help me test. I'm on to something here, I know it!"

"Fine. First thing Monday morning. If frix season ain't started by then."

Friday came, and with it, the mathletes event—as mind numbing as Laine had suspected it would be. Dustin couldn't seem to grasp that just because Laine excelled at something didn't mean he had to like it. He was very good at washing the dishes—there wasn't a single dirty plate in the Riven household— but that thankless task was also liable to kill him from the drudgery of it all.

Laine suffered through, confident he'd answered

all the questions correctly from the way Dustin and Principal Kim beamed at him every time he hit the buzzer. There was also a measure of satisfaction to be had at seeing the tears—of rage or sorrow, Laine couldn't quite be sure—that the team from New Little Rock struggled to hold back as the scoreboard kept rising in Ethaba's favour.

A nervous energy thrummed through Ethaba High in the hours between their decisive STEM victory and the upcoming sports match. Dustin couldn't stop grinning at him and winking, and various members from their lacrosse team fist-bumped Laine when they passed him in the halls. Laine himself was looking forward to the after-party; maybe somebody would even dare to spike the punch.

The time came, and Laine tumbled into the locker room, half kitted out already.

"Couldn't wait to suit up, eh?" Jacques teased as Laine grabbed the rest of his stuff from his locker. The blocky goalie had been rather disappointed when Mariola had accepted his Fall Formal proposal only to later say she'd gone with him as a friend and wasn't ready to date. But Jacques had quickly gotten over his heartbreak when Yoon Ah had introduced him to a friend of hers, and the locker room was always a cheerful place when he was in it, bolstering the team spirit one smile at a time.

Laine clapped Jacques on the shoulder.

"We're gonna win. I can feel it." He tugged up the laces on his cleats and made sure every piece of his gear was strapped into place.

Yoon Ah dropped by the locker room—sporting bubblegum pink hair—to deliver personally wrapped bottles of lytorade and gush about how full the stands were.

"Practically the whole town has come out to see you guys! Make Ethaba proud, you hear?"

"Aye." Andy pecked her on the cheek. "Now hurry back 'fore you lose your seat!"

Yoon Ah gave Andy and Laine a thumbs up and vanished into the hall.

Laine chuckled at Andy's joyous expression—it'd been a painful few weeks that the two had been on break, and not even Jacques had been able to completely lift the gloom which had hung over Ethaba High until they'd kissed and made up—and went back to applying his face paint. Mom had mentioned that red was a good colour to add to their normal eye black when readying one's self for battle.

"You ready, team?" Andy hollered, and the boys let out a resounding war cry. The announcements over the P.A. wound down, and Principal Kim's voice broadcast over the loudspeakers:

"And now, presenting what you've all been waiting for, the New Little Rock Condors versus Ethaba High's very own Ospreys!"

The doors swung open, and the team poured out, headed by Andy. Yoon Ah cheered bombastically when she saw him, waving a homemade sign and a flashy ribbon.

The teams took their places, the referee gave the signal, and the match began.

The first few minutes the ball zipped back and forth between the two teams, until Jacques snagged it just before it would have smacked into the goalie net and whipped it over to Andy who passed it to an attackman who promptly scored. A deafening roar rose from Ethaba's side of the stadium, and the game raged on.

Second quarter came, and Laine jogged off-field to guzzle down some lytorade. The scoreboard showed a tie: one-to-one, neither side giving an inch.

"Stiff competition," Laine remarked.

Andy bounced on his toes, all full of adrenaline ready to be unleashed.

"They trounced us in every big match the last few seasons. But with me as captain this year an' you as our secret weapon, there's no way we can lose tonight!"

The second half of the game proved even more vicious than the first. Players and sticks clashed together, steel meeting flesh, masks butting and clanging.

Laine had never felt more alive. Black, sparking clouds roiled overhead, lending an air of urgency to the frantic plays Andy called, and for one euphoric moment, Laine was almost glad Mom and Dad had brought him to Thorunn. He bit down harder on his mouth guard, grinning at the fallen form of a Condor he'd body checked, and rushed back into the fray.

As fast as the ball flew, verbal insults zipped about even faster, each team attempting to throw the other off their game, whether by a general bashing of the entire team, or by direct attacks on individual players. Laine let loose a particularly colourful stream of insults at Jersey Number Seven as the Condor blocked every step he took. He could see Andy directly behind the opposing player, cradling the ball and dancing out of the path of several large midfielders as he tried to get a clear shot.

"And yet for all your big words, I see no ball in your stick," Jersey Number Seven said, crowding Laine too closely for Andy to make the pass. "You know what they say about—"

"What they say about the pitiful math students from New Little Rock who have too many XX's and not enough Y's to get a single question right?"

The split second Jersey Number Seven took to process Laine's rebuttal was all the time Andy needed to snap the ball hard and fast. Laine snagged it out of the air from behind his back, getting halfway down the pitch before the sputtering player could respond. Another attackman had a clear shot to score, so Laine flicked the ball his way, but the team from New Little Rock swarmed his teammate—Tom, sporting a nine on the back of his jersey—knocking him head over heels and regaining possession of the ball.

Laine gnashed his teeth at the loss. The scoreboard taunted him with its glowing display of the tied points. He couldn't tell if the wetness on his skin was sweat or the first drops of rain promised by the rumbling clouds above, but they needed to net at least one more goal before either the timer ran out or Principal Kim called the game.

Laine glanced at the stands, seeing Yoon Ah waving the giant banner she'd made for Andy. The rising wind whipped up her hair, and when it settled he glimpsed Mom right behind Yoon Ah, her bright, intricately beaded necklace glinting under the harsh spotlights, and—the sight sent a shock through his entire body, jolting him hard enough that he thought for a moment a Condor had slammed into him—Dad! They'd both come to the game after all.

Laine stared.

Despite his many promises, Dad had never made it to one of his school events before. The euphoric feeling crept back, and Laine turned his attention fully to the game. They'd win. The surety of it settled into his bones, the mocking laughter of the Condors utterly unimportant.

Nine seconds.

Laine bolted towards the New Little Rock teen who currently cradled the ball, his loose strides betraying a reckless confidence Laine couldn't wait to obliterate.

Seven seconds.

He battered the player's crosse with all the force he could muster, throwing in a few tricks Andy had taught him to fake out his opponent. All around him, New Little Rock players rushed to defend their teammate, but Andy rallied the other Osprey midfielders, cutting off the Condors.

Six seconds.

The ball dropped, and Laine scooped it up, dashing towards midfield to get it in play again.

Three seconds.

Laine's cleats had barely touched the line before he pivoted, bringing his stick up in front. He wished he could look to the stands again, could confirm that Mom and Dad were watching his greatest moment. He was more than a screw-up with an accidental overdose on his record. His medical records anyway—they'd done him a solid in not reporting the details of the incident to the school.

But every last bit of his attention needed to be focused on this one singular moment. The opposing players were still converging on him. If he missed, none of his work to redeem himself in Andy's eyes meant anything.

Two seconds.

With arms trembling from excitement, Laine forced all his energy into one last, furious throw, whipping the grass-stained ball towards the muddy net at well over one hundred miles per hour. At least, it looked that fast, blurring past the other players and straight towards the goal almost quicker than his eyes could track.

One second.

The goalie snapped out his overlong stick, the ball meeting it, and Laine's heart stopped.

And restarted as the ball smashed right through the reinforced aluminium, catching in the net and rolling to the ground mere inches from the reaching fingers of the stunned goalie.

The counter flashed zero as the crowd screamed, every Ethabite in the stands jumping to their feet as the score ticked over to read two-to-one, favouring the Ospreys.

Laine almost stopped breathing. He'd done it! His desperate long shot had won them the game. He stared at the scoreboard for a long moment, but it didn't change. They'd really won! Laine brandished his crosse towards the sky and let out a wild victory whoop before his teammates dogpiled him and hoisted him high to face the shrieking crowd.

Jersey Number Seven had gone pale, and tears streamed down the cheeks of his teammates, but Laine could hardly find it in himself to care about their hurt feelings, especially as it was the first game the unbeatable Condors had ever lost. A little defeat built character, or so Gordon was fond of saying.

The team from New Little Rock walked solemnly off the field, leaving it empty for the Ospreys' victory lap, and Andy, Jacques, and the others hooted and hollered every step of the way.

The constant cheers from the stands drowned out any booing from the New Little Rock supporters— Laine figured those who'd come out to see a good game had also joined in the celebration, excited to see a team win, no matter which town's it was.

He looked up to where Yoon Ah bounced excitedly in front of his parents, displaying a giant banner reading: OSPREYS ROCK, CONDORS CAN EAT A SOCK! in all capital letters. Laine chuckled at the thought that she'd been so confident of their victory she'd made the sign beforehand and hauled it into the stands despite it being fully twice her size.

About to turn back to his ecstatic teammates,

movement behind Laine's parents arrested his attention. Security he could understand—tensions had run hot before and during the match and weren't showing any signs of winding down—but why were Skytown military forces here? Why were they walking towards his parents?

The men—similarly uniformed with close cropped hair, bulky light-grey jackets, and glowing sols strapped to their hips—reached Mom and Dad and took Dad by the arm. He stood, pulling Mom with him as she clung tightly to him. Already pale due to too many long nights at the lab, Dad's face drained of what little colour remained as he said something in response to the soldiers, jerking back when another gripped his other arm. He shook his head furiously, motioning to Mom to get behind him, and Laine felt sick.

How was no one else seeing this? Even Yoon Ah, standing right in front of them, hadn't noticed the awful scene unfolding behind her.

"Let me down!" Laine yelled, beating his fists at the players holding him up. "Let me down, my parents!"

Andy glanced in the direction Laine gestured at, let go immediately, and Laine tumbled to the ground. When he regained his footing, the soldiers had Dad in cuffs, tugging at his ear, replacing his clip with the dark-grey prisoner model Earth had recently outlawed.

Mom was reaching towards Dad, the soldiers having wrestled her away, and the words "promise breaker" rose up like bile in Laine's mind. Rage pushed down the nausea—whatever Dad had done to get himself arrested couldn't be good, and on top of that he had to go and drag Mom into his moment of betrayal—and Laine ran for the stands. The officers held his mother far too tightly when she hadn't done anything, wasn't guilty of anything except loyalty to a man who let them down over and over again.

As the soldiers marched his father to the exit, Yoon Ah finally, *finally* noticed the commotion behind her, turning in time to catch Mom after the uniformed men shoved her away from them. Laine ran faster, pushing his weary legs to the limit, trying to ignore the spasming in his left calf that threatened to turn into a full-blown cramp. He was almost to the stairs leading to the stands when thunder boomed, lightning sparked, and the first drop of frix fell, down, down, down, hitting the ground mere inches from him.

Laine stopped short, eyes drawn momentarily to the tiny bursts of electricity raining from the sky. The school staff jumped into action, hitting levers that rolled rubber-coated covers over the stadium, artificial lighting brightening to compensate for the darkened interior.

When he looked back at Mom, she'd collapsed in Yoon Ah's arms, and the Skytown soldiers and Dad were nowhere to be seen. Laine ground his teeth and slammed his fist into the nearest wall over and over again, lacrosse stick forgotten on the ground. He faltered only when Andy pulled him away from the cracked concrete, staring in horror at the blood dripping off the exposed bone of Laine's knuckles.

"Saint Ailbhe, what have you done to yourself?" He lifted Laine, ignoring his thrashing legs and beating fists, and started carrying him away from the stairs, going under the stands to a tunnel Laine hadn't seen before. "We've got to get you to hospital. You an' your mum!"

They met Yoon Ah by the dim tunnel, which lit up within minutes as an emergency vehicle barrelled towards them. The medical staff who poured out took one look at Laine's hand and bundled him into the hover-ambulance alongside his mother. After a brief conversation, Andy and Yoon Ah joined them, and they sped away, sirens wailing.

"What's wrong with my mom?" Laine asked, paying little mind to the med tech wrapping his hands. He shook his head when the woman offered him some painkillers. "What happened?"

"I'm not sure," Yoon Ah said. Andy took her hands in his as she struggled to get the words out. "One moment she was trying to get to your dad, the next she was seizing in my arms."

Laine's eyes went wide. "Seizing?" he choked out, casting a terrified glance at Mom, who lay deathly still on the stretcher in the middle of the ambulance.

"Yes, but Min Soo's given me extensive medical emergency training, so I knew to get her in a safe position."

"Min Soo?" Did Yoon Ah have another sibling Laine hadn't met? Unless they'd done some creative restructuring of their family photos, which seemed unlikely. "You mean Peter?"

"He started going by that after Mom . . . Anyway, I always forget if someone doesn't say it first. How's your hand?"

Laine held up the heavily swathed limb. "Hurting. Where are we anyway?"

Granite walls whizzed past them, the darkness offset by soft lights embedded every few feet. The tunnel stretched on and on, no end in sight. Ethaba High's relative position to absolutely nowhere in town, especially Ethaba General, was maddening. They'd hooked Mom up to the oxygen supply, but it could run out before they reached the hospital, and what would they do then?

"The old tunnels," Andy replied. "They're only used during frix season an' in emergencies, rest of the year they're sealed. Too many kids got lost an' died down here. Dustin didn't tell you?"

"While he insisted on reading the student handbook to me, I may not exactly have been listening." That had been the week Laine had finally gotten clearance to link his clip to the edda-net, and he'd spent every day of it scouring the network for music, movies, and risqué images. Dustin's annoying facts had been the last thing on his mind.

"Back when the first explorers found a hole in the storms," Andy began, tapping at his clip and projecting a slide show that looked like something he'd put together in eighth grade, "and landed at the base of Mount Lalethusl, before Skytown was built, they cut down trees an' fashioned shelters from the steel-like wood. Figured it was best to keep the ships intact case they somehow got enough fuel to go home. But then frix season came, raining down fire from the heavens, burning their homes, an' forcing them underground. Destroyed the spacecrafts too.

"Against overwhelming odds, they survived an' eventually managed to ship over enough rubber an' such from Earth to get around during frix season. But 'til then they used the tunnels to travel safely from place to place, an' every town had them—though these days, y'can only get in if you have proper clearance."

Andy's expression darkened, and Laine couldn't help it, he flinched a little at the lines furrowing Andy's brow.

"It's a sore point with us an' Earth. They know we need rubber coating to survive the next few months—'specially as frix burns right through most everything else, even steel if it's out long enough—but they refuse to sell to us at a reasonable cost, despite how plentiful such materials are back there, an' the price for being caught smuggling is too high for most sane men to risk it."

Come to think of it, Laine did recall seeing a big rubber-coated umbrella in Gordon's hallway—he hadn't paid it much mind, since it hadn't rained in the months he'd been on Thorunn, but he could see how it'd come in handy during storm season. He shivered, recalling how the drops of frix had sparked and fizzled out on the ground in font of him before the school staff had finished pulling up the stadium covers.

"I almost got hit out there."

Andy chuckled. "Don't look so frightened, mate. A drop or two won't do y'much harm. Frix is more like static electricity than anything else. It's the fact that it accumulates—poison from Sigyn's bowl some say—turning much deadlier when combined with rain. Long as you've got some good boots, you can nip out here an' there."

Laine shuffled his feet. His green-stained lacrosse cleats wouldn't do him much good against the downpour he glimpsed as the ambulance rose up a large shaft and docked in a covered shelter just outside the ER.

The EMTs sprang into action the moment they stopped, trotting Mom inside and down the hospital's corridors at breakneck speed. Yoon Ah was the only one able to keep up with them, given Andy's and Laine's exhaustion after their exacting game.

One of the medical personnel thrust a holoscreen at Laine, and he filled in the required information. It was a little concerning that most of his mother's details were already in the system, and he hesitated before hitting the confirmation dialogue. The choice was taken out of his hands by the staff member, who grabbed the device from him once they noticed he'd answered all the remaining blanks.

"I got where they took her," Yoon Ah said, half out of breath as she came running back towards Laine and Andy. "But it's authorised personnel only."

"They can't not admit me!" Laine protested.

But the team outside the doors baulked when Laine couldn't produce his ID, and Laine swore violently. It was still in his school bag, in the locker room at Ethaba High, alongside his clip, which contained a digital version of the card, so despite his pleading they adamantly refused to let him through.

"Please," he begged, clutching at the dark grey scrubs of the stern-faced attendant. "I'm her son. I just freakin' filled out all those stupid forms. You gotta let me in!"

The nurse—shorter than Laine but an imposing figure somehow, in spite of her stringy, blond bob and smoke roughened voice—shook her head.

"Sorry, sweetie, rules is rules. If y'fetch some ID, I can help ya, but not 'til then."

"You don't understand!" Laine yelled, close to putting his other fist through the wall. Her behaviour was exactly why he couldn't stand dealing with adults. They all looked down on him—doubtless the staff had all heard about his little incident and were jerking him around for fun. Probably didn't believe he was trustworthy; after all, addicts were all liars right? He was likely after the drugs in the OR.

A familiar voice cut through Laine's spiralling thoughts. "It's okay, 'Xandra."

Laine's legs went weak. He was no friend of that voice, but at that moment it sounded sweeter than all the lollipops in Dustin's collection.

"I can vouch for him. These two as well, since this's my little sister and her boyfriend."

Peter waved them over, and 'Xandra stepped aside to let them pass, pursed lips showing her displeasure at being outranked. Laine could care less what one disgruntled nurse thought. Peter, wonderful, lovely Peter had granted him access to Mom.

Peter continued to lead them forward until the group reached a room with large windows. The nurse put a hand on Laine's shoulder as he made for the door.

"Not yet." He pointed out the cluster of medical professionals surrounding Mom. They had her all hooked up to different machines and were drawing blood and administering fluids through an IV. "Once those guys give us the all clear we can go in. There's a wash station and gloves in that room there. Sit tight, and wait 'til they call you. I'll be back."

He fixed each of them with a stern look before taking off, pressing his clip and speaking hurriedly. Since there were no chairs in the corridor, Laine, Yoon Ah, and Andy slid to the floor.

"Can they really help her?" Laine asked. He couldn't get his words above a whisper, throat tight with emotions that he clamped back.

Yoon Ah hugged her arms around her knees. "I don't know. I hope so. She was so cold when I touched her."

"Gonna assume that's not good."

"You tell me—it's December, the start of first frix. If anything, I'd've expected her to be suffering from heat exhaustion. But I've never—" Yoon Ah swallowed. Her next words came out muffled as she ducked her face behind her knees. "I've never felt someone be that cold."

Laine shuddered. Over and over again, he kept seeing it, Mom clinging onto Dad in the stands and then being tossed aside like so much trash when the soldiers dragged him away, not even bothering to look back at her crumpled form. Pain lanced through Laine's unbandaged hand, and he looked down to see that his knuckles were white from how hard he clenched his fist.

Yoon Ah caught the grimace that flashed across his face, and took his hand in hers, gently uncurling his stiff fingers.

Andy let out a low whistle. "You're one plucky nut. Here we are, medicine central, an' you've not taken anything fer the pain."

Laine shrugged. The ambulance EMT had wrapped his shattered hand well enough that it wasn't bleeding all over the place. A nano-diffuser could wait until he knew what was wrong with Mom.

"I don't do pills. Not after . . ." The other teens nodded understandingly, and Andy had the good sense to cast his guilty gaze away from Laine.

Peter returned shortly after, and moments later, a doctor poked his head out of the theatre to announce that Mom had stabilised, and they could come in and see her once they'd washed up. Even better, Mom was awake.

"Don't let them linger too long," the man said to Peter as Laine scrubbed the dirt off his skin. He stepped back from the rushing water to hear more clearly. "The woman needs her rest."

"It's starting isn't it?" Peter said quietly. "Thought she had until Christmas before she reached this stage."

"She'll be lucky to make it until—" The doctor cut himself off, suddenly aware that the water no longer ran, and three round-eyed teens hung on his every word. "We'll move her upstairs in a little bit and make her comfortable as best we can."

He stopped talking, leaving as Peter ushered them into the room.

"I'm glad to hear your voice, Mrs. Riven," Yoon Ah said after Mom greeted them all.

Laine wasn't. That weak, low tone didn't sound a bit like Mom. She was soft-spoken yes, but not quieter than a breeze on a still, summer day.

"It's okay, Mom," he said, squeezing her hand. He cleared his throat several times. He would not cry, not in front of his friends, and most certainly not in front of all the strangers in the room. "Don't speak, it's okay."

Mom's eyes flicked over to the white strips enveloping Laine's wrist. "Hand," she croaked.

"I'm fine," Laine protested, though the stabbing pain in his fingers begged to differ. The sharp biting sensation came and went, but he could ignore it to focus on Mom. "Don't say anything; save your strength."

"Dad?" Mom asked, and Laine shook his head.

"Gone. It's just you and me again. Like old times." His eyes blurred suspiciously, and he blinked away the wetness, suddenly furious.

How dare his father go and get himself arrested and cause Mom to have this attack? Wherever he was, good riddance. The soldiers could lock him away for a very long time. He and Mom had roughed it on their own before; they'd be fine without Dad.

Mom tried for a smile, eyes fluttering shut as she gave Laine's hand a feeble squeeze in return. It was more like a gentle press really, the movement so faint Laine thought he might have imagined it, but she repeated the action once more before lapsing back into unconsciousness.

Laine too, drifted off at some point, waking to Peter's hand on his shoulder and a room empty of all but the most essential nurses and doctors.

"Yoon Ah and Andy went home," he explained, taking Laine upstairs to get his hand looked at. It turned out he'd done more damage to his hand than simply mangling his knuckles, an X-ray revealing hairline fractures running throughout his wrist and fingers.

After setting the breaks, Peter treated Laine to another encounter with a nano-diffuser, this time on an even lower setting than he'd used at the Kim residence. It would heal slower, but the pain would be more manageable, Peter told him, and the gratitude Laine had felt towards him started to dissipate at the pity in the man's eyes. If Laine could go one day without someone reminding him how bad he'd messed up, he'd, he'd make peace with Gordon or something.

Laine tried to return to Mom, but the attending doctor was firm in his denials, and not even Peter could change his mind, so Laine headed to Gordon's, detouring by Ethaba High first to change out of his lacrosse gear and collect his things. Neither the hospital nor the school had any extra umbrellas to lend him for the lengthy trip, so Laine held a paper bag over his head and dashed from building to building, hoping the frix didn't kill him before he got back. The haze created by the mix of water and frix reduced visibility to almost nothing, and after he got turned around a few times, Laine finally stepped through the doors of a convenience store about halfway home.

"Rub your hands on this," a sales associate said, handing Laine a dry towel. "Gently—I don't need you getting shocked every time you touch something and starting a fire in here."

Laine rolled his eyes but towelled off, the screen in the corner catching his attention. The news was on, a pretty TCBNN anchor—who pretended to battle the elements in front of a decent green screen—reporting on an unprecedented power surge in New Little Rock. It seemed ridiculous to cover such an obvious story, given the frix coursing down around them, though Laine kept watching, heart pounding as he waited for the scrawl to feature his father's arrest.

But the perfectly safe and dry newscaster continued to blather on about New Little Rock, and never once did Laine see mention of a Doctor Jack Nathaniel Riven.

The house was silent and dark when Laine entered, the flowers he'd bought at the store a little crushed from where he'd stashed them under his jacket, so he jumped about a mile high when he flipped on the kitchen lights and was greeted by the sight of Gordon hunched over a bottle of whiskey, the strangest expression on his face. His sol for once wasn't strapped across his chest, sitting instead on the table, inches from his hand.

"You're back," he stated in a flat tone.

"Ye-ah," Laine said. He grabbed a drink from the fridge and approached his uncle. "Why were you just sitting there in the dark looking ready for a fight?"

Gordon slid a piece of paper along the table towards Laine. "You'll want to read that. Where's Alanna?"

Laine took the paper in lieu of answering. *Notice of Arrest,* it read. The listed charges were incredibly serious, and Laine reached for a chair to steady himself.

"Wilful negligence. Conspiracy to destroy government property. Collusion with the Cabal?" Laine waved the notice around. For Dad to have been charged—and convicted without trial it seemed—he had to have really messed up. Which didn't track with all his talk about starting over and making a new life on Thorunn.

"Gordon, you've been with him at the lab and in the field everyday—these charges can't be true. Not all of them."

"Jack's my little brother, Laine. I want so badly to believe he's innocent. I risked everything bringing him here, and he promised, he promised!" Gordon's voice cracked, and he turned away from Laine, shoulders shaking. "But I keep thinking of all the questions he was asking and the digging around he wouldn't quit doing, and it all points to the same thing."

"I don't believe you."

Did Gordon think Laine was stupid? He'd placed second on his team in the mathletes competition and won the most important match of the year for the Ethaba Ospreys, all in the same day. The crimes Dad was accused of on the bit of paper—he'd have to have turned his back on everything he stood for, and despite his less than stellar track record, Dad wouldn't have done anything to put Mom in danger, even simply by association.

A frisson of worry shot through Laine, and he dropped into the chair he'd been holding, scanning the list over and over, willing the words written on it to change.

"How do I know you didn't set this up somehow 'cause you're tired of us being in your space?"

Gordon certainly complained about "Jack's freeloading family" often enough, and if Laine had overheard him that one night, maybe Dad had too and called him out on whatever sketchy plans he and Doctor Frenally were working on.

"You have no idea," Gordon said, stabbing a finger at Laine, "the long hours I worked, the nights I went sleepless, the comforts I sacrificed to bring you and your family here. Why on Earth would I have my own brother arrested after doing everything in my power to give him the best life possible?"

Laine shrugged. So long as Gordon was in cahoots with Doctor Frenally, he couldn't trust a word out of his mouth, and since Laine couldn't confront his uncle with what he knew, admitting he'd spied on him, they were at an impasse. One thing was certain—he couldn't stay another minute in his uncle's house of lies.

He pushed the chair aside and left the kitchen. "I'm taking the umbrella. Don't wait up."

Laine's walk back to the hospital was slow, each step measured to keep him inside the protective circumference of the heavy rubber umbrella. He checked in with the staff and was pointed to a room on the second floor. The elevator moved like molasses, the doors getting stuck halfway through opening, and Laine had to squeeze himself through the small gap, the roses in his hand crumpling even further.

Unlike the confining first floor, the second had long, wide hallways set with floor-to-ceiling windows. Any other time of the year, Laine imagined they'd provide ample natural light. As it was, the view outside was only of the frix streaming down, an unearthly glow dancing about at street level, not quite light enough to fully illuminate the greying buildings. An occasional flash seared the sky, balls of lightning rolling green through the turbulent heavens, and Laine wondered for the nth time what had possessed Mom and Dad to move to Thorunn. The hospital probably had backup generators for their generators, but he hated to think what would happen if a particularly directed strike of lightning caused even those to fail.

As Laine rounded the corner, catching sight of the room number he'd stored on his clip, he heard murmuring voices that sped up and dropped in volume before coming to an abrupt stop. When Laine peeked into the room, Mom was clutching the hospital blankets tightly, face as white as the curtains tied back to the wall. The doctor she'd been talking with gave her a little salute and bowed out, leaving them alone.

Mom smiled when she saw him, making an effort to relax while he arranged the wilting flowers by her bedside.

"Laine. It's late, sweetheart. You should be at home."

"I couldn't be there with Gordon. He had this paper—" Laine still held it, he realised suddenly. He'd never put the notice down, and now it was a soggy, crumpled mess in his hand.

Mom saw and reached for it. Laine shook his head, but when she fixed him with a look, no less stern for her trembling, wan countenance, he handed the paper over and watched her anxiously as she read the writ inscribed upon it.

"It can't be true," she said in a faint voice. She smoothed out the document, unwrinkling each corner. "Your father would never."

Laine bit his lip. Maybe. Maybe not. Mom was

biased towards Dad, being his wife and all, so of course she'd think the allegations were false. Gordon, on the other hand, was his uncle, Dad's older brother—someone who should be in his corner no matter what—and he'd been sitting alone in his house, drinking away the news. Would he have done that if convinced of Dad's innocence?

Peter popped into the room while Mom was still reading and steered Laine out with a strength that belied his wiry frame.

"Heard you were in again; thought I'd catch you here. Look, this isn't my ward, but I figured the news'd be best coming from me 'stead of anyone else."

Peter's dark hair fell into his eyes, and he brushed his fringe aside as he led Laine to the second floor's waiting room. It was a small, cramped space, and Laine eyed the nearly full candy jar sitting on the glass-topped coffee table in the middle, the assorted sweets reminding him he hadn't eaten since before the lacrosse match, hours that seemed a lifetime ago.

Peter lowered the volume on the large holoscreen set into the wall, gesturing for Laine to sit in one of the chairs adorned with the ugliest upholstery Laine had seen outside of a thrift store. The nurse dropped into a chair opposite and took a piece of candy but didn't eat it, fiddling with the wrapper before speaking.

"Alanna, your mother, she—" Peter stopped playing with the clear plastic and put the candy onto the table. It *plinked* softly upon touching the glass face.

Peter took a deep breath and looked Laine right in the eyes.

"I'm sorry, Laine, but your mom's been very ill for some time. What she's got—it's incurable. We'd initially estimated until a little before second frix, but I'm afraid our new prognosis gives her only until just after New Year's. Maybe a few weeks longer, if she can find the strength to hold on."

"What's she got?" Laine asked, ignoring the part about "incurable" and "just after New Year's." Cancer had been thought incurable, but they'd finally cracked that a few decades ago—doctors were wrong all the time. As soon as Peter was done, he was getting a second opinion.

Peter swept his hair back from his forehead again, stopping halfway through as he let out a long sigh.

"It's bad, Laine. Bowman's disease. Named for Edward J. Bowman, an army doctor who came over with the original colonists in 2203. He wasn't the first person to contract the disease, but he documented it meticulously, describing first the symptoms his patients complained of, and later, what he himself experienced. His research proved invaluable in early identification and treatment of the disease—"

"Treatment?" Laine interrupted, a faint hope clutching at his heart. "So if they catch it early enough, you're okay?"

Peter took a long moment to answer. When he did, his voice had taken on that tone Laine hated, piteous, compassionate—gentle in a way that suggested Laine wasn't grown enough to handle facts delivered without sugarcoating.

"The most we can do for anyone is alleviate pain and make their last days comfortable."

"There's no cure? No way to fight this?"

"Everything we've tried to counter Bowman's causes it to spread that much more aggressively. The only pain medication that even remotely works is narprolepscene, which—as you've experienced—is lethal after only a few doses."

Laine jerked forward and swore, the harsh four-letter word punching the air the same moment the bowl of candy tumbled to the floor. Peter jumped up, but not in time to stop Laine from upending the table, tiny fragments of glass flying everywhere as the top shattered on the unforgiving linoleum floor.

"Laine!" he barked. "I know you're upset"—he barely dodged the fist Laine threw his way, getting an arm around Laine and pinning him to his chest—"but you can't go around destroying property—in a hospital no less!"

Laine wriggled and struggled, managing to break free when Peter activated his clip, no doubt to bring security down on his head. He swore at Peter again, screaming at him while staying just out of reach. An alarm went off—the lights in the room flashing red—and Laine bolted.

But by the time he'd skidded around the corner and dashed back down the long corridor, it became very apparent he wasn't the cause of the alarm. He stopped short, gasping at the sight through the large windows. The whole town was lit up in red, people running about the streets with or without their um-brellas, and what looked like Ethaba's entire police force had turned out, forcing smoking vehicles higher and higher through the damaging frix.

The Outpost Terrorist—he's here!

Or it was the lokians. Laine didn't know which was worse, the shadow wreathed cat-like aliens ru-moured to transform into twisted mockeries of men and steal away babies, stabbing their screaming mothers to death and then vanishing—he hadn't slept easy for a week after Dustin had told him that one—or the very real savage who'd been working his way through each town west of Mount Lalethusl for the last few months.

Laine slammed his fist against the glass. Not here. Not now. Not when Ethaba General was right next door to the Ethaba Scientific Research Centre, making it a prime target. He cast a glance at the room where Mom rested, too ill to get out of bed and run away, and made up his mind.

Lokians, terrorists—whoever. They weren't getting close enough to lay a single finger on her. He snatched up Gordon's umbrella and rushed outside, baulking when a crack of lightning struck not five buildings over.

Before Laine could head back inside, an utterly drenched middle-aged man dressed all in black gripped him by the shoulder.

"Know how to shoot?"

Had Laine been second-in-command of the Or-quídeas? He nodded, hiding his bum hand behind him, and was rewarded a moment later when the man pressed a sol into his other hand and clapped him on the back.

"Good. We're forming a police-sanctioned militia and need every able body we can get. Heck, I'll take someone in a hover-chair if they can shoot."

"What's going on?" Laine asked as he jogged alongside the man. More and more people ran towards them, some covering the hospital, a greater number heading for the ESReC.

"The Outpost Terrorist finally slipped up is what. Hit New Little Rock 'bout an hour ago, but one of their communication lines held out long enough to get a message through 'fore they went dark. We tried to wire the capital, but this awful frix means the edda-net's down, and 'sides, Skytown's too far away for them to be any help. Best we can figure, we got about ten minutes before all hell rains down on us."

"Not like it ain't already," Laine muttered, bracing the sol against his shoulder.

The man laughed darkly. "Just wait 'til second frix. You ain't seen nothing yet, kid."

For several long minutes, Laine and the other assembled members of the militia waited, sols at the ready, peering through the rainwater starting to eat away at their umbrellas. Although the news always reported on the Outpost Terrorist in the singular, the devastation he left in his wake was too large to have been caused by one man. Laine pictured him about Gordon's age, a nasty scar twisting his face into a permanent snarl. Stringy, greasy hair, a well-worn leather jacket, and massive amounts of weapons—mostly knives—completed Laine's mental image.

But those with him, Laine had no clue how to imagine. Maybe they looked the same, outlaw bounty hunters, running from the government they'd turned their backs on. Maybe—Laine grimaced thinking it—the Outpost Terrorist had worked an unholy alliance with the lokians rumoured to live in the forest a couple hours north of Ethaba. The very same ones spoken of in hushed tones whenever the disappearance of the Apollo XXII colony was mentioned.

Perhaps the news had it all wrong, and the Outpost Terrorist was a woman, disgruntled with a life gone wrong. She still looked the same in Laine's mind, only with longer, unkempt hair, and curiously enough, a missing arm.

The attack caught Laine and everybody with him by surprise. A bolt of concentrated frix striking the ESReC's radio tower was their only warning before half a dozen hovercars swooped down, outmanoeuvring limping police vehicles with ease. The stricken radio tower caught fire, the flames casting enough light into the gloom to make it absolutely impossible to see, and the militia shot blind against a foe better armed and equipped than they.

Still, Laine ran towards the cloaked shapes whose outlines he could just make out, ringed as they were by the layer of frix that settled against every solid surface. He fired—once, twice—but got nowhere, his metre showing only a few charges left.

The enemy transports that were clustered around

the ESReC kept blasting away, splitting off whenever the police got too close. Another minute and they'd have the whole place in ruins. How catastrophic that would be for the hospital Laine didn't wait to find out, abandoning the militia and running for the roof of Ethaba General.

He tucked the sol into his waistband and pocketed his clip before gritting his teeth and dropping Gordon's umbrella. Then he scrambled one handed up the fire escape, twitching at the stinging frix that drove like tiny bullets into his exposed face and hand. Laine dropped into a crouch upon gaining the roof—no sense in painting a target on his back—and headed for the line where Ethaba General tipped over into the ESReC. Most of the monitoring equipment had been blown to bits already, providing Laine with ample cover as he darted from one twisted hunk of metal to another. The attackers wouldn't shoot again at an object they'd reduced to a charred, smoking mess the first time round.

That was the theory Laine clung to at least. Lightning might strike the same place twice, but the frix pouring out of the terrorists' weapons hadn't so far, and Laine crossed his fingers that the trend continued.

The building shook, large parts of it sheering off in the front. They'd hit the structural supports. A few more good blasts, and the ESReC would crumble, taking Ethaba General—and Mom, lying helpless on the inside—with it. Laine seethed with a rage which built until he could no longer feel the frix that sizzled against his skin.

A quick check of the settings on the sol he'd been loaned revealed a laser guided crosshair, and after a test to ensure the aim was true, Laine dashed to another misshapen block, throwing himself into a forward roll before bouncing up and waiting for a hovercar to circle around again.

The instant one of the cube-shaped transports pointed its rounded front his way, Laine fired, but his shots slid off its nose, and he cursed. Figured the Outpost Terrorist would have commandeered costly military-grade vehicles.

No wonder the weapons on the police hovercars weren't doing any damage—they'd have to disable the shields first. And of course, the attackers had taken out the radio towers in their opening salvo, so there was no way to send a signal to lower the shields remotely. Given that the manual control sat inside the protected cockpit, defeating the Outpost Terrorist and his private army was looking more and more like a pipe dream.

But there was a small window—literally—of opportunity that Laine could exploit. Every time the Outpost Terrorist's gang fired upon Ethaba they rolled down their windows to expose their weapons, which exposed the instrument panels. Their erratic movement made hitting the hovercars next to impossible, but if Laine could snag a ball out of the air when it was moving at close to a hundred miles an hour, he could target and destroy the control switch.

Cradling the sol to his chest—two charges left, he

had to make them count—Laine dashed towards the single remaining piece of undamaged machinery atop the ESReC. His pulse jumped so high it felt like every nerve in his face was on fire, and he could clearly hear his heart over the incessant drumming of the rain and the near-constant thunder. He slipped behind the still-intact structure, praying his slim shape went unnoticed as a ship slowed its approach and the window began to slide down.

Three things happened then:

The tip of a wicked-looking rod poked out of the crack.

Laine released the breath he'd been holding, and squeezed his sol's trigger.

Wide, bright blue eyes transfixed Laine—their very human, male owner no older than him—as the bright cutting beam hit the instrument panel dead on, the shields dropping instantly.

So shocked was Laine by the youth of the enemy that he almost missed his last shot, which hit the unprotected ship's propulsion system.

The grey vehicle dropped from the sky so fast and so close to the ground it didn't even have time to go into a tail spin before crashing into the narrow alley between the ESReC and a neighbouring building, causing the other ships to scramble and vanish, gone as suddenly as they'd appeared.

Laine vaulted off the roof, barely catching onto the rain-slick metal of the fire escape as he dropped towards the ground. Once at street level, he snatched up his abandoned umbrella and sprinted towards the smoking vehicle. The crackling frix made it impossible to see if anyone had survived the collision, stray sparks setting the downed transport alight within moments. Laine flung an arm across his face to shield his eyes from the harsh glare, coughing as the smoke reached his lungs.

He wasn't five feet from the wreckage when his foot slipped on oil, the thick black substance floating atop the quarter inch or so of water pooling in Ethaba's streets. Laine snapped the umbrella out in front of him, but the unstoppable, incandescent explosion—its sound swallowed up by a particularly large boom of thunder—flung him into the wall of the alleyway, unforgiving stone cracking hard against his ribs.

Laine couldn't move.

The end of the alley narrowed to a point, and above the flames he could just make out members of the militia dashing down the street beyond in the direction the hovercars had gone, the police vehicles now fully disabled, forcing their officers to continue the pursuit on foot.

"Wait!" he managed, reaching weakly towards them. "I'm here. Help. Help me."

A horrible cough seized Laine, forcing his lungs into his throat, and when his chest finally released him from the convulsions that banged his head against the grimy concrete, he tasted the iron-wrongrust of blood. The viscous liquid dribbled thick over his lips, bubbling forth with each wheezing breath, and a terrible pain stabbed him just under his heart.

Laine was no doctor, but if he had to guess, one of his ribs had broken and punctured a lung.

If he'd had any breath left, Laine would have laughed at the irony. Here he was, head lolling against the side of the ESReC, no more than a short walk from the best medical care credits could buy, and he was going to choke to death on his own blood.

But the thunder was quieting, and so was the solfire. Whomever Laine had brought down, it had demoralised the others enough to flee, halting the assault on the ESReC, and by extension, the hospital. As far as Laine could tell, both buildings yet stood. Mom was still safe. He'd saved her, and if that meant he bled out in an alley, he'd take it. He doubted the smoke would dissipate enough for anyone to find him before the end.

Another cough racked Laine, his vision blurring out at the edges, the frix distorting what little sight remained to him. He only hoped they wouldn't tell Mom right away. That whoever did end up coming across his limp, battered body could muster up enough kindness to spare her the news for just a little bit. He'd caused Mom too much grief while he was alive—he didn't want his death to be the last terrible thing he did to her.

I hate this. I hate this planet. I hate that Dad is gone, and I hate that you're dy—that you're—

That I don't get to say goodbye. Hope this reaches you, Mom.

Love you . . .

7

Two pairs of eyes watched from the shadows as the boy who'd shot them down went flying into the wall when their stolen transport exploded, bits of metal, fibreglass, and various plastics spraying everywhere, the debris sharp and deadly.

"That's one problem taken care of," Bo whispered, words practically a purr, "no witnesses."

"Bo!" Kenton exclaimed, shaking his shoulder in recrimination. They'd gotten so close to home without a single death. If the figure lying crumpled within the alley truly had met his end, then no matter that he'd succeeded in disrupting the scientists' plans, he'd failed in his sacred duty given by the Innah, and he didn't know how he could face the Council of Elders.

"Ken," Bo hissed, "we've got to go."

Kenton shook his head and started towards the boy—an adolescent really, not much older than himself if he had to guess. Bo stiffened, ears pinned flat against his head.

"Let the humans take care of their own." He sounded like he was chewing on rocks. "It was the explosion what killed him, we were never here."

"We can't get past Ethaba's gates on foot—if we save him, he might help us," Kenton said, trying to ignore the way Bo had shredded the tips of his gloves.

He knelt next to the unconscious teen. Bright red blood stained his lips, rattling breaths faint and fading with each moment. His exposed skin was rubbed raw with frix burn. Kenton retrieved the discarded rubber umbrella, the gaping holes blown into it rendering it almost useless, and shrugged off his frix-proof jacket to stop the electric barrage against the teen's clammy skin.

"Help me get him up."

Bo grumbled but wound his tail around his waist and got his hands under the teen's legs, and they carried him swiftly across town, ducking behind trash cans and dumpsters whenever Bo's sharp eyes spied someone walking their way. Not that there were many people about—most of the soldiers on the streets had headed towards the long cold trail of the Igis Chosen.

Kenton wasn't worried. The military hovercars they'd stolen would be well on their way to the Hinnom Forest, and by dawn Seri and the others would be safe and sound with Tribe Osinan, no danger of falling from the sky once the frix did enough damage to the shields.

Kenton stopped as close to the town wall as he dared, uncovered a shallow depression in the ground, and bade Bo follow him inside. Together they laid the ashen Ethabite on the ground before Kenton replaced the concealed hatch.

"What is this place?" Bo asked, rubbing the blood

off his suit in disgust.

"Annie and I used to play pirates down here when Umama was cooking." Kenton touched the rusty cover. "It wasn't sealed off then."

"There enough ventilation?"

"It'll last us the night. We have to hope he can move by morning."

Bo threw one last withering look the injured teen's way before pulling out his med-kit and tossing it over to Kenton. The regen-rig inside wasn't as powerful as Leida's, but it would heal the worst of the damage. Throughout the entire process—the incisions Kenton made to alleviate the pressure and stem the blood loss, the broken ribs he removed and the liphiz blossom serum he injected to jumpstart the regenerative process, the spinner-floss he used for stitches, and the rolls of gauze he covered the entire mess with—Bo chattered on, keeping up a constant stream of complaints.

Kenton let him. Ever since his accident, when Leida had forbidden Bo from shifting, the young klia'an had struggled to express himself without the easy body language that came naturally with his s'hinoian form and had developed a habit of talking nonstop to make up for it. Kenton found the continual muttering soothing, drifting off once he finished his work.

His sleep was fractured, night terrors showing him his parents' faces slicked with blood, the soldiers who'd beaten them to the ground shooting Annie in the head over and over again. He woke several times with the certain knowledge that Bo had slit the Ethabite's throat in the night, only reassured once he heard Bo's snuffling snores and the soft murmur of the teen's breath, stronger with every moment.

It took longer to get back to sleep each time, and as dawn approached Kenton stopped trying, watching over his patient with aching eyes instead. He knew Bo wouldn't actually sabotage their only shot home, but he couldn't get his instincts to respond to logic and settled for ruffling his hand through Bo's soft mane, the silky strands comforting after their exhausting night.

———————— ● ————————

Bo stretched every limb upon waking, claws popping out as his fingers kneaded the air.

"Way to use up the whole med-kit," he said, once he'd finished smacking his lips after a huge yawn. The human Ken had insisted on saving looked much recovered, which was most disappointing. "He good to talk?"

Ken dabbed a soft rag at the traces of blood crusted onto the Ethabite's lips and forehead. "In a few minutes, I think. Can you pack our things?"

"Always making me do the grunt work," Bo teased. He wrinkled his nose at the sickly-sweet scent of various bodily fluids clinging to the boy's ruined clothing.

"You're not the one who spent several hours patching him up and then watching to make sure all that hard work didn't go to waste."

Very true. Ken knew better than to expect Bo's assistance with the enemy. If they didn't need his help to get back—and really, Bo figured he could get them both safe out of the city if he truly put his mind to it—Bo would've had zero qualms about leaving the kid to the tender mercies of fate. Bo touched his chest, where scars matching Ken's sat hidden below his fur. His best friend's inability to walk away from anyone in distress was a double-ended quirn.

"Lanae's whiskers. We're gonna have to steal a bunch more supplies," Bo said as he rifled through what little Ken hadn't used on the enemy. "Plus, we gotta find a way to charge this—" He hefted the regen-rig. "Not like we can exactly knock on someone's door and ask to use their frix jack."

Ken hummed but kept quiet, continuing to dab at his patient's forehead and checking his pulse every so often.

"Is it weird, being back here?" Bo asked when the silence got to be too much.

"Like you can't imagine. The walls might be taller, the buildings bigger, and the people different, but Bo, I know these streets. I could point out the exact spot where I found the broken string of my mother's pearls on that awful morning." Ken's voice dropped to almost nothing, Bo's keen hearing troubled to pick out the words, and he couldn't help himself, he lurched forward and caught Ken in his arms, purring for all he was worth.

"Every night I see it," Ken gasped, "the sol they put to Annie's head before they blew her away. She was only five, Bo, five!"

Ken buried his face in Bo's chest, sobbing, and it took all of Bo's willpower not to reach forward and slash through the sleeping boy's throat. Had he been older, Bo might well have, but as much as he hated to admit it, a kid his and Ken's age couldn't be responsible for what had happened to his family.

Or Bo's for that matter. That'd been an interesting night, the Innah coming back to the village with chunks of her mane pulled out, her clothes torn in grief, and a tiny human child cradled in her arms. Noticeably, Bo's father hadn't returned, making him and his brothers orphans. He'd thought Ken at fault for a long, long time.

Bo wiped away Ken's tears. "You an' me, maybe being here's what we need to face the past and finally let it go."

"And you were upset"—Ken's voice sounded a little stronger now, that was good—"that we got shot down."

Bo hissed at the recollection, and Ken shook against him in barely repressed laughter before suddenly sitting ramrod straight and then digging in the ground like a mad person.

"Have your nightmares gotten to you at last?" Bo asked, cocking his head at Ken's inexplicable actions. "How concerned should I be?"

"I told you, me and Annie used to play pirates. We'd bring our treasures and bury things—hand me my quirn."

Baffled, Bo did as Ken asked, watching while his

friend scrabbled at the dirt until he hit something.

Ken's frantic pace slowed, and a few minutes of careful digging unearthed a small wooden box. Whatever it was treated with had preserved it fairly well, though the wood showed signs of wear at the edges, dirt forever stained onto the tops and sides no matter how fastidiously Ken wiped at it. He finally realised cleaning the thing was a lost cause and eased it open, a look of hurt flashing across his features when the flimsy lock popped off, although, what had he been expecting, given how rusted the metal fastener was?

The inside had remained intact, and Ken's hands shook as he pulled out a small photograph. In it, two chubby cheeked children stood together, the boy—he had to be Ken with his blue eyes, pale skin, and fair hair—had his arms thrown around a little girl's neck, hugging her with an easy affection that showed even through the slightly blurry print. The little girl—a baby really, with pretty dark skin, round, curious eyes, and curly hair styled into lots of tiny puffballs—had her arms wrapped tight around Ken's waist.

"That's Annie?"

Ken nodded, his fingertips trailing over the tiny faces. When he spoke, his voice was rough, the tears obviously not finished coming. "This must have been taken only a month or two before—"

Bo laid a hand on Ken's arm and drew him back against his chest, starting his rumbling purr again, but before he could speak, a groan from the dark-haired human stretched prone on the floor distracted him.

"The sleeping royal awakes."

Ken chuckled at that, slipping the photo into a hidden compartment in his pack. "But not at the first drop of frix like Lady Lanaekim. I think our patient here has had his fill of being shocked."

"Maybe so. Let's see what we can get outta him," Bo said, popping his claws. "I've always wanted to interrogate a human."

———————————— ● ————————————

Laine felt like someone had punched him in the chest. A jumbled mess of images and emotions blurred through his mind—crackling frix in rain-slick streets, a fiery explosion, the certain feeling he'd never see Mom again—and he jerked upright, immediately doubling over as pain stabbed him in the stomach. He touched his fingers to his mouth, but they came away dry, no trace of the blood that had spilled out earlier.

Laine sucked in a lungful of musty air. The pain, while sharp and brutal, was bearable. It faded further with each new breath, letting him pay attention to his surroundings, and as his eyes adjusted to the dim lighting of wherever he was, two figures—one human, one decidedly *not*—came into focus. He felt around, but the sol he'd had during the attack was gone. He was at their mercy, reduced to the weapons of his words.

"So my craziest theories were right, and the Outpost Terrorist is a lokian lover."

The two individuals looked at each other, hissing fiercely before approaching Laine. He shrank back at the gleaming fangs and outstretched claws of the yellow-eyed lokian.

"What is your name?" the human teen asked, articulating each word slowly and carefully, as if long out of practice speaking English. His accent was odd—Australian or European maybe.

Laine kept silent even when the lokian growled at him, its tail swishing angrily back and forth and the teen asked again, producing a long rod that crackled with frix at the end—one of the weapons he'd been using to destroy the ESReC.

Laine gulped but held firm. He'd defeated them and somehow still lived to tell the tale, a little concentrated frix didn't scare him. Much.

"Monsters like you don't deserve my name," he said.

"I could say the same about our healing tech, but we still administered it to you."

So that was why he felt so good. But who knew what horrible alien things they'd injected into his body while he'd been unconscious?

"Yeah, well I didn't ask you to, so you can get outta here with your quid-pro-quo nonsense."

The lokian was suddenly in his face, hot breath gusting foul into Laine's nostrils, the tips of its claws scant inches from his eyes.

"Bo here is very eager to maim you in rather . . . creative ways. I suggest you answer."

Laine swallowed again. "Fine. I'm Laine, Laine

Riven."

"Kenton. Do you know how to get past the gates?"

"Sure, but I couldn't help you even if I wanted to. I ain't got clearance yet."

The lokian—Bo, Kenton had called it—poked Kenton in the arm and vocalised a series of short, bitten off sounds. Kenton responded in kind before turning back to Laine.

"But you know someone who does. You can have them help you, and thereby, us."

"I really don't see how this is any of my business," Laine said, picking at the edges of his sleeves. He felt a little stronger; his hand had stopped throbbing, and even the would-be bruises from the lacrosse game had been wiped clean from his skin. If he rushed them he could wrestle the strange weapon away from Kenton, stun both him and the lokian and alert the militia before they had a chance to run.

"You made it your business when you shot us down," Kenton said, grip tightening on his weapon.

"Yeah, well you made that my business when you attacked Ethaba General." That statement was met with a blank look. "You know, the hospital?" Laine stressed. "Where all the sick people are—including my mom?"

Kenton blanched. "I didn't—I didn't know the science building was attached to the hospital."

"What, you thought the giant plus on the front was painted there for fun?"

"What's your mum sick with?" Kenton asked, ignoring Laine's pointed question. "I can heal her." The lokian hissed. "Once we stock up on supplies."

Laine laughed until he started coughing, eyes watering. "That's the best joke I've heard all year, and trust me, Jacques is full of them. My mom's got Bowman's. It's incurable."

"Bowman's?" Kenton tilted his head, looking oddly like his feline companion.

"You can't possibly be new to Thorunn like I am, so cut the act, 'less you lived under a rock or something before destroying all those towns."

"Or something," Kenton said. "Humour me—what are the symptoms?"

"They're . . . Uh. She . . ."

He didn't actually know. Peter had gotten as far as pronouncing the prognosis terminal but hadn't managed to say what that entailed before Laine had flipped the table and rushed away—and then Kenton and his pet lokian had attacked, and there hadn't been time.

"Can you take me to her? I promise, if it's something I know how to heal, I'll do so in exchange for safe passage for us through the gates."

Kenton had to be lying, trying to manipulate Laine into letting him go. But his face was open and earnest, one hand outstretched in front of Bo, stopping it from pouncing on Laine. Course, that could all be a ploy to gain Laine's trust and then murder him the moment he turned his back. However, if there was even the most minuscule of chances he was telling the truth and Mom could be saved, Laine had to agree. Plus, the air was getting hard to breathe, and

Laine didn't fancy expiring so soon after being patched up.

"Fine, but that lokian doesn't come anywhere near her." Laine thumbed on his clip and checked his map. "My uncle's place isn't far. He's almost never home, and he doesn't go into my room."

That was one small advantage of having a relative who hated him so much he refused to touch anything belonging to Laine. He'd probably burn the umbrella once Laine returned it, not that the worn object was much use after the abuse it had sustained.

Laine started shrugging back into his clothes, a little creeped out that Kenton had undressed him, though it'd probably been necessary to treat his wounds.

The lokian vocalised loudly, and Kenton said, "We can't go now, too many people about."

Laine paused in the middle of zipping up his still-damp jacket. "What with your little stunt last night, everyone's gonna be either at the ESReC cleaning up or at the hospital making sure the attack didn't kill their loved ones." He spat the words with as much venom as he could muster. "And do you really wanna risk waiting 'til dark and then running into my uncle coming back late?"

Kenton sighed and turned to the lokian, his quick gestures accompanied by the weirdest set of sounds Laine had ever heard a human make. It was almost as if Kenton were talking to the thing, using a language that sounded like a mixture of foreign words and all sorts of growls, hisses, and cat-like chirps and meows. The lokian bristled, puffy fur making it look twice as large as it yowled back, stamping its booted feet a few times before crossing its arms and looking away.

Kenton powered down his weapon and strapped it onto his back. "We're already packed. Lead the way."

The trip to Gordon's house was rather laborious, since Kenton and Bo insisted on ducking down whenever the hint of a shadow crossed their path, and by the time the two-storey dwelling came into view, Laine was about ready to strangle the two of them, crazy weapons and promises of magical cures notwithstanding. He very nearly ran right into Kenton when the teen stopped smack in the middle of the street, rooted to the spot despite the lokian tugging him forward. Laine really wished he had the frix-proof suit that allowed Kenton to stand in the open without getting shocked.

"That's my—" Kenton stepped forward slowly and rested a hand on the small fence that ran around the property. "This is new." He looked up. "And so's that. Amazing. They didn't even bother to raze the place. Just replaced us."

Laine shoved him onward. "You sound like a crazy person—acting it too. You're not exactly inconspicuous standing out here like this."

The frix did a lot to obscure Ethaba's streets, but the upside of being hardly visible to the denizens of the town came with the downside of not being able to see anything themselves. The sooner the Outpost Terrorist and the lokian got inside, the easier Laine would breathe.

"So, I'm sure you're hungry," Laine said as he led them into the kitchen, ignoring Kenton's sharp gasp when he caught sight of the curtain in front of the stairs leading to Laine's room. "But don't take anything from the fridge. Gordon will notice. You can stash your stuff here, Kenton."

"Won't your uncle see?"

"I was thinking; it'll be harder to hide both of you, so once the edda-net's back online I'll fix the school records to make it look like an extra New Little Rock student got left behind. S'not like they can easily come back for you through the frix."

Kenton nodded, handing his weapon to Bo. He took a can of pineapples out of the pantry as the lokian disappeared down the stairs.

Laine grabbed the can from him and stuck it back on the shelf.

"You and your little friend can eat once you've seen my mom and told me how to fix her and not a moment before."

"Hi, Mom," Laine whispered as he entered her room. "I came as soon as I could."

The flowers he'd left yesterday had been placed into a vase and water added. All the dead petals had been picked off, and—no longer wilting—the red and yellow blossoms had regained their cheering effect.

"I've been crazy worried about you. Peter told me yesterday you have Bowman's disease, but the ESReC got attacked before he could tell me what that means."

"In a moment. How are you? Were you safe last night—who's this?"

Kenton came haltingly into the room, shoulders held tight and high, hair falling in front of and obscuring his face as he kept his gaze on the floor.

"I'm fine, and this's Kenton," Laine started, nudging the other teen when he realised that was all the name he had.

"Oso."

"Kenton Oso," he finished. "He's from New Little Rock and got stranded here once the frix started, so he's staying with us for a bit."

"That's so nice of you, darling."

Laine pulled his lips into a smile that was all teeth and no heart. All the times he'd lied to Mom and never felt any guilt—why this occasion felt any different, especially when he was looking to save her, he didn't know. But the uneasy feeling sat heavy on his chest despite knowing the truth wouldn't benefit anybody. There weren't supposed to be cameras in the rooms, but Laine wasn't taking any chances. He didn't want to be the next to get dragged to Skytown.

"Anyway, Bowman's disease, what should I be expecting?"

Mom sighed, her eyes filling with dark clouds.

"I'm so sorry you had to find out like this, darling. I can try to explain, although there's a chart at the foot of the bed with all the details."

Laine tapped the holoscreen he found there, and a

list of symptoms related to Mom's condition popped up. Easy bruising. Weakness. Fever and headaches. It got worse and worse as the chart listed all the terrible things preceding the ultimate result written in pronounced capitals at the end.

"Dehydration, vomiting, IV rejection, and . . . rapid bone disintegration?" Laine pressed his finger to the penultimate words on the list, his stomach turning over at the images and information displayed on the holoscreen. Deformed heads and sunken chests with pools of blood and bits of skin and muscle extruding from bodies collapsed under their own weight. Small wonder they'd put Mom on the strongest pain medication available.

Worst of all was the phrase "all known treatments for osteomalacia and hypophosphatasia ineffective in treating Bowman's Disease, currently classified a terminal illness."

"That's wrong."

Laine almost cracked the holoscreen at the shock of hearing Kenton's voice. He'd forgotten he was in the room.

"We call it Raxilsish. 'Mush bone' would be the closest translation, I think. Your doctors are wrong. It is curable."

Mom's eyes widened. "Laine, who is this boy? He's not from New Little Rock."

Apparently Kenton didn't care about keeping his identity secret, and Laine had been outed as a liar yet again. He went over to the door and checked that it was locked before sitting right at the head of the bed.

He kept his voice low, just in case.

"I didn't wanna worry you, cause you any more stress, but uh . . ." Might as well go for broke. If Kenton wanted to expose his identity, Laine wasn't going to keep anything back. "This's the Outpost Terrorist who attacked the hospital yesterday."

From the way Mom gasped and put her hand to her throat, that might have been the wrong thing to say. Across from him, Kenton had his eyes screwed shut, like he couldn't believe Laine had revealed that.

"Putting aside the fact that the most wanted person on all of Thorunn is sitting at my bedside"— Mom's fingers inched towards the call button, and Laine quickly snatched it away—"how could he possibly know of a cure to Bowman's, or that it even works?"

"Because I contracted Raxilsish and had the cure used on me. You're much further along than I was, and by the time we get the ingredients together to, what's the word, synthesise the serum, there's no guarantee you'll be able to walk without assistance ever again. But you will be alive. I promise."

Laine could hardly grasp what he was hearing. A cure existed! And all it cost him—if the other teen was telling the truth—was getting Kenton and Bo out of Ethaba undetected. Not the easiest task to be sure, but neither was lock-picking Doctor Frenally's secret, illegal basement lab.

"How long do you think it'll take?" Laine said, looking Kenton in the eyes and daring him to lie to him.

"A month or so, by your reckoning," Kenton said.

"The doctors think I can hold on until February if I keep fighting this. Will that give you enough time?"

Kenton nodded and took Mom's hand to press a kiss to it. "We'll save you. You have my word."

Not to be outdone, Laine stood and leaned over to kiss Mom on the forehead. "I refuse to let Bowman's tear us apart. Me letting you down ends now."

And Mom smiled at him, something like hope glistening in her eyes.

8

Bo was going crazy.

He'd been confined to Laine's room for the last week while the human and Ken went out in search of materials to synthesise the cure for Raxilsish, with nothing to do except watch reruns of old Earth television. Which wouldn't be so bad if, one, they didn't show the same five programs on a loop, and two, if Bo understood English a little better. Ken had taught him bits and pieces over the years, but the people on the shows went too fast in their ugly, incomprehensible language for him to keep up.

The knock on the doorframe before Ken padded down the stairs had become the highlight of his day, sad as that was. Bo combed through his mane again, wishing he could shift and groom himself properly. Klia'an form was just not that flexible, and he dared not freshen up in the upstairs bathroom too long in case the scientist who owned the house unexpectedly returned in the middle of the day. Laine had assured them that wouldn't happen, but he'd also told Ken about the man's private lab two floors up, and Bo couldn't trust that the teen's uncle wouldn't choose to work from home on a whim.

He'd heard the man creeping about at night,

always after Kenton and Laine had fallen fast asleep. If Bo listened hard enough he could make out a soft murmuring, but the words themselves were jumbled, phrases like ". . . a surprise if he thinks . . ." and ". . . monitor . . . right time . . ." floating around without any apparent sense or meaning that Bo could parse out.

Bo uncoiled from Laine's soft bed and inspected the med-kit. It remained the same as the dozen or so other times he'd checked it, as did their ration packs. His and Ken's quirns were hidden inside their travel bags, in turn stuffed under Laine's bed, the space between the frame and the ground draped about with the human's dirty laundry. He hated reaching through the stinking garments every time he retrieved his quirn to remind himself that they'd get home.

Bo vividly remembered the day he'd forged the weapon. Irjah had presided over the affair, watching as he heated and shaped the metal, following the elder's instructions to the most minute of details as he laid the circuitry. Getting approved to carry his final design had been one of the best moments of Bo's life, and it wasn't fair that he'd been reduced to hiding out in a human's basement, not even able to shift to banish the aches and pains in his body. He glanced at what passed for a clock in Ethaba.

Twenty minutes down, three hundred and thirty to go.

<hr>

"When you suggested undercover infiltration I wasn't exactly picturing volunteering for cleanup duty at the ESReC," Laine said as he picked up another piece of debris. All around him and Kenton other Ethabites were hard at work sweeping away rubble and filling large trash bags, returning the building and its perimeter to something resembling respectable.

"I'm open to suggestions that'll get us close enough to liberate some kitterstone samples," Kenton said. "In the meantime, we start here and work our way inward."

Kenton wasn't keen on their course of action either, not after all the trouble he'd gone through to destroy the labs in the first place, but what they sought was likely buried somewhere amidst the sizeable chunks of metal and rubble, and they needed a plausible reason to be digging around. They couldn't just ask Gordon Riven for help, given that that scientist's destructive ambition was the whole reason Kenton had left the Hinnom Forest in the first place, and he'd be in quite a predicament if they were arrested for looting and the alias Laine had created for him placed under scrutiny. But with a solidly established cover as a concerned citizen trying to help after the attack, it wasn't himself he worried for.

"Bo's not dealing well with being isolated in your room."

Laine ran a hand through his hair and blew the dust off a bent piece of machinery. "You're telling me that what amounts to basically an overgrown house cat can't amuse itself for a couple hours?"

"How would you feel in his position, forced to spend all day hidden away with nothing but repetitive shows for entertainment?"

Television was not something Kenton had missed in the Hinnom Forest. Not that he'd watched much of it before his old life had been torn away, but he greatly preferred acting out the myths and legends of Tribe Osinan or reciting the old stories late at night over a flickering fire. Holographic displays, no matter how immersive, had an unnatural quality to them that bothered him every time he went downstairs and found Bo staring listlessly at the senseless violence happening on-screen.

"Super irritated," Laine replied, "but you know what? I'm not Bo, so, not my problem."

The detritus in Kenton's hands crumbled to nothing as he struggled to resist striking Laine for his callous words. Ever since he and Bo had taken up residence in the boy's uncle's house, Laine had treated them like Ls'sa—outcast. He also spoke rudely of his uncle, bitterly of his father, boasted about his athletic prowess and the fact he'd shot them down, and griped continuously about his classmates and the school he attended.

"Don't you care about anybody?" Kenton asked, drawing a surprised look from Laine—who was doing his best to stay under the alcove and away from the stinging frix.

"Mom, obviously."

"But do you, really?" Kenton pressed. Laine

seemed the type to want accolades and the prestige that surely would come with being the first human with the cure to Raxilsish. It was a shame the early settlers from Earth had been so distrustful of Tribe Osinan. They could have spared themselves decades of suffering.

Laine straightened, jabbing a finger in Kenton's face. "How dare you insinuate I don't care about her, after everything I'm doing—putting up with your company, secretly housing," he spat, "a lokian, not to mention our little deal. What kinda heartless jerk do you take me for?"

Kenton met Laine's gaze and held it. "If you don't change how you treat others, you will lose everything." Laine grabbed at his jacket, dragging him close.

"That a threat, lokian lover?"

"One doesn't reach inside a nest of wild bees expecting not to get stung."

Laine rolled his eyes, let go of Kenton, and threw rocks into his bucket with greater force than before, muttering under his breath about Confucius aspirations and delusions of grandeur.

Farther inside, beyond the shattered glass doors of the ESReC, Kenton could just make out snatches of conversations had by the other volunteers.

"Our team was this close to a breakthrough y'know? Even with Doctor Riven's arrest, we still had enough data to forge ahead, but this attack's set us back to square one."

Kenton couldn't help the smile that stole over his

face. The dry, dusty months of travelling, the carnivorous creatures they'd encountered, and the long night flights in stolen vehicles, it all was worth it. The Igis Chosen had hit the settlements posing the greatest threats and made it safely back to the Hinnom Forest just as frix season had started.

Kenton only wished they'd had the manpower to risk a strike on Skytown, but even if the scientists started their tests right back up the minute they got their equipment working again, they couldn't possibly do much before second frix, and after that season passed, Kenton didn't think the Innah would be opposed to him and Seri leading another crop of Igis Chosen against any renewed efforts, constantly crippling the outposts until they ran out of money and resources to rebuild.

"I heard they found some pieces of the stolen ships in the alley," one of the male volunteers said. "Blown to bits. There wasn't even enough DNA to identify who or whatever it was that'd been inside."

His companion let out a long string of muttered curses. "I'd ha' liked to be the one to bring that ship down. The Outpost Terrorist put my little cousin in the hospital, and they still can't tell me whether she'll pull through."

The smug, cutting look Laine sent Kenton, both eyebrows raised as if to say, "Look what you did," told him the teen had heard the same exchange, and Kenton's chest tightened. He only had the means and opportunity to help Mrs. Riven, but he wished he could do more for the others he'd inadvertently hurt.

In no other town had the hospital been directly attached to the Scientific Research Centres, and with the dark and rain, he truly hadn't known when he'd given the order to open fire, no matter what Laine insinuated.

Each new bit of news that unfolded regarding his assault on Ethaba made Kenton increasingly regret the decision he'd made after they'd left New Little Rock. The attack had been decided in haste, a combination of eagerness to reach home and misplaced confidence in his ability to hit two towns in one day and wrap up his long mission with a double success. Still, if he'd delayed, they'd have been caught in the frix, and Ethaba's ESReC would yet stand.

Kenton was beginning to understand why the Innah often told him a leader's shoulders were burdened with the weight of choices that walked a line between upright and necessary and how sometimes a choice made with the best of intentions—with eyes wide open—led its maker into a dilemma they could not have predicted, no matter how detailed they'd been in imagining the outcome beforehand.

Kenton stared at the rocks he'd just picked up. Yes, assisting with the reconstruction of the very place he'd sought to destroy was the last thing he thought he'd be doing when he'd told the Igis Chosen to set a course towards his childhood home.

"Hey, this what we're looking for?"

Laine thrust a hand into Kenton's face. A glossy red rock fragment sat in his palm, and Kenton plucked it from him to inspect the crystalline chunk.

"Yes, where—?"

"There's a whole box of this stuff buried under one of the collapsed support struts. How much d'ya think we'll need?" Laine led Kenton to the spot he meant and dragged out a hefty metal crate, warped on one side by the crushing weight of the pillar.

"Better take the whole thing." They needed only a fraction of the shimmering kitterstones, but they'd lingered long enough at the ESReC, their luck reaching nearer its limit each day that passed and no one stopped Kenton to interrogate him and watch his flimsy backstory fall to pieces. "It's safer than coming here again."

Laine started stuffing the rocks into his jacket, at which Kenton brushed him aside and hefted the entire crate.

"What?" he said, when Laine threw up his hands in exasperation. "We'll tell anyone who asks we're running an errand for your uncle."

"And when Gordon asks me why he apparently needed a whole bunch of magic rocks?"

"Tell him you intended to sell them and didn't want an accusation of theft hindering you. You dislike him enough for him to believe you'd callously use his reputation to profit yourself." Kenton shouldered the box and strode away from the ESReC, leaving Laine to turn in their volunteer badges.

They stopped by one of Laine's classmate's houses on the way back, picking up a large crate of books of all reading levels for Kenton and Bo. From the way Bo's pupils rounded in interest when Kenton showed him the box, it had been a good decision—perhaps the kindest one Laine had made since they'd started staying with him, though "kind" might have been too generous a word to describe what Laine had given as the reason.

"I'm not gonna be able to concentrate thinking about your little friend getting tired of the drivel that passes for TV on Thorunn, roaming the house, and getting discovered by Gordon. Luckily, I've come up with a solution."

That the books were mostly in English—though Kenton had spotted a "My First German" text and a Spanish counting book among the mix—would be a challenge for Bo, but Kenton rather suspected his hatred of all things human would be tempered by how bored he was, and had no doubt Bo would pick up the language by the time they'd put the cure together. Hopefully a better grasp of English would assuage Bo's fears and stop his insistence that he heard Gordon whispering at night of "getting rivers arres tit," "the caval," "nooses drawn dighder" and other such things that made little sense.

Laine was going to throttle his uncle. Sometime after the conversation with Doctor Frenally he'd eavesdropped on, Gordon had upgraded the security on his lab. A thick steel door set into an equally sturdy frame and linked to a tamper-proof palm scanner greeted him at the top of the stairs.

How Gordon could've afforded the installation on a scientist's salary, Laine had no idea, but it was yet another suspicious mark to put on Laine's "Gordon's up to no good" tally. Close inspection revealed that anything he did would set off a series of alarms, and Laine slid to the floor of the landing in defeat.

"That's it," he said and slammed his fist against the carpet. A stupid door was all that stood between him and Mom getting better. "It's over."

Even if school weren't locked during break, the labs in the chem room were too far for him and Kenton to go and come everyday without attracting notice. Laine drove his fist into the floor again, regretting it when a stab of pain shot through his still-tender hand.

A whirring sound made him look up. Kenton had extended his weird weapon, the end of it crackling with blue-white frix.

Laine scrambled back from the entrance. "Are you crazy?" he hissed, shielding his eyes against the glow. "You touch that door, you're gonna get electrocuted!"

"I've lived on Thorunn almost all my life. I think I understand how frix works."

Kenton tapped the tip of his weapon against the wall before letting it pulse gently against several different spots, then powered it down and strapped it onto his back again.

"Try it now," he said, a slight smile on his face.

"How about, no?"

Laine knew a trap when he saw one. The moment his fingers brushed the smooth steel, he'd be knocked out, and Kenton would take the lokian and all their money and flee. Laine's extremely sensible refusal caused Kenton to huff and stride over to the door himself. He set his fingers in the fine seam between the two panels and pulled.

The door slid apart, smooth as butter, and Laine jumped to his feet, a hand on one of the panels before he could snatch it back. No shock followed. No alarms sounded.

"How did—?"

The grin on Kenton's face got bigger. "I just, how do you say it again? Demagnetised it. Simple."

"Then what on Earth do you need my help with the gates for?" Laine asked as they stepped into the lab, leaving the door open so they could keep an ear out for Gordon. "The locking mechanism works on exactly the same principle."

The words flew out of Laine's mouth before he realised he should have kept that information to himself, at least until Mom's cure was safe in his hands. Kenton however, didn't bash him over the head and take off towards freedom, electing instead to clear a small space on one of Gordon's worktables and choosing some different apparatuses from the various kits sitting close to the displays projected onto the walls.

"Using my quirn to try and unlock Ethaba's gates would be like trying to cut down a tree with a knife. No, I need a different way."

"Maybe you just need a bigger knife." Laine tossed some kitterstone chunks at Kenton. "Start working on this, and I'll go get in touch with someone who might be able to help." But whatever solution he could cook up with Andy—without letting on what he was actually doing of course—he'd be sure to keep under wraps until Kenton delivered on his end of the bargain. He still didn't trust the "Outpost Terrorist," couldn't even consider it really, until he knew the cure worked.

The blond caught Laine's wrist before he could duck out onto the landing.

"I'll need your help for at least the first stages. Pass me that beaker? And light the burner, will you?"

Laine grumbled but handed the glass container to Kenton who directed him to crush the dark red kitterstone while he mixed small drops of green and silver substances into a clear vial filled with a milky fluid. When he shook the vial, the mixture within fizzled, small, popping bubbles forming a froth at the top.

"Quick, the kitterstone, in the pan!" Kenton said, and Laine tossed the ground up particles into the sole steel container in the lab. Its outside edges were burnt and flaking, but it worked as intended, and the powdered mixture turned molten within moments.

Kenton immediately poured a precise amount of the liquid he'd mixed into the pan and set the heat to low after a bright flare expulsed from it, casting the room in sickly green tones that reminded Laine of Doctor Frenally's basement of horrors.

"Now you can go." Kenton shooed Laine towards the door. "I have to wait until this settles before I can use the, the separator machine."

Centrifuge, he meant the centrifuge—which looked new and hideously expensive—tucked into the back of the room. Laine had been looking rather closely at the Riven family finances of late, trying to figure out how they were supposed to pay Mom's hospital bills and still have enough to eat each week. Dad hadn't made that much, and he and Gordon had worked at the same place. It didn't make sense that Gordon could have the money for his shiny new toys or even still be working, given how much damage the teen grinding up a new batch of kitterstone had done to the ESReC.

But his absence was their gain. Much as it galled Laine to have the Outpost Terrorist and his Alien Freak sleeping under the same roof as him, he couldn't deny the thrill he got in pulling one over on Gordon.

After that first break-in, Kenton and Laine made sure to remagnetise the locks each day, hiding their work and restoring the lab to how they'd found it, and the man never noticed a thing out of place. He didn't seem to notice the beers Laine had been liberating from the fridge either, so Laine kept at it, growing bolder each day that passed and still Gordon said nothing. It might be his uncle's house, but Laine was done playing by his rules.

December flew by, each day mostly the same. Unless they were working on the cure, Laine spoke little to Kenton, and to the lokian not at all. Every now and then Laine volunteered at the ESReC to steal this or that item—whatever was needed to replace what they'd used up in Gordon's lab—and poured over a way to deactivate the gates. He didn't need Kenton or Bo in his room a minute longer than necessary. A musty stench that had to come from the lokian seemed to hang about the place, and Laine found himself sleeping on the living room couch or at the hospital more often than not.

Christmas sucked.

That hag 'Xandra had refused to let him put up the decorations he'd begged off Jacques in Mom's room, citing "sanitation issues" as the reason. Peter had agreed with her, apologising, but obviously not meaning it, as he hadn't even tried to change the other nurse's mind. Laine hadn't even had enough credits to buy the next audiobook in the one series Mom enjoyed, and they were stuck watching old *Task Force: Mars* episodes on Christmas Eve since the only other channel wasn't worth trying to watch through the static.

Mom had fallen asleep before nine, her once-thick hair falling out in waves, paper-thin skin mottled with bruises, and Laine had gone home in a rage, by-passed the locks on Gordon's fridge, raided it for all the alcohol he could find, and subsequently spent much of the next day on his knees in the bathroom.

School was scheduled to start again a day after the New Year, the frix supposed to taper off and stop by then according to the news. But the end of the miserable lightning season was the last thing on Laine's mind New Year's Eve, as he raced up the stairs and almost collided with Kenton on his way out of the lab.

"I figured out the gates!"

"It's finished."

Their words tumbled out at the same time, and Laine very nearly slipped down all fourteen steps when Kenton's statement sunk in.

"Lemme see!" he demanded, scrambling to his feet. Kenton ushered him into the lab where ten vials filled with a sparking red liquid sat in neat rows inside a leather satchel.

"This's a month's supply," Kenton said, hands on his hips, chest puffed out a little. "I've written up precise instructions so you can replicate it exactly the way I was taught it. I'd suggest you start the next batch soon, given how long it takes to cure."

Laine picked up a vial. The mixture inside seemed almost to glow. He ran a finger along the smooth surface, wondering that within was a substance strong enough to reverse almost death itself. For the first time, something like admiration for Kenton and the knowledge of the lokians stirred in his chest. It was just possible that they weren't all the savage, backward forest-dwellers the school handbook made them out to be.

"How many months do I need?"

"You start your mother on this now, and she'll be free of Raxilsish in less than three. But you must administer it in precise amounts. Too little won't have any effect at this stage in the disease, while too much . . ."

"I get it," Laine said softly. "Thanks. And as promised, I've come up with a way for you and the lokian to bypass security and get back to your home."

Kenton's face shone with a rare smile—he normally looked so serious it was a wonder his face hadn't frozen like that. Laine quickly stepped back before the teen got any ideas about hugging him. They weren't friends and never would be.

"Don't look so happy—if the cure doesn't work, I'll burn your forest to the ground."

"It's laughable you think Hinnom trees would kindle so easily."

Kenton was still smiling, the wide grin unsettling Laine to his bones, and he gathered up the satchel and brushed past Kenton.

"C'mon, show me how t'fix my mom."

A chaotic blur greeted Laine and Kenton when they arrived at the second floor of Ethaba General. They turned the corner to reach Mom's room, only to be met by Peter striding hurriedly towards them. His eyes widened when he saw them, a grimace flashing over his face before he reached them and clapped a hand on each teen's shoulder.

"I was just about to call. Alanna's been rushed into emergency surgery."

Every nerve in Laine's body froze, skin prickling. Waves of terror rushed through him, churning through his stomach and dropping his legs out from under him. This couldn't be happening, not here, not when the cure for Bowman's sat nestled inside his jacket. He clutched at Peter.

"Take me to her. Now!"

Laine's heart hammered in his chest as he and Kenton raced behind Peter through the hospital, taking all the back corridors and "staff only" staircases. Peter grabbed Laine's arm just before he pushed open the large double doors leading into the hallway outside the OR.

"You can't cause a scene, you understand me? One peep and they will throw you out."

Laine nodded. He didn't think he could force a single word past the constriction in his throat anyhow. It seemed hours that the doors took to swing open, revealing the harshly lit hallway with wide windows in the wall opposite, behind which a blood-spattered team of doctors huddled over a teal draped body that Laine knew instantly as his mother.

He staggered and fell to his knees, clutching at Kenton for support.

"This only happens in zero-point-one percent of patients, but her spine underwent sudden rapid disintegration, the broken pieces severing her spinal cord." Peter closed his eyes and sat, as if relaying the information were too hard to do standing. There hadn't been any chairs added since Laine had last been in the surgery halls, and the nurse looked almost a comical sight, cross-legged in soft grey scrubs on the floor. "I'm sorry, kid. She doesn't deserve this."

"Just tell me they can save her," Laine whispered, pressing the heels of his palms to his eyes in an effort to stop the tears he could feel welling up.

"We're doing all we can," Peter said and patted him on the shoulder before going to stand watch by the door. Kenton took his place.

"It's worse than I thought—but we can still save her. She will be"—he darted a quick look at the nurse, who had folded an arm, resting his chin atop a pensive fist—"paralysed. Permanently. But she will live."

"There's still a chance? These aren't useless?" Laine pressed a hand to the vials stashed just over his heart. "You're not just jerking me around to get your ticket outta here?"

"As long as your mother still draws breath there's hope."

Laine turned the words over in his mind. Permanent paralysis was a frightening concept. He tapped his leg, wondering what it would feel like to not be able to run or walk again. This new development would rob Mom of everything she enjoyed. Cooking and gardening and dancing. Moving to the heartbeat of life as drums played rhythmically in the background.

All the steps she'd painstakingly showed Laine; and she must have been in so much pain, never letting a hint of it slip onto her face as she carefully corrected his movements and waited quietly for him to return when he got frustrated and stormed off. How beautiful she'd looked, spinning around in the one ceremonial outfit she'd had room to pack in her suitcase, her long black hair flowing out around her as beaded necklaces and earrings caught the light. How every press of her feet must have felt like stepping on a thousand needles—and now, she never would again.

But she'd be alive. If Kenton was telling the truth, Mom would be alive to smile at him when he came home from school with the highest grades. Alive to cheer him on at his next match, and to talk with him at the end of a long, tiring day. Laine felt again for the soft edges of the leather satchel concealed beneath his clothes. As much as he disliked Kenton, Laine had to trust him. Without the cure, Mom would die anyway.

"You don't leave Ethaba until I see for my own eyes that this works."

"Then we better distract those nurses so we can inject the serum."

Laine pulled himself up and looked around. The OR team consisted of two surgeons, a few nurses, and one very eager med student who ran back and forth fetching things and recording everything on his holo-screen.

"That guy's about your height," Laine said to Kenton. A cart of medical supplies sat unattended in the hallway—or at least it would be once Laine had finished hacking into Ethaba General's paging system using a trick he'd learned from Andy. "Think you can hold him down long enough for me to stick him?"

Kenton nodded and sidled up to the door, Laine heading to the cart. He surreptitiously read the labels behind Peter's back while he waited for the signal he'd sent to go through. They only had one shot at getting his plan right, and it wouldn't do to hit the unsuspecting intern with adrenaline by mistake.

The minute Peter's pager chimed, sending him running down the hall, Laine grabbed everything off the top tray and ducked below the windows. He broke the first set of needles and cartridges he tried to load, and dropped three syringes. The judgy look and frantic gestures from Kenton didn't help; Laine could very well figure out for himself that the med student was getting ready to leave the OR again at any minute. Aware of the clock ticking over their heads, Laine sucked in a deep breath and steadied his hands, succeeding on his third attempt just in time.

Their victim turned and let out a squeak when he took in first the dishevelled medical cart and second, Laine poised to strike, syringe at the ready, but Kenton clapped a hand over the student's mouth, and Laine stabbed him through the first vein he could find. They quickly stripped the young man of his scrubs as he fought against the effects of the medication. The hallway suddenly felt very hot, every thrashing struggle of the intern magnified a thousand-fold in the quiet space. Laine really hoped the lead surgeon had a predilection for listening to music while he operated.

By the time he and Kenton had dragged the intern to a nearby closet, the man had gone limp, and Kenton shrugged into his clothes, accepting a new syringe loaded with a fraction of the kitterstone cure. He pocketed what he needed and slipped into the OR while Laine attempted to restore the cart to normal, trying not to think about what would happen if Kenton failed. He risked a peek after a couple minutes. Kenton gave him a thumbs up from behind one of the doctors and hovered about in the background until he was sent out, no one the wiser to the switch, and exchanged clothes once more.

They left the intern propped up against the wall and ran for the exit before he could wake and turn them in.

"Even now, the healing properties of the serum should be taking effect," Kenton puffed as they jogged through the halls to Mom's room, careful to keep out of the way of the nurses. "I had to go between her toes so the doctors wouldn't notice, but it works fast, and I wouldn't be surprised if they return her here within the hour."

It ended up being a tense two hours, Laine jumping at every little sound, certain that Peter or 'Xandra would burst in and scold them for traumatising the med student, but the doctors wheeled Mom back to the room without any fuss, leaving once she'd been safely tucked into bed. The lights dimmed, and after Laine had ripped up a piece of flooring and stashed a plastic-wrapped syringe in the cavity below, just in case, he and Kenton curled up in the straight-backed chairs opposite a large holoscreen and fell asleep.

"—aine, Laine?"

"Mom?"

Mom! Laine jumped up, almost tripping over Kenton, who'd decided the floor was more comfortable than the corrugated plastic chair with its meagre cushion. Laine's back had gone numb, so maybe Kenton had the right idea. Dusting himself off, he dragged his chair over to Mom's bedside.

"Sorry, I was sleeping. Adrenaline crash." He jerked a thumb at Kenton. "We got you the cure."

Laine pulled out one of the vials from his jacket and offered it to Mom. Her fingers twitched, but she made no move towards it.

"I, I . . . can't," she whispered, a hitch in her voice as she turned glassy eyes on Laine. "Why? Laine, what's wrong with me?"

Permanently paralysed, Laine heard in Kenton's voice. He swallowed, tucking the vial away.

"Peter said, he said you suddenly took a turn for the worse. They managed to stabilise you, and with this"—he patted his jacket, feeling the vials bump gently against his chest—"we stopped whatever was going on, but not in time before . . ."

"You'll never be able to walk again, Mrs. Riven," Kenton said, having woken due to the chatter. He drew up the other chair. "Physical—how do you say it?—therapy might help your hands and arms, but the damage to your legs was too severe for even kitterstone serum to counteract. I'm sorry."

He looked genuinely upset too—strange for someone who'd had no qualms about attacking upward of a dozen towns in his quest for vengeance.

"Don't be. I'm alive, I'm with my courageous son"—she smiled at Laine, her face bright for the first time in weeks, gaze sweeping the room as if just now seeing the place properly—"and the pain, the pain is gone. Thank you, Kenton."

Kenton flushed and looked away, but not before Laine caught the guilty expression on his face. No matter that he'd helped save Mom, he was still the Outpost Terrorist and had traded his lifesaving knowledge for safe passage out of Ethaba. Laine couldn't quite find it in him to respect Kenton's motives, even if they produced wonderful results.

"How long before it starts hurting again?" Mom asked, brow pinching a little.

"It won't—"

"We made enough of the cure—courtesy of Gordon's lab," Laine cut in, "to keep you going a month straight. I don't intend on letting it run out." He leaned forward, blinking his eyes to stop the stinging at the rush of emotion that swelled up within him. "Mom, you're gonna live. You can come home."

"Home," Mom said, drawing out the word like a loving caress. "That reminds me—I've been meaning to ask, how's your uncle taking living with Kenton?"

"Oh, they haven't met." Shame really, Laine had gone to all the trouble of creating a backstory for Kenton, and hadn't had a chance to use it. "Gordon's like, in love with work or something. Stays at the ES-ReC all day, and according to Kenton's loki—uh, um, well, apparently he comes home real late and just works upstairs all night."

Mom turned troubled eyes on Laine. "In the same lab you created this cure in?"

"He's got no idea we've been in there," Laine reassured her. "We put everything back where we find it, and Andy wrote me a loop program that overrides all kinds of camera footage. Trust me, Gordon is completely in the dark about this."

"He may know more than you think." Mom's hands twitched, like she wanted to fold them together, so Laine moved them into her lap, careful to keep his movements feather-light as Mom's condition had so progressed that the gentlest of touches could cause deep bruising.

"With everything else going on, I'd almost forgotten—you know how my mind is these days. He came to see me once. Just the once. He talked to Peter a long time before coming in. I remember . . ." Mom trailed off, the recollection clouding her eyes. "He wasn't sad. He wasn't happy. He just said it looked like he'd have the house to himself again soon. I wanted to remind him you live there too, but something about his face frightened me, and I couldn't get the words out."

Laine ground his teeth. His uncle had no right; what kind of cold-hearted, despicable waste of space would visit a sick person solely to scare them?

"I'll handle Gordon, don't worry, Mom. Get some sleep. I'll be back tomorrow." Laine stood, then stooped to kiss her, lips brushing like a breath on her forehead.

Once Mom was better he'd be able to reveal how he'd healed her. Kenton would be long gone by then, and the doctors would look at Laine as a saviour, not a traitor. Maybe they'd even give him a medal. He'd be known throughout Thorunn as the boy who cured Bowman's disease—Laine Alexander Riven would be a household name, and that would rankle Gordon like nothing else. Gordon's face would still look best smashed through the floor, but since Laine didn't fancy getting arrested for avnucide, avulcucide—whatever the word was that meant killing one's uncle—he'd settle for his undying hatred in the face of Laine's success.

"Guess this means I gotta show you how to get out, huh?" Laine said as he and Kenton wended their way back through the frix. It had eased off to near nothing, but Laine still carried the tattered remains of his uncle's umbrella with him. Not for the first time he envied Kenton's sleek jacket, pants, and gloves that repelled the worst of the damage and kept him dry.

"It'd be appreciated, yes," Kenton replied, glancing at the sky where the sparking clouds had thinned, no longer black and intimidating. "We can be ready as soon as this evening." When Laine hesitated to respond, he added, "Or when we get back."

"Nah, you should have one more decent meal and a chance at a nap," Laine said. He was eager to have the free-loaders gone, but Kenton had delivered on his promise, and Laine was feeling magnanimous after their success at the hospital. "Bring in the New Year right."

As they approached Gordon's, Laine put out a hand to stop Kenton.

The garage door was open.

"It's not like your uncle to be home so early," Kenton said, one hand going to the weapon concealed under his jacket. Gordon's Blackline sat tarpless in the middle of the tidy space, shiny like it'd just been washed and waxed.

"Go round the back. I'll let you know if it's safe to come in," Laine said. He'd made it so far without having to explain Kenton's presence to his uncle—one more day, and he'd never have to mention it. The teens backtracked, and Kenton took off running the minute they were sure he wouldn't be spied from the windows.

Laine hurried up the front steps and banged open the door—hopefully the lokian would hear and know to stay quiet. More than that, he was furious with Gordon. Ever since Mom had mentioned his uncle's little visit, he'd been simmering with a low-grade anger that flared hotter and hotter as he thought about Mom, pale and alone, cowering under the weight of the imposing man's cruel words.

He found Gordon sitting in the living room, watching a Thorunn Crystal Broadcast News Network special on the history and dangers of the Cabal. Apparently they'd been a thorn in the local government's side for close to four years.

"What are you doing here?" Laine said, gripping tightly to the doorframe to stop himself from attacking the man. He couldn't afford to fight with Gordon, not with the slight weight of the vials in his jacket that would surely be crushed if Gordon put him on the floor again.

"I wasn't aware it was a crime for a man to enjoy television in his own home?" He stood and tapped his clip to switch off the holoscreen. "But it's good you're dressed. C'mon, we're going out."

"What, why?"

Gordon brushed past Laine, crowding the teen into the narrow space, and snagged his keys off the ring by the door.

"Heard y'had a scare with Alanna today, thought I'd see how you were doing. Or don't you want to ride my Blackline?"

Laine glanced over his shoulder as he hurried after the man. Kenton's head popped up, features blurred through the back window, and Laine beckoned him in, miming that he was going out with Gordon. Kenton and the lokian could pack, eat, and rest in the meantime.

"I thought you didn't want me touching your precious vercycle?" Laine said as they reached the garage, where Gordon tossed a spare helmet at him.

"Frix's dwindled to almost nothing, and after a month of not being able to ride my baby, guess I'm feeling a bit . . . magnanimous." He paused, helmet in gloved hands, looking Laine up and down. "That could change if you keep up the attitude."

"No, no, I'm grateful, really!" Laine insisted.

The words felt foreign in his mouth, but the longer Gordon was out of the house, the higher the chance he'd actually succeed in getting Kenton and Bo out of Ethaba with no one the wiser. They couldn't risk dismantling the locking system in broad daylight anyway, so he might as well while away the time with Gordon. And he couldn't deny that he'd lusted over riding Gordon's vercycle since the time his uncle had so rudely tossed him out and stranded him in the middle of the Thorunn wilderness.

Laine hopped on eagerly, and they took off, the sleek machine eating up the wet streets with ease, and before he knew it, they were at a dimly lit pub calling itself "*Skaði's*." Laine goggled a bit at the wide variety of alcoholic beverages sitting on every table and in the hands of the colourful flock of rather underdressed patrons.

"Aren't I a little young for this kinda place?" he asked.

"Eh, this's Thorunn, not Earth," Gordon replied. "'Sides, I figured if you knew this place was here, it might stop you from stealing my beer."

He might know more than you think.

Mom's words came back to Laine, and cold ran spiderlike through him, his cheeks growing contradictorily hot. If Gordon knew about the beer then— no, it wasn't possible. Beer was a quantifiable object. They'd start the week with ten and end with two. In hindsight, maybe he should have realised Gordon might miss the bitter, watery drink.

In contrast, he and Kenton took almost nothing from the lab upstairs; not even a speck of dust was out of place, and what they did use up they replaced with supplies stolen from the ESReC. Gordon was trying to scare him for whatever reason, just like he'd tried to scare Mom. He wouldn't let his uncle play these mind games with him.

"Two please," Gordon said when they reached the bar. "The usual."

The drinks arrived, and they sat in silence for a

while, taking in the sounds around them. Laine's beverage was flavourful, not nearly as bitter as his normal fare, and he drank half the mug before he made himself slow down. Gordon had already drained his and signalled for a refill. He turned to Laine once his second drink was in hand, as if he needed the relaxing qualities of alcohol to hold a conversation with his nephew.

Laine scowled. He wasn't that difficult to converse with. Was he?

"Look, I know we didn't start on the right foot, and you hate me—not without cause probably, I know I ain't the cuddliest guy on the block—but Jack's gone. I've tried, but there's no getting him outta the mess he's in, and your mother, she's not much longer for this place."

Yes, thank you, Gordon for recapping every horrible thing that had overshadowed Laine's life recently. Bang up job he was doing with his apology or whatever it was supposed to be. Laine gulped down more beer, hoping it would help him tune out the man's droning, drawl thicker than normal. It reminded him of Dad, when Dad was trying to be genuine, and that made Laine's hackles rise.

"Soon it'll be just you and me, an' I know we ain't each other's favourite people, but you're family, an' family's got to stick together. Whaddya say?" Gordon extended his hand. "Put all this bad blood behind us?"

Laine stared at his uncle. The olive branch he held out probably had a nest of hornets hidden beneath, and if he didn't trust Dad when he got like this, he most certainly would not trust Gordon.

"You expect me to just, forget all the difficulties we've had?" Laine's voice rose and cracked in incredulousness.

"I ain't asking you to. I'm telling you t'be an adult. You're about to go through something awful, an' I should be there for you. What kind of uncle would I be if I didn't at least try t'bury the hatchet before then?"

"An even worse one than you already are?"

Gordon laughed, noticeably looser because of the second drink he'd already finished. "Think about it, okay? If we can't solve our problems like men, we're no better than those blasted, meddling lokians."

Laine hummed noncommittally. Until Gordon started being nicer about Mom, instead of treating her like so much trash, he wasn't ready to even attempt to make peace. But he could pretend for one evening while he tried to suss out Gordon's true intentions. And if Gordon was paying, the anlo steak on the menu looked mighty appetising.

———————— ● ————————

Bo lay curled around Ken, the two of them barely daring to breathe when they heard the lock click in the front door and the heavy boots of Laine's uncle, followed by clinking and shuffling sounds in the kitchen that meant the Riven men had returned.

Less than five minutes later, Laine swept aside the curtain, calling for them to come upstairs. Bo shouldered his bag and followed Ken into the kitchen, glad to leave the dark, cramped space behind.

Brilliant light flooded the kitchen despite the late hour, and Bo's pupils shrank to tiny slits against the harsh glare. Loud snoring filtered through the open door from the living room, and he narrowed his eyes further, wanting to hiss at Laine's negligence. He could have waited 'til his uncle was safely abed before fetching them.

"You can tell your pet not to worry about Gordon," Laine said to Ken, still labouring under the delusion that Bo couldn't understand him. Bo *might* have fostered that belief by ripping a few of the books to shreds once he'd finished with them. That had been a fun fight between himself and Ken.

"He's had like twenty beers. He's not going anywhere."

If Bo squinched his eyes any more he'd not be able to see, so he hissed quietly instead, baring razor-sharp canines at the boy.

"Before you go, I want one more thing," Laine said. "A guarantee you'll leave Ethaba alone." Ken nodded before Bo could tell him not to make any such promise. "Your frix-proof suit. Everyone keeps saying that second frix is way worse, and since you caused Gordon's umbrella to get shredded, I'll need something to get around."

Laine crossed his arms and stared challengingly at Ken, and if his best friend hadn't held him back with a quick shake of his head and a hand to his shoulder, Bo would have torn the teen to pieces, secret to leaving Ethaba or not. The Innah was right. Only a disgusting human would take and take and *take* until decent people had nothing left to offer except the clothes on their backs, and then take those as well.

"It's such a small thing," Ken murmured to Bo. "Please, don't cause a commotion now. In less than two days we'll be home, and I can always make another."

Bo growled low in his throat and turned away, unable to watch as Ken stripped off his jacket, pants, and gloves, exchanging them for some clothes Laine held out.

That matter sorted, they locked the door softly behind them and started the long walk to the gates. The frix had all but vanished, only a few stray drops *plinking* down here or there. The glow that had previously bathed Ethaba's streets was non-existent, aiding their silent trek through the mostly unoccupied streets.

"I'll need both your quirns," Laine whispered once they reached the wall, the gates of Ethaba looming large above them. As tall as several houses, and twice as wide as the Laika River, it seemed impassable on foot and yet had been so easy to fly over. Once home, Bo was going to pester Irjah until he let him start building hovercars. With the imminent threat the humans posed, the elder probably wouldn't withhold his permission too long.

"Your quirn, Bo," Ken repeated in Klia'an, and Bo grudgingly handed it over. The human pulled two bulky devices from his jacket and attached them to each corner of the gates. The quirns he settled against the middle of each device—power amplifiers if Bo had to guess—and pressed two small buttons to each, but left them dark and moved over to the unguarded palm scanner, a glowing projection from his clip hanging in the air in front of him.

"We got a tiny window before the gates slam shut again, so be ready to run," Laine said.

Once everyone was in position, the human gave the signal and the temporarily remotely controlled quirns flared to life, the heavy steel doors humming low and sonorous, the vibrations shaking Bo to his bones. Following Ken's example, he set his fingers in the seam and pulled, putting all his strength behind the movement.

The doors budged a claw's width, then stopped.

"Sorry!" Laine called. "Let me adjust for the automatic gears."

He did something to the scanner, and the doors started moving again. Bit by bit, Bo and Ken forced the giant doors open, stopping when the crack between them was large enough to slip through.

Bo grasped Ken's wrist. The moment had been a long time in coming, but the Hinnom Forest lay on the other side of the narrow gap, and Bo was determined to get back, even if it meant running all night and into the next day.

"Ready?" he asked.

"Here's to finally going home."

They dashed over to their quirns. The heavy doors started to grind together the moment the glowing weapons lost contact with the devices, the strange humming vanishing.

Bo ran like he'd never run before. The gates weren't just tall but thick, and he didn't much like the idea of being smashed between them. His tail was tightly wrapped around his waist, the resulting loss of balance a necessary sacrifice if it meant leaving Ethaba with all his limbs attached.

The thin space dwindled, and Bo upped his pace, quirn still sparking with frix, no time to deactivate it. He pushed faster, passing Ken, and reached out a hand to drag him along. The doors slammed shut moments after he and Ken tumbled through, and Bo flopped onto the muddy, red ground in relief. They were free.

The sound of rumbling yanked Bo into instant alertness.

Ken still slept—having been forced to rest sooner on their return journey than Bo would have preferred on account of his weakened heart—and his human ears hadn't yet picked out the vibrations that whispered across the drying Cerado. Bo shook him awake, pointing at the shimmering mirage on the horizon that shouldn't be there, given they travelled along no route customary to the people of Ethaba.

"Another scientific expedition?" Bo wondered aloud. The last of the bad weather had dissipated overnight, the sky its customary rich blue, and the blinding sun obscured the vehicle drawing closer and closer.

"Can't be," Ken said, snapping his quirn into his hands and ducking behind one of the large boulders scattered about the wide expanse between Ethaba and the Hinnom Forest. "I've been sabotaging the ES-ReC's transports for the last month."

"Then"—Bo's mouth went dry—"it's Skytown soldiers sent to attack the tribe in revenge."

Ken shook his head, risking a glance around the boulder. It wouldn't provide cover much longer, not against a flying vehicle, but they couldn't chance making a break for it across the fathoms of empty space between them and home.

"We crippled the outpost towns too badly for them to turn their remaining resources on us right now—they don't even know we're behind the attacks. Besides, there's only one hovertruck, look."

Ken crouched lower, Bo almost flat on his belly next to him.

He too, had his quirn out, newly recharged and hot with the sun's energy. His fur stood on end, and it was a good thing he'd already turned his gloves into fingerless versions of the ones he'd left home with, given that he couldn't help the instinctual popping of his claws. The transport drew nearer still, the humming turning into a roar. Bo waited for it to pass, ears pinned flat against his head.

But the engines abruptly cut to half power, quiet enough to hear a human voice give the command to open fire.

The boulder they'd been hiding behind shattered, and Bo sprang aside, dragging Ken with him. His best friend had a dazed look about him, forehead bleeding from where a small chunk of stone had glanced off him.

It's us they're hunting, Bo seethed internally. *That no good lying vana'byss of a human turned us in the moment he got what he needed from us.*

"I told you we shoulda let Laine Riven die in that alley," Bo hissed at Ken after they tumbled behind another rocky outcrop. "We're gonna die out here like prey because you had to help him."

Bo peeked around the outcrop and fired a few quick shots at the now stationary military-grade hovertruck. The sun still glinted blindingly off its exterior, but hard squinting revealed two sets of heavy-duty sol-cannons mounted atop the boxy shape, a smaller emergency vehicle strapped to its side. If it stayed still just a little longer, he could eat through the shields with the frix and show those ignorant humans that klia'ans were not to be trifled with.

Bo's desperate shots caused smoke to rise from the hovertruck, but a panel of blue lights flared to life along the bottom, auxiliary power units, if it was anything like the vehicles the Igis Chosen had appropriated all those months ago. Bo gnashed his fangs and fired again, to similar effect. The sol-cannons on the transport started to charge once more—they had to move before the enemy could obliterate his and Ken's current barricade.

"I would have failed the mission—" Ken started.

"Hang the mission!" Bo snarled, reverting to guttural S'hinoian. "What's the point of saving a human—who hated and wanted to kill us—if you're gonna wind up dying out here anyway?" Bo's vision blurred, tears spilling over that had welled up out of nowhere. "I lost P'rraa to humans; I can't lose you too!"

"And I can't lose myself!" Ken yelled back. "Okay, now. Go, go!" They shot a concentrated stream of frix at the main sol-cannon, and it backfired in a spectacular explosion, smoke and steam billowing out thick and fast. "I wouldn't be worthy of passing Igis if I sacrificed what I believe in to selfishly save my own life."

Ken had a point—his steadfast, earnest integrity and fierce sense of right and wrong was what had drawn Bo's interest in the first place, once he'd gotten over his hurt that the village elders had approved a human living with Tribe Osinan. But in times such as they found themselves in, when the solfire flew hot and deadly, Bo really wished Ken could be persuaded to compromise his values. Then he hated himself for thinking that. Ken wouldn't be Ken anymore if he changed so fundamentally, even over a small matter—and saving someone's life wasn't a small matter at all.

Ken gasped suddenly, one hand clutching at his chest. "I'm fine, fine," he said, waving off Bo's concern. "Have you noticed, they haven't fired any truly lethal shots?"

Now that Ken mentioned it, Bo discerned how the solfire had driven them into a corner. Pinned them down. Exactly the sort of thing he'd have done when hunting on the banks of the Laika River.

"Oh, so instead of dying now, we'll die in pieces in a cold lab when they've finished pulling us apart." Bo popped up and let loose with his quirn, taking a dark satisfaction in the resulting screams. As far as he was concerned their mission had ended at Ethaba, and he could shoot whomever he wished with impunity. "How is that an option that puts a smile on your face?"

Ken glanced in the direction of the Hinnom Forest. It appeared deceptively nearby, a bright green smudge that stayed the same distance away no matter how hard they'd run towards it over the past few hours. For how far they'd travelled since leaving Ethaba, the horrid town still seemed to loom close at their backs. And now, trapped between the brittle, frix-ravaged shrubbery and a group of rock formations about to be blasted to smithereens by their enemies' secondary sol-cannons, home seemed like a dream they should have abandoned long ago.

"Because if they are pulling their shots, hoping to take us alive, I've an idea. See that vercycle near the back?"

Bo nodded, grasping what Ken was getting at.

"We'll have to run straight at them, and run fast if we wanna grab it before they realise it's what we're after."

"Just get the locks disengaged," Ken said, ratcheting up the power on his quirn. "I'll take care of the rest."

He gasped again, and Bo pegged the culprit as the

increased voltage. Any higher and his quirn's protective casing would fail—if it hadn't started to already. Bo's pulse jumped as images of Ken going into cardiac arrest tormented him. No matter how much Ken insisted he was fine, the sheen of sweat coating his ashen face and trembling hands told a different story.

Ken pushed against the ground to steady himself.

"On my mark, three, two—now!"

They dashed headlong at the hovertruck, several blasts coming very close to searing off Bo's ears before the humans started yelling and the shooting ceased. Bo kept up a steady stream of frix, stopping only when he gained the small metal ledge jutting out from the vehicle's side. Several concentrated bursts made short work of the locks that kept the slim vercycle magnetised to the side, and Bo wrested it to the ground mere moments before the transport fired its hoverdrives, lurching into motion.

Bo dropped flat, the whirring engines passing harmlessly over him, the force they generated pressing him hard into the unforgiving earth. He surged up again in an instant, activating the vercycle, and circled around to catch Ken. A savage burst of pride shot through him at the comforting weight of his friend settling against his back, and he opened the throttle, the lightweight machine speeding away from the attacking hovertruck.

Less than ten seconds later however, the vercycle started to whine and dip dangerously close to the ground. Their speed slowed, and their pursuers began to close the gap.

"Go faster, you Lanae-cursed piece of junk!" Bo yelled at the sputtering vercycle. The enemy transport drew close enough that it blocked out the sun, its shadow falling cold over them.

"This vercycle wasn't built to carry more than one person," Ken said. Each breath sounded like a hard-won victory, and Bo craned his head around to check on him.

"Will it last to the forest at least?" he asked, dreading the answer. Ken didn't look like he had much time left. But short of hijacking the hovertruck itself—and they didn't have enough charges between them to disable its remaining sol-cannons—they had no other way to get to safety before Ken's heart stuttered out.

Ken turned his quirn to max power, the electricity so thick Bo could taste the hot metallic sparks dancing at its tip.

Everything happened in slow motion after that, Bo powerless to move as Ken reached out a gentle hand and cupped Bo's face, an achingly tender expression spread across his.

"No, no, Ken, please," Bo gasped out, his own hands locked onto the vercycle's handles in a death grip. He wanted to rip them away, to block Ken's determined course of action, but adrenaline trapped him within his body. Bo could only flail helplessly inside his mind as Ken pressed a kiss to his forehead, his long, blond hair whipping about in the shifting currents caused by the uneven pace the limping vercycle had done its best to achieve.

"You've been the best friend I could ever have hoped to have." Ken smiled despite the horrific amounts of pain he had to be enduring, the hand that gripped his quirn bleeding profusely, and Bo's heart spilled out of his chest. "Get home for me."

Then Kenton Oso Frix turned and launched himself off the vercycle, hurtling through the air bright and deadly in an arcing maelstrom of raw, blistering energy.

3

arly Monday morning—the first day back at school and the beginning of the third day since Mom had taken the cure and started getting noticeably stronger—found Laine rushing about at a frenetic pace, trying to gather his school things without stepping on Gordon's toes.

The man had been weirdly present, lips quirked into a permanent smirk ever since the previous afternoon, but Laine didn't have time to dwell on his odd behaviour or he'd end up late to school. He really should have gotten his things together the day before, but it'd been his last free day before school sucked up all his time, and Laine couldn't think of a better place to have spent it than at Mom's side, watching the colour return to her face.

"Yo, you seen my jacket?" Laine called as he swept up his lacrosse gear from the hallway. He thought he'd taken it down to his room with him last night, but then he spotted it hung over the back of a chair. "Never mind, got it." Laine shrugged it on and dashed off without waiting for any kind of response.

The walk to school felt blissfully short, the frix gone, the sky bluer than he'd remembered it being. If he hadn't actually wanted to make it on time, he'd have spent a few minutes more gazing at Frey and

Freja as they hung full and bright in the early morning sky. The almost month of hazy darkness—punctuated by violent flashes of lightning—had seemed to go on endlessly but disappeared the moment Kenton and Bo had left Ethaba. Frix season had come and gone with them, and Laine was glad to have both nuisances out of his life.

"Dustin, my man," Laine called upon arriving in class. He still had to figure out a way to explain the shredded piles of paper in his room that were once classic works of literature. Was it possible Dustin wouldn't remember he'd loaned Laine the books if he "forgot" to return them for long enough? "Ready to cause a little ruckus?"

"If by 'ruckus' you mean taking this spring's mathletes competition." Dustin grinned, dangling the medal from December in front of Laine, who batted it away.

"Not gonna happen. With Mom sick, I can't do two time-intensive activities, and sorry, but"—he clapped a hand on Dustin's shoulder—"lacrosse club's the only time I see the guys."

"I'm a guy!" Dustin protested, a look of hurt in his eyes. Laine valiantly held back a laugh.

"I see you in class every day. All day. I get at most, maybe two hours with Andy and Jacques and the rest. Plus, spring season's short because of second frix or whatever, so we gotta make the most of it."

Dustin shivered. "Second frix. I'm not looking forward to it. What if the Outpost Terrorist strikes again? We barely survived the first time."

He spoke faster as the seconds ticked down until their homeroom teacher would appear and popped a lollipop into his mouth, offering one to Laine. It was lime green, so he accepted, the clear wrapping crinkling as he tore it off. It tasted unexpectedly sour.

"Don't worry, I think we're off their hit list for now."

"Their?" Dustin shot him a questioning look, but Laine was saved from answering when the homeroom teacher strode into the room.

As soon as Laine stepped through the door after classes finished, the locker room exploded with sound. Crackers popped and noisemakers sounded, and an armful of confetti hit Laine dead in the face.

"What the—?" Laine spluttered on the glittery flakes. If the choking stuff settled in his lungs, he was going to kill somebody. Probably Andy. "What's going on?"

"Do you or do you not remember scoring the winning goal for us in December?" Jacques demanded, trying to look stern, but failing, his excitement getting the best of him.

"That was weeks ago!" Laine shook his head, trying vainly to rid himself of the annoying shreds clinging to his hair.

"Yes, but then your mama fell ill, and the Outpost Terrorist attacked, and school was closed, and long story short, this is the first time we've been able to properly celebrate."

"So you decided to chuck glitter in my face."

"It's confetti with glitter in it," Andy said, as if that really made a difference. "We thought you'd be a touch more enthused, mate."

Laine looked around, seeing for the first time the "Laine Riven, MVP" banner hanging over his locker, a golden-ish trophy on top, as well as the table in the back with boxes of what passed for pizza on Thorunn stacked rather high. Several large bottles of lytorade sat beside the delicious-smelling food, an assortment of different coloured cups just behind the refreshments.

Every member of the team was there, Jacques, Tom, Andy, and the rest, and Yoon Ah's handmade sign from the game sat proudly in front of the table.

Laine felt his throat grow tight at the care Andy and the other Ospreys had put into the surprise party.

"Yeah," he said. "I'm just, with Mom and all—I, I wasn't expecting—this is really cool, guys." Laine cleared his voice and blinked rapidly. The longer he stared at the food, the hungrier he became, and who was he to turn down a party in his honour?

"We get it, mate." Andy clapped him on the shoulder, fixing an earnest look on Laine. All the hard feelings from their fight seemed to have dissipated entirely, though Laine wished he could've gained back his captain's favour on the merit of his skill alone, and not everything else that had happened. "That's why I petitioned Principal Kim to skip practice for today—we've the whole hour to hang here an' celebrate. Long as we clean up after. Don't want any skreet infestations."

"Enough talk, let's eat!" Tom said, edging around Jacques to get to the food. Laine couldn't help but agree, and they had at it.

"Here's to another good season." Laine raised his cup of lytorade.

"Aye, it'll be short, but intense," Andy said, lifting his cup to Laine's. "Be ready to run like you've never run before."

Principal Kim's voice over the intercom cut through the jovial atmosphere in the locker room.

"I need Laine Riven to report to the principal's office straightaway. Again, Laine Riven, I need to see you in my office immediately."

The PA system clicked off, and everyone in the room turned to look at Laine, half-eaten slices of pizza in their hands. Their wide eyes would have been comical if Laine's heart didn't feel like it was being squeezed in a vise. Only Andy looked serious, immediately grasping the gravity of the situation.

"Need me to come with?" he asked.

"Sure." Laine's voice trembled, and he put down the pizza.

He felt cold.

It was only his first day back, and he'd been in classes all day. His grades had been fairly good last semester, and running around with Kenton during the break had kept him out of trouble. There was only one reason why Principal Kim would be summoning him if it wasn't to reprimand him.

Laine checked his clip, but there weren't any messages.

"Look," Andy said as they jogged down the hall, "I hope to Saint Ailbhe this isn't what I dread it to be. But I want you to know, if it is, I'm here for you. We're here for you, me an' Yoon Ah. Whatever you need. Everything else's in the past."

They came to a stop in front of Principal Kim's office. Laine had managed to avoid the place after his accident, but if he remembered correctly from the few times he'd had to have a concerned talk from the school head, the room was small, a large mirror on one wall reflecting the window on the other side, brightening and enlarging the space.

Laine was still trying not to think of worst-case scenarios, but even if Bo and Kenton's secret stay had somehow been discovered, he wouldn't have been called to the office. More likely soldiers would have shown up and dragged him away like they did Dad, before presenting Gordon with another damning document. Somehow he didn't think Gordon would be too sorrowful over the news. Since he was still at school and not in the back of a military police hovercar, that left only one other alternative, and Principal Kim had sounded too serious for anything other than the awful option that had Laine's hair standing up on each arm.

He nodded to acknowledge Andy's offer and gestured for him to wait outside. He didn't want to see the pity on Andy's face if, if—

Laine couldn't even think it. He stepped inside after pushing the door open. It took a long time to swing shut.

"Please, sit." Principal Kim indicated the chair in front of his desk. A pretty Indian lady about his mother's age stood next to him.

"I'd rather not." Laine crossed his arms, letting anger rise to stamp down the fear beginning to creep along his bones.

"Mr. Riven, please," the lady said. She looked vaguely familiar, someone from the student guidance office perhaps. "I strongly advise it."

Laine remained standing. "Who's this?" he asked Principal Kim. The man was mid-fifties and usually sported a genial smile, which softened his age lines, but at that moment, the furrows wrinkling his brow and the pinched press of his lips added at least a decade to his worn appearance.

"This is Mrs. Padeem." He spoke each word as if they were heavy stones, reluctant to pass his lips. "Ethaba High's grief counsellor. She's here to help you through this difficult period."

"Yeah, no thanks. If you're here about Mom, you're wasting your time." Laine forced every ounce of confidence he could muster into his voice. He wanted to rage, to scream, to destroy something, if it meant he could take back the truth he could see written in the adults' eyes. It shouldn't be possible though. Kenton had promised. Laine had seen Mom getting better with his own eyes, and she hadn't been lying about the pain being gone.

"She's been on the mend the last couple days."

Principal Kim closed his eyes. He appeared visibly struck, like Laine had reached over the desk and punched him in the chest.

"I'm so sorry, Laine," he said. His eyes when he opened them again were a little wet.

Laine took a step backward, but the next words arrested his movement, curdling every bone in his body, and he knew—for a fraction of an instant—the vomit-inducing torment Mom endured.

"The hospital called, trying to reach you."

Laine's hand flew to his clip again—still nothing. He was sure he'd given the front desk at Ethaba General the right frequency. He'd listed himself as the first person to reach in an emergency, and they should have called him before the school the instant anything changed. Dread settled cold and thick in Laine's gut, and he could only listen numbly as Principal Kim finished delivering the news.

"Your mother has a half hour at most. Mrs. Padeem will escort you to the hospital so you can say goodbye."

Laine stormed out of Principal Kim's office, leaving a broken chair embedded in the wall and a stunned Mrs. Padeem next to Principal Kim. Broken glass littered the floor from where the now useless chair had struck the long office mirror. He'd probably get a suspension—expelled even—but Laine couldn't bring himself to care. Not when the sharp shards kept them from rushing after him.

Andy reached for him, but Laine shoved the older teen away and ran for the entrance.

"Pro tip," he heard Andy say from behind him,

"don't tell Laine Riven bad news 'less you've someone to hold him down."

He caught up to Laine sooner than he would have liked, grabbing hold of him and jerking him to a stop.

"Your mum, I presume?"

"She's—I gotta get to the hospital," Laine choked out.

"You'll never make it on foot." Andy pushed Laine outside to the school's vercycle charging stations and towards a bright orange vercycle he remembered Andy saying had been a Christmas present from Doctor Frenally so he didn't have to keep borrowing the family vercycle when running errands. Flashy white and green stripes ran down each side, and it gleamed in the sunlight, unfairly beautiful in contrast to the horrible news consuming Laine's thoughts.

Andy fired up the engine and patted the vercycle's second seat. "I told you, whatever you need."

Laine hopped on, and they zipped through the air, rising higher and higher, rooftops flying dark and fast below them. When they reached the landing pad atop Ethaba General, Laine rolled off the vercycle and disappeared through the rooftop doors before Andy had a chance to cut the power.

He didn't bother running down the hospital stairwells, instead jumping entire flights of stairs at a time. There wasn't room to go into cushioning rolls at the bottom, and his feet ached by the time he burst onto Mom's floor, heels bruised and tender. He couldn't stop touching his jacket as he ran, assuring himself that the extra doses of the cure were in there.

Seven, eight, nine.

Nine?

Laine stopped dead in the middle of the hall. He was supposed to have ten. With a sick feeling, he remembered his frantic search for his jacket earlier that morning. The dread which had seized hold of him back at school snaked through him again, freezing every drop of blood in his body. The missing vial had something to do with Mom's sudden relapse, he knew it.

The gut-churning thought spurred Laine into action, and he careened down the wide halls, heedless of his near collisions with nurses and patients and of the upset medical supply carts he left in his wake. He about ripped the door to Mom's room off its hinges—earning a cold look from the doctor hovering by the entrance—and ground his teeth at finding Peter hunched over Mom's bedside. Hadn't he said he didn't work on this floor? And yet he was always, always underfoot.

"Laine!" the nurse said, as if not expecting to see him. "I wasn't sure you were going to make it—I passed the message on to Dad, but Ethaba High is so far across town I did worry."

Mom lay deathly still, skin paper dry. Laine wanted to reach out and touch her, but she looked like she'd flake away if he did.

"You could have called me," he gritted out, shooting Peter a disdainful look.

"I did—tried you every way I could think of; figured your clip must have been in a reset cycle."

Only, Laine had disabled the reset cycle weeks ago, not wanting to miss anything important. Like Mom relapsing in the event something went wrong.

Which it had.

Curse everything.

Mom was dying.

A red mist descended upon the room, the walls seeming to waver from the force of the anger coursing through Laine.

"Everybody out!" he screamed. He had a handful of minutes left. He had to act, get the hidden syringe. They'd brought her back from the brink before, he could do it again.

"Give the kid a couple minutes," he heard Peter say as the man ushered the other nurses through the door, closing it almost all the way as he stepped outside. "It's not quite the end yet."

Laine tried to ignore the sluggish beeping of the monitors as he ripped up the floor tiles. An empty cavity greeted him. The syringe was gone.

No. It can't be!

Laine continued to destroy the floor, hoping the syringe had merely wedged itself in a hard-to-reach place. But at the end of his frantic searching, only dust, cracked plaster, and damaged linoleum surrounded the hole in the ground. Laine glanced at the door. There was no way he could get past the doctors and nurses in the hall, steal more medical supplies, and get back in time.

His eyes fell upon the IV lines attached to Mom. If he could introduce a bit of kitterstone serum into one of them, she might yet be saved.

Laine wasn't ready to face life without her. Dad was gone. Gordon had made some half-hearted attempt at reconciliation, but he trusted that as much as he did the guy who'd sold him out on his last joyride back on Earth.

Mom might have offered less smiles and more disappointed looks the older he got, but she believed in him, despite everything he'd done. And with Dad out of the picture, they'd been getting close again, bonding over the fresh betrayal. She was just starting to understand him. He couldn't lose that. Wouldn't lose her.

Laine's hand was on the IV, about to disconnect the tubing so he could rig it up with the life-saving serum, when a soft sound from the bed stopped him.

"No."

Laine barely caught the whisper over the beeping. He spun around, startled to see Mom's eyes open the tiniest bit.

"You can't . . . save me."

"What are you talking about?" Laine's vision blurred, and he patted his chest. "I've got the cure right here!"

"Oh, sweetheart," Mom whispered. Her face was very still, lips barely moving, but Laine heard the smile in her words. It drained away with the next sentence. "He c-came. Came back. Used your . . . hidden, hidden needle. Tr-triggered this."

Mom's eyes suddenly opened very wide, pupils blown huge and gone a milky white. Forgetting about her fragile state, Laine grabbed her hand, frightened. All traces of the sweet perfume she used to wear had vanished, a stale, sickly smell hanging over the room.

"Who came, Mom, who? Who did this?"

She didn't answer, seized in a rictus of agony. Tears that Laine couldn't stop spilled over, wetting where his hands clasped hers. Dimly he heard the creak of the door, light flooding the room as Peter and the doctors returned.

"Mom, answer me, please."

The tears ran thickly, his throat tight like he would never again breathe, and his heart felt as though someone had ripped it from him and was striking it over and over. The weight of the useless vials of serum sat heavy on his chest, Thorunn's greater gravity overcoming him at long last. Laine pressed Mom's slack hand to his face, trying to transfer warmth to her.

"Mommy, don't leave me." He tried to close her fingers around his. "Mommy, Mommy, please. Please!"

Then there were strong arms pulling him away, turning him so he could no longer see his mother. He screamed and thrashed, beating his tear-stained fists against whoever held him, but their grip was steadfast, and a moment later he heard Peter's voice in his ear.

"You don't want to see this. The end of Bowman's is never pretty."

Laine redoubled his efforts, fighting until a sound

reached his ears that promised to stalk through every dark dream; a massive sucking squelch that drowned out everything else. The horrific sound of a body collapsing in on itself. Moments later, one of the monitors ceased its intermittent beeping, and a long, single tone filled the room.

Laine fell limp in Peter's arms.

"Time of death, 4:23 p.m.," the attending doctor announced. Laine heard the rustle of something large.

Peter released him, and Laine wrenched around to see that a white sheet had been drawn across the bed, Mom an unmoving outline beneath. Streaks of dark red began to run out under the cloth, mixing with the long black locks that were all Laine could see of her. A foul smell filled the room, a stench so awful Laine had no words for it, and he only then noticed the bottles of bleach sitting next to buckets of soapy water, sponges listing about inside.

He waited for his feelings to catch up to the situation, expecting wails to let loose from his mouth. None came. Laine's head ached from grief, pounding as if his skull would split apart, but no more tears fell, his dried-out eyes stinging from the salt they'd already shed.

The room was a-flurry with movement, the doctors and nurses doing whatever it was they did after they let someone die on their watch. But all Laine felt was nothing.

Numb.

The thing on the bed wasn't his mother.

There was nothing left for him anymore.

Unnoticed amidst the commotion, he turned on his heel and walked out.

The time after that was curiously void. When Laine came back to himself, frix-damaged grass tickling his arms in the open field he'd stumbled into, all he remembered were flashes. Andy's worried face as Laine left him behind. The cloying looks of pity and sympathy from each person he passed. The ping of his clip until he turned it off—what good did it do him for messages to come through now?

Gordon found him in the field, long after still-foreign constellations had risen in the sky, and pulled him to his feet. Laine went with him, unresisting, not really seeing the road in front of them as his uncle steered him back to the house. He said nothing when Gordon draped a blanket around him in the kitchen, muttering about shock, and, "I should have known this would happen; no matter, you can work with this."

Laine stared blankly ahead as the man went about heating water. A slow blink later, a steaming mug of hot chocolate sat in Laine's hands, hot enough to scald, but Laine welcomed the burning. It was the only thing he could feel. If the frix still fell, he'd have discarded the jacket he'd received from Kenton and let the elements eat away at his skin.

She was gone. The one person he loved. She was never coming home again. He'd never hear her laughter again. Never dance with her again.

Laine's fingers crept up to his clip, but he couldn't bring himself to access a picture of her. His heart would crack, and he'd shatter, right there on the floor. He pressed the blistering mug to his tight throat and wondered where the tears were.

"Sorry about Alanna, kid."

Laine would have jolted out of his seat—he'd thought Gordon had left the room—but the heavy emptiness inside him kept his limbs rigid under the blanket, and only his eyes flicked over to acknowledge Gordon.

"I would've come to find you earlier, but you know how busy work keeps me. Not that they're paying me, but hey, essential services gotta keep running, right?"

Laine managed the tiniest of shrugs. Whatever lies Gordon spouted, they only further drove home the fact that his uncle didn't care. Not about Dad, not about Mom, and certainly not about him. He'd probably only spoken because the silence was crushing, otherwise.

Gordon slumped into the chair across from Laine, making it impossible to ignore his presence.

"This has got to come at the worst time, kid, but I've been looking at my finances recently, and the current situation?" He shook his head, looking deeply sorry, though there was a queer set to his shoulders that made it seem like he held something back. Laine had the oddest feeling it was laughter. "Well, Thorunn ain't any place for a kid like you t'be half-orphaned, and I ain't parent material—heck, my garden was dead 'til Alanna revived it."

He'd slipped back into that cajoling tone Laine despised.

"I've arranged it with your mom's side of the family, and they've agreed to take you in. Interstellar travel's possible again now that frix season's over, and there's a seat with your name on it on the next shuttle out."

The mug slipped from Laine's hands, and only Gordon's quick reflexes—or maybe he'd anticipated Laine's reaction to the news—saved it from becoming a mess of pottery shards and hot liquid on the wooden floor.

"Shuttle leaves tomorrow, so pack anything you don't want left behind."

"I thought—" Laine tried to gather the scattered fragments of memories floating through the pea soup fog of his mind. "I thought we were putting the past behind us? Solving our problems like men, being better than lokians?"

Gordon's expression turned indecipherable at that, the edges of his mouth pulling tight. Laine rushed to get the next words out before his throat constricted around them.

"What was all that if you were just gonna offload me on distant relatives the minute things got even slightly hard for you?"

"I meant what I said at the bar, Laine. I did want us to move forward as uncle and nephew, but see"—Gordon clapped one heavy hand on Laine's shoulder, opening his eyes wide in a show of earnestness—

"that was before I got the hospital bill. Between that and the legal issues tied up in Jack's arrest, plus the way work has been going around here, I can't keep you fed and clothed any longer."

"I can get a job," Laine said, voice rising as the anger he'd been holding onto since the hospital started spilling out along with tears he'd thought expunged. "School just started. You can't ship me off to people I barely know. Mom isn't even buried yet!"

Laine's hand swept across the table, the mug ending up on the floor after all. He swore at Gordon, wishing the man would react as he spat out the nastiest words he could dredge up. The most he got was an eyebrow raise as Gordon deliberately folded his arms.

"I'm staying right here, and nothing you can say or do will force me from this house."

"I've already made the arrangements," Gordon said, towering over Laine as he stood. He rummaged around in the fridge for a beer, a clear dismissal as he spoke his next words. He'd dropped all pretence of niceties, the soft Virginian drawl stripped almost entirely from his haughty, condescending tone.

"You will be on that shuttle tomorrow." Gordon tapped his ear meaningfully. "I'll know if you're not, and I've no qualms about calling Ethaba's finest to assist me in rounding up my wayward nephew. Now, go. Get packing."

He headed upstairs, flicking the light as he went and leaving Laine alone in the darkness with the fractured, rust-glazed mug.

Laine buried his head in his hands, clutching hard at his hair. There wasn't anywhere in Ethaba he could go that the police wouldn't eventually find him. He still had the devices he'd used to help Kenton and Bo escape the city, but without a quirn, he had no way to power them. The tunnels had been sealed again—he could probably crack the locks, but he'd have to surface eventually for food and water, and anyway, that was the first place they'd think to look.

If he wasn't at the spaceport tomorrow morning of his own accord, he'd be marched there in cuffs. Forced to come to Thorunn and forced to leave it. Shipped Earthside before Mom's broken body had even cooled.

He'd never forgive Gordon for this.

He'd just been starting to settle in and make friends who didn't demand he participate in petty thievery—and more—to prove himself to them. And Dad . . . if he left Thorunn now, he'd lose all hope of ever seeing him again. Not that Laine was sure he wanted to, but the choice shouldn't be ripped away from him. The horrible planet was stealing both his parents from him, and he had nothing left to push back with.

Laine pulled the blanket tighter over his shoulders, contemplating whether he could outfox Gordon after he got to the spaceport. Not all the shuttles went to Earth—he seemed to recall Dustin saying something about his dad working on a mining colony on one of Thorunn's moons. If Laine could somehow get to a Frey-bound craft he'd at least be within view of the ground where Mom would be buried. He could find work, save enough, and sneak back someday. He couldn't let himself be sent half a universe away.

Decision made, Laine stood, letting the blanket pool into the chair, one long end trailing onto the floor and soaking up the lukewarm hot chocolate. Laine let it. Gordon could deal with the mess. His uncle's irritation was worth the unpleasant crunching that sent a shiver through Laine as his booted feet ground the biggest shards against the wet wood.

Once in his room, Laine began to fill his duffle. He left anything non-essential on his bed and stuffed the basics in his bag—clothes, electronics, his passport, a blanket, and some hygienic items. The stack of books he still hadn't returned to Dustin caught his eye, and he popped some of them in as well. He might be able to trade them for a few extra credits upon reaching Frey.

Upstairs, Laine grabbed some canned and dried fruit from the pantry. The first aid kit sitting at the back of the third shelf caught his attention, reminding him of the accident he'd had, the incredibly strong painkillers he'd overdosed on.

She'd known then that she was sick, hadn't she? All that time, and she'd kept her suffering to herself, hoping not to worry them. It was possible that since Dad had been arrested before Mom's collapse that he still didn't know.

Laine almost broke the wooden shelf from how hard he gripped it upon the realisation that he and

Dad had something in common. They'd both lost the woman they held closest to their hearts. Laine sank to his knees, only the hand clutching the shelf keeping him from fully collapsing.

Mom couldn't be dead. She couldn't be. Laine's eyes blurred afresh, and a muted wail escaped him. He crammed his fist into his mouth to keep any more sounds from escaping, holding each breath until they burst from him in long, noiseless sobs. Even though he'd been there, held her hand 'til Peter had torn him away, it didn't feel real. Laine kept replaying the nightmarish scene in his mind, hunched double and crying until he was gasping for air.

How could Mom be dead? His lovely, kind, wonderful mother? The universe had to be playing a cruel joke on him. He was just dreaming, and if he opened his eyes, she'd still be there. Sick, pale, paralysed, but there. Alive.

Hours and hours had passed since the doctors had thrown a sheet over her ruined body and made their cold pronouncement, but time seemed to have hardly shifted at all. It felt as if, maybe, if Laine went back to the hospital, she'd be back in her room, smiling softly at him. An irrational, overwhelming urge to go and check, just to be sure, seized Laine, and he wondered whether Thorunn had finally driven him crazy.

Despite how badly it would hurt to see the truth written out, Laine clenched his teeth and accessed his family's information on his clip.

Laine Alexander Riven, the holo-projection read, *Sixteen years, student. Doctor Gordon Gray Riven, forty-*

*three years, developmental technician. Doctor Jack Nath-
aniel Riven, further details suspended from public record
pending trial. Alanna Jane Riven, homemaker, 2194-2231.*
Not content to simply display the beginning and end
years for Mom's too-short life, below the unfeeling
numbers blinked a word in red. *Deceased.*

Agony rippled through Laine. He beat at his chest;
but the tearing void remained.

He stared at the words, willing them to change,
pleading that they'd read something else when he
blinked back the tears that leaked out his entire soul.
But they stayed stubbornly the same. No matter how
much Laine wished it, Mom wasn't coming back.

Laine tried to get himself under control, staggering to his feet. He didn't know how long he'd been
sobbing in the cramped space, but he had to finish
packing. He needed to be well rested if he wanted
any chance at succeeding with his plan to stow away
to Frey.

Deceased.

Laine's head throbbed something awful, and he
ducked it under the tap in the kitchen sink, then wet
a cloth and pressed it to his sore eyes. It didn't stop
the constant flow of tears, but the pressure from the
swelling seemed to ease.

Deceased.

Mom had taught him that trick. Back when Dad
had practically abandoned them and she'd cried all
the time. She'd scared Laine—only a little kid then—
and after he asked if she too was going away, she'd
started keeping cool wet rags around to alleviate her

red-rimmed eyes, reassuring him that she'd always be there for him.

Deceased.

Some cruel whim of fate had reached into Laine's very core, torn out his heart, set it on fire, and shoved it back inside, still burning. He was about to collapse in on himself like, like—

Laine retched into the sink. He hadn't eaten since the pizza party at school, and chunks of pepperoni and pineapple forced themselves back up his throat, scraping it raw as his insides turned themselves out. He felt worse after and sank back to the ground, pressing his cheek to the cool wooden slats. The water continued to run.

Laine lost time again, peeling himself off the floor when a little strength trickled back into his aching limbs. He shook off the prickles of his waking nerves and peered through the window. Frey and Freja sat doubled in the sky, so close together they looked like intertwined wedding rings.

Mom had loved Thorunn's night sky. It was so completely different from Earth's, but she'd insisted she could make out some of the same constellations, delighting in telling Laine all the legends behind them, both Greek and Native American. She'd been so excited when Laine had told her the kitterstone serum would have her home and able to stargaze from her own garden again in only a short time.

But she wouldn't. Every word out of Laine's mouth had been a lie. He started to sway and pressed his hands against his eyes to stem the fresh onslaught of tears. He had to get out of the kitchen or he'd spend all night crying. With trembling limbs, he forced himself into the hall, trying desperately to think of something, *anything* else for long enough to make it outside where the night air could clear his head a little.

Pens. Pens were safe to think about. Permanent, washable, frustrating when out of ink. Laine had just closed the door behind him when a memory struck him, knees buckling as the rest of his body locked up. He'd gotten caught stealing office supplies the year after they'd moved to L.A. Dad had been at his new job, so it'd fallen to Mom to collect him from the precinct.

"You shouldn't have been stealing at all," she'd said on the way home, voice quiet and disappointed, "but pens, Laine? You know if you need something you have only to ask."

Thirteen years old, and embarrassed at being discovered and detained so easily—not to mention he'd failed the dare from his new friends—Laine had sullenly pressed his face into the window and refused to speak for the remainder of the drive.

What he wouldn't give to hear that gentle reproof one more time. He'd never hear her voice again. Never hear—

Never . . . never.

Laine almost crumpled to the ground once more, but he couldn't be crying outside where anyone could see him. He surged around to the back of the house, in retrospect, a terrible idea, since he was confronted with the sight of Mom's garden, fallen into a state of disrepair while she'd been in the hospital. Some of the flowers still bloomed under their protective covering, the only thing Laine had remembered to do for the garden during frix season, but most of the plants had died.

A raw cry like that of a wounded animal wrenched itself from Laine, and he turned away, pushing his forehead against Gordon's rough stucco walls. He peeked at the garden again, but that brought a fresh wave of tears, and thereafter, couldn't bring himself to look anymore. He pounded his fists against the wall instead, slowly sinking, sinking, sinking, until he crouched against the frix-charred plaster, mucus mixing with the steady, teary stream that collected at his chin and watered the ground beneath.

The touch of cold metal against the base of Laine's skull arrested his next muffled sob, foggy senses suddenly on alert.

"Not a sound," an unfamiliar voice hissed in his ear, though Laine knew intimately the cadence of that growl. "Or I'll light you up 'til your brain liquefies."

10

Laine swore under his breath and raised his hands, craning his neck around to get a good look at his assailant. Yeah. It was what he thought. The glowing eyes, bared fangs, and angrily lashing tail confirmed it. The good-for-nothing, promise-breaking lokian—that somehow spoke perfect English, add that to its list of lies—had returned.

"Come to gloat?" Laine snarled, face growing hot at the creature catching him with tears still trailing down his cheeks. "It's not enough you crippled our town and poisoned my mom, you have to come here and rub my face in it?"

The pressure eased a bit, enough to let Laine fully face the dark-furred lokian. It gripped the end of its quirn too tight for Laine to have any chance of wresting the weapon away—especially given his focus-breaking headache.

"Poisoned?"

The lokian should not sound that indignant, not when Laine was still suffering the terrible effects of its malicious handiwork.

"Your mother was already dying when you shot us down. Still would be if Ken hadn't taken pity on her."

Laine surged forward, the end of the lokian's quirn digging hard into the dip of his throat.

"She was getting better! But you just couldn't leave well enough alone, could you? You had to finish the job."

"What're you on about, human?" Its razor-sharp canines gleamed in the moonlight as it narrowed its eyes. "Ken promised to cure your mom, and as much as I hate your kind, I'd never go behind his back like that."

"Then how do you explain her death?" Laine choked against the pressure on his windpipe. The crushing force eased up when the lokian faltered at his words, and Laine took advantage of his slip, hand darting to his clip before the lokian could activate the sparking frix stored inside the slim rod.

"You have five seconds before I call the police." Laine allowed himself a sneer, the closest he'd come to a smile since the locker room party that now seemed so long ago.

The lokian slid its thumb over a button and the weapon hummed to life.

"To finish what you started?" it said, turning Laine's earlier words back on him. "It wasn't enough we were leaving Ethaba in peace, you had to send them after us?" It jabbed the quirn harder into Laine, his skin stinging where it split under the chafing. "Go ahead, call them. Be responsible for their deaths. Ken's not here to stop me."

"I never sent anybody after you," Laine said, backing into the wall as far away from the active quirn as he could. He let his hand drop from his ear. He might not like the officers, but their families didn't deserve to go through losing their loved ones.

"You're the only one besides your mother who knew who Ken really was, the only one who knew I was here. For what you did, I came back to make you suffer, and suffer slow. You do know some of my kind like to toy with their prey before putting it out of its misery?"

Laine glared at the lokian, eyes no longer wet, his tears long dried.

"I never"—he ground out each word deliberately, hands coming up to grasp the end of the quirn despite the low-level burn that seared his palms—"sent anybody after you. Mom means . . ."

Laine stuttered mid sentence but collected himself. "She meant everything to me, and I wouldn't break my word where it concerned her."

"And I didn't kill her, couldn't, when I was running for my life. You seem like you're suffering enough already, so I'd almost be convinced to leave you be if I believed you wouldn't immediately call your soldiers."

"And maybe I'd be more inclined to take your word for it that you didn't trigger Mom's relapse if you weren't a despicable lokian, but I swear, I had *nothing* to do with whatever mess you got yourselves into. You can check the call log on my clip if you . . . don't . . ."

Laine trailed off, the image of Gordon tapping his clip earlier that evening flashing into his mind. He'd implied he'd know if Laine wasn't at the spaceport later, and though Laine had disabled the GPS function, any hacker competent enough could turn it back on—hijack the device even, to watch and record his every move.

If Gordon had been doing that, then he knew everything. And likely he was the one behind what had happened with Mom.

———————— ● ————————

Bo watched the human come to some sort of realisation, his eyes widening and mouth gaping, before he slowly and clearly telegraphed his intent to remove his clip and hand it over.

"Go on," Laine said, one hand still keeping Bo's quirn off his throat.

Not a fun way to get a scar, Bo could attest to that, but every little bit of hurt the human wanted to inflict on himself was fine by Bo, so he turned up the power a fraction and said nothing.

"If you can speak flawless English, I figure you can work that."

Bo chuckled. The human had realised he wasn't an ignorant savage after all. Palming the small device, Bo quickly navigated to the information he was looking for, keeping a wary eye on Laine in his peripheral vision.

"Fine, I believe you," he said. The call logs showed a back and forth between Laine and the hospital, and when he dug deeper—looking for messages the human might have deleted, trying to cover his tracks—

Bo found only a series of previously undelivered communiques from Ethaba General. He kept hold of the clip as he lowered his quirn.

"Do me the same courtesy. Just look at me." Bits of his fur had been burnt away, the cut across his cheek just beginning to scab over, crusted blood still clinging to its edges. "Look at my clothes."

Scorch marks marred his frix-proof suit, solfire not quite strong enough to eat all the way through the resistant material at a distance. He'd ripped pieces off here and there to fashion bandages for the wounds he'd sustained when his stolen vercycle had exploded, and day-old dust covered what remained. The human's eyes darted up and down, taking everything in before he nodded, some of the fight going out of him.

"The facts are these," Bo said, easing his quirn out of Laine's blistered hand, and powering it down as keeping his weapon hot at night was a waste of energy. Laine didn't make a move—a shame really, Bo would have loved an excuse to leave him twitching in urine-soaked jeans in the small garden.

"Ken and I were attacked when no one should have known about us. Your mom died when she should have lived. Neither of us is responsible for the other's misfortune, but someone did this." He thought of the teen's uncle skulking around late at night. The overheard snatches of conversation he'd been puzzling over. "Maybe the same person."

"Only nine vials," Laine muttered. "And my jacket wasn't where I left it."

"Gordon?" It was a terrible thought, that the human's uncle was responsible for the death of a member of his own family, but humans—Ken excluded—were generally terrible, in Bo's experience.

"Very possibly," Laine said, hunching in on himself.

"He in there?"

"Yeah, but we'd have to go through his lab to get to his room—no way he wouldn't hear us coming. He keeps his sol on him at all times, and he's friends with a lot of the soldiers 'round here. You'd wind up dead, I'd wind up in cuffs for my entire trip back to Earth, and Gordon walks free."

"Earth?" Bo asked, ears flicking forward in spite of himself.

Laine's brows knit tightly together.

"He's shipping me off tomorrow. Any move I make to act against him, he'll know."

"Sucks to be you." Bo started off towards the back wall, sparing a glance for the double image of Lanae and Lanaekim. The moons had shifted, and he had maybe another hour left before he risked detection. Perhaps a bit more than that, since the human teen had escaped his wrath for the time being.

"Wait, where're you going?" Laine demanded, running to catch up with him. "You've still got my clip."

"To rescue Ken from Skytown." Bo turned off the clip and tossed it at Laine. He didn't think Laine would alert the authorities now that his anger had been directed onto another target. "Don't worry. I'll be back to kill your uncle."

"I'm coming with you."

Bo slowed his pace, twisting to throw the human an incredulous look.

"My uncle's stronger than me and better with a sol. No way I take him in a fight." The words came slowly, haltingly, forced out through clenched teeth. It probably physically hurt the human to admit when someone was better than him.

"Even if I did somehow get a weapon and surprise him, he's a renowned member of the community—without proof he did it, I might as well turn the sol on myself."

"Still not seeing why you want to tag along," Bo said, crossing his arms, ears flattening.

"The proof—I just said! He's shipping me off to-morrow; I can't prove he k-killed her before then. I need, I just need a little more time. Time I won't get if I stay here." Laine drew himself up to his full height, squaring his shoulders. He still stank of grief, but beneath that Bo caught a note of determination. "I'm coming with you."

"I don't need you dragging me down." Bo turned and started to scramble over the wall. He had to admit, some help would be nice, but he didn't trust Laine the least bit.

"Take me with you or so help me, I'll call the guards."

Bo spun back around. Sure enough, Laine had re-activated his clip and brandished it in one fist, thumb at the ready. Bo's quirn was in his hand and crackling again the next instant. He'd made a mistake in not crushing the stupid thing; he didn't doubt Laine would make good on his threat. His red-rimmed eyes were a little too wide, the sorrow pulling down his mouth a little too raw for him to be anything less than desperate.

Bo quickly ran through different possible ways the standoff could end. If his choices were arrest by the Ethaba police—and then most likely torture before death—versus an extra hand helping him get to Ken, he supposed it wouldn't hurt to let Laine try to keep up for a while. Once beyond Ethaba, he could always cut Laine loose if he proved too troublesome.

"Fine," Bo said and let his weapon power down. "I'll show you the way in I discovered. Put that thing away."

Laine did so and thrust out his hand. Bo shook it, still amused by the quaint human custom. No one in their right mind negotiated peace by clasping weapons together, but he supposed the humans did lack the claws to turn their hands lethal.

"Let me grab my pack."

"Be quick about it."

Laine nodded and disappeared into the house, leaving Bo outside with his thoughts. He hoped the boy wouldn't take too long. Ken was still out there, captured, undergoing who knew what.

And it was Bo's fault. If he hadn't stupidly handicapped both of them back before their mission had even started, he'd have been able to shift. Ken wouldn't have had to face their pursuers while fighting off a heart attack. Together they could have, would have, destroyed every last one of their enemies. Instead he was stuck on a one-klia'an rescue mission, with the most annoying creature in existence insisting he had to come along.

"I'm ready," Laine announced, his bag and sports' stick strapped to his back. The latter probably made him feel special, even if the stick didn't store frix like Bo's quirn. "But we can't leave town just yet."

"And why ever not?"

"I gotta grab something of my mom's from the hospital before they"—Laine choked and ducked his head—"before they burn or repurpose her stuff since I know Gordon won't claim it."

Bo rolled his eyes but gestured to the human to lead the way.

Ethaba's streets were filled with shadows, not even a hint of a glow lingering from the departed frix. The few undamaged streetlamps did their best to aid the light thrown from the moons, but ample cover remained, and Bo and Laine slid their way undetected to the entrance of Ethaba General. The ESReC next door still had reconstruction pallets piled around it, and Bo couldn't help a little burst of satisfaction at that. Even if he had screwed up rather badly where Ken's wellbeing was concerned, they'd at least managed to complete the mission.

"Up for a little B and E?" Laine asked.

"Time is short. Don't waste it with dumb questions."

"Pushy," Laine replied but let Bo's words slide and

tripped the fire alarm attached to the side of the building. Within minutes, patients and staff were streaming out of the doors, the two teens slipping inside during the commotion.

"Ethaba's too small to have a separate place for the crazies, so they house 'em all in a part of the hospital overlapping the ESReC," Laine said as they hurried to the hospital storage rooms. "Course, that means someone's always escaping, and there was at least one alarm pulled a week when I was visiting. While they're searching for whoever they think it was this time, we get a good ten minutes unfettered access to the rooms nobody cares about."

Bo struggled not to grind his teeth as Laine prattled on. He sure did like to hear himself talk. Rushing footsteps sounded ahead, and Bo cut Laine's babbling short as he yanked the human into an empty examination room. The frantic pounding faded quickly, and Bo and Laine continued on, unhurried amidst the shrill ringing.

The room labelled *Patient's Belongings* was locked when they arrived, and Bo's ears pressed themselves flat against his head again.

"Don't get your whiskers twisted," Laine said, fiddling with the panel that held a palm scanner. "I wouldn't have brought us down here if I couldn't crack this pathetic attempt at security."

Despite his words, the human spent what felt like an inordinate amount of time messing with the circuitry to grant them access. It had always looked so easy on television. The longer the doors stayed stubbornly closed, the more Bo felt an uneasy itch creeping under his fur. The alarm would only screech a few minutes more, and they still had to exit the place.

"Stop with the growling," Laine said. The doors slid open and the vault lights flickered on. "We're in. Grab whatever you want."

Bo began to wander about but stayed close to the entrance while Laine started going through boxes, scattering them in his haste. He made a noise of exultation when he found what he was looking for, a beautiful, multicoloured beaded necklace that he slipped around his neck and tucked beneath his jacket before shoving his mess haphazardly back into the various boxes and drawers he'd been rifling through.

Bo eyed the clutter with distaste. Even if the personal effects in the room hadn't belonged to sick or dying people, he still couldn't have lowered himself to take human things. The locks clicked shut after they exited, and Laine led the way to a disposal chute on the next floor that discharged outside the hospital. The alarm had ceased its wailing and the flurry of activity had slowed, staff trickling back inside as he and Laine made their escape.

"Ouch! These chutes were not designed with people in mind," Laine grumbled as he wedged himself down the angular shaft.

"Speak for yourself," Bo said, twisting his lithe bulk easily down the smooth metal after Laine.

"You're a stupid cat, course y'c'n fit," Laine rejoined, petulant as ever.

Bo welcomed the cool nighttime air after the

scraping friction that had claimed some of his fur, but the relief it brought was quickly trod upon when a shocked face—illuminated by the glow of a clip projection—confronted him and Laine as they scrambled out of the dumpster they'd landed in.

"Laine? What are you—?"

Bo knew he shouldn't have gone along with the human's ill-advised plan—this wasn't much better than having the soldiers called down on him. Two teenagers, one decidedly not human, climbing out of a garbage chute in the middle of the night? The nurse would be insane if he didn't immediately turn them in. Bo's hand went to his quirn as Laine darted in front of him.

"I can't explain right now. Peter, please, you've helped me out a bunch before. Can't you look the other way one more time?"

The man's eyes softened, but he shook his head, grinding the cigarette he'd dropped under his heel. Apparently medical professionals disregarding health advice wasn't just something invented for television.

"Is this creature the reason Tracey started babbling last week about two kids stealing his scrubs? Laine, if you've been ensnared by some sort of magic making you do crazy things, I have to report this, for your own safety."

Peter's hand went to his clip, and Bo pounced, razor-sharp claws closing around the man's neck.

"Bo!"

So the human did know his name. A small victory,

but one Bo would take knowing that pressing his claws any deeper into the man's neck would probably cause Laine to call the guards. The human was obviously desperate to get away from his uncle but grief-maddened enough that he'd sabotage himself out of spite if Bo pushed too far.

"Sweet dreams," Bo hissed, stabbing his quirn into the man's side, earning another strangled exclamation from Laine.

"Oh, quit your whining." Bo dragged the unconscious man behind the dumpster. No doubt he'd be found when another nurse came out for their break, but the confusion caused by the alarm might delay even that inevitable discovery long enough for them to quit the city.

"My quirn was set to disable, not kill. You got your precious necklace; we gonna get outta here or what?"

"One last stop," Laine promised, holding out his hands to ward off Bo's warning growl. "Unless you want my uncle tracking our every move?"

Bo gave Laine a mocking flourish, but bared his teeth behind the human's back after they started off again. He looked forward to ditching him in the Cerado.

●

A strange tapping at Andy's window pulled him from the deep sleep he'd been enjoying. He rolled over and glanced at the analogue clock face projected onto his wall. Too early o'clock to deal with whatever had woken him. Andy snuggled back under his blankets and was just nodding off when the tapping sounded again, more insistent this time.

"For the love of—" he muttered, threw off his blankets, and snapped his fingers for the light. He very nearly tumbled off his bed in shock at seeing Laine Riven perched outside on his second-storey windowsill, dressed all in black. He wasn't alone.

The unmistakable gold eyes of a lokian peered out from under a dark hood, its fangs glistening in the low light of Andy's room.

"Open up!" Laine mouthed, arms windmilling as he gestured for Andy to let him in. Half convinced he was dreaming and too stunned to do much else, Andy released the latches, and his window clicked open, allowing Laine and his inhuman companion to tumble into his room.

"The heck are ya doin' here?" Andy demanded, scrambling back onto his bed, not quite able to believe what he was seeing. "An' with one of them?"

His back hit the wall, nowhere to go, when the lokian snarled at him. Curse his sleep-addled mind. Yoon Ah would box his ears when she heard about his stupidity. Andy's eyes slid over to the lacrosse gear stashed on the other side of his room. He wasn't confident he could lunge for it without getting his head bitten off, but if he could keep Laine talking, he could edge his way within arm's reach. He might even be able to snap his friend out of whatever trance the lokian had him under.

"Remember how you said you'd be there for me,

whatever I needed?"

How could Andy forget? He'd been up half the night worrying about Laine after he'd vanished from the hospital following the wrenching loss of the gentle soul that had been Alanna Riven.

"Well, my uncle's hellbent on shipping me off to Earth in about"—Laine glanced at the glowing clock hands to Andy's left—"five hours, and my only shot at getting a head start away from this place lies in your hands."

"You're leaving?" Andy eased off the bed and sidled closer to his sports gear.

"Not by choice. Gordon's gotten sick of me. He's behind what happened with Mom—probably set up Dad too, now that I think about it—and if I don't get away from Ethaba before morning, I'll never be able to get justice. No, not justice—" Laine shook his head, eyes seeming to take on an otherworldly glow, and Andy threw a sidelong look at the lokian standing with arms crossed near the window. "Vengeance."

Laine detached his clip and held it in a loose fist, offering it to Andy.

"He made a comment that niggled at me 'til I realised he's been tracking my every move. It's how he knew about—well, that doesn't matter now. Only getting safe out the city."

Andy rubbed at sleep-bleary eyes, still not quite processing the shocking—bordering on outlandish—information. "An' you want me to—?"

"Take this, and leave it at the spaceport. It'll have logged my visit here of course, but with any luck

Gordon'll think you were just a stop on my farewell tour. I mean, you are." Laine stepped forward and folded his clip into Andy's hands. "You gotta say goodbye to Yoon Ah and the team for me, but I refuse to go back to Earth. I'll see you again after I expose the truth."

"If your uncle wants you off-planet as badly as you say, like as not he'll hire bounty hunters once he realises you're gone. There's nowhere y'can go they won't find you."

Andy inched closer to the lacrosse stick sitting innocuously by the door. The lokian had definitely enthralled Laine somehow. A good whack over the head might shock him back to his senses—if it didn't completely addle him. He'd have to measure his strength carefully.

"Meantime, I'm on the hook for aiding an' abetting a criminal. Laine, I could be sent to prison fer this. Adult prison!"

Laine jerked a thumb towards the lokian. "And his friend—Ken, I don't know if you met him while he was here—he got taken by the soldiers, and he's definitely in adult jail. Possibly worse. We're off to rescue him as well."

Andy gritted his teeth, wishing Laine hadn't appealed to his protective side. He couldn't stand the thought of someone being mistreated; Laine had discovered that the hard way.

"I can't," he said, voice wavering. "I want t'believe you, but the lokian—"

"Isn't influencing me at all." Laine let out a bitter

laugh. "If anything, it's the other way around. Bo here is *not* happy about me inserting myself into his rescue mission. Check the logs on my clip after I leave. You're better at computers than me; if you find it's been tampered with, promise me you'll take it to the spaceport?"

"You're leaving no matter what, huh?" Andy sighed and briefly closed his eyes. But Laine and the lokian still stood there, shadowed figures in the dim lighting of Andy's room. Andy had half hoped he was dreaming the whole thing, but the nightmare gone wrong was very real.

"Please," Laine said, "for my mom."

The desperate crack in his voice finally broke through Andy's defences, and he abandoned his plans to retrieve his crosse, setting the clip on his desk next to his computer instead.

"I'll do it, but I'll have to wait fer daybreak since I don't have nighttime clearance at the gates."

A small, sad smile tugged at the corners of Laine's mouth. "I owe you. Double, since I don't know if I'll be back before second frix to play with the team."

"Hey, I promised. Whatever you needed." Laine nodded roughly, and a thought occurred to Andy. He put out a hand to stop Laine before the younger teen could climb through the window. "The gates are locked, an' no way can you use a vercycle this time of night without attracting attention. How are y'getting out?"

"Same way I got in." The lokian's voice was low and gritty, his unexpected speech startling Andy into banging his hand against the wall. He goggled at the creature. Its English was flawless, accent strangely Californian.

"There's a lot Laine hasn't told you, I bet," it said, popping its claws out and inspecting them in an utterly blasé manner before turning eerily glowing eyes on Andy. "But in the interest of getting outta here before we run out of time"—its tone turned venomous, the glare it shot Laine laced with poison—"I came in through the tunnels on the northeast side of town."

Andy gasped as Laine turned a shocked look on the lokian.

"Those tunnels are toxic!" Laine blurted. "Gordon was always telling Dad to stop digging around out there. Didn't you see the signposts?"

"Tch, as death-like as they smell, they're perfectly safe. Someone's probably using those false warnings to hide something," the lokian said. "Nothing I care to figure out, nor do we have time to." It emphasised the words with a jerk of its head towards the slowly lightening sky beyond Andy's window.

"Let's go." It directed the last bit at Laine and pushed past him to the outside.

Laine looked at Andy and shrugged. "I stay here, I'll never even get to visit Mom's grave. Worth the risk to me." He started to clamber through the window, but backed up suddenly, rushed towards Andy, and hugged him fiercely before Andy could react.

"I'll call when it's safe."

Then Laine was out the window and gone from sight, leaving Andy reeling from all the insanity he'd just experienced. He looked at the clip sitting on his desk and pressed his fingers to his forehead, hoping to alleviate his building headache. Yoon Ah was going to kill him when he didn't show up at school later. At least his record was perfect, and the fool decision he'd made wouldn't screw up the rest of the school year too badly.

Andy blew out a long breath and started getting dressed, unable to get his mind to quiet at the worry consuming him for his friend. Laine was gone to parts unknown with a lokian at his side, and Andy was going to have to smile and pretend he hadn't played a crucial part in his disappearance when the Ethaba police came round to question him. But he had promised, and Frenally men didn't go back on their word.

He just hoped Laine wouldn't get himself in too much trouble beyond Ethaba's walls.

11

The hovertruck was noisy and cramped, but even if there had been room, Kenton doubted he'd have been able to move. His calves spasmed painfully, and each breath came as if he'd run the final Igis course five times over. His tongue had swollen, a thick presence in his mouth, where he'd bitten down by accident before the medic had rolled him onto his side, and his limbs felt heavy and sluggish.

They'd left him in his mud-stained clothes, and Kenton tried not to let hot prickles of embarrassment creep over his cheeks at the wetness he could still feel in his pants, where he'd lost control after passing out.

His fingertips felt odd, cold and constricted due to the little rectangular devices clipped atop them. Their wires led to a device fastened to his wrist just above the manacles cuffing his hands together. A small, attached display seemed to be measuring his pulse and breathing.

Kenton tested his restraints again, but he'd been strapped into the hovertruck, legs also cuffed, forced to lie on his back, the stretcher below him elevated at an angle, his head and neck cushioned. But even if he'd had the strength to rip himself from the bands keeping him shackled, there was nowhere to go.

The transport's interior was windowless, lit by a

thin panel of lights running across the top of each side, and it vibrated almost excessively—quite a contrast from the smooth flight of the hovercar he'd once piloted. But then, that too had rumbled distressingly before its final plunge towards the ground, and the unstable rocking of Kenton's current method of travel had to be due to the damage he and Bo had wrought upon the sizeable machine. That made him smile, even if the action caused his cracked lips to split and bleed.

"Please, water," he gasped, a dry pit of thirst claiming him.

The men in the vehicle only laughed, some spitting at him, telling him to be grateful he got even that.

"Beg real nice, and maybe I'll have mercy," another said, coming to stand over Kenton, hunching in the confined space, unpleasant breath a little too close.

Kenton begged.

He wasn't above it, not when he gained nothing by trying to be strong. After all, they'd saved him when his heart had betrayed him, crippling agony dragging him into the dirt, so they must have some sort of interest in keeping him alive. He shivered at the thought of where they must be taking him. The one place that Kenton and the rest of the Igis Chosen had avoided, the mountainside city too remote, too heavily guarded for them to attack without amassing serious causalities.

The soldier snickered and took a swig from his flask, letting water gush out of the sides and over his stubbled face, the droplets landing on Kenton's chest. He strained towards them, but shrank back when the soldier caught his motion, expression turning cruel.

"When the people of Ethaba begged, the people of Amahn and Smoketown and New Little Rock, did you show mercy?" The man crouched to meet Kenton's eyes, stowing the flask at his hip. "You don't deserve the spit we're wasting on you."

"Please," Kenton said, struggling to hold on to what little composure he had left, his eyes burning from the glare of the lights. He suspected the man stood where he did to purposefully flash the reflections of his shiny buttons into Kenton's blurry vision. "I never . . . never intended to hurt anyone."

The soldier raised an eyebrow. "You stormed our cities and towns, destroyed millions of credits worth of labs and equipment, and attacked a hospital. And still you have the gall to look me in the face and protest that you didn't mean to cause harm."

The man backhanded Kenton hard, the sudden blow snapping his head up with a sick cracking sound. Vision swimming, Kenton flinched back from the next strike, the unyielding material of the soldier's gloves tearing open the bruised skin under his eyes. The man punched him in the gut, forcing up bile, and Kenton choked and coughed, unable to breathe.

The soldier readied himself to attack again, and Kenton closed his eyes, willing himself to endure the pain. His home was safe—Bo was safe. He'd be back in the Hinnom Forest by now, completing the last rite of Igis and receiving his mark of adulthood. Seri and the others too; and with the hovercars, they'd be able to move more freely and counter further incursions into their home.

Doubtless, many years of warfare lay ahead, but Kenton's gambit had gained them the upper hand, and they could ultimately come out the victors. That was worth the agony, worth the pain of his skull breaking apart.

"Aii! Jennin, that's enough!"

The soldier was shoved aside by a furious dark-haired man before he could beat Kenton any further.

"Seriously, I close my eyes for two seconds after saving this boy from the grave, and here you are undoing all my hard work. Tchaa!"

Kenton's vision swam too much to read more than half of his saviour's name off his uniform—Álvero, he guessed. He tried to hold on to it. Information was his only weapon with his body out of commission, and he hoarded each little scrap.

A cool cup of water pressed against Kenton's lips, and everything else faded as he gulped the stale liquid down. It didn't do much to lesson the hot flush on his face, but it was decidedly better than being beaten and spat upon. He mumbled a word of thanks.

"Just doing my job, like the rest of you idiots should be." Álvero pointed an accusing finger at the other men in the transport. "We're 'sposed to get the boy to Skytown alive. No matter what grudges you hold against him, he's the Consul's to deal with, not ours. Mark my words, Jennin, this incident is going in my report."

The soldier growled something unintelligible and retreated to the far end of the truck, his compatriots joining him in sullen silence. Their saliva had long dried on Kenton's face, but he knew that that unpleasantness and the vicious beating Álvero had interrupted were only glimpses of what was to come. If Tribe Osinan had captured someone attacking their village, they'd have been turned over to the council for interrogation, and Kenton didn't think his fellow humans were much different. He shivered, thinking of the probable torture ahead.

He didn't want to break.

Hours crawled by, the miles eaten up in the hundreds at the speed the hovertruck sustained despite its damaged condition. The soldiers' muttered conversations confirmed that their travel took them towards Skytown and they expected to be there well before the next sunrise. Álvero stayed by Kenton's side, his presence dissuading further physical attacks, though the medic said nothing to rebut the increasingly distasteful insults the soldiers hurled once they'd gotten over his sharp reprimand.

Through it all, Kenton kept quiet except to ask Álvero for sips of water. He forced himself to push past the fog his brain floated in, gleaning all the information he could in the airless space. A long-forgotten lesson from the Innah drifted back to him through the haze.

"*A noisy captor is a treasure trove,*" she'd said, tapping her pipe against her lips. *"Talk too much, and you'll reveal everything to your prisoner. So, aye, children, you must always have a plan when speaking with or around one of the accused."* She'd personally taken the Igis Chosen to the Jail Pit that day, watching them watch the guards divine truths and falsehoods from the most recently arrested thieves.

Kenton had thought it fascinating at the time, never an inkling crossing his mind that someday, he'd be the prisoner, desperately soaking up each precious bit of knowledge that passed his way. He continued to keep quiet as the miles wore on—listening, observing, internalising—each rumble of the hovertruck carrying him farther and farther until his home of near the last decade was naught but a forgotten speck.

Kenton popped his ears as best he could when the vibrations that had set his teeth on edge ground to a halt. The relief of sudden stillness almost outweighed the uncomfortable pressure in his head from their abrupt descent. From what Kenton could gather, the vehicle had docked deep underground in the bedrock of Mount Lalethusl. After years of living free in the Hinnom Forest, perched high above the floor in the welcoming treetops, Kenton's skin crawled with claustrophobia.

The door to the truck slid open, the harsh glare of the lights beyond blinding Kenton. Black spots danced in his vision before his eyes adjusted, and in that time, Medic Álvero detached the stretcher from the hovertruck's interior wall and wheeled him out into a narrow hallway, its whitewashed walls repressing any sense of hope.

"I can't lie to you," Álvero said, tugging at Kenton's bindings to secure them. "Going to the bowels of the Hexagon—I wouldn't wish that on nobody. I don't know what choices led you here, but my heart breaks seeing you like this. You should be in school, getting in trouble for doing dumb senior pranks, not out terrorising an entire planet. You won't find much mercy beyond my hands. I can only hope to make the journey there a little less unpleasant."

Kenton felt something prick his skin, and then a long, needle-thin rod slid inside him. The world started to blur out; he'd been injected with a sedative. Panic jolted his heart painfully, and he fought against the numbing effects, expending whatever strength he'd regained on the long trip to keep himself awake as the stretcher trundled down the halls. Halls that seemed to fold in, their shadowed endings reaching for him, hungry for his terror.

Kenton clung to a consciousness that never quite left him as Álvero continued to wheel him along. He thought the man might be talking to him, words about not resisting the pain penetrating through the muddled mess of Kenton's thoughts. But his voice also faded out, the soft, not-quite-comforting tones replaced by harsh jeering he recognised as Jennin's.

As the sedative started to wear off, Kenton found himself being manhandled into a room so small he couldn't stretch out lengthwise in it. Not that he had the chance, his arms pinned roughly against the wall and locked into the manacles hanging there, his bare feet—when had they taken his shoes? How had he lost so much time that they'd managed to switch out his ruined pants, jacket, and undergarments for the soft, grey fabric that hung loosely on him? His toes barely brushed the cold concrete beneath.

Not content to leave Kenton's muscles to burn from the strain of dangling from the wall, harsh hands slipped a rope around his neck, pulling it tight, forcing him to hold himself aloft if he wanted to escape the strangling hold.

And then nothing.

For hours.

He held himself up as long as he could, the bruising pressure around his throat stealing his air whenever his strength failed him. Each time that happened, the room grew smaller, the walls squeezing together, threatening to crush him. And each time, Kenton somehow summoned the energy to prop himself up again, gasping for air, only taking in half breaths, the pain too great for anything else.

He welcomed the burning. After a while it was all he could feel, his arms having gone numb long ago, his back a formless thing that existed solely to keep his frantically pumping heart inside his body. If someone cut him down, he'd collapse in a heap on the floor. He began to see visions of himself lying there, armless, legless, only a head attached to a useless torso, unable to do more than hump along the floor, bleeding out onto the unfeeling grey.

The hallucinations became more and more vivid until the door of his cell opened, and a hand emerged from the light, gripping a glowing sol. A burst of pain surged through him, an intense strike to the shoulder.

He'd been shot! But suddenly the pressure around his neck loosened, and after the initial dizzying oxygen rush, Kenton's vision cleared enough for him to perceive the situation better. There was no sol, no smoking wound in his shoulder.

The hand, however, was real. It belonged to a woman with dark red hair that tumbled to her shoulders. She had a face that should have been pretty, but the sneer across it twisted her features into something terrifying. The pain in his shoulder emanated from the knife she'd stuck there. She pulled it out slow, twisting it as she went, wringing a scream from Kenton.

Blood—his blood—beaded down the length of the blade, and the woman smeared the flat of it across Kenton's face, dancing the edge dangerously close to his right eye. She turned the knife just as she finished drawing it over his cheek bone, nicking the bruised skin there, and Kenton bit back a cry.

"Don't be afraid to sing for me, darling," she said, before taking a soft cloth from a tray of nasty looking tools behind her and wiping the bright steel clean. "I'm the best at what I do, and we've got eons before I'll have to call in the medics. Until then"—her smile was wicked, and Kenton trembled—"let's play."

Hours bled into days.

Who are you? Where are you from? Were you working alone? Who else was with you? How many were there?

First, the knife. It cut, struck, *carved* into soft flesh, coaxing more blood from Kenton than he knew he had. He half suspected they kept replenishing it just to watch him pour out his life even faster.

How did the Cabal get you your resources? Where did you steal your weapons and equipment? How long have you been a spy?

Next, his nails. Crushed, pulled off, peeled away. Fingers and toes suffered the same treatment, the woman never stopping no matter how Kenton begged.

Who is "W"? Who's feeding you your orders? How was the Cabal communicating with you? How did you choose which cities to attack?

After that it was water. Kenton lost count of how many times he drowned, brackish streams running into his nostrils and down into his lungs, the relentless trickles staying with him even when that torment was discarded for another.

What are the names of your compatriots? Who is Seri? Who's Bo? Have you been working with Iokians? Have you been living with them? Have you been living in the Hinnom Forest?

She pressed him. Tied him to the floor, legs strung up since there was no room for them elsewhere, and set heavier and heavier weights on his chest.

Sometimes they heated the iron weights before placing the blistering blocks on his bare skin. The cold ones were almost worse, the metal sticking to him and ripping away bloody at the end of it.

What do you know about the Apollo XXII colony? How did you acquire your weak heart? What is Igis? What's a quirn? How does it work? Who is "W"?

Then it was the knife again, cutting, slicing, flaying. He was awake the day she flipped him over and pinned him face-down, ignoring his struggles as she shaved away a section of his hair and pierced his skull.

Kenton would never forget the touch of her knife to his exposed brain. In the rare moments she left to give herself a brief reprieve, he twisted to trail numb fingers against the jagged stitches holding together edges that promised to scar thickly. That stopped when she caught him at it and broke his arm. His legs too for good measure.

Who leads Tribe Osinan? How many lokians are there? How many adults? How many children? Will hinnom sap truly help our forces cross the sea? Who lives across the sea? Why did you leave the forest? Why did you stop in Ethaba?

Sometimes she just beat him.

And always, in between the torture, while the medics healed him to almost as good as new for the next round—the pain that brought its own excruciating torment—came the questions, the endless questions.

What do you know of Jack Riven? What is your connection to "W" and the Cabal? How did you escape Ethaba? Why did Laine Riven help you? What's the cure to Bowman's disease?

"You've wrung him dry, Lynn. We've pulled

everything from inside his head."

"Except who "W" is."

"No need for that tone, Cousin. Look at him. The boy truly doesn't know."

Kenton struggled to lift his eyelids, but failed to manage even that small action. The last beating had swollen them almost completely shut, day old blood crusting over to form an unbreakable seal. His eyes burned with unshed tears.

He had tried, tried so hard not to yield any information. None of the trials of Igis had prepared him to withstand such torment. Piece by piece she'd cut his soul from him, pushing him until he sobbed out whatever she asked of him, desperate for the pain to stop, for even half a moment.

He'd thought they'd kill him quick. He'd never imagined such malevolence. They kept healing him over and over, presenting him to her a fresh, blank canvas. She delighted in peeling away his knowledge one strip of skin at a time, ofttimes not stopping even after the traitorous words had streamed out of his abused mouth, obviously thrilling at causing him pain just for the sake of it. Kenton wished he didn't know what his own exposed muscles looked like.

And now she knew everything. The Hinnom Forest wasn't safe anymore. Kenton had wanted to save them; instead he was their destruction. If he ever managed to escape, there'd be nothing but ashes waiting for him.

"I'm not convinced, Rolv, he—"

"You'll kill him if you keep going. I have plans for

him."

"You think your pet scientists can still make something out of that sad sack of broken bones?"

"Better him than good soldiers, Lynn. If they can make it work with someone that mangled, then we can conscript our healthy men and women into the program."

Kenton had thought he was beyond feeling, but prickles of terror ran through him at the implications of what the man and his tormentor discussed. When she whistled and rough hands grabbed at him, Kenton thrashed with all his might.

"Thought you said you'd beaten the fight out of him?" the man said, and a forceful blow struck Kenton, cracking the bones in his face. His ears rang, her next words filtering in one at a time.

"He's lived with the animals so long he's one of them."

The door slammed open, the boom of it bouncing around in Kenton's skull, and he mustered up what little strength he had left, hoping to enrage her enough to end him before they delivered him up to the scientists. Blood leaked from his newest wounds, his mouth tasting of ash and copper, and the viscous feel of it sparked one last idea. He would not allow himself to be their slave.

"You'll never, n-never get me to tell, tell you about 'W'."

Steeling himself for the next blow, Kenton bit down hard when it came, the sudden gush of blood closer to pleasure than pain at the horrified gasp when she realised what he'd provoked her to.

Let her think he'd died protecting a secret she had a burning desire to uncover. Never mind that Kenton didn't have the slightest idea who "W" was, had never heard the moniker before the Torturer had first whispered it to him.

He began to laugh, the sound bubbling out of him until he started choking on his own blood, and his tongue slithered forward, landing with a plop at his torturer's feet. In one small thing at least, he'd won, and she couldn't take that away from him.

She couldn't take anything from him ever again.

12

"This is such tripe," Laine complained, wading through the waist-high brackish water Bo had forced him into. "Not like they'll be tracking us with dogs."

Dustin had told him that even when they managed to survive the long space travel, man's best friend reacted poorly to frix season, and Earth had given up trying to send them to Thorunn.

Bo rolled his eyes. "I'm not worried about the soldiers, idiot. I told you, if we wanna reach New Little Rock without attracting every predator on the Cerado, we gotta stop smelling like tasty snacks."

Laine held up his sol. "You saying I stole this off the guards by the tunnels for no reason?" Poor saps had never seen them coming, half asleep on their watch, fear of radiation poisoning driving them far enough from the entrance that he and Bo had easily snuck up on them.

"And if we run out of charges or crack the, the sun-trapping parts—"

"Solar panels—"

"Then we're down to a single usable weapon between us—and no, your sports stick doesn't count."

Laine rolled his eyes. The stupid lokian had spent

all its time in his room while he and Ken had worked on the cure. It didn't know just how good Laine was with his crosse. But since Bo held a fully charged sol—the new Cloud 47 for that matter—and a quirn, depowered and slung over its shoulder but within easy reach should Laine antagonise Bo too much, he didn't argue the point, switching subjects instead.

"You never said, what exactly are we hiding our scents from?" Laine grimaced at the odorous mud clinging to his pants and jacket. He'd need three showers, or ten, to get the stink off.

Bo responded with a set of angry hissing sounds, throwing in a snarl or two for good measure.

"Least that's what we call them," the lokian said, its steps carrying it towards the bank—finally, Laine had been cold and wet for way too long already. "From what I saw on television there's a reserve on Earth somewhere with similar creatures—vela, ve-loraptor, I think they were called? Ours are bigger, with more teeth, an impenetrable hide, and a highly developed sense of smell."

Laine snorted—poor creature had gotten reality and fiction mixed up—before a frisson of fear swept through him. The prospect of the long-extinct anim-als existing, no thriving, on Thorunn made the muddy water take on a whole new appeal.

"Can they swim?" He hurriedly splashed more of the nasty-smelling stuff onto his neck and chest.

"Oh, yes." Bo grinned, flashing its fangs at Laine.

"Yet another fact conveniently left out of the hand-book," Laine muttered, hauling himself onto dry land. Sól had risen only a few hours ago, casting off the night's chill, and Laine's arms and clothes started to dry right before his eyes.

Bo flicked an ear. "You humans have been here for less than thirty years flying your noisy ships and ver-cycles around; little wonder you missed a few things."

"Since you're the expert, any more death creatures I should know about?" Laine asked, brushing drying mud off his jacket sleeves. The dirt came away easily without leaving a stain. He suspected the garment wouldn't shrink either, unlike leather.

Bo looked Laine dead in the eye, the glee in its own a new level of unnerving. "Does something that lays poison eggs and can vanish from sight count?"

By midday, Laine's and Bo's clothes had dried fully, but the strong, musty smell lingered. Laine struggled to match the relentless pace Bo set, alternating between a creeping shuffle and an all-out run, forging their way through rock-strewn, scrub-like terrain. Laine's jacket protected him from the worst of it, but his palms stung all over from tiny cuts inflicted by the patches of stabbing grass they'd army crawled over, and he kept finding little pebbles pressed into the grooves between his fingers.

His left knee was numb from where he'd knocked it against a boulder on an unlucky misstep, but the lokian refused to slow down to let him recover, only huffing and pushing Laine to go faster, and eventually Laine gave up on asking. He wiped sweat away from his forehead with dirt-stained fingers.

"It can't be good we've veered so far from the river," Laine panted. He kept his voice low as they crept past a large anlo herd. He'd eaten the meat of the pre-historic-looking animals plenty of times at school, but he'd never seen them in the wild, the leathery creatures making their home quite some distance from Ethaba.

"River's the first place they'll check after your uncle records you missing," Bo shot back, careful to rearrange the grasses to cover their trail as they went along. "But there's plenty of water holes, and the anlo will lead us right to them at dusk if we stay close."

"The soldiers found you and Kenton easy enough, and you weren't on the road."

"We thought ourselves safe, else we'd've covered our tracks better," the lokian hissed and raked its claws through the packed earth. "I've no intention of getting ambushed again, so quit fretting. They could search for days and never find us, and by that time they'll assume something nasty got you and call off the hunt."

Laine started to answer when a hard-shelled insect took that moment to catapult into his mouth, and he choked violently, spitting out chaff and dust and crushed leg remnants. The bitter taste of bug guts filled his mouth, and Laine gagged, his frantic coughing prompting a hard whack from Bo.

"Cover your freakin' mouth, you moron!" Bo thumped him a few more times for good measure, then stilled, all the fur that Laine could see on it sticking straight up. "Lanae's whiskers," the lokian whispered, eyes going wide and round before hauling Laine to his feet and dragging him along at breakneck speed.

Laine's bruised knee protested the rough treatment, but the puffs of dust rising from the Cerado and the ground starting to vibrate beneath his stumbling feet told him a truth he didn't need to look at to confirm. He glanced back anyway, pounding heart lodged fast in his throat. His ill-timed coughing had disturbed the anlo herd, and they'd begun to charge.

That's it. We're dead, Laine thought, hysteria creeping through him. No, he was dead. The lokian had outpaced him, its claws having slipped off Laine once Bo had gotten him up and moving. Despite being on two legs—and not for the first time, Laine wondered why the lokian didn't just shift to its jaguar-like form, if its species really were stronger and faster that way—Bo quickly left Laine in the dust, aiming for a small copse of withered trees about half a mile ahead.

Bo would make it, Laine had no doubt, but Thorunn's higher gravity had stolen away his five-minute mile, and not even the gruelling training sessions with Andy and the team had managed to push him back to his top speed. He'd never run down the pitch with a heavy pack thumping against him with each desperate step either. Not to mention the field at Ethaba High was flat, carefully maintained, and free of debris, nothing like the ankle-breaking rocks and holes strewn about the Cerado.

The rumbling increased in step with the shaking

ground. Even if Laine didn't put a foot wrong, the juddering was liable to knock him flat within minutes, and he still didn't have a hope of getting to the scraggy tree that Bo had halfway reached before the stampeding herd caught up with him. One hand went to his hip, lingering on the Cloud 47 strapped there. He could pull it and perhaps get a few shots off, but Dustin had told him the beasts often required a whole hunting team on account of their thick skins. Laine would run out of charges long before his solfire had any effect.

No matter which way he flipped the equation, it ended the same, him trampled to a smear beneath an anlo's crushing bulk.

"I can't make it!" he sobbed out, and Bo whipped around, doubling back so fast the lokian must have strained something.

"What are you doing?" Laine gasped as Bo pulled up alongside him. "You just threw away your shot at rescuing Kenton!"

"He wouldn't be much happy to see me if he found out you got yourself killed on my watch. I've got a plan—ever hear of the Minoans?"

"The who what now?"

Bo lifted his face to the sky, managing to look utterly done with Laine despite the fact that they were running for their lives. The lokian grumbled something about pitiful human education systems— clearly intending Laine to hear, since the words were in English—then said, "Long story short, we're gonna grab their horns and vault onto their backs."

The lokian was certifiably insane. But Bo was also stronger than Laine and wrenched him around to face the enraged lumbering beasts, their dark hides making them appear like frix storm clouds rolling topsy-turvy along the ground.

"Jump when I say. We've only got one shot at this."

"Ya think?" Laine tasted blood at the back of his throat. The grass-inflicted wounds on his hands seemed so paltry compared to the thousands of tonnes of snorting anlo thundering towards them.

He could picture it easily, his lithe form skewered on the massive horns on the lowered head of the lead anlo. The tips wouldn't even need to be sharp at the barrelling herd's breakneck pace. Slamming into anything at that speed would snap it in two. But somehow Laine was still running straight at the crazed beasts, muscle memory taking over, his body thinking it was facing off against enemy lacrosse players instead of certain death.

"Now!" Bo shouted—and Laine had to face facts, Bo was a person, only a person would attempt something so crazy, when even wild animals would flee when presented with the might of hundreds of near-invulnerable anlo—and launched himself into the air, his lokian nature lending him a grace Laine couldn't hope to even half-achieve.

Laine jumped.

The half a second he flew through empty space was the longest fraction of a moment in his life.

Legs in the air, committed to an action he couldn't

take back, Laine watched himself rise in slow motion, arms flung forward, wishing in desperation that he'd taken up basketball instead of lacrosse. His hand touched the horn of the anlo he'd leapt towards. The front horn. He'd aimed for the two higher ones; he'd arrived too low.

In another instant he'd be tossed aside and trampled, if he weren't impaled first. But Laine's upward trajectory continued as he slid past the side of the anlo's face, not quite having sprung at it head-on, and his feet skimmed against a slavering mouth. Laine kicked off the anlo's snout, propelling himself up, up, up! And his fingers gripped the top of a brightly coloured crest. Eyes blurry from sickening relief, Laine pulled himself over, away from the glassy gaze of the creature, hanging on until his fingers went white, already-bruised skin starting to split and bleed as the jostling threatened to spill him to the treacherous earth below.

Sweat slicked his grip, and fear of falling had Laine throwing a leg over the anlo's neck, sitting astride it as the herbivore bucked and jolted, not understanding the new weight of its terrified rider. Breathless, wind buffeting his face, Laine looked across to see Bo clinging to a nearby anlo, his claws dug into its sides, blood streaming out under the lokian's fingers. His eyes were wide as he met Laine's, and he looked very much like he would vomit, the mad nature of his plan—and the improbable reality that they'd survived—only just setting in.

"I didn't quite expect that to work," Bo mouthed,

pupils rounder than they should be in broad day-light.

Laine shrugged, a delirious laugh overtaking him as the herd thundered on, carrying them swiftly away from Ethaba, the Kansor Mountains looming ever closer with each reckless mile.

———————— ● ————————

The anlo herd ambled along, the thundering that had shaken the Cerado long quieted. Bo and Laine had discovered that pressing on the sensitive left and right sides of the Anlos' colourful crests encouraged them to turn to escape the pressure, meaning they could steer the animals where they wished. Annoy-ingly that meant Laine had navigated his way over to Bo and was attempting to strike up conversation.

"If soldiers do find our tracks, they'll definitely think we've been trampled."

"If your friend did his job, they won't know to send a search party to look for you until this evening at least, and thanks to the anlo"—Bo reached down and patted his mount—"we can be at New Little Rock by sunset, even on foot."

Laine scrunched his face at that. "More walking?"

"Unless you want to announce our presence by showing up riding a creature your kind thinks un-tamable?"

An attractive idea, to be sure, but Bo wasn't in a hurry to get caught by the humans of New Little Rock, no matter how awestruck they'd be by his new-found ability to master the horned creatures. Knowing them, they'd put it down to sorcery, and really, the baffling notions the humans invented to explain what they didn't understand was both the bane of Bo's current existence and an endless source of amusement. He kept recalling the stricken look in Laine's friend's eyes and chuckling to himself.

The shuffling pace of the anlo ground almost to nothing as the exhausted creatures began to spread out and graze. Bo nudged his mount over to a low-hanging branch attached to a sturdy looking tree and pulled himself onto the thick limb, Laine following suit.

"Let's rest here until the heat of the day—and the herd—has passed," Bo said and shook his hammock out of his pack. "We'll continue closer to dusk to mask our approach."

"You got an extra?" Laine gestured to the thick piece of cloth Bo secured to a "Y" split in the wide trunk.

"Nope." Bo popped the "P" and smugly drew forth a sheer, spinner-floss sheet, tossing it over himself after he climbed into the hammock. He tucked his pack between his arms in case the human got any ideas about stealing. "Not my fault you brought your sports gear 'stead of a wilderness survival kit."

Laine made a hand gesture Bo assumed was meant to be insulting, but he ignored it and slipped into a light sleep, ears flicking at the flies that landed on him.

Bo roused himself when the oppressive heat began

to fade. The air always felt so sticky after first frix, but it was more bearable on the vast plains of the Cerado than in the dense Hinnom Forest. The shade they'd sought was a welcome relief from the piercing sun and the hot, stinky hides of the anlo that had brought them so far. The hulking beasts had vanished, and after he'd stowed his hammock, Bo shook Laine awake. The human teen had wet streaks running down his cheeks that he dashed away, tan face reddening at Bo catching him in the aftermath of a doubtless upsetting dream.

"My legs," Laine groaned, almost falling to the ground. "I need a few more minutes."

"If you want, but I'm going." Bo couldn't afford to linger. Not when Ken's fate weighed on his mind, gnawing at him.

At this very moment the humans of Skytown could be doing terrible things to Ken. They'd likely interrogate him—it was what Bo would have done with a threat. He knew Ken abhorred the Jail Pit on the outskirts of their village, but Bo liked to visit, liked to watch as the guards coaxed all manner of confessions from those too uninspired to evade discovery and arrest for their crimes against Tribe Osinan. Ken was a soft soul. He'd have broken under the methods La'aisa and the others employed, and they did their best not to be overly cruel.

Humans had no such compunctions. After what they'd done to Ken's family, Bo held very little hope they'd show kindness to one of their own. His journey might end up being futile—Ken might already be dead. But Bo couldn't show his face at Tribe Osinan without trying, not when he owed Ken his life.

"Any ideas how we'll get through the gates at New Little Rock?" Laine asked, having managed to catch up with Bo. He looked like he hadn't slept much, dark circles under his eyes hollowing his face.

"We're not. Going in, that is. They've got several vercycle charging stations outside the walls, and it'll be easy enough to steal a couple."

Laine snorted, an ugly, indelicate sound that made Bo's hackles rise. He could abide many things, but that horrible assault on his ears wasn't one of them.

"Way things have been going, we ain't gonna come within miles of easy."

Bo shrugged, and they trudged on in silence, keeping away from the main road but not particularly bothering to hide any longer. Odds were good any parties searching for them would turn back once they discovered the crushed grasses left by the anlo stampede—if they even managed to trace his and Laine's tracks that far.

"I gotta sit." Laine's words were clipped, tone tight.

Bo glanced up. The sun hadn't yet dipped behind the mountains and he wanted to get as close to the walled town as he could before it set. Before the hunt started.

"Give me five minutes, and I won't ask again, I swear."

"Fine. When we reach the crest of that ridge

ahead."

Laine limped quickly in front of Bo, crossing his arms as he blocked Bo's path. "My legs, ankles, knees, are all swollen. I can't walk that far, not without a quick break right now."

"Then crawl." Bo moved around the human and continued on. "Stop here, and you'll be cursing your-self for resting out in the open when the chsaa-rhee come."

"The what?" Laine asked, eyebrows pinching to-gether.

"Oh, did I forget to mention them earlier?" Bo didn't repress his smirk at Laine's irritation. "The chsaa-rhee." He let the syllables slither between his teeth, relishing Laine's minute shudder at the loud hiss accompanying the name of the death creature. "Massive. Wings. Stabbing mouths full of teeth, too many eyes, and best of all, almost impossible to see coming."

"That describes, like, half of everything you did tell me about."

Bo shook his head. "There's only one chsaa-rhee. Their ferociousness, their, their—what's the word—malevolence; s'why my people try to avoid travelling alone across the Cerado. The vyss'ngryr we can out-run. Not so much death from above." Though with the hovercars the Igis Chosen had stolen from Smoketown, that might not actually be a problem anymore.

"Then we'd better hurry."

"Astute observation," Bo said and gestured to the

shadowed recesses barely visible on the cliff-face of the Kansor Mountains. "They'll come from there, but there's enough cover ahead that they should pass by even if we do stop a moment."

They reached the ridge's crest shortly thereafter, New Little Rock finally coming into view, and Laine collapsed gracelessly to the dusty ground. He wasted no time grabbing his canteen from his pack, spilling much of its contents over himself, and Bo might have chided him if they weren't so close to the outpost town. He refreshed himself from his own waterskein, legs trembling as he allowed them a brief reprieve. For all his harsh words and not-so-hidden ridicule of Laine's halting pace—though the teen's pant leg strained so tight around his left knee, perhaps his complaints had some merit—Bo had also grown weary of their relentless march.

"You should pull your muscles," he told Laine, who lay prone, arms and legs thrown out every which way. Laine tipped his head up to lock eyes with him and then rolled over, giggling helplessly.

"Pull your muscles," he gasped out between each laughing breath. "P-pull!"

Bo ignored him, stretching first one arm, then the other. Laine had obviously known what he'd meant. He didn't have to mock him over it. In fact, he rather deserved the cramps that would result if he ignored Bo's suggestion.

Bo rolled his shoulders, feeling keenly the loss of his s'hinoian form. If he could just shift, he could easily banish the aches and pains that lingered in differently sized body parts. But the outcome was almost certain death, and he couldn't risk it, not unless he ended up in a situation where he'd die anyway.

Bo settled for using a large boulder as an anchor to twist his back this way and that, feeling his spine re-align with each crack. Laine's laughter died down as he started to imitate Bo, a slight scowl on his face.

"I'm so stiff," he groaned, kneading his arms and legs.

A sudden rustling caught Bo's attention, and he looked up, eyes widening.

"Laine!" he hissed, pouncing on him mid-stretch and rolling Laine to the ground. The human pro-tested, but Bo forcibly turned his head in the direc-tion of New Little Rock, the town on display at the foot of the Kansor Mountains. "Look."

Laine's mouth dropped open. "What the—?"

Chsaa-rhee. Hundreds of them.

All a-flight, a black mass that wriggled its way through the sky, wings a papery whisper that cres-cendoed into the sound of a river rushing over rocks, interspersed with eerie clicking cries, like a newborn startled into tears.

"I, I've seen one of those before," Laine breathed, as they watched the winged wake circle in front of the caves for several long minutes. "It must have been a baby."

The chsaa-rhee swooped and dived, rising back up in lazy spirals until every last flier had left the roost. As one, they fell silent, sunlight glinting off their beating wings in such a way they almost vanished from sight, the sounds their flight made the sole clue to their whereabouts.

"Where are they going?" Laine had a hand on his brow, squinting to catch a glimpse of the near-invisible mass of writhing bodies.

"Hunting."

"I see why you wouldn't let me stop earlier."

"And you best be grateful. Keep still. If we're quiet, they should pass us by."

"Should?"

Bo thumbed on his quirn. "The frequency this gives off might be able to disrupt their elocutio—" No, that didn't feel like the right word. "Echolocation. It won't make them notice us more, but hopefully they'll notice us less."

"Not really filling me with confidence right now," Laine groused.

Bo shrugged. "You're the one who forced me to let you tag along. You get to deal with the consequences."

"I don't wanna be pterodactyl chow! Wait—are they turning?"

The wake of chsaa-rhee had indeed began to bank, flickering into sight again. That was different from what he and the other Igis Chosen had observed before.

"Something's wrong," Bo said, ears flicking forward. "Last time we came this way the chsaa-rhee favoured the Cerado for their hunting grounds."

"Who cares, if they're not hunting us."

"They're creatures of habit. For them to change

their pattern they'd need to have found easier prey elsewhere."

"Elsewhere, like, New Little Rock elsewhere?" Laine pointed at the town ahead, his voice biting and accusatory. "What did you do?"

"The city had energy shields we had to destroy before we could take down the science centres," Bo said, recalling the moment he'd realised why their attacks were bouncing harmlessly away from the outpost. "Which is how they had enough time to warn your fellow citizens; but in our haste to reach Ethaba before your militia could properly organise, we didn't stop to consider why—when no other town did—they had shields and some sort of sonic disrupter attached to them in the first place. After all, such things would be useless against the oncoming frix."

"And when you disabled the systems keeping them at bay, the beasts acquired a taste for human flesh," Laine surmised.

"Seems so," Bo said. He adjusted the straps of his pack, making sure his Cloud 47 was primed and ready. His quirn sizzled quietly in his loose grip. "Means we won't have to wait 'til nightfall to sneak over. In all the confusion, we can grab some vercycles and be on our way before the lookouts ever see us coming."

"Innocent people are gonna get killed, and you want to take advantage of that? Just when I thought your kind couldn't stoop any lower." Laine shook his head in disgust.

Bo scrambled up and started down the other side

of the ridge. If the humans hadn't rebuilt their defences by now—when they knew what was out there—that was hardly a concern of his. Any and all obstructions keeping the human's eyes off the Hinnom Forest could only be a positive thing in Bo's estimation.

"I presume they've got tunnels to hide in, same as Ethaba. Now c'mon, we're wasting daylight."

Bo could hear Laine protesting behind him—apparently the few minutes they'd spent resting had done little to ease the teen's aching limbs, but Bo couldn't care less whether Laine would be able to drag his weak, human body along at the punishing pace. He'd welcome it if Laine gave up. However, as they approached New Little Rock, Laine gained a second wind, and Bo sighed, resigning himself to travelling with his straggler a little while longer.

So close to the city the chsaa-rhee were about to besiege, the ground became less scrubby, the vegetation dwindling to almost nothing, walls rising out of a desolate landscape of rocks and dust.

"Wait—" Bo ducked behind an outcropping—the last large one before the empty stretch that surrounded New Little Rock. He tugged Laine with him. It wouldn't do to outpace the giant avians flying full tilt at the city.

The sound of the wake's wings had been swallowed up by the early evening breeze, and the setting sun cast deep shadows over the town, the light bending around the silent force, rendering their approach almost undetectable. But the chsaa-rhee were creatures that didn't deviate much from routine, and though the humans couldn't possibly see them, warning claxons began to shrill, probably timed to the minute, anticipating the daily attack.

Most of the chsaa-rhee were still too far from the town to be reached by the defensive fire of the soldiers on the walls, but a few eager birds had flown on ahead, and some lucky shots tumbled them from the sky. Injured, but undeterred, they dragged themselves on damaged wings towards New Little Rock.

"How will we get past those?" Laine asked in an unsteady murmur, hands trembling around a sol glowing with a ready charge.

Bo scanned the scene quickly turning bloody before them. Try as he might, he couldn't see any vercycles, and he had the sudden, sick fear that they wouldn't find the fleet, lightweight transports they so desperately needed at the outpost town after all.

The wake rippled into view, a black, writhing mass that dropped, shrieking, like a massive inkblot onto the hapless town. The men and women on the walls did their best, solfire blazing as they dodged stabbing beaks and shredding claws, but despite their efforts, soldiers were knocked off the walls and ripped into by some of the grounded fliers, guts spilling out across the dirt. Some of the rocks they bled out onto weren't rocks at all, but bleached bones of human and monster alike, the bleak remnants of former bitter battles.

Laine gagged, and Bo's insides also rebelled at the sight, forcing him to breathe deep to quell his stomach's roiling. The wounded chsaa-rhee on the ground that hadn't stopped to feast on the doomed soldiers reached the gates and began to savage the thick steel.

"Those gouges are crazy deep," Laine breathed out, voice low and incredulous. "They must have been attacking New Little Rock for days. Weeks, even."

"Stop trying to guilt me," Bo replied. "You know I happily would let all of your kind burn. Except for Ken," he amended before Laine could challenge his statement. He brought a hand up to his eyes, but no matter how hard he strained, he couldn't catch sight of the charging stations he'd noted back when he and Ken had completed their final fly-by before heading to Ethaba that fateful night on the eve of first frix.

Bo's heart sank further as he realised that scattered amongst the dead bodies surrounding the town were twisted hunks of metal, shine dulled by the dust blown thick over them, pits and scars testifying to weeks-long frix damage. He and Laine couldn't steal any vercycles because there were none. They'd all been destroyed, most likely when the chsaa-rhee attacked the first time and the soldiers had attempted to mount a defence from the sky.

"I'm not seeing these so-called charging stations," Laine murmured, watching the fighting on the wall grow more intense. Tingling spread throughout Bo's body, stomach doing funny little swoops at the uncomfortable truth that confronted him.

"They're gone." Bo struggled not to lash his tail in anger-tinged mortification at the look Laine turned on him.

"You assured me so many times your plan was foolproof. Now we're gonna die, and it's a toss-up whether thirst or the birds get us first."

"We can still swipe a couple vercycles and make our way to Mount Lalethusl," Bo gritted out between clenched teeth. "We just have to get over that wall."

"The one directly behind the open terrain filled with murderous beasts and rampant solfire?"

"The very same."

"That's like, a quarter mile empty space, where we'll be easy targets," Laine said. "You're crazy to think we'll make it to the wall, much less over it."

"My friend, my best friend is in the hands of savages!" Bo snapped, rounding on Laine, claws popping out. "Because of me. They could be killing him. Or worse. I already wasted enough time when I let anger drive me back to Ethaba . . . I need a vercycle from behind those walls."

Bo jumped up and dusted off his jacket, readying himself to run. "I'm getting into New Little Rock. Whether or not you join me is your choice."

Laine would of course. The human teen seemed to fear being abandoned, and every time he'd wanted to stop, Bo had let the threat of leaving him behind hang over his head, although it truly made no difference to Bo if Laine carried on or let himself perish in the Cerado.

Laine got to his feet, a resolute expression settling over his features. "How are we doing this?"

"The fighting seems to be mostly at the fronts, so I

think we can scale the south side without being seen. I'll go first, throw you a line."

It would be quite amusing to not lend Laine a hand once he reached the top and watch him flail about in terror upon realising that Bo truly didn't care about any other humans who weren't Ken. Bo wouldn't give into the urge—mostly because he didn't want to see the disappointed look in his best friend's eyes once he found out—but it was a pleasurable thought amidst the disappointments of their current predicament, and Bo let it spur him on as he dashed out towards the shadowed side of the town, Laine hot on his heels.

They made it a quarter of the way, then half, but New Little Rock still seemed so far, the hot bursts of solfire and the screams of creature and man alike ringing harsh in Bo's ears. Shots glanced off bones and metal, and Bo spared a longing glance at a damaged vercycle thruster as he sped forward, pushing himself to go faster, faster! Again he cursed his inability to shift. Four legs would have had him to the walls by now, removing the fear that a chsaa-rhee would swoop down and pluck him up or that the soldiers would see him and direct solfire his way.

Bo stumbled on the debris-strewn ground, falling flat on his face. Though he recovered a moment later, back on his feet just as Laine passed him, that didn't stop the jolt of terror that pulsed through his hammering heart. If a chsaa-rhee had bounced its echoes his way and picked up on his display of vulnerability—!

No, he had to banish the distressing thought. New Little Rock's walls loomed before him as the taste of blood seemed to rise in his throat, accompanying the burning that seared his lungs with each gasping breath. He was almost there.

As if summoned by Bo's anxious thoughts, a shadow spread out before him—so wide he couldn't see his own blurry shade—and the sudden absence of the setting sun on his back left him cold and stumbling.

Bo froze.

Instincts waged war on logic and won, his limbs turning to stone, shackling him in place. *Not again,* he thought, a tear rolling hot down his cheek. He was a prisoner in his own mind, battering at a door that would free him of his paralysis if he could just break it down. But it was not to be.

Here, in this moment, Bo was the prey.

Despite the crackling quirn in his hand, all Bo could do was cower and quiver, and desperately hope he'd blend in with the ground. A mantra of, "Don't notice me, don't notice me, DON'T NOTICE ME!" ran through his scrambled brain, though he knew it to be useless. His blue-black fur—dappled with patches of light brown and a few tufts of cream atop his ears—perfectly camouflaged him in the forest, hiding him from even the vana'byss amongst the deep shadows cast by the Hinnom trees.

In the north-eastern Cerado, against the stark white and grey of the bone-littered landscape, the dark of his clothes and fur was unmistakable, easy pickings.

A strangled cry in the form of the human boy's name wrenched itself from Bo's throat, a last frantic clawing at salvation. Barely ahead of him, Laine twisted around at the exclamation and staggered back at the sight of what Bo knew to be his certain death.

Laine jerked his sol up—too late! The hot, rotten stench of the creature's breath gusted onto Bo's neck, and he squeezed his eyes shut, waiting for its maw to crunch through his spine.

An otherworldly, triumphant shriek rent the air, just as heavy claws came down on Bo's pack. The weight of it crushed his face into the ground, and he choked on dust. He'd been so close; after the flier tore him to pieces, there'd be no one left who could save Ken. He'd failed him.

But the expected shock of the killing blow never came. Instead, hands on his arms pulled him out and up from under the chsaa-rhee, its discordant hissing aborted mid-screech, and rather than devouring Bo, it started thrashing in deadly, unmistakable death throes.

"—oly smokes!" Bo heard Laine say, and strangely enough, felt a pair of very human arms wrap around him. The embrace ended as abruptly as it had begun, Laine's face—when Bo gathered himself enough to look at him—flushed quite red, though whether from excitement or embarrassment Bo couldn't tell.

"I hit it a bunch of times, but nothing was working, and I only had a couple charges left—if it hadn't screamed like that . . ." Laine trailed off, but Bo understood. The bird's vicious victory cry had been its undoing, gaping mouth a perfect target for the high-powered blast Laine had let loose.

"Dude, what happened? You just froze."

Shame crept over Bo as he stood on trembling legs, dropping to the ground again when they gave out under him. He clutched at his chest, drawing in a shaky breath and wondering if this was how Ken had felt, the last time he'd seen him.

"I, I—" Bo stuttered, the foreign cadence of English failing him as he struggled to collect his composure. "My instincts, I couldn't, couldn't help myself."

Laine shot him a pitying look, which twisted the feelings of shame towards anger. "Well, while you were falling to pieces, I made the second-best shot of my life. Really reconsidering coming out here. I think I might just have been able to take Gordon after all."

"Weren't you trying to avoid prison?" Bo reminded him, and Laine's face fell.

"Can't you let me have my moment?"

"I would if you hadn't foolishly drained your sol."

Laine waved the now-useless weapon in the air. "This is the thanks I get for saving your sorry hide?"

"You need me to get over that wall. I'll thank you when you act without having an ulterior motive." Not that Bo planned to ever again put himself in a position where he needed a human's help. He'd had a moment of weakness, that was all. It wouldn't be repeated.

Laine cocked his head thoughtfully, looking at the still-twitching chsaa-rhee. "On that note . . ." He unslung his lacrosse stick and poked at the fallen creature. It jerked a few more times before stilling for good.

"Swell." Laine grinned. "I've an idea that'll get us the rest of the way to the wall without risking another attack." He put his crosse and sol away before lifting one leathery wing and ducking under it, gesturing for Bo to join him.

Bo wrinkled his nose at the stink exuding from the dead thing, but acquiesced, seeing—but not liking—the wisdom in Laine's proposition. It rankled him that he hadn't thought of it first, though it sucked to have to rely on the thing that had almost killed him for safety. Swallowing his discomfort, Bo stowed his weapons and shouldered the sizeable but surprisingly lightweight carcass between himself and Laine.

Shuffling along under its bulk slowed their progress, but it worked to keep them safe from the warning shots that glanced off the chsaa-rhee's tough hide. The other chsaa-rhee circling above left Bo and Laine unmolested as well, unable to make sense of the echoes bouncing back to them.

"I don't see that the guards have much beyond personal lights," Laine remarked upon reaching the foot of the wall.

"The city's beacons were also hooked into the system we disabled. Terrible design flaw." Propping up one floppy wing with his quirn, Bo unstrapped his pack and began rummaging through it for the rope buried somewhere within.

"Kinda concerning they didn't fix something so vital in all this time, but if it gets us inside undetected, I ain't complaining."

Bo's hand finally closed around the braided steel cord. "Sit tight 'til I give the signal."

He tugged off his boots; the walls looked scalable enough, but it couldn't hurt to have the full set of his claws at his disposal. He didn't leave his quirn or footwear with Laine however, instead knotting the laces into his belt and restrapping his weapon to his back before taking a running leap at the rough stone.

He slipped the moment his fingers and toes caught the flat surface, wringing a yell from Laine. He almost sounded alarmed—if Bo wasn't so intently focused on not falling, he'd tell him to shush up. While the chsaa-rhee's attention had been diverted to the westward wall and the soldiers might not be able to see them, a cry at just the wrong moment would surely attract notice from both groups.

With the last of his strength, Bo dug his claws deeper into the unforgiving stone. His arms burned with the strain, shoulders ready to burst from their sockets. He gritted his teeth and jumped to the next handhold, where he wedged a hand into a narrow crevice and let himself dangle a moment before swinging his body higher.

Bo's fingers almost gave out on him twice more before he reached the top, a muffled gasp from Laine following both occasions, but he narrowly recovered, heart leaping each time he didn't plummet to certain death. The relief that flooded him when his hand struck the edge was like a sudden release of steam from a high-pressure cauldron, and Bo hauled shaky limbs over the top, almost collapsing as his bare feet touched the smooth walkway on the other side. He took the briefest of breaks to jam his boots back on before securing the cable he carried, winding a bit of the cord around his hips to be on the safe side.

He had no sooner tossed it over than a sharp yank told him Laine had started scrambling up, and Bo had to brace himself against the waist-high wall to keep from being tugged over. He distinctly recalled telling Laine to wait until he was ready for him, but it seemed the human was determined to ignore every bit of good sense Bo foolishly handed him.

"This's military-grade stuff," Laine said, smoothing one hand along the steel rope as he clambered across the wall. "Like the hovercars, huh? Pick it all up at the same place?"

"Help me pull up the slack," Bo responded, ignoring Laine's attempt at small talk. His shoulders still burned from the abuse he'd put them through, and he wound the rope into a loose coil with unsteady hands. He really didn't appreciate it when Laine clapped a hand on his strained muscles, oblivious to, or more likely—knowing the human—utterly uncaring of his injured condition, despite the fact that without him, Laine would still be stuck on the ground.

"Don't look at me like that. We made it! Time for us to resupply, recharge, and get the heck outta here with a sweet ride."

"Not on my watch."

Bo caught the sound of a rather hefty sol whining

as it was turned to full power and berated himself for letting his attention lapse after his successful climb.

"Hands up. Turn around. Slowly."

Each word was deliberately spoken, brooking no room for argument.

Bo complied, Laine doing the same, and they pivoted to face a slight, well-armed woman in military fatigues, blonde hair braided to keep it out of her face. The sol she pointed at them was nearly half her size, and the tension that had been bleeding away came rushing back, standing every strand of Bo's fur on end. He looked closer through the gloom, nose picking up the tang of sorrow she exuded, her eyes red from more than weariness.

"Look, lady—" Laine began, but shut his mouth with an audible click as one by one the panels on the side of her sol lit up bright blue. If he had dared move, Bo would have elbowed Laine for his stupidity in provoking someone so clearly unhinged by a barely restrained grief.

"One word, one step out of line, and so help me, I'll blow you both clear to Freja, understand?"

Bo and Laine nodded furiously.

"Sols. On the ground. Now. That staff, and your lacrosse stick too, kid."

Bo glanced at Laine as they unstrapped their weapons. He'd tried to keep his head low, but his hood had fallen as he'd scaled the wall, and he hadn't thought to replace it given the darkness. It was probably too much to hope that the light from her giant sol hadn't highlighted his eyes, and she'd probably be watching for any sudden moves from him in particular given that he still had his fangs and claws even after disarming. Plus, she was a soldier—he couldn't just jump her like he had the nurse back in Ethaba. Not without getting Laine killed and himself severely injured in the process.

"So since you're out here all alone, and you haven't called for backup even after seeing Bo here," Laine said after they'd slid across their weapons, "what do you want with us?"

The woman's mouth tightened into a hard line.

"Revenge."

13

"I'm not an idiot. I know you're a member of the Cabal terrorist force that attacked us before Christmas—though the lokian reveal is an unwelcome addition to the narrative."

"Whoa, hey!" Laine interjected, irritated that the woman—Woodley, going by the label on her jacket—had mistaken him for Kenton. "The Outpost Terrorist is blond, blue-eyed, and white. I'm not." He gestured at Bo. "I don't even like this guy!"

"You like him enough to save his life," Woodley said.

She'd seen that? She'd been watching them?

"It's a long story."

"Bullet points, then." Woodley carefully picked up the weapons they'd handed over as she spoke. "Start with how you know what the Outpost Terrorist looks like."

Laine rolled his eyes. Like he was really going to spill everything to a stranger who'd happily hand him back to Gordon.

"He's my best friend," Bo said, and Laine glared at him. "We got shot down over Ethaba by this guy, and he agreed to help us escape in exchange for curing his mother of Bowman's."

"Impossible!" the woman breathed.

"It wouldn't have been if the cure we gave her hadn't been sabor, sabat—messed with and my friend, the Outpost Terrorist, taken by soldiers."

"And good riddance," the woman muttered, drawing a snarl from Bo. The lokian took a deep breath and continued.

"I thought this guy had done it, and he thought I'd killed his mom, but when both of us realised someone else was responsible for our misfortunes, we decided to team up, see if we couldn't help each other."

"Don't take that to mean I like him in any way," Laine said. "You're right to hate him. He and his buddy Kenton trashed my hometown and put a lot of people in the hospital. We're only travelling together 'cause we have to."

"When have I ever needed you?"

"Excuse me, who just saved you from becoming pterosaur chow?"

"Tch, weren't for me, you'd have been crushed to death in the scrublands."

"Boys. Hey, hey! Boys!"

A warning shot flashed between the two, singeing Laine's jacket and crumbling a chunk of the wall beyond. He and Bo snapped to attention.

"I don't care who's saved who. I'm the one holding the sols, so it really doesn't matter what ridiculous story you've concocted. I'm willing to let you go."

Laine jolted at the words, waiting for the catch.

"If you kill every last rheas maximus." Woodley

circled around him and Bo, and motioned for them to start walking in front of her.

Laine didn't want to get his head blown off, so he just grumbled under his breath and obeyed.

"Our shields have been disabled since the terror attack, and a lot of equipment was subsequently and permanently damaged during frix season. We put in the request for new parts a month ago, but far as I know, the mooks in Skytown haven't even processed the paperwork yet."

They went through a narrow walkway and stumbled down the steep set of stairs at the end of it.

"You boys want to know what does happen to be impervious to frix?"

Laine's eyes darted over to the wall where the chsaa-rhee still attacked, their double rows of eyes glowing from glaring solfire. The deepening dusk made them easier to see, wings shimmering that phosphorescent green Laine remembered from Doctor Frenally's basement lab of illegality.

"Every day since Christmas we've lost one more person to the rheas maximus. Soldiers, farmers, teachers, men, women, kids—the birds don't discriminate. Less than two weeks ago, they took"—Woodley's voice cracked, her next words a whisper Laine had to strain to hear—"they took my husband."

The three of them passed through more dark streets, lead gathering at the bottom of Laine's stomach as he stared at the rubble piled up at the mouths of alleyways.

"And today they took my little girl."

Laine caught Bo's eyes. If the lokian felt guilt, he hid it well. *See what you did?* Laine tried to communicate his thoughts with an accusatory look. *See?* How Bo could still believe his actions were justified was beyond Laine. The lokian disgusted him.

"Lady, I don't know how you think we can help," Laine said. They paused in front of a rundown apartment building recessed into a shadowed alley. The windows were dark, glass from an upper one lying scattered on the ground beneath.

"It's lieutenant," Woodley snapped. She glanced around before pressing her palm to a scanner to unlock the apartment. "Get inside."

The door opened to a homely space. A cross-stitch of a pond hung above a small sink, and inspirational quotes surrounded a family portrait sitting on a dresser next to a pair of guitars. A child's finger painting adorned the fridge, the whole scene a jarring contrast to the staggering array of sols, grenades, and other such weapons stacked behind the glass doors of a locked cabinet opposite the entrance.

Before Laine could comment or resist, the lieutenant cuffed him and Bo to her kitchen table and set down her sol, looking relieved to be rid of the heavy weapon. But she didn't rest for long, fastening bulky, grey clips onto his and Bo's ears despite their protests.

"I'll uncuff you now, but those prisoner clips are wired to my vitals. You attack me, and the whole of New Little Rock will be out for your blood before dawn. Try to remove them on your own, and . . ." She mimed their heads exploding.

Laine sulked as she unfastened him from the table and rubbed at his sore wrists, not daring to attempt an attack. She'd been too matter-of-fact to be bluffing.

"The brass in Skytown refuse to let us clear out the roost in the mountains—something about not disturbing precious minerals and making new advances into secret tech—and so long as we had the shields, we were content to play by their rules. But now"—Woodley unstrapped the weapons on her person and began attaching them to Bo and Laine—"my husband's dead, my baby was dragged away, and I've got nothing left to lose."

She unlocked and opened the cabinet before pulling out an alarming number of what Laine assumed to be explosive devices.

"I was prepared to break my parole and try to blow up the mountain myself—not that I'd get far with this thing on." Woodley tapped her ear, and Laine startled to see a modified clip not dissimilar to the ones she'd forced on him and Bo.

"But as I was getting ready to go over the wall and run for it, I saw you two and got a better idea. No one's tracking you—'cept for me, now—so you can get inside and destroy the roost without being caught, court-martialed, and sent to Skytown in disgrace. Not to mention if that happened that cursed mountain range would still be standing. Our people would still be dying. But hey, at least we'd have followed the rules, right?"

Laine wouldn't have thought such a petite woman

could be so bitter, but if she felt even a fraction of the way he did after losing Mom, her anger and resentment made perfect sense.

Mom. In all the excitement, Laine hadn't spared a thought for her. He touched his fingers to his throat, to the intricate beading of the heavy necklace lying there, its textured surface a comforting presence. And a painful one.

The familiar sting of tears burned Laine's eyes, and he turned his back on Bo. The lokian didn't need to see him falling to pieces. Again. Why couldn't he just hold it together, get through one day without succumbing to the grief that kept his throat tight and thoughts reeling?

"Mom," he whispered. "Mom." The dryness of his mouth stole away any other words, but it didn't matter. Nothing would bring her back, not the remaining vials of kitterstone serum he still had tucked into his jacket, nor the blackness in his head that threatened to stop him in his tracks. She was gone and worse, it hadn't been natural—if such a debilitating disease could be called natural—instead she'd been, been . . .

A hot spike of anger lanced through Laine. He could just imagine Gordon smiling like a cat that had caught an unfortunate bird. He'd behaved much the same, toying with them, causing pain one unpredictable blow at a time, until finally, he'd gotten everything he wanted. And the way he'd done it—no one would ever believe the charges Laine wanted to bring against the double dealing waste of space.

"We'll do it."

"I'm not giving you a choice," Woodley said, packing yet more bombs into a vest she'd secured around his jacket. She'd also given him back his crosse—and Bo his quirn—as well as their sols, freshly charged. Laine had a feeling they'd need to use every bit of their arsenal before the night was out.

"I know, but I want to. Someone I love was t-taken away from me too, and after killing that chsaa-rhee earlier, I'm feeling up to a mass extinction spree. Might as well give you a little closure while I'm at it."

"Dragged away, you said?" Bo hadn't spoken much since explaining their situation, and his unexpected speech arrested Woodley's movements. "There wasn't a body?"

The lieutenant shook her head. Bo bit his lip, obviously mulling through something.

"Sometimes, chsaa-rhee carry smaller prey back to their nests for their chicks. Your daughter might not be dead." He paused to let Woodley take in the words, the sudden, fierce hope they must have sparked prompting tears to spill down her cheeks. "If we can bring her back . . ."

"Amnesty, refuge, transport, supplies—anything that's in my power to grant, it's yours."

"You'll still let us go at least, if we find her too late?"

"I'm a woman of my word." Woodley's gaze turned beseeching. "It's a long shot, I know; but if she's alive—if you can save my baby—!"

She jumped up, ushering them out of the apartment and towards the north side of the city. The chsaa-rhee had begun to retreat as night settled in, but enough of the gradually dissipating solfire lingered to muffle the sound of Woodley's hovercar. She settled the transport in an shadowed alcove near a unguarded but heavily locked door before drawing a clip out of her jacket pocket and handing it to Laine.

"This's Tom's—rest his memory—which means the commander's going to get an alert the instant it goes off. I can disable that from mission control long enough for you to reach the base of the cave, so wait 'til I give the signal before using it to bypass the locks."

Woodley put a hand on each of their shoulders. "My daughter's fate rests with you. Blast those murdering creatures from the skies."

The entire scheme was madness. A fast and furious dash across the open plains under the cover of darkness, then what promised to be an hours-long climb through unexplored cave systems, the shape of them only vaguely mapped out on the schematics Woodley had transferred to their clips; Laine shook his head as he listened to the lieutenant go over the last-minute details.

"Now remember, Shannon Beth is tiny, like really tiny for her age. She might be hard to find in there."

Laine studied the picture that popped up on his clip. The child had adorable round eyes set above chubby, dark cheeks and shoulder-length tumbling curls. Two bottom teeth were missing in her shy smile. Laine quickly committed the picture to memory and switched off the glowing projection. The chsaa-rhee might not be on the hunt anymore, but it didn't hurt to be safe.

"We'll probably lose comms once you boys are inside," Woodley said. "The mountain is chock-full of onite, and signal is always patchy for a month or so after frix season. One more time, the code for the bombs is?"

"3216A," Laine and Bo responded together. "We prime, then set."

"Correct. After that you'll have about five minutes to clear the blast radius before the mountain crumbles on top of you."

"Exciting stuff. Kinda feels like we're in the middle of a *Task Force: Mars* episode, right, Laine?"

Laine fixed Bo with an unimpressed glare, but before he could reply with what he thought of the asinine series, Woodley chimed in over the comms.

"You like that show?"

"Seen every episode," Bo replied, smirking at Laine. The jerk knew how much he hated *Task Force: Mars* and was needling him on purpose. "That part in season seven when Detective Josef had to stay behind to give everyone else a chance to escape the base before it was vaporised? I cried."

"Took me a solid month of avoiding the rerun cycle before I could bring myself to watch again after that."

Idiots, the both of them. They were on a suicide mission to rescue the lieutenant's daughter, and she and Bo were chatting like good friends about old-as-the-hills television with bad special effects.

"You know they filmed all the scenes on location?" Bo said to Woodley, sounding genuinely excited he'd found a fellow fan despite the fact that she was human, and Bo supposedly despised humans. "Won them an Emmy."

How? How much television had Bo watched while trapped in Laine's basement?

"Can we focus?" Laine snapped. "I'd rather not get blown up because you guys are too busy chit-chatting to pay attention to the mountains of explosives strapped to us."

"Excuse me for wanting some small comfort in the middle of the worst week and a half of my life."

Laine's head exploded with pain, and he dropped to his knees, the agony radiating from his ear all consuming. It cut off, accompanied by the crackle of Woodley's voice on the line.

"Consider that a warning, and keep your smart comments to yourself."

Laine grunted his acquiescence, unable to unstick his jaw. An awful metallic taste filled his mouth, and as the last of the pain at his temples vanished, a new, bright throbbing started in his right cheek. He probed the inside of his mouth with his tongue and spat out blood, continuing to listen to the lieutenant's directions in petulant silence.

Laine and Bo wound their way to the dark recesses ahead, sticking to the shadows cast by rock formations that increased in height the nearer they drew to the mountains. The line crackled more and more, and just as they slipped into the low opening, static filled their ears.

Laine looked at Bo, who shook his head before tapping his clip to lower the volume.

"We're on our own."

Laine thought back to the gaping maw high in the cliffside that marked the entrance to the chsaa-rhee roost. It had looked to be twice as tall as the walls of New Little Rock and half of that again. He wasn't looking forward to the climb.

The moonlight illuminating the mouth of the cave winked out as Laine and Bo rounded a bend, the flashlights on their clips barely denting the overwhelming blackness. Laine didn't think even Bo's sharp eyes could make out much in the oppressive nothingness they trudged through. The rocks Laine kept banging his sore knee against were the only things convincing him they hadn't entered some nightmare void that stretched endlessly into nowhere. It was like being in space—only that emptiness was still punctuated by stars.

When Bo turned to face Laine, he nearly screamed. He couldn't see the lokian's face at all, his golden eyes looking like they were floating in air with nothing tethering them down.

"Don't do that!" Laine hissed, clutching his chest as Bo's features settled into place, though he wished they hadn't as Bo's fangs came into view, and Laine had the fleeting, irrational thought that Bo was about to devour him alive. He rather suspected Bo savoured his discomfort, but tried to push it down, asking why they'd stopped.

Bo pointed to the ceiling inches above their heads. "The passageway dead-ends here. Wedging ourselves up that shaft is the only way forward."

"You sure? We can't call for help if things go wrong," Laine said. "We get stuck, we're dead."

"Don't get stuck then," Bo said, as if it were that easy.

"You can say that, you've got liquid bones," Laine complained and craned his head up to look into the narrow tunnel. The walls weren't uniform or particularly smooth, and crevices and nooks abounded. Perfect for handholds.

"Careful!" Bo whisper-shouted as Laine jumped for the lowest ledge. His hand struck the lip of the rock, and it shattered, sending him tumbling to the ground in a hail of loose stones.

"Onite can be surprisingly fragile," Bo said as he stripped off his boots. He carefully set and armed a few large bombs at the bottom edge of the tunnel wall before leaping nimbly into the darkness.

If only he had claws—Laine caught himself. First he'd been forced to travel in filthy clothes alongside Bo, next he'd saved his life, and now he was wishing he could be him? At this rate it wouldn't be long until he was ready to hold hands and sing campfire songs with the lokian.

Laine smacked his face a few times to banish the insane thoughts. He tried again after Bo had scrambled his way up, succeeding at his second attempt.

The climb was slow, impeded by the fragile sheets of onite lining the vertical tunnel and the chalky, spindly spiders that skittered directionless about the walls. Some dropped suddenly onto Laine's face and eyes, while others lay in wait in giant webs, invisible until Laine put a hand through them and got sharp stings through his gloves for his efforts. He hoped the numbness in his fingers was from the cold of the cave and not venom.

As Laine and Bo ascended, the shaft closed in around them, and Laine went from a free climb to bracing his legs on either side of his body and thrusting up, gaining more ground inch by agonisingly slow inch. The walls hadn't narrowed enough to prevent a fatal plunge if his legs failed to hold him up, and Laine had to twist until his back was braced against the uneven surface, one knee at a time pressed into the hard rock in front of him. Only the thick suit he'd gotten from Kenton kept his skin from being torn to shreds.

Laine's left leg throbbed, hot spikes of agony shooting into his toes each time he brought it up to push off again, and he bit back a curse whenever he shifted his weight. But when he risked a look down, the end of the tunnel revealed nothing but inky blackness, the cool air so thick it was a tangible thing. Even if he wanted to go back, he couldn't. One misstep, one hand placed wrong would send him freefalling down the tunnel, and a drop from that height would leave him paralysed, if it didn't kill him or trigger the explosives Bo had left behind.

"Lights off, quick," Bo hissed, the shaft dimming with little warning.

Laine fumbled with his clip, managing to get his tingling fingertips to comply, plunging them into utter darkness. He tried to ask why as the black settled in around them, but Bo soundly shushed him. Their progress stalled, time seeming to stretch out longer and longer with no noise except their soft breaths. Laine was about to pinch Bo to see if the lokian was still there when he spoke again in the faintest of whispers.

"I think—I can't be sure—but I think we're close. How quiet can you move?"

Laine shrugged before realising how pointless the action was in the lightless space. "Not very, at the pace we've been keeping."

"Great," Bo muttered. "Who knows how much longer this'll take."

A soft scrape sounded, and Laine took that to mean the lokian had began to climb again. Laine squirmed his way up so slowly, trying to muffle the sounds of his progress, that he began to doubt he was actually moving at all. His arms trembled from the strain, each higher increment he clambered tedious and hard won.

"Lanae's whiskers!" Bo exclaimed softly, and some rocks pattered down onto Laine. A few rolled over his shoulders, bouncing off the walls on their way down.

He never heard them hit the bottom.

"What happened to keeping quiet?"

A sudden light shone in his eyes, and Laine squinched them shut, then eased them open, the grey spots in his vision clearing until he could make out Bo's luminous amber eyes staring down at him. The sight still unsettled him, but Laine thrust away his discomfort when he realised Bo looked down on him from the lip of the tunnel. It ended just above Laine's head, taking a sharp left and creating a horizontal surface. Bo flattened himself against the flaking stone, and as Laine's eyes adjusted to the dim light, he saw that some of it came from beyond Bo.

"I can see the nest," Bo whispered, "and this part's wide enough to let us crawl side by side. We made it!"

The lokian grinned, and Laine wished he hadn't. A mouthful of bright, gleaming fangs wasn't the most reassuring sight after their gruelling climb. Laine pushed himself towards Bo, looking anywhere but his face.

And then.

He couldn't.

Laine couldn't push himself any higher. His knee had stuck, refusing to budge. Wedging his shoulders against the walls, Laine slowly—trepidation creeping through his bones—let his legs drop. They dangled there, his body held up only by his chest, shoulders, and the unforgiving line of his lacrosse stick. He collected himself, braced his feet, and pushed again.

But nothing happened. He didn't move up, and if he tried to shift down and lost his leverage, he'd plummet uncountable feet to the ground below.

The oxygen seemed to drain out of the confining space, Laine's breath constricting in his lungs. "Bo, I'm, I'm stuck."

"Oh, no, no, no," Bo said, peering down at Laine. "Don't do that. If I can hear how fast your heart's going, *they* might too."

"I'm trying."

Laine couldn't help that his pulse ratcheted up with each second he couldn't work himself free. This wasn't good. They were so close. Bo had already struggled out of the shaft. Stupid cats and their ability to twine through impossibly tight spaces.

"Calm down. Deep breaths, Laine. We're gonna get you outta this."

Laine shook his head. He was going to die there, in a dark hole, with only a lokian for company. Worse, it wouldn't be a quick death. Bo might be able to feed him some scraps of food—if he didn't leave Laine to rot, or decide to take some small mercy on him and blow up the mountain with Laine still inside—but what they had wouldn't last three days between them, and they'd drunk the last of their water hours ago.

Thirst would set in first. His lips and tongue would get dry, so dry. Laine could feel it already, no saliva left to wet his mouth, cave dust settling in a thick film across his lips. He would get dizzy, and direction would lose its meaning. Up, down, forwards, and backwards—like being suspended in water, upside down and right-side up all at the same time. He would fast run out of energy, no strength left to save himself even if he could shake his body loose. His muscles would waste away, skin turning sallow, and one by one, his organs would begin to fail, until he went into shock and shut down completely.

If it was still cool in the cave, Laine couldn't tell. His face and hands felt aflame, blood rushing around his body as his heart thrummed faster until Laine was sure it would burst from his chest. A thought occurred to Laine, and hysterical laughter burbled out of him. At least he and his mother would have something in common. They'd both have died horribly.

Bo whisper-yelled at him to shut up, though when it became apparent that Laine's frightened giggles—now turning into hiccupping sobs—were beyond his control, he reached down and shoved a sock into Laine's mouth.

The unexpected taste and texture of thick cotton startled Laine into silence. Bo swayed towards him, slim enough to hang in the narrow tunnel without touching the wall on either side, anchored by his clawed feet to the ledge above. The lokian popped out the claws on his hands with a soft *schnick,* and Laine would have flinched away if he could have moved.

Bo was going to slit his throat to keep him quiet, dump him like the dead weight he was, rescue the lieutenant's daughter, and go on his merry way without Laine to slow him down. But the sharp tips didn't land on Laine's neck, Bo bypassing his head and going for his pack instead.

"Breathe out and lean forward as much as you can," Bo instructed, hooking his claws under the straps and slashing through them. "Brace yourself."

Laine yelped when Bo shoved his face into the wall, crushing his nose and causing blood to trickle down his upper lip. The rough material of his backpack scratched and cut the side of his face as Bo dragged the pack free and gripped it between his fangs.

"There we go. Now your arm."

It hurt. Worse than the time Laine had skinned his knees falling from his hoverboard before he'd learned to ride it properly. Worse than the time he'd jumped from a moving hovercar after his middle school friends had stolen a cop's vehicle and gone for a joyride. Bo had his claws dug into his arms, through the upper layer of flesh into the muscles, and was pulling with all his might.

Laine bit back a scream, and tears stung the corners of his eyes as Bo wriggled backward, tugging Laine free a bit at a time.

"I'm not gonna lie, this is going to hurt."

Laine scoffed internally. Pain already consumed his senses. Bo couldn't add much more. Then Bo shifted one of his hands onto Laine's wrist, piercing through his gloves to the soft skin beneath, and Laine was suddenly, eternally grateful for the nasty sock shoved between his teeth. He couldn't see Bo's face, eyes streaming and blurry, and muffled sobs gasped their way out of Laine's chest as the lokian tried to tug him loose.

"Push," Bo said around the pack in his mouth. "C'mon, help me out."

"I can't," Laine whimpered, his words almost lost behind the foul-tasting sock gag. "I can't, I can't, I can't."

"Never took you for that much of a quitter," Bo said, narrowing his eyes. "No wonder you couldn't save your mom."

"Shut up!" Laine snarled. How dare Bo insinuate that he hadn't done everything he could to keep Mom alive? Anger-fuelled strength welled up in Laine as he surged towards Bo, wanting to wring the lokian's head from his neck. No one was allowed to speak that way of Mom. She'd been kind and gentle and good, and didn't deserve to die—to have been murdered the way she was. Her painful struggle didn't warrant the callous way Bo spoke of her.

Laine lunged again and got a bit closer to the sneering lokian, hyperaware of the pain blossoming in his nose, wrist, and shoulders. The force with which Bo yanked him up was going to rip his arms from their sockets.

"That's it!" Bo crowed, digging his claws in deeper, heedless of the blood that ran in rivulets down Laine's forearm. Laine willed all his remaining energy to his legs and with one last burst came close enough to swipe at Bo's triumphant face. He missed and his hand came down on the edge of the ledge, blood-slicked gloves almost slipping from the smooth rock.

Bo retreated farther back, tossing Laine's pack into

the flat space beside him, and then readjusted his grip, retracting his claws and handling Laine's bruised limbs with a gentler touch.

Laine hauled himself the rest of the way up, the fight flooding out of him as he flopped onto the relative safety of the horizontal surface, only pausing to fling the sock away, spitting to rid his mouth of the taste.

Bo stared at the slimy cotton in disgust and elected to slip his boots back on without it. "Now we're even."

Laine rolled over and propped himself up in the low space, accepting the roll of bandages Bo tossed his way. He wrapped his wrists tightly to stem the bleeding, then shot Bo a murderous glare.

"Never do that again."

"I wouldn't have had to if you hadn't given up on me back there."

The lokian had a point, though it pained Laine to admit it, so he ignored Bo and crawled instead to the other end of the tunnel, towards the soft, grey-blue light he could see at the opening.

They had indeed made it.

The smell hit Laine first. A rancid, putrid odour that had him clapping his hands over his nose and mouth.

"That'll be the half-eaten spoils of their raiding parties," Bo whispered as he came up beside Laine.

Similar to the debris-strewn ground outside of New Little Rock, the floor of the cavern Laine gazed into was littered with bones. Rock ledges jutted out from the moonlit walls, large nests perched atop them. Chsaa-rhee flew unceasing through the large entrance, giant shadows that Laine shrank from. Pairs united above some of the nests, hissing and snapping at any who dared approach too closely. Laine watched in fascinated revulsion as the giant avians regurgitated bits of flesh that their greedy offspring gobbled down.

Loud squeaks from the entrance caught his attention. Clutched in the thick talons of a massive chsaa-rhee was a small rodent that looked like a cross between a rock hyrax and a guinea pig. It shrieked furiously, its side covered in streaming wounds. Its captor didn't bother stopping, instead opening grasping talons and dropping the rodent above a nest from what had to be ten feet up.

Laine shivered at the rodent's aborted squeal after it hit the edge of the sturdy structure and tumbled to the ground. Another chsaa-rhee, evidently deciding the miss meant the tiny animal was fair game, hopped over to the stunned creature and poked at the rodent a few times before snatching it up and crawling on the knuckles of its wings to a different nest.

The huge chsaa-rhee that had originally dropped the rodent descended on the usurper with a savage fury, hatred burning in its many beady eyes. It stabbed and clawed at the smaller chsaa-rhee until the bird lay still, blood gushing from its ruined breast. But during the vicious confrontation, the little rodent had woken and squirmed free, darting to the far side of the cave wall and disappearing into one of the many crevices there.

"That'd be a good place to set the charges," Bo remarked, watching the chsaa-rhee gnash its toothed beak at the loss of its prey. It attacked and killed several more of its brethren in its rage.

Laine couldn't bring himself to feel sorry for the chicks that would go hungry that night. They'd all be blown to bits by morning.

"Or maybe to hide a little kid."

Bo nodded and inched to the edge of the tunnel, stopping just shy of poking his head into the large cavernous expanse beyond. He flashed his clip's light: once, twice, a third time. Nothing.

He repeated the action, but cut the beam when a chsaa-rhee appeared to turn its leathery head towards the source of the blinking. Bo waited a few minutes before trying once more, swivelling his ears back and forth and listening intently as he watched the light, but there was still no response, and Laine's heart fell.

He didn't realise how much he'd been hoping that Bo was right and Woodley's daughter had survived. That had been a foolish dream. Hours had passed since the chsaa-rhee had taken her, and more likely than not, she'd been torn to shreds by the hundreds of chicks all clamouring for their next meal.

"Little else we can do now except wait." Bo sounded as defeated as Laine felt. "They'll settle down as dawn approaches. We can make our move then."

Laine glanced towards the bit of moon he could see from the mouth of the cave. Morning was a ways off yet; he and Bo had some hours of waiting ahead of them. His prodding exhaustion made itself fully known, the knowledge that he could finally rest for a while turning Laine's limbs leaden. The long, gruelling walk to New Little Rock across the Cerado's uneven terrain, the narrow escape from the chsaa-rhee, the terrifying climb through the Kansor cave systems—the adrenaline from the non-stop action crashed to a halt, leaving him drained and achy. If he survived their current predicament, he'd sleep for a month.

Laine jerked awake at Bo's insistent shaking.

"I've got one energy bar left. Here." Bo handed the snack to Laine. "We need to be ready at any moment. I can't have you falling asleep on me."

"Dude, five minutes won't hurt."

"That's five minutes we could be planning our exit." Bo looked out at the noisy cave. "I honestly wasn't sure we'd get this far. That you'd get this far."

"Yeah, and making it down might be harder than getting up."

Laine's attention was drawn to the fresh carcasses of the unfortunate chsaa-rhee in the middle of the cave. They weren't the only ones, just the newest casualties in a graveyard of dozens. The immense number of differently sized chicks in the yawning caverns made sense, given how mindlessly the creatures slaughtered each other. Their numbers would probably be abysmally low if they didn't constantly reproduce.

Bo wrinkled his nose. "I'll be glad to leave this

foul-smelling place. This is exactly the stink lingering in the tunnels in and out of Ethaba. All the trouble I've run into; sometimes I wish I'd never left the Hinnom Forest. Ken wouldn't be suffering at the hands of those who murdered his family, and I wouldn't be stuck inside a freezing cave."

"I wish you hadn't either. Mom would still be . . . gone, but I wouldn't have had hope dangled in front of me only to have it snatched away. Why couldn't you have just stayed where you were? Long as you didn't bother us, we didn't bother you. Heck, I think we'd just about forgotten you existed."

"Tch. Your uncle hadn't. Ken and I overheard him and a bunch of other scientists, way back before first frix at a research camp they'd set up on the edges of the Hinnom Forest. They were planning to strip the trees and force us out if we resisted. We had to strike first."

Laine tried to suppress an uncomfortable squirming at Bo's words. Laid out so simply, he couldn't quite disagree with the lokian's reaction to the threatened destruction of his home. He had to remember the situation wasn't so simple.

Lokians were behind the disappearance of the Apollo XXII colony. And Dad had been on Gordon's research team—surely his father, for all his flaws, wouldn't consent to the genocide of an entire people. Especially not over a few trees they could grow anywhere.

Kenton must have misheard. All the ruin and terror of the months leading into frix season could have stemmed from a terrible misunderstanding.

"What made Kenton want to live among lokians and not humans?" Laine crumbled his energy bar and forced the dry bits past the ever-present lump in his throat one piece at a time.

"We were all he had left." Bo shook his head. "Your kind, your capacity for cruelty is . . . astonishing. What happened to Ken's family—well, it's why we responded so severely at the first confirmation of our suspicions. We won't be used to further a ruthless conquest. Neither will we be victims. We will not be erased."

Laine could respect that, even if he didn't agree with the terror attacks, with the trauma the lokians had inflicted.

"Maybe after you find Kenton our people and yours can come to some sort of agreement?"

Bo laughed quietly for a long time at Laine's words.

"I'll believe that's possible when our ghosts return from the pasts where we've buried them. No, I don't foresee peace. For all the towns we hit, we didn't come away with a real win. We just bought ourselves a little more time in an endless war."

———————— ● ————————

Morning brought clouds that gathered at the very edge of the horizon, ready to be blown out to the coast. Bo had watched as black faded into deep blue, then into grey. The last of the chsaa-rhee had entered the cave and nested down hours prior, but Bo had waited until he was sure they'd succumbed to sleep after a long night of hunting. Laine had drifted off despite Bo's efforts, and he'd stopped expending energy on the slothful human, though he did poke Laine whenever he started snoring a little too loudly.

"It's time," Bo said, shaking Laine awake.

"Wha—?" Laine rubbed at eyes that struggled to stay open.

"The chsaa-rhee are all asleep, but we gotta keep quiet. We can't risk rousing them before we've cleared the cave."

They still didn't have a safe escape route. The outer cliff-face was sheer, and Bo's cable only went down two thirds of the way. The drop remaining would be enough to break his and Laine's legs. Bo began to climb cautiously out of their tunnel, racking his brain for other means to flee the mountain without getting caught in the blast radius.

The irony of the situation wasn't lost on him. If Ken or Seri or Lanae forbid, the Innah, were here, they'd have choice words with him about his complicity in wiping out an entire species. Especially when the birds were only acting according to their nature. But when faced with choosing between Ken's life and those of the murderous chsaa-rhee, it really was no choice at all. Bo couldn't even begin to consider wavering from his decision. He had to carry on, one bomb-laden step at a time.

Bo slipped a few times on the gently sloped walls of the cavern, heart jumping into his throat at each fresh shower of onite fragments. Behind him, Laine struggled not to cough at the clouds of black dust they stirred up. Yet the birds remained quiescent, worn out by their nighttime excursions, sleeping soundly on full bellies. As they passed the motionless chsaa-rhee that had died during the moonlit hours of the morning, an idea struck Bo.

"What if we used them to get down?"

"Like . . . like hang gliders or something?"

"Exactly. The blades the lieutenant gave us should be able to cut through their wings; then it's just a matter of popping out the bones and slotting my quirn and your lacrosse stick in place."

Laine recoiled, a look of disgust crossing his features before he schooled himself and reached for the large knife belted to his hips.

"What the heck. Beats tryna rappel down an entire mountain in five minutes."

They crept over to the dead chsaa-rhee, Bo breathing shallowly so as not to expel the contents of his stomach at the rotting odour. He drew his own blade. The bright steel glinted in the sunlight as he sawed through thick wing membrane. Bo used his steel cable to bind his quirn to the wings, and wonder of wonders, Laine's sports gear actually came in handy, a long length of extra netting ending up lashed around the human's lacrosse stick.

Makeshift gliders completed, Bo and Laine crept through the ankle-high detritus of the cave floor to the wide entrance and set the contraptions close enough to the edge that a running start would carry them up and out. Then they shuffled back to the shadowed recesses at the rear of the cave, explosives in hand. Divesting themselves of all the remaining munitions Lieutenant Woodley had strapped to them, Bo and Laine began to prime and set armfuls of the devices, spreading them out for maximum effectiveness.

A sudden burst of movement froze Bo. A small, furry body darted past him and Laine, its squeaks echoing shrill and loud, too loud, in the hushed space as it disappeared over the lip of the cave and down the side of the mountain. The likshish had survived and like them had waited 'til day to flee the awful place. Despite his mounting concern that the chsaarhee would stir and attack them, Bo couldn't help smiling at the animal's tenacity.

"Bo. I thought I saw," Laine began, voice very low in the silence left by the likshish, "that guinea pig looking animal had a bandage on its leg."

Bo stiffened, chest squeezing painfully at the implication. "You're certain?"

Laine shook his head no. "It's dark in here, and my eyes are still blurry, so could've been wishful thinking."

Bo wedged a few more sticks of TX-99 explosives into the cracks, priming and then setting them. The counter in his gloved hand blinked up at him, glowing a soft green in the dimly lit space.

"You have to be sure. We can't enter the detonation code if there's even a sliver of a chance."

"Shannon?" Laine's words, quiet as they were, rang like a claxon in the expansive cavern. "Shannon

Beth?"

"What're you doing?" Bo mouthed, throwing up his hands.

"Making sure. The bombs ready to go?"

"They'll start counting down soon as I transmit the code."

"Good. Operation 'Rescue Shannon' is back on."

Laine called the little girl's name again, and Bo winced at his raised voice, eyeing the distance between them and their getaway gliders. A few chsaa-rhee twitched, and Bo flinched towards the cave mouth.

"Shannon, your mommy sent us to find you. We're here to take you home."

Laine walked back and forth in front of the various narrow crevices, repeating himself over and over. Bo hurried after him, intent on getting Laine to lower his voice before they woke the chsaa-rhee.

The human teen came to a standstill in the middle of the cave, and Bo tumbled into him, almost knocking the two of them to the floor. Bo's tight grip on the remote detonator kept the small device from slipping, but his thumb almost pressed the countdown button as he scrambled to keep his flailing limbs from hitting the macabre piles of bones strewn all about.

Amidst the ungainly scuffle, Bo caught a high, lilting sound. He suddenly saw himself from the outside, all pinwheeling legs and arms, a comical sight had it happened on an episode of *Task Force: Mars*. The musical noise cut off when he swivelled his ears and head towards it.

"There." He pointed as Laine looked at him with furrowed brows. "Between those two nests. I heard giggles."

The nests in question rested on a ledge near fifteen feet from the floor of the cavern. They would come up to Bo's shoulder if he stood next to them. Only about an arm's length separated the nests, one of which had a slumbering chsaa-rhee settled atop.

Bo struggled to keep his breathing under control as he and Laine picked their way over to the source of the laughter. He'd been fine with the dead fliers and confident even when they kept to the back of the cave, but the closer they got to the very much alive chsaa-rhee, with its stabbing beak and shredding claws, the harder Bo found it to keep moving forward. He touched the sol at his hip to remind himself that he still had a weapon, even if his trusty quirn was out of reach on the other side of the caverns.

Maintaining his composure was easier said than done upon viewing the nests up close. Sticks and vines, bits of brush, and clumps of stone and clay made up the large structures, stuffed with bits of dried moss. Bo also spied hunks of fur and hair and bone, both animal and human, woven in. He wondered if the remnants of some unfortunate klia'an might be part of the oldest nests, from a time before humans came to the planet they'd re-named "Thorunn."

Lieutenant Woodley's bombs would ensure that no living creature fell prey to the chsaa-rhee in the future.

The rocks below the nests provided rough handholds that Bo and Laine used to haul themselves up. Bo held his breath as they crawled through the tight space between the nests, hoping that the drops hitting his back came from the natural moisture of the cave and wasn't the sleeping chsaa-rhee's spittle. With a last look back at the creature, Bo wriggled forward and tapped his clip's light on.

There, in the void at the back of the wall was a natural vent, similar to the others he and Laine had been stuffing sticks of TX-99 into.

"No way I can squeeze in there," Laine said.

"Keep watch then." Bo set his own travel bag outside the tunnel, still clutching the detonator, and folded his way inside. The confined space was a little larger within, allowing him to rise into a crawl.

"Shannon Beth?" he called, voice loud as he dared. He shuttered his eyes to make them appear less frightening in the gloom. It was one thing to tease Laine, but scaring a little girl was just cruel.

"Shannon, we're friends of your mom, Lieutenant Woodley." Bo tilted his head back and forth, sweeping the light over the area. A thrill ran through him when he saw the small figure huddled in the furthermost corner of the crevice. He kept his tone soft and encouraging. "We're gonna get you away from this place. We're gonna get you home."

He knelt next to the tiny child, who shrank away at his approach.

"You're a lokian." She sounded terrified, lisping her "L's" and "R's'," pronouncing them like "W's."

"Are you gonna eat me?"

Shannon's eyes filled with tears, and Bo hurried to reassure her before her sobs could spill out. She might be a human, but she was only a baby, and children were children, fur or no.

"I'd never do that. You've been very brave. How'd you even get in here?"

Shannon looked at him with mistrust, and Bo mentally smacked himself before withdrawing the softie the lieutenant had given him from his jacket. Shannon's expression brightened and she reached one brown little hand for the stuffed animal.

"Lovey!" she cried, grabbing the toy.

Bo noticed that her other arm hung at an unnatural angle, and she'd covered it with colourful bandages. He supposed the likshish must have run into the same vent where Shannon had taken refuge, and she'd patched it up while it was still too stunned to refuse her ministrations. Another quick look around revealed more tunnels in the rock wall, too small for Shannon, but the right size for the rodent, explaining how it had reappeared at a completely different spot before it had quit the caverns.

"How did you get away from the birds?" Bo asked again. The soft toy seemed to have allayed Shannon's suspicion of him, and she answered without hesitation.

"The rheas maximus dropped me, and I fell and hurted my arm, and then I fell again and ran in here, and they tried to get me, but they couldn't reach."

"Well, you've been very courageous, and Lovey

needs you to be brave a little longer. Can you do that for Lovey?"

Shannon nodded, curls bouncing vigorously.

"I'm going to back out, and then I need you and Lovey to get on my back, okay?"

Shannon nodded again, and Bo retreated from the cramped space, Shannon inching after him. She clambered onto him and hugged her good arm around his neck, making it a bit hard to breathe, but Bo ignored the choking sensation, and reached in his pack for his chishish-vine rope to secure her tiny form to his.

It was time. Bo pressed his detonator and pushed between the nests to the edge of the ledge, the words on his lips to tell Laine.

Empty space greeted him. Laine was gone.

All of Bo's fur stood on end, and he ground his teeth. The human wouldn't—would he? A quick glance towards the mouth of the cave revealed the gliders, both of them, still gleaming in the sunlight, but Laine was nowhere near them. He wasn't any-where Bo could see.

And then he heard him. A shout, followed by harsh screeching that rent the air and disturbed the eerie quiet of the caverns.

Laine came tumbling over the edge of the other nest, a needle-thin beak stabbing the spot where his head had been, and leapt for the ground. He smoothly rolled onto his feet and ran for the entrance. He grabbed Bo's pack as he went, and Bo chased after him without thinking, drawing a startled cry from

Shannon.

"Did you activate the code?" Laine yelled, not bothering to keep quiet.

"If I hadn't before, I certainly would now!"

"Run then; they're waking up!"

Bo tried not to look around, focusing his gaze on their escape route, doing his best to block out the angry hissing that rose in fervour as he dashed towards the mouth of the cave. He caught up to Laine within moments.

"What idiot thing did you do?"

Without stopping, Laine unzipped the pack he clutched to his chest to show several cream coloured eggs nestled atop his belongings.

"There was all this space in there after I took the netting out, and you were taking so long, and nothing was guarding the one nest, and I just thought, well . . ." Laine floundered, as if only at that moment realising how foolish he sounded. "It seemed like a good idea at the time?"

"When we get off this mountain, I'm going to make you wish the chsaa-rhee had gotten you."

With that, Bo grasped hold of the glider he'd reached and took a running leap, launching himself from the cliff's edge. Shannon shrieked at the sudden drop that immediately followed.

"No, no, no, c'mon!" Bo yelled as he went into a spiral, too heavy for the wings attached to either end of his quirn. Out of the corner of his eye he saw Laine angling his body against the rushing wind and did the same, gasping in relief as the current caught him and Shannon, and they levelled out, orienting their flight towards New Little Rock.

The outpost town shone like a beacon, enough of the cracked solar panels on the guard towers remaining that they momentarily blinded Bo's sensitive eyes. He breathed out an exclamation of wonder. If he ignored the still-smoking grey walls and rubble-littered streets, the town was beautiful from above, morning sunlight lending an ethereal air to a place Bo had only experienced by night.

"Yes! Told you we'd get you home."

Bo grinned despite the small arm clamped around his neck. He almost couldn't breathe from how tightly Shannon clung on, but he wasn't about to ask her to loosen her grip when they were still so far from the ground.

A faint crackle in his ear alerted Bo that their rapid descent had carried them far enough from the frix-charged onite deposits that communications with the lieutenant had been restored. He risked lifting a hand to his ear to increase the volume, slamming it back to his quirn when even that quick action caused his glider to wobble and lurch against the buffeting winds.

"Lieutenant, come in, come in, Lieutenant. This is Bo. We foun—"

"Watch out!" Laine followed his warning shout with a burst of solfire, and Bo banked sharply left in time to catch sight of a furious chsaa-rhee heading his way. Wounded but not in the least deterred, the monstrous creature shrieked as it dove at Bo and Shannon, the sound standing Bo's fur on end, bringing back the dread-inducing memory of a dark shadow stretching over him.

The chsaa-rhee opened its mouth to scream a second time, but Laine dropped into a dizzying spiral and blasted the bird's gaping maw, solfire searing it from the inside out.

"Hah! Looks like you owe me one again," Laine crowed at his success, and Bo shot him a withering look.

"Course the one of us not holding a child feels free to pull death-defying stunts."

"Who else is gonna keep these pieces of scum off our backs 'til the mountain blows?"

Laine threw him a rakish grin, seemingly thriving on the dire stakes they faced. He swooped and dove and circled and flipped, riding the currents with a reckless ease, something wild alight in his eyes as he fired blast after blast at their murderous pursuers.

In his peripheral vision, Bo could make out two, four, ten of the dark, shimmering shapes—not the whole wake, not yet. The counter squeezed between his knuckles showed seconds remaining before Lieutenant Woodley's explosives remade the Kansor Mountains. They just needed the rest of the chsaa-rhee to stay put until that happened.

"Cover me then!" Bo yelled, straining towards New Little Rock on a fast, cold current. He screwed his eyes shut for a moment, Shannon's arm clamped tight across his pulse point vividly alerting him to the blood pulsing through his veins. He could feel it pounding at the base of his ears, the hot rush drowning out the whistling wind and the harsh screams of every chsaa-rhee Laine shot down.

A muffled boom roared behind him, cutting through the dulled fog of Bo's hearing, and he knew, with a gut-wrenching certainty, that they'd run out of time.

Chunks of charred onite, some larger than Bo's head, spewed from the mountain, striking a few of the chsaa-rhee and felling them instantly. Bo winced at the sick crunch of their bones breaking, first at the initial impact and again as they slammed into each other before plummeting downward, now-useless wings fluttering like trapped moths.

A second boom rumbled out, and Bo felt the wave of heat mere moments before the concussive blast slammed into him, shooting him towards the town much faster than before—but also towards the ground. Knocked so violently about, with nothing he could do to correct their plunge, Bo abandoned his attempts to steer and tore his arm away from the makeshift handle of his quirn, reaching desperately to cover Shannon's head.

"Don't look," he told her, before trying one last time to angle them at the walls. If he smashed into the unforgiving stone, the cushioning of his body might give Shannon a chance. But even as he thought it, Bo could only see one ending to the harrowing descent.

He clutched Shannon tighter and braced for the impact that nothing short of a miracle could avert.

14

Lieutenant Jenna Woodley started to pace the moment she lost Bo's and Laine's signals. She'd already been mouthing at her short nails, chipping away what little paint was left. She'd been alone in the Mission Control tower since she'd pulled rank and dismissed the soldiers, her sole companions the quietly beeping display panels and static-filled radio. Periodically, she interrupted her jerky steps to grab a cup from the desk and gulp down bitter mouthfuls of imitation coffee.

So many things could go wrong. Her plan had so many variables, known and unknown. Was she a fool to risk putting so important a mission into the hands of two teenage boys—one a lokian at that?

A commotion on one of the holoscreens attracted Jenna's attention, and she sighed upon seeing the displeased look on her commander's face as the woman strode down the halls to Mission Control, soldiers clearing out of her way. Another holoscreen showed the sun just beginning to rise. The teens had been gone all night with no word, and the mountain still stood, not even a hint of an explosion. Jenna tried not to torture herself with worst-case scenarios, but it was hard not to, when so much else had gone wrong.

She'd thought she'd known pain when the rheas

maximus had first attacked, littering the Cerado with the bones of her brothers-and-sisters-in-arms.

She'd thought she'd known pain the morning she'd kissed her husband goodbye and come home to a body bag that night.

But when Jenna had dashed home to grab her gear after the rheas maximus had attacked yet again, determined to do something despite being on suspension-pending-review, and had seen the shattered glass of her second-storey window—Shannon Beth's window—when she'd screamed and run inside to find a trail of blood leading from Shannon's big girl bed to the splintered sill and turned the place upside down with nary a trace of her only child!

She'd thought she'd go mad.

She'd known it wasn't exactly safe to leave Shannon by herself, but the child had been sleeping, and Jenna had needed to get out of the apartment, away from the memories of Tom, from the thousand constant reminders that she'd never see him smile at their daughter again. Her negligence had been rewarded with the most awful of consequences, and if Bo and Laine hadn't appeared before she'd quit the town, she'd most likely have let the birds have her—although not before destroying as many as she could.

Heavy pounding tore Jenna from her musings, and she couldn't calm her racing heart at seeing the stern visage of her commander. The holoscreens with the outside displays showed the mountain still untouched. She'd have to stall and hope Bo and Laine would pull through in time. Jenna's finger hovered over the button for the PA system. Then she stabbed it, wincing at the tightly controlled anger in the commander's voice.

"Woodley! You don't open these doors right now, you're looking at a court-martial and five years hard labour in the Mount Lalethusl mines. This is your final warning."

Jenna closed her eyes. She could keep the commander out longer, but being sent to Skytown meant she'd be separated from Shannon, if the boys really could find and rescue her. Jenna crossed the room, flipped each latch, and stood aside as the doors burst open and the commander strode in, eyes blazing.

"My sister-in-law you may be, but you have sorely tested my patience this morning, Lieutenant."

"Shannon Beth," Jenna said in response, the commander drawing up short upon hearing her niece's name.

"Explain yourself," the commander demanded. The hall behind her was packed with battle-worn soldiers and terrified cadets. Jenna stepped back, and as the commander followed her deeper into the room, the onlookers poured in, getting as close to Jenna as they dared without risking the wrath of the commander.

"They took her." Jenna's hands trembled no matter how hard she clenched them, the combat gloves she wore biting into the creases of her joints. "The rheas maximus."

Gasps rippled around the room at her pronouncement, pity and shock mixed into the low murmurs.

Jenna swallowed back the tears clawing at the words she pressed out.

"After losing Tom, I couldn't bear, well, I—" She took a deep breath and stood to attention, forcing herself into her soldier's mindset. She wouldn't be able to say what she meant otherwise.

"Ma'am. The moment I realised Shannon was gone, I lost all control of myself. I was prepared to wipe out every last rheas maximus in revenge. And before you say anything, yes, I know"—she tapped her clip, thankful they'd only modified her existing one instead of springing for the prisoner clips she'd attached to Bo and Laine—"with this thing on, I wouldn't have gotten halfway across the Cerado.

"So I sent someone else instead. Two teen boys I spied trying to infiltrate New Little Rock. They promised to blow up the Kansor Mountains, and I promised them immunity."

The commander folded her arms in the hushed pause that followed, her long locs spilling over her forearms. Her dark eyes dared Jenna to continue speaking, to damn herself that little bit more.

"I would have promised them anything, after they told me they could rescue Shannon."

The moments stretched out, Jenna standing with her head lifted, willing herself to keep eye contact with the commander, hoping that for once, the woman would overlook her fierce devotion to her job and focus her sense of duty on her family instead.

A range of emotions shifted across the commander's face before she seemed to settle on no emotion at all, expression a blank canvas that left Jenna reeling. She remembered seeing the commander like that at Tom's funeral. The two had been thick as thieves, yet the woman hadn't cried once, buttoning up her feelings under the guise of an unflinching, combat-weary soldier who'd lost too many men and women to shed any more tears over them.

She opened her mouth to speak, to doubtless condemn Jenna, when a shout cut through the tension in the room.

"Look! On the holoscreens!"

Everyone squinted, trying to see past the sunlight glaring off the mountainside. It had been undisturbed so long that Jenna was startled to see the almost-invisible shapes of rheas maximus emerging from the cave mouth high in the cliffs. In front of them flew—no, glided—two dark shapes, looking very much like the predatory avians; but something was off about them.

"Lieutenant?" The radio on the desk crackled with something other than static, and Jenna leapt for it, turning up the volume. "Come in, come in, Lieutenant. This is Bo. We foun—"

"Watch out!"

That was Laine's voice, sounding panicked, and the lokian abruptly cut off, shrieking and solfire transmitting from his clip.

Jenna gripped the edge of the desk to steady herself. Still trembling, she dared to rip her eyes away from the screen long enough to meet the commander's discerning gaze. She didn't need to say anything; everyone in the room had heard clearly enough.

"We'll discuss the actions that led to this later," the commander said, striding over to the main console. "Enlarge that screen," she commanded a tech. "You and you, outside, get the rest of our forces to the north wall."

Someone else wheeled over a chair, and Jenna sank into it, transfixed by the images on the screen, both dreadful and elating. Solfire glanced off shimmering mirages, shielded wings turning a visible, ashy grey as one rheas maximus after another fell from the sky, blood streaming into the air above.

Jenna felt—rather than heard—the first explosion, and she gasped as the top of the mountain began crumbling away, debris spraying into the cloudless sky and narrowly missing the boys, one of whom had split off towards New Little Rock. A closer look revealed him to be Bo, barrelling unevenly towards them.

That was when the rest of the bombs kicked in, and the Kansor Mountains exploded.

Somebody screamed at the unmistakable image of Bo spiralling towards the ground. Jenna clapped her hands over her mouth when she realised the awful wail had come from her.

But there was her baby! A small, shivering lump atop Bo, clinging to the lokian as they fell and fell and fell, faster with each unavoidable second. The bone-breaking impact with the ground—or the walls, whichever they reached first—would kill them both.

Jenna was going to watch it happen, and nothing she could do would save her child.

And then a miracle happened.

One final blast shook the violently disintegrating mountain, splitting it in half from bottom to top, sending out a rippling shockwave that bounced Bo and Shannon away from the carcass-littered ground.

Jenna jumped from her seat and ran for the door before the commander could stop her, dashing down the hall beyond to get outside. She couldn't just watch the holoscreens anymore. She had to see Shannon with her own eyes.

Upon arriving at the north wall, Jenna snatched a pair of 'nocs from a very young, very shocked cadet and turned the dial as high as she could, not breathing until Bo and Shannon came into sharp relief. The lokian's grim, determined countenance was closer than she'd anticipated, and although Shannon's face was buried into Bo's shoulder where Jenna couldn't see her, slung around the lokian's neck was a small, brown arm Jenna would know anywhere.

She tossed the 'nocs back to the cadet, no longer needing them as Bo and Shannon approached the walls at terrifying speeds.

Laine wasn't with them, never having regained his original trajectory, eyes wide as he plunged towards the ground, and behind her Jenna heard the commander mobilising troops to gather outside the town with nets, the teen's only hope at the end of his dizzying fall. She didn't doubt they'd catch him just in time, so didn't waste another minute worrying over

Laine and instead rushed to the very edge of the wall where moments later, Bo skimmed over the top and slammed into her, all three of them tumbling down.

"Lieutenant," he gasped, appearing unhurt despite the bruises he'd doubtless have later. "Your daughter, as promised."

Jenna burst into tears.

"Shannon Beth," she moaned as Bo unstrapped her darling from his back and handed her over. She began to cry, shaking from how close she'd come to losing her, and hugged her hard. "Shannon. My baby."

"Careful, Lieutenant. I believe Shannon's arm is broken," Bo said.

Jenna jerked back, scanning her daughter, and saw a large lump bulging in Shannon's right arm, the stretched skin turning eggplant purple underneath a plethora of brightly coloured bandages.

"Baby, I'm so sorry. Mommy didn't know," Jenna said, gathering Shannon up with gentle hands. "I'm just so happy to see you. I thought, I was so frightened, I thought—"

"It's alright, Mommy. The lokian saved me," Shannon said and brandished the stuffed animal she held in her good hand. "He brought Lovey, so I wouldn't be scared. I love him, Mommy."

Jenna laughed despite her tears. "Yeah, baby, I kinda love him too. Thank you," she said to Bo. "You've more than proven yourself." She deactivated the prisoner clip, and it fell to the ground.

When Bo bent to retrieve it, the soldiers surrounding them lifted their sols.

"Put those down," the commander snapped as she approached the scene. "Didn't you all hear my niece say this lokian saved her?" She reached Jenna and brushed some of the dust and debris out of Shannon's curls.

"Goodness, child, you've had an adventure. Why don't we go down to medical and get you checked out? All of you." She included Bo in her arching look, and Jenna had never felt more grateful to be related to the woman.

They left the walls, Shannon burying her head against Jenna's shoulder, Lovey tucked in the crook of an arm, her little fingers intertwined with Bo's as he walked beside them.

Jenna kept mouthing "thank you" at him, struggling to see through the tears of relief still streaming down her cheeks. Not even the aching weariness starting to set in could dampen her joy.

———————— ● ————————

"Laine! You're alive! Gordon said—We thought you'd been trampled."

Laine chuckled, then winced as his recently re-healed ribs protested the sudden movement. It still hurt to recall the moments before the world had gone black, flashes coming back to him of a large net and blurry faces before the gusting winds had slammed him down hard.

"Nearly was. And a whole bunch of other things besides."

Andy cut in over Yoon Ah, who was dabbing at her eyes. "You do look a bit poorly, mate—wouldn't have anything to do with those reports of the Kansor Mountains blowing up, would it?"

"Guilty as charged." Laine struggled not to laugh at the matching grimaces on his friends' faces. "Fun upside of nearly getting smashed in half—I'm now a legend. A legend among legends. Laine Riven, the rheas maximus slayer." He spread his hands apart like he was unfurling a banner.

"A rheas, what now?"

"Remember the ptera-whatever in your dad's basement?"

Andy swallowed and ran a hand uneasily through his hair. "Funny you should mention that." Beside him, Yoon Ah went very still, sitting ramrod straight, the couple's discomfort obvious despite the somewhat hazy connection of the projected holoscreen.

"The day before the news broke about your landscape reconstruction, Dad rushed home in a panic. He was so flustered he left his lab unlocked when he was called back to the ESReC later that night. That's never happened before, an' given what we all know is down there, I couldn't help wondering."

"You checked it out."

"He called me first," Yoon Ah said. Her voice was choked like she was holding back tears. "The poor thing was half dead, hooked up to all sorts of wires and testing equipment. We couldn't do anything for it."

"After seeing that, I hacked Dad's systems. I almost wish I hadn't."

Laine propped himself up a little more, leaning closer to the projection. The movement prompted a coughing fit, which lit a line of searing pain down his spine.

"Still trying to undo medical's hard work, I see."

Laine turned his head and saw Bo standing in the doorway of his hospital room, holding Shannon's hand. The tiny girl had a colourful bouquet tucked into the bend of her cast. She disengaged from Bo and ran to Laine, presenting him with the flowers. Bo caught her before she could climb into Laine's lap.

"Remember what we said about being careful?"

"Sorry! These are for you. Here!"

"Thanks," Laine said, taking her offering. He rolled his eyes at Andy and Yoon Ah's bemused expressions.

"And who's this?" Yoon Ah asked, eyes crinkling at Shannon's irresistible cuteness.

"I'm Shannon Beth. Laine is my best friend!"

"I thought I was your best friend?" Bo growled and pulled a mock sad face, before tickling Shannon until she was shrieking laughing. "Anyway, we delivered the flowers, and Laine's busy with his friends, so let's go see the baby birds, alright?"

"Baby birds!" Shannon yelled, all but dragging Bo out of the room. "Bye, Laine! Bye, Laine's friends!"

"Still hanging with that lokian, I see." The grin slipped off Andy's face.

"I owe him. 'Sides, soldiers from Skytown have been prowling around outside the walls ever since we killed all those rheas maximus, so he's kinda stuck here—the commander keeping everyone off our backs—'til they leave, and then we can go. Once I get done this stupid physical therapy."

"About that. As I was saying, I got into Dad's systems, figured out what he was doing with that creature."

"Wild guess—something to do with their vanishing ability?"

Andy nodded. "Just so. He was trying to replicate it, make it wearable. If he'd succeeded, well. Imagine the havoc an invisible special forces unit could cause."

"And Bo and I blew all that sky high. No wonder your dad was freaked."

"To put it mildly. He's convinced the Cabal blew up the mountain, an' we'll do all we can to keep him thinking it."

"Yeah, if Gordon finds out I'm alive, that I'm here—" Laine shook his head and wished immediately that he hadn't, as a sudden headache reverberated through his skull like a thousand needles stabbing his brain.

It had been days, but the pain still lingered as nano-diffusers could only do so much at half power. The doctors had explained that pushing the healing any faster could send him into shock, and Laine grudgingly accepted his slow recovery. Centuries ago, he'd never have walked again given the severity of his injuries—if he'd even have survived such a harrowing a fall to begin with.

"We've got your back, mate. Yoon Ah's already started doing some digging, an' you won't believe the crazy things she's discovering about Skytown. I just wish my dad weren't caught up in all this."

"Adults always lie," Laine said softly.

Even Mom had kept secrets from him. The more he thought about it, the more he realised she must have known she was sick for weeks, months even, before she collapsed. She'd told them she was fine, that the medicine was helping, but nothing except Kenton's cure helped Bowman's.

Laine couldn't be too badly angry at Mom though. Every time he gritted his teeth into a smile and told Shannon, yes, he felt better today, he realised he'd have done exactly the same.

"We have to go," Andy said, his eyes sympathetic, expression burdened. "Too much longer an' someone'll get suspicious. Can't have this line traced. Call you tomorrow?"

Laine nodded and made his goodbyes before disconnecting on the clip he'd been loaned. He wasn't looking forward to the rest of his day. New Little Rock's medical rations were pretty awful, and his physical therapist was trying to kill him, he was sure.

The days Laine spent convalescing were filled with mixed reactions from the citizens of New Little Rock. The soldiers—Woodley's friends and those of her late husband—always had a kind word for Laine whenever they stopped by the hospital or met him in the street after his discharge. They didn't openly gawk at Bo anymore, and he in turn stopped flashing his fangs and claws at the slightest provocation, though Laine thought that playing babysitter to a star-struck five-year-old contributed quite a bit to the slow lowering of Bo's defences. He didn't have to hide anymore—couldn't, in the wake of his heroic and very public rescue of Shannon Beth, and continuous exposure to humans seemed to be wearing his generally caustic attitude into something approaching grudging tolerance.

Others however, went out of their way to cross the street if they saw Laine or Bo walking towards them, and quite a few of the teens Laine's age whispered mockingly as they passed. Laine only smirked at those encounters. They were just jealous they still had to go to school, envious of someone in their grade being better than them at everything.

It probably didn't help that Laine carried his lacrosse stick wherever he went. The sturdy piece of equipment had survived the fall, and Laine saw no shame in flaunting the item that had helped him escape the Kansor Mountains. The dark looks from the New Little Rock High Condors when they realised he'd been the cause of their crushing defeat before first frix bolstered Laine's spirits on the days his healing injuries kept him flat on his back from the pain.

He continued to call Yoon Ah and Andy when he could, keeping updated with Yoon Ah's progress on digging into the Cabal and her new apprenticeship under Andy's mom. Ostensibly it was to learn the ins and outs of professional accounting, which sounded like the worst job in the world—all the things a person could be on Thorunn and someone chose managing other people's money? But really she was trying to uncover any evidence she could about what exactly their parents and Gordon were hiding.

It had burned Laine to hear of the paltry excuse for a funeral the man had arranged for Mom, Yoon Ah's voice going very small as she'd described the lonely affair only her family and Andy's had attended. Laine spent the night after that call making friends with a bottle of something strong he'd discovered at the back of Woodley's fridge.

The lieutenant had offered to take them in while Laine recovered, a daily regimen of physical therapy helping him to regain mobility—though the doctor had been apologetic and realistic about the possibility of permanent damage to his knee. Laine suspected Woodley was glad to have some company to fill the empty space left by her husband. He caught her many times, when she didn't think anyone was watching, tracing the face of the dark-skinned man in the pictures hung about the house and pressing her fist into her mouth, trying to be strong for Shannon.

It reminded Laine of the lonely days he'd endured with Mom when he'd been little, of the sympathetic looks her friends and family had given her, advising her to leave when they'd thought him out of earshot. But like Woodley, Mom had an iron core of strength that had kept her going through the difficult days. Laine didn't doubt that Woodley would raise Shannon with that same strength of will. How many other little girls could say they'd survived being taken by the rheas maximus?

And yet, despite her terrifying ordeal, the child didn't seem afraid of the chicks that had begun hatching at New Little Rock's *Scientific Research Centre*, begging Bo and Laine every day to take her to visit. Somehow, most of the eggs he'd almost died getting had survived intact, and the *Laine Riven Rheas Maximus Propagation Program* had been up and running at their crumbling science building all of three days into Laine's hospital stay. The half-reconstructed building wasn't exactly a safe place for a little kid, but the eggs had been cordoned off in a relatively undamaged corner of the SreC, and Laine couldn't help grinning at how Shannon pressed her face all the way up against the glass of the incubators in her unbridled enthusiasm.

He and Bo ended up watching over Shannon more often than not when Woodley was out patrolling or on a supply run to the nearest outpost, given that the destruction of the chsaa-rhee roost meant the New Little Rock soldiers were free to come and go as the commander pleased, no longer constrained to guarding their town's defences day in and day out. Laine didn't mind it, but as his leg and back healed and his bruises faded, he found himself itching to do more than babysit a five-year-old. He couldn't just sit around, not when Gordon still walked free.

And each day that passed while Laine was recovering his strength was another day Bo grew more anxious, the haunted look in his eyes growing ever deeper.

The lokian had managed to connect a call to the stolen hovercars his fellow lokians had taken back to the Hinnom Forest but learned no help was forthcoming on his rescue mission. A lokian Bo named as Seri had spoken to him for a long time, Bo becoming increasingly angrier during their conversation, ears pinned flat to his head and nothing but growls and snarling hisses spitting from him. He'd disappeared for a whole day after that, coming back to Woodley's apartment in the early morning, growling about, "stupid elders and their anlo dung decisions."

Apparently, the tribe didn't want to risk losing any more lokians while they prepared for an attack they were certain would come by second frix. Bo was on his own.

"Can't help but notice you ain't ditched me yet," Laine remarked as he and Bo walked back to Woodley's apartment after a particularly gruelling physical therapy session.

As always, the teen at the receptionist's desk had glared daggers at the two of them. He looked familiar, but whether Laine had beaten him at the mathletes competition or on the lacrosse pitch, Laine couldn't remember. He made sure to flash the other boy a peace sign and a wink every time he saw him, laughing at the narrowed eyes his actions prompted.

"We kinda blew up a mountain if you recall. The road to Smoketown's still crawling with soldiers who obviously don't believe the commander's insistence that she has no idea who or what caused it. The others might have given up on Ken, but I refuse to leave him in Skytown. I have to rescue him. Can't do that if I get myself killed trying to go it on my own right now. I may be reckless, but I'm not stupid."

"So you admit, you need me."

"Tch." Bo spat, swishing his tail in annoyance. "Your value lies in getting me up Mount Lalethusl and into Skytown. Nothing else."

"I'm worth more than that. I've kept your secret after all," Laine said, not bothering to lower his voice at the irritated look Bo shot him as they pressed through a crowd, some of whom skated around them like the touch of them was toxic. "Or are you saying"—Laine reached over and flicked Bo's ears, receiving a swat for his daring—"that these adorable little guys won't endear you to the people whose towns you destroyed?"

Bo shushed him, a growl underlying the sound. "Keep that up, I'll rip your ears off. And be quiet. No one knows my tribe had a hand in that. I'd like to keep it that way, particularly given your kind's, what's the word, irrational distrust of me and mine."

"Irrational? What about the Apollo XXII colony?"

"You know very well your own people did that."

"Yeah? Where's the proof?" Laine said. "You can't think I'll believe something so insane as our own soldiers being responsible. That would be like, like the commander turning on everyone here and then saying the rheas maximus did it. It's completely senseless."

"As you and yours have ever been."

They turned down the street that led to the alley adjoining Woodley's apartment. Shannon Beth saw them from the window and ran outside to meet them before they reached the door, her arm in a brightly coloured cast.

"Hey, kid," Laine said. He scooped her up and held her upside down while she giggled.

"Mommy says I get my cast off tomorrow!" she announced once Laine set her back on her feet. "And look! Another tooth falled out!"

"It did indeed." Bo crouched to her level, very seriously inspecting the new gap Shannon pointed out. "Did you put it somewhere safe?"

Shannon nodded and tugged on Bo's arm to lead him back to the apartment, talking excitedly the whole time.

Laine followed, pasting on a smile for the sake of the happy child. He wasn't sure he'd ever been that carefree. He left Bo to entertain Shannon with stories of his life in the forest and grabbed a drink from Woodley's fridge before settling on the woman's couch and putting a call through on his loaner clip.

Laine massaged his sore legs while he waited for his friends to answer, grimacing at the prospect of returning to the physical therapist's office the next day.

"It's happened, Laine," Yoon Ah said with absolutely no preamble as soon as the signal connected. "I was just about to call. He knows. They're coming for you."

15

Kenton guessed about a week had passed since he'd failed to kill himself.

In retrospect, it wasn't the most terrible thing to fail at, but it did mean he'd been watched every minute of every day since then. They'd ceased questioning him, instead sending him along to the Hexagon's labs for alterations. His useless heart had been stripped out, replaced entirely with a device of their making, a state-of-the-art piece of machinery that looked—and felt—organic but one which they controlled, could shut off and restart at will.

Kenton was so, so tired of fighting them. They'd dug deep; *She'd* scraped every last secret out of him, and after he'd woken on the operating table to the sight of his scarred heart going grey in a steel pan on the cart next to him, whatever strength he'd had left had absconded, leaving only his dull shell behind.

He went where they put him, moved where they moved him, ate, slept, bathed, and dressed all according to his captors' every whim. He hardly even had the energy to worry about Bo. He wanted to, knew that whatever respite his actions as the "Outpost Terrorist" had bought them wasn't enough, wouldn't last beyond a couple months before the men of Ethaba devised some way of putting the Hinnom Forest to the torch.

But the concern Kenton tried to muster up slipped from him like oil over ice. She had done more than peel his flesh from his bones. She'd reached into the very seat of his feelings, plucked out every last, clinging emotion. He didn't know who he was anymore.

Kenton couldn't even be sure he was still human.

He traced the blue glow that sparked through his veins, lighting his arms from the inside out. As with so many other procedures, he'd been awake when they'd inserted the implants, rewiring his nerves, searing his blood with a fire he'd thought would never quench. He hadn't screamed however, knew better than to beg for mercy as they'd laid his skin open, pumping blood into him faster than it could gush out, integrating his bones and muscles with a queer, almost-incomprehensible technology. They'd denied him anaesthesia, but Kenton had blacked out from the shock alone, and by the time he'd regained his senses, the deed was done.

He still couldn't fathom the purpose for the callous experimentation, but given that he rested in a clean room, dressed in loose training clothes after having been fed a nourishing meal, he supposed he'd find out soon.

At that moment, the door slid open, and a soldier stepped through it.

"Cybernetic boy's awake," he remarked, tossing an energy bar and a juice packet at Kenton, who almost didn't catch them in slow, still-aching fingers.

How could he not be awake? The days of torture,

of vivisection, the constant thrumming from whatever they'd embedded into his body—he remembered everything. Couldn't scrub it from his mind, phantom pain keeping his limbs numb and senses alert.

"Reflexes still active. That's good. You'll need them in the Tomb." The soldier snapped his fingers twice, indicating that Kenton should follow him.

Kenton didn't want to go, didn't want to face whatever fresh torments waited in a place named after a grave, but he rose to his feet. The sly smirk on the soldier's face told him he'd be leaving the room one way or another, and Kenton would rather walk than be dragged to his execution. He had at least that much dignity left.

Kenton shaded his face as he hurried along behind the soldier, wondering if he'd ever grow used to the harsh lights illuminating every hallway. He ate as he walked, trying to ignore the impression of ash crumbling on his tongue. The doctors had reattached it, but taste had been slow to return. Given that they'd painstakingly put him back together, better than before, after tearing him to shreds, Kenton had to assume his lack of sensation had been a deliberate oversight—a punishment.

The juice went down thickly, an unpleasant slime that clung to the back of his throat, but it washed away the chalky crumbs, so Kenton bore it, and it wasn't much later that he arrived at the Tomb. The doors were different than the others he'd passed, very wide and tall and overlaid with a beautiful dark wood.

The soldier stepped up to the palm scanner, but paused before activating it.

"Smile, and hold nothing back. She'll know if your efforts are half-hearted. Make sure you smile, okay?"

Kenton barely heard the words, struggling to breathe through the clawing fear the mere mention of his torturer elicited, chest too tight for him to draw more than shallow gasps of air. Before he could gather his composure, the soldier shoved him into a small chamber that seemed to be an in-between place. Someone fitted him with lightweight body armour, combat boots were shoved onto his feet, and an old quirn was placed in his hands. All the while, a blank -faced scientist stood off to one side, incongruously out of place with his long, white coat, recording everything on a holoscreen.

A second set of wood-overlaid doors greeted Kenton on the far side of the room, and he was pushed beyond them before he quite realised what was happening, finding himself blinking up at rows of blinding lights. The noise hit seconds later, excited yells and cheers and raucous music, and as Kenton's vision cleared, his surroundings came into sharp focus about him.

He stood at the edge of a large arena, circular in shape and ringed about by rows of stands, the seats of which were packed almost double with screaming spectators. The ground alternated between sandy, grassy, gravelled, and paved sections, with a small pool dead centre. Middling-sized trees and large boulders had been artfully arranged throughout the space, and although the smells of food and bleach and sweat filled the air, covering any lingering scents of blood or vomit, Kenton could still see dark-stained grains of sand.

Movement from above caught his eye, and he saw himself projected larger than life on four massive holoscreens hanging from the two-storey high ceiling. Loudspeakers blared excited yammering from two young men in a glass-enveloped box that sat on a protruding balcony to Kenton's left. After general news, they started announcing the beginning of the match.

Kenton still didn't know who or what he was to fight or how he was supposed to put on a convincing show with a decrepit quirn and limbs that felt encased in tar, but the cameras feeding the holoscreens had focused on him, powerful enough to showcase his worried blue eyes. There was something he was supposed to do. Something in addition to the fighting. Something that would make the white-coated scientists high in the stands—observing from near the shadowed exits—look favourably on him and carry a good report back to Her.

The noise quieted as Kenton stood motionless in the sand at the edge of the arena, a puzzled hush that stretched out as the moments lingered on and Kenton made no move away from the wall.

A grinding rumbling sounded opposite Kenton, a gate he hadn't noticed before beginning to lift. It stopped halfway—as if waiting—as one of the whitecoats rose to his feet, in his hand a device Kenton knew would send a painful jolt through him. Thinking of the expression the man might wear in response to Kenton's imminent distress broke through the fog in his mind.

Kenton smiled, letting his lips part to reveal his teeth.

The gate rose, the crowd roared, and something blurred towards Kenton so fast he could only discern a giant clawed foot slashing at him before he swung his quirn around to block the vicious assault. More furious attacks followed, Kenton dodging, parrying, and blocking instinctively, too hard pressed to figure out how to activate the unfamiliar quirn in his hands, too stunned to think much beyond the fact that they'd put him—a tired, broken boy with a false heart—into an enclosed space with the most dangerous predator to ever roam the Cerado.

Kenton kept ducking, staying just beyond the creature's reach. As a child, he'd goggled over carefully preserved fossils, had known the name of every long-extinct animal they belonged to. But Earth had never quite had something like the vyss'ngryr. Just thinking the hissing, grinding name sent a shiver through Kenton.

Fully four and a half metres from slavering snout to twitching tailtip and taller by half than Kenton himself, its scaly hide scarred—chunks missing from it, visible bite marks marring the jagged edges of healed-over wounds—the hulking vyss'n was the last thing Kenton had ever thought he'd encounter in

Skytown. He'd deliberately taken a circuitous route through the Cerado to avoid the bone-strewn hunting grounds that indicated a colony's presence, had made it to Smoketown and then almost to the Hinnom Forest without stumbling into a single vyss'n, and somehow, here he was, deep underground, fighting for his life with a useless quirn and unwanted implants about as helpful as sheets of paper.

He could feel the energy bubbling beneath his skin, almost burning from how it roiled under freshly healed incisions, but he had no idea how to summon it, or what it would even do if he could.

Kenton rolled to the side and sprinted for the far wall of the Tomb, the vyss'n not two paces behind. Most of Kenton's focus was on the path directly in front of him, on not tripping over the protruding rocks and uneven sand, but out of the corner of his eye, he spied the centre pool again, four cracked cobblestone walkways extending out and away: north, south, east, west. It was his only hope.

Vyss'ngryr feared nothing. Not men with their tranquillising darts, not chsaa-rhee with their stabbing beaks, not klia'ans with their frix-charged quirns, and certainly not others of their own kind. Yet for all their haughtiness they disdained water, keeping their hunting grounds far from the brackish pools and streams that dotted the Cerado. If Kenton could just gain the shallow pool he'd be safe. At least until the beast's hunger got the better of it. But those few moments would buy Kenton precious time.

Reaching the water—that was the problem.

Kenton was barely keeping ahead of the vyss'n as he sprinted around the edge of the arena, each step jarring him, shooting pain through his knees. If he stopped or slowed to angle his course towards the middle of the room, the hissing raptor would snatch him up halfway.

Less than that even.

But he couldn't keep running.

Maybe if he'd had the chance to have more than one proper meal, to have rested free of nightmares, or to have two weeks between him and the last surgery they'd performed on him instead of two days—maybe then he'd have had a chance.

The vyssn'gryr was big. Heavy. Its thudding pace wasn't meant to last long. In normal circumstances Kenton might have been able to push himself until the vyss'n wore itself out. But this was the furthest from normal Kenton had been since that fateful day when he'd lost everything.

And he couldn't keep running.

He'd step wrong, or a cramp would seize him, or he'd stray too close to the wall, collide with the hard plaster, and tumble to the ground. Within moments it would be over, and his blood would be the next to stain the Tomb's floor.

But he couldn't keep running.

One of the arena's scraggly trees loomed ahead, and Kenton didn't let himself think or second-guess his actions. He simply jumped, up, up, *up*, right hand reaching for the springy branches, his fingertips catching them, slipping, and then holding fast. He swung himself around to face the creature as it screamed, but far more dreadful than that was the unmistakable sound of powerful hind legs propelling the furious vyss'n off the ground, tooth-filled jaws stretching wide to snap at Kenton with bone-crushing force.

Despite everything he'd endured, a terrible fear flooded Kenton, and he had to fight against his every instinct to hold himself still until he felt the creature's fetid breath hot upon his face.

Quick as flashing frix he dropped out of the tree, rolling as he hit the ground, and bolted for the centre of the Tomb. Behind him, the vyss'ngryr gnashed at air, slower to recover in its confusion at being denied certain prey.

Kenton enjoyed mere seconds of reprieve before crashing footsteps informed him the vyss'n pursued him once more. It sounded louder, the thundering growing closer, rage forcing the raptor into a frenzy that lent it a nightmarish speed. It could smell him, could scent his fear, and it would have Kenton's flesh. He dared not look back.

He was almost to the pool—near enough that his nose wrinkled at the brackish odour of the stagnant water—but he could hear those clicking talons and knew he was too far, still too far. He heard it again, that awful noise, like rotten tree limbs splitting and falling to the forest floor, the one that meant the vyss'ngryr had launched itself at him, and Kenton threw himself forward, right hand reaching desperately towards the murky water, pleading with aching limbs for enough strength to gain the refuge before it was too late.

But above him, the raptor's hulking body blotted out the harsh lights of the arena, and he couldn't stop himself. His nerveless hands dropped the rusting quirn as he twisted onto his back and curled into a ball, arms raising in an "X" to cover his face. In his mind he saw the next few moments in stunning clarity. He envisioned the vyss'n landing on his powerless body, saw it ripping him apart, scattering pieces of him around the Tomb, mauling him, devouring him alive between one heartbeat and the non-existent next.

Now Kenton knew how Umama and Pa must have felt before the soldiers had murdered them. Soldiers sent from the very town that was his prison. The place that would be his grave. No one had been willing or able to help his family, and despite the hundreds, maybe even thousands of eyes watching Kenton, nobody would help him. They couldn't even if they'd wanted to.

Then, Kenton heard the Innah's voice in his mind. A memory from when he and Seri had been very young.

The sturdiest trees eventually give way to frix fire. But when the blaze dies and the ash is swept away, do you not uncover the flame-defiant shoots ready to grow into trees that will last for eons? Remember this, my children. Destruction and resilience walk hand in hand.

Kenton let his eyes close.

He shut out the screaming from the stands, the excited jabbering of the sportscasters, the hissing screech of the vyss'ngryr a hand's-breadth away, and reached deep inside himself. He thought of his home. If he let himself succumb to the urge to stop fighting, if he died upon the unfeeling sands of the Tomb, he surely would never see it again, would never be able to escape Skytown and gaze upon the dark waters of the Laika River.

Kenton thought of those he had yet to protect and those he still needed to avenge. In his mind's eye he saw Seri, saw the Innah and Bo, saw his mother and father and little Annie, and somewhere deep inside of him a string of determination stirred. A string he yanked on with all his might.

Blue-white frix, brilliant as any that had ever burst from his quirn, sparked along Kenton's forearms, and the vyss'n's claws rebounded off a shield of pure, blinding energy. It attacked again before Kenton could quite comprehend what had happened, only to be rebuffed once more in a crackling shower of frix.

Shocked to still be alive, Kenton stared in astonishment at the two energy shields emanating from his arms, sparking from his shoulders forward and around to his elbows, flexing with his movements and keeping the vyss'n at bay. The shields looked like the slyrs gifted to those Igis Chosen who performed exceptionally well in the trials—two sharp-pointed triangular planes that flared out and met with a gentle curve just below his fists.

But the slyrs Kenton gazed upon in wonder had no handholds to grasp. They weren't made of wood or steel or even the fibreglass and carbon composite materials Tribe Osinan traded for with the klia'ans across the ocean. The frix slyrs were weightless, blistering in their intensity, and Kenton knew it would only take a thought for him to command them.

He quit gawking and sprang into action, taking advantage of the frix-generated barriers to smack the vyss'n as hard as he could, scooting backward in the stunned pause that followed until his legs touched water. The slyrs vanished, and Kenton cringed, loss seeping into him at their sudden disappearance. But the brackish water protected him, filling him with some sense of security. He realised that while he remained within the pool's boundaries, he didn't need the shields, so they would not come.

The vyss'n screamed and postured and shook its head as it tore up the earth outside the pool, but it stayed just beyond the water's edge, and Kenton breathed deeply, limbs trembling, trying to recover his strength and plan a counterattack, some strategy to let him leave the Tomb alive. He looked away from the screens starting to replay the last few moments, trying to ignore the whispered commentary from the excited sportscasters, jarringly loud over the broadcast system.

Everyone else was quiet, almost tumbling out of their seats while they waited for what would happen next. Even the vyss'n had fallen silent as it stalked around Kenton, wary of sudden splashes.

He wondered if he could douse the creature with water and fry it with frix, the way he'd done with the monster that had tried to snatch Bo in the Cerado. No. The vyss'n would dart out of reach before he ever came near it, and besides, its leathery hide was so thick that for electrocution to work, he'd have to force the raptor into the pool and pin it down until its skin softened enough to cease insulating it against the frix Kenton planned to pour into it.

Besting a vyss'n would be impossible under normal circumstances. Kenton chuckled to himself, again having the thought that normality had absconded from his life months ago. He needed to stop hoping for its return and focus instead on winning the fight and enduring whatever else came after. The slyrs could bring him victory. Kenton's arms burned where the frix danced in writhing blue lines below his skin, almost whispering to him, and knew what he had to do to call the slyrs forth.

I must be mad, he thought, stepping out of the pool and bracing himself.

The vyss'ngryr eyed him curiously, then lunged faster than he could jump back to safety. But Kenton had no intention of playing it safe. He snapped his arms up—almost too late—and the vyss'n screamed as the humming, newly re-appeared shields caught it across its sensitive snout. Kenton advanced on the raptor, hammering away at it, ducking its seeking talons as he bashed and bashed, striking it with as much strength as he could muster, forcing his blows to punch past thick scales to the bones and muscles beneath.

A particularly vicious blow caught the creature on

its left shoulder, and there was no mistaking the sickening snap of bone almost drowned out by the vyss'n's agonised shrieking.

Kenton ducked back to the pool to catch his breath, confidence surging through him, even as his legs trembled in exhaustion.

"Did you see that, Brett? He broke its arm!"

Kenton glanced towards the booth where the two sportcasters clutched each others' arms while pointing at the battle below. The moment played again and again at all different angles on the holoscreens, and Kenton turned away in disgust, angry that they were portraying his desperate struggle to stay alive as mere entertainment. He couldn't block out their voices however, and the running commentary grated on him as he steeled himself for his next attack.

"I mean, I have watched every, count 'em, every single one of the TK-97's battles, and no one except Shadow has ever gotten in a hit like that before!"

"'Cause everyone else tried to slice through unsliceable skin."

You don't try to saw through concrete, Kenton thought, shaking his head at the foolish actions of those who'd apparently gone before him. *You take a sledgehammer to it.*

He reached for the energy within, preparing to leave the refuge of the water once more. Somewhere out in the stands the whitecoats lurked, doubtless recording the events with exhilaration. Their new weapon was outperforming their wildest expectations. But Kenton refused to let himself be used, to let what had happened to him be repeated upon bright-eyed cadets with no idea what they'd signed up for. He would make it through this battle, but he wouldn't give them what they wanted.

The slyrs whispered to Kenton of hope, of a future where someday, somehow, he could frustrate his captors' intentions and burn the Tomb to the ground. He savoured the image of that far-off day in his mind and, gathering his strength, stepped for a final time out of the pool.

"Tell me I'm seeing this right, Brett? He isn't gonna!?"

"'E is! The Tomb's newest figh'er is runnin' straight at our resident murder machine!"

"Those weird energy shields of his aren't even active anymore—does he have a death wish?"

"I don't think 'e can control it, Matt. The two times the shields 'ave popped out were when the TK-97 was attackin' 'im."

"Then let's hope they kick in again, 'cause it's about to get bloody up in THE TOMB!"

Kick in they did. Unprepared for its prey to charge head on, the vyss'n hesitated, all Kenton needed to close the gap. Seizing it about the neck, he began whaling on the startled beast.

He broke its carpals and metacarpals. He cracked its tarsals, femurs, and scapulae. He pounded until a section of its skull collapsed in, and he shattered each protruding knob of its spine. He drove the sharp points of his slyrs through the vyss'n's eyes and pressed his sparking shields to its hide until the dulled scales started to smoke and char.

Kenton took out his anger and frustration on the creature, beating it in equal measure for every punch and kick he'd received since his capture. He couldn't hit the soldiers who'd spat at him, the scientists who'd opened him up and turned him into a conduit for the violent frix flowing through his bones, and he couldn't hit Her, so he struck the vyss'n in their place, venting all his rage and helplessness in a storm of savage fists.

He drove the vyss'n—insensate with pain—to the pool, forced it into the water it so hated, and sliced open its underbelly the instant its scaly skin softened enough to allow his slyrs to pierce the leathery hide. Blood gushed from the raptor in an almost black red into the churning waves.

Kenton could have stopped there.

It would die, whether or not he delivered the killing blow himself. He'd gone too far, seeing in place of the wild animal the faces of his captors and torturers. The vyss'n still struggled weakly, trying to bite at him with a jaw missing most of its teeth.

Kenton let the slyrs dissipate, calling the burning energy back into himself, and knelt beside the once-mighty creature's head, running a hand gently over the mangled, deformed skull.

"You didn't deserve this," he whispered to it, struggling to hold back tears. "I am sorry."

But he couldn't leave the broken animal to the tender mercy of the whitecoats. No one else would suffer by their hands if he could prevent it.

He let the vyss'n's head loll into the tainted water and flooded the pool with frix. It glowed dimly at first—his nerves twisting in pinching pain as he pushed the burning energy through himself one last time—before shining so brightly it blocked Kenton's face from the ever watchful cameras. A white blank filled the hanging holoscreens and the growing brightness obscured him from the hushed crowd.

He continued to hold the creature as it died, pressing his forehead against it, begging over and over for forgiveness for the ghastly death he'd inflicted upon it. The vyss'n twitched and jerked and lay still, and Kenton let a tear trickle down his muddy cheek before he wiped it away to rise and face the crowds.

He felt awful. He was tired, aching, and he'd just killed, in the most horrible way, a creature only trying to survive. It hadn't known any better. It'd been just as much as a victim as he.

But compassion for the vyss'ngryr was the last thing his captors wanted to see. If he was to win their trust and undermine them from the inside until he could bring about his freedom, he'd have to stay the course they'd laid out for him. He needed to pretend to be pliable and agreeable, someone other than himself. So Kenton raised a fist to the ceiling of the Tomb in a mimicry of victory.

And he smiled.

16

"You have to leave New Little Rock as soon as we're done talking. Doctor Riven placed a bounty on your head, and he's not the only one."

"But our ruse worked—he'd given up looking for me!" Laine jumped to his feet, too agitated to sit in the suddenly too-small apartment.

"That was before you blew up a mountain, you idiot."

Laine cringed. Yoon Ah wasn't partial to insults, even when people deserved them, so her harsh words meant the situation was much worse than her clipped tone implied. He projected his borrowed clip's display, taking in Yoon Ah's worn appearance when her face flickered into view.

She looked older than fifteen, her current hair colour matching the redness of her eyes. Behind her, Andy was busily typing away, though he waved once he saw Laine had connected the visuals, and Laine realised the two of them had called him from Doctor Frenally's nightmare-inducing basement lab.

"The commander's been keeping it secret I'm here, how—?"

"Maybe if y'didn't tick off so many people they'd be more inclined not to snitch, mate. Far as I've been able t'figure, your whereabouts an' what you did to the Kansor Mountains was leaked from a computer system registered to New Little Rock High."

"Jersey Number Seven," Laine muttered darkly. He clenched his jaw as he pictured the lacrosse player's scowling face. It had to be him, still stinging from his defeat months prior, and Laine abruptly found himself wishing he hadn't laughed so openly in the faces of the New Little Rock students.

"How'd you even find out about this? And why are you holed up in your dad's lab?"

"Ever since you left, I've been scouring the edda-net, watching for anything that could help. Andy also set me up with a program that lets me listen in on any of the official channels—and some of the unofficial ones."

Yoon Ah paused, biting her lip and scrubbing at her face with a shaking hand. "I've heard more than I ever cared to about the Consul's plans to root out the Cabal—enough to make me think maybe we've got that situation all upside down and backwards. But nothing with your name ever popped up. Until today.

"You're packing, right? You're not just standing there? I mean it when I say you have to get out of town. Andy's blocking all attempts to hijack our conversation, but even Doctor Frenally's security won't hinder Skytown's best for long. The bounty's high, Laine. Your uncle wants you—the Consul wants you and your lokian friend, and I don't think either of them much mind in what condition they get you."

Yoon Ah's face filled the screen, her eyes brimming

with an intense urgency.

"Andy's scrubbing all evidence of our conversation here, so get in touch when you're safe, if you can get a secure-ish line. We'll be listening. But they're on their way, so go!"

Laine stood in shock for a moment before he dashed to the kitchen-turned-guestroom he and Bo had been sharing and hastily stuffed all his belongings into his pack while shrugging on his jacket. Bo appeared in the doorway, Shannon perched on his shoulders.

"I heard voices—" Bo's gaze landed on the half-zipped bag in Laine's hands, and his brows knit together, ears flattening.

"Get Woodley," Laine instructed, thoughts all a-jumble as he started gathering up Bo's things as well. "Yoon Ah called—"

"Our time in New Little Rock just ran out," Bo finished for him. He set Shannon down and ran for the stairs.

Woodley ushered them through a shadowed alley, Shannon Beth on her hip, a charged sol glowing brightly in her hands. They'd left the likely-compromised clip on the kitchen table, stuffing food and weapons into their bags while Woodley had paged her sister-in-law. Despite having a plan in place for just such an emergency, the commander hadn't sounded happy her hand was being forced so soon.

"Hold your breath," Woodley told them, pressing an oxygen mask to Shannon's tiny face as she slid away a grate set into the paving at the very end of the alley. "These tunnels are saturated with lethal levels of carbon monoxide, but they're the fastest way to Mission Control without being seen."

Laine stared into the dark entrance, lit only by the weapons they carried. The last time he'd gone willingly into a small, dark space he'd almost not made it back. He inhaled and exhaled, trying to gulp down as much oxygen as he could, both to heed Woodley's warning and to try and keep himself calm. Still, his hands shook as he took a final breath and stepped after Bo, ducking to keep his crosse from scraping against the low roof.

Laine ran, his muscles protesting at each jolting step, his head pounding, as still-tender lungs screamed for him to breathe. So much of his life revolved around running—from danger, into it, *through* it—would it ever end? The months before Mom had fallen ill had been the most peaceful days he could remember, and he'd been starting to accept his mostly trouble-free life—enjoy it even. He should have known the reprieve wouldn't, couldn't last.

Oxygen blurted from Laine, and he gasped in air before he could stop himself. The gulping breaths didn't ease his dizziness, and he stumbled and fell to his knees, wheezing and nauseous.

Where was the end of the tunnel? It had been in front of him moments ago, but a dull grey was all he could see. He heard muttered exclamations in a language he didn't understand, and then Bo was there, hauling him out of the darkness and into an almost-too-bright room.

"Cutting it close, Lieutenant," the commander said.

Laine blinked, sucking in deep lungfuls of uncontaminated air. And promptly vomited all over the commander's boots. He wiped his mouth and shuffled back, cheeks burning. Laine kept his head low as he accepted Woodley's oxygen mask, not wanting to meet her eyes and see the pity doubtless gathered there.

Before Laine could quite recover, he and Bo were bundled alongside Woodley into the back of an armoured hovertruck. They sped out from New Little Rock alongside two other identical vehicles that split off, heading north and northeast. Their truck headed south before turning east, the route chosen to throw off any pursuers watching for them.

"Hope this isn't the last I see of you boys," Woodley said, gripping the handle that hung from the roof as the hovertruck swayed back and forth. "Skytown; it's not a place I'd go on a good day, and there aren't many of them in that city."

"There's no good places with Mom gone," Laine replied, angry that Gordon had once again forced him to flee a place he'd just been beginning to enjoy. He'd have liked not to have made Shannon Beth cry when he and Bo bid her a hasty goodbye. He knew if he touched the lokian's fur, he'd find it still damp from where she'd sobbed inconsolably against Bo's shoulder.

Woodley curled her hands into fists. "I get what

you mean. Some days I wish I'd never heard of Thorunn. Tom might . . ." She trailed off, staring out of the slitted windows for a long while before turning to address Bo.

"The climb up Mount Lalethusl is a hard one, and Laine hasn't fully healed from that fall he took. We'll stall the soldiers and bounty hunters long as we can, and hopefully they'll follow the decoys until you boys reach Skytown, but, watch out for each other? You saved Shannon, and I can't bear the thought of anything happening to you."

Bo and Laine nodded, and the transport sped on in silence, rendered almost invisible by the chsaarhee wings the New Little Rock soldiers had scavenged from the dead birds. Laine breathed slowly, still feeling the aftereffects of inhaling so much carbon monoxide.

Bo, on the other hand, seemed to grow more and more excited with each mile, ears and tail twitching as his hands clenched and unclenched.

Laine hoped Kenton was still alive, else Bo might just burn down Skytown before he could find evidence of Gordon's treachery. What proof there was to be had in the capital he didn't know. But as long as his uncle pursued him, he had to keep pressing forward. Laine reached beneath his jacket and touched the beaded necklace that sat heavy against his chest. Even if it took him one year or ten, he'd make Gordon pay for what he'd done.

And . . . he might see Dad in Skytown.

Was he ready for that? Could he face Dad, with all

of their history between them, and tell him that not only had Mom, had Mom, that she, well, that what had happened had happened, but that his own brother was responsible? Laine shuddered, face flushing as his eyes started to prickle, and he pressed his forearm against his face, turned his back to the others, and willed himself to think of other things until he could shove down the hot feelings twisting his stomach into knots.

The hovertruck shuddered to a halt as the last of the sun's rays began to fade on the western horizon. The landscape had changed dramatically, and New Little Rock was nowhere to be seen. Gone were the open, flat plains and the misshapen outline of the Kansor Mountains. Instead, the thickly forested slopes of Mount Lalethusl towered misty and forbidding above them. Laine couldn't help noticing they'd come to rest far from the trailing path leading up the mountain.

Woodley chuckled when she saw him looking.

"I shouldn't think I have to warn you boys to steer clear of the road? This is as close as we can come without being stopped and questioned." She let out a long sigh as Laine and Bo clambered out of the hovertruck and checked that their packs were secure.

"Hopefully," she continued, "the Skytown soldiers won't think to check this side of the mountain until they've worn themselves out chasing after the commander's diversion." Woodley placed a hand on Bo's and Laine's shoulders, a firm yet comforting touch in the face of the unknown wilderness they were about to brave.

To Bo she said, "If even half of what you told me about your friend is true, I hope you find him," before hugging him and then Laine. "I meant what I said earlier. You both mean more to me than I can say, and I just really need you to be okay out there."

With that, she strode back to the grey vehicle, started it, and rumbled away, leaving Laine and Bo shading their faces against the dust and debris the engines kicked up.

"Smoketown has vercycles," Bo said as he trudged alongside Laine to the edge of the forest waiting eagerly to swallow them up. "It was the first place we hit for that reason, since New Little Rock's barrier was still up at the time, and the other outpost towns would have noticed half of their fleet going missing."

"I take it Smoketown's too large to notice the loss of two more?"

Bo hefted his pack and brushed aside some low hanging branches, stepping carefully into the woods proper. "With all eyes looking for us, we can only hope."

He let the branches spring back, and Laine spluttered as twigs scraped across his face. He swore, but Bo had already forged ahead, forcing Laine to keep up or be left behind.

The light dimmed rapidly after the sun set, the forest canopy high above not letting even a sliver of moonlight penetrate the shadowed ground they tramped, and Laine struggled to keep track of where

Bo was, trying—and failing—not to be envious of the lokian's ability to see in the dark. More than once Laine started to reach for his clip to check the hour but stopped short each time upon remembering it was speeding through the stars to Earth, safely nestled in the bag of some unsuspecting traveller. He'd probably never get it back.

He kept climbing. Each step hurt. New Little Rock's physical therapist had wanted him to push himself harder, but Laine didn't think she'd imagined he'd go and trek up another mountain, at least not before he'd fully recovered.

But he refused to complain. Bo would just mock him, thinking him a weak, fragile human, despite all they'd been through. Resolving to ignore the pain that stabbed through him every time he put his foot down, Laine gritted his teeth and carried on, following Bo through miles of endless, uphill forest until they reached a massive tree with a trunk like smooth stone.

"Here," Bo said, pointing to the vines twined about it. "We can go up and sleep unmolested."

"It's so quiet," Laine remarked as he pulled himself up to the large branches, wide enough for him to lie on without fear of falling. "Is your forest like this?"

Bo shook his head, illuminated the tiniest bit by grey light filtering down through a gap in the tree-tops. "Our forest is alive. This . . ." He shuddered and ran a gloved hand over the curiously smooth bark. "This place is dead. Your people killed most of the klia'ans that lived here and drove the rest away. We tried to help. We sent"—Bo swallowed, struggling with the retelling—"sent messengers over the sea, but either our trading partners didn't care or the distance and storms kept them away. Regardless, there are no more klia'ans here now."

Laine's nausea made a sudden reappearance as he processed what Bo was implying—no, outright stating. No matter how many times he heard it, he struggled to fully accept the purported crimes of Thorunn's first settlers. The planet was supposed to be a place for people to learn from their mistakes, not repeat them.

"That's—first you tell me Kenton's whole family, along with the entire Apollo XXII colony, was destroyed for daring to side with lokians, and now you're saying the Consul would sanction what, genocide, xenocide?"

Bo waved a hand. "Whatever you wanna call it. Tribe Anshi was here, now they're not. And the ones responsible have done a—what's the word? Meticulous. A meticulous job of covering up the truth and poisoning the unknowing against us. Or can you truly say you wouldn't have killed me in a heartbeat the night you shot us down, just for being who I am, if you hadn't been injured?"

Laine couldn't. He remembered how good it had felt to watch Kenton and Bo's hovercar spiral out of the air, remembered the absolute exhilaration that had thrilled through him when he'd realised he'd bested a lokian. If Mom had known of his deep disdain for the lokians she would have been more deeply disappointed in him than for anything he'd ever done, and she'd come to collect him from the back of a police transport too many times to count.

She'd raised him better than that; she'd tried to teach him through her own example to be compassionate and kind, merciful and considerate. Laine had spurned her gentle reproofs, her love, rejecting her attempts at reasoning with him, all because she'd let go of her hurt towards Dad. Laine had let the man's broken promises fester and build inside of him, growing angrier at each kind word Mom had for his father, taking it for granted that she'd always be there, that he'd have a chance in the future to make it up to her.

There were no more chances now.

"Get comfortable," Bo whispered into the stillness, interrupting Laine's thoughts. "I'll take first watch."

———————— ● ————————

<u>*January Sixteen, 2231, Day Two of Testing:*</u>

"Subject 742 remains co-operative, thus today we are measuring stress response levels."

The taped footage from that first awful day at the Tomb was playing on the monitors again. It was as if Kenton's captors hoped the sickening visuals would inspire him to perform for them while they avidly recorded everything. He fiddled with the wires attached to him and tried to block out the sounds, glancing everywhere in the average-size lab except at the holoscreens.

The whitecoat who'd been speaking tapped his holoscreen, and the treadmill Kenton stood on started to move, forcing him from a measured jog to a tight sprint in a matter of moments. They ran the room slightly too hot, and sweat trickled down Kenton's neck as he tried to keep his breathing under control. His forearms burned with restless energy pulsing just below the surface, yearning to be set free.

Kenton clamped down on the feeling. The whitecoats could never know he could control the slyrs at will. No matter how much his skin felt like it was blistering from the inside out, he had to maintain the fiction, his only advantage when they'd taken everything else from him.

> *"Heart rate at 120 BPM and climbing.*
> *130, 135, 140—still no manifestation.*
> *Variables will now be introduced."*

Kenton hardly had time to ponder what the whitecoat meant before a hard sphere the size of an orange shot at him. A twisting dodge took him out of harm's way, but Kenton lost his footing and went flying off the end of the treadmill, crashing into a cart of test equipment, and landing in an ungainly heap amidst newly shattered beakers and overturned boxes of balances and cylinders. The slyrs threatened to burst from Kenton's arms—that was the closest his captors had come to surprising him into manifesting them—but he bit back both the fear and the almost overwhelming urge to trace the writhing blue lines which sent tingles racing through his fingertips and clambered to his feet.

He had to centre himself, to ignore the sensation of so many shards of glass scraping his muscles raw each time he forced the frix back. Using them was almost effortless, holding them back a torment. At least he could attribute his heavy breathing and the look of agony screwing up his features to having been thrown halfway across the room. Small mercies, Kenton supposed.

January Eighteen, 2231, Day Four of Testing:

"Subject 742 continues to display a remarkable ability to adapt to ever-increasing high intensity scenarios. Manifestation remains elusive, so live combat has been introduced."

Kenton crunched down on his apple. At least they were feeding him, keeping him in tip-top shape to get the best results from their testing. He hadn't told them he was starting to taste again, the juices of the crisp fruit running down his tongue with just a hint of its full sweetness.

A fresh faced Hexagon soldier—a new cadet by the wide-eyed look of her—walked into the lab, Kenton's cue to shuffle into the padded space that took up a large square in the middle of the room. Boxing ring ropes ran along each side, swaying gently as Kenton clambered over them.

The cadet, looking apprehensive yet determined, also climbed into the ring. She was young, not more than a few years older than Kenton if he had to guess, sporting close-cropped, blue hair coiled in tiny, intricate curls.

Kenton lunged at her, landing a soft blow before skipping back to assess her reaction. The soldier's arms had instinctively moved to block her face, and Kenton shook his head at the poor training she must have received.

"You had three opportunities to strike me just now," he said, tapping his neck, torso, and groin in quick succession. He deliberately turned his back on the soldier to address the whitecoats, whose eyes were hyena-wide at his precise demonstration of control.

"This is the level of sparring partner you pit against me? Has she even finished her training?"

The cadet took that moment to try for a surprise attack, but Kenton had been listening for the rustle of her training fatigues; oddly, there was a jangle too, likely concealed jewellery of some sort. Before she could react, Kenton whipped around and caught her forearm, twisting it out and away from her body, putting her on her back with a ruthless efficiency that made pride bubble up in him. He pushed the heady feeling away, determined not to let hubris overtake him.

The soldier struggled to regain her footing, but Kenton pressed her back to the ground until she yielded, keeping his voice soft as he whispered some advice to her.

"I don't know what they've been teaching you, but consider that when a stronger opponent turns his back on you, it's not because he's being foolish."

The soldier nodded, and Kenton stepped back, offering his hand, which she accepted despite the humiliation burning in her eyes, and they took their places again.

January Twenty-One, 2231, Day Seven of Testing:

"Subject 742 holds his own against multiple combatants, easily dispatching groups of five or more with a fighting style having no exact equivalent to what we've seen before.

Manifestation is close, and testing has been modified to allow nightly fights at the Tomb, with the public none the wiser regarding the true identity of Skytown's newest sensation.

Kenton had to give credit where credit was due, the whitecoats were nothing if not persistent. They'd come close—precariously close—to forcing Kenton's slyrs to erupt. But each near success only taught Kenton how to further suppress the frix, to push it deeper and deeper until the constant burning was almost an afterthought, just another ache to add to the long list of pains plaguing him from the torture and rapid healing he'd undergone.

The frustration on their faces at each inevitable failure was a small comfort in the living nightmare that was his every waking moment. He did everything else they wanted but never that, and no matter how much they poked and prodded, Kenton's slyrs stayed stubbornly inside his arms. Only when they pushed his pulse close to two hundred beats per minute did the crackling frix start to emerge from his skin, and each time they tried that, Kenton clamped down so hard on the impulse to release the electricity that he ended up convulsing on the floor, convinced the alien heart grafted inside him would finally give out.

"Please," said one of the scientists Kenton had come to think of as "Assistant Whitecoat II." "Just give us something." The electrodes he placed on Kenton were cold, as always. "I'd really like to be off this rotation."

And Kenton wanted to be free, but neither of them could give the other what they wanted. Another nameless, faceless whitecoat would be brought in soon enough in any case; the testing controllers switched out the teams whenever extreme fatigue started to get the best of the scientists. Kenton wasn't above trying to draw out each session as long as possible—outwardly in the name of being helpful, but the long hours inconvenienced everybody, so the weariness that overwhelmed Kenton at the end of each day was worth even the tiniest and most subtle of victories.

"What makes you think you'll be taken off this rotation if my slyrs do show today?" he asked Assistant Whitecoat II.

The man scrubbed at his beard and let out a long sigh. "No, no, you're right. Getting the results they want will probably mean more work for me."

He'd dropped the pleading note from his tone, the despondence that crept in causing Kenton to look at him sharply. He had the same nervous energy as the others, but less manic somehow, more—afraid?

The man observed Kenton with bloodshot eyes, his mouth pulled tight at the corners, a permanent frown seeming to have settled on a face that might otherwise be inviting. A pale strip of skin encircled his ring finger where a band must once have sat, the dark brown of his eyes familiar in a way Kenton couldn't quite place. As he scrutinised the man further, he noticed a prisoner clip attached to Assistant Whitecoat II's ear, similar in model to the ones Kenton kept deliberately shorting out and then blaming on his inability to control the latent frix the scientists sought so desperately to harness.

Who was this man?

"I never did get your name," Kenton voiced softly, startled to see panic flash across the man's face before he ducked his head.

"Ah, what's in a name?" he said, continuing to fiddle with the nodes that would send biological information to the computers clustered in the corner of the room.

Everything, Kenton thought. *That's how they break you, how they unmake you.* He hadn't heard himself referred to as anything other than "prisoner" or "subject 742" since they'd forcibly gifted with him with the frix slyrs. He ached to be called something, anything else. Even "Outpost Terrorist" would do in a pinch. At least that title conveyed something other than his utter meaningless beyond the experiment they'd turned him into.

Assistant Whitecoat II patted his arm. "That's the last of them. Anyhow, make today the day?"

Kenton shrugged. "Make your tests properly threatening."

They couldn't throw anything less than an entire army at him and expect him to cower. Not after he'd faced a vyss'n and walked away unscathed.

Day eight of testing passed—a new rotation of scientists taking over the monitoring—then day nine and day ten, and still Kenton soothed the lightning running through his veins, growing stronger bit by bit with the constant training, supplemented by the proper rest and nutritious food they allowed him, hoping a healthy Kenton could be pushed harder and further until they got what they wanted.

Assistant Whitecoat II eventually returned, looking more harrowed and ill than before. As he bent to attach the customary monitoring devices, Kenton said, in a very low voice,

"You're a prisoner here, like me."

Assistant Whitecoat II jerked back, the whole array

of instruments going with him and clattering to the ground, the crash drawing the attention of every person in the room.

"626!" the lead whitecoat barked, his stride promising punishment as he approached Kenton and the trembling man. "Do you know how much money you've just cost us? How much time?"

He backhanded 626 across the face. An instant bruise blossomed on the man's sallow skin. "Clean this up, and reset immediately! No more of this nonsense, or She'll hear about it. Is that what you want?"

626 mumbled an apology and got to his knees, none of the others coming over to help him. He gave Kenton a look that strongly suggested he should stay put when he made a move to assist.

The only upside to the situation was that the sudden change in tone made it very clear to Kenton which whitecoats worked willingly on the testing and which had also been coerced. Not all the men and woman who were there under duress wore prisoner clips, but their tight, drawn faces gave them away, and even when order had been restored, they moved like skittish deer, afraid to jar anything and attract the ire of the project leader.

"Have they been punishing you for my inability to manifest?" Kenton asked quietly.

A single nod was his only answer.

"They send you to Her?"

"Not yet," the man whispered back. "I haven't screwed up that badly. But they have been threatening us with it."

Kenton closed his eyes, a sick feeling beginning to churn in his stomach. His refusal to turn loose the frix inside him was actively hurting other people, other prisoners like him. It would be so easy to let go, to stop the pain that had him clenching his teeth to keep the sparking frix at bay.

But each time Kenton even began to entertain the thought of releasing his slyrs outside of a scenario where he was believably frightened for his life, his mind swam with visions of hundreds—maybe even thousands—of frix-enhanced Skytown soldiers storming the Hinnom Forest and burning it to the ground. As long as the whitecoats thought the frix they'd implanted in him manifested unpredictably, they'd be wary of repeating the procedure, and Kenton would not, *could not* reveal otherwise, not even to spare the prisoner whitecoats from further torment.

"Alright, last one today, and we're done." The lead whitecoat shook his head as he flicked his finger to scroll through the day's test findings on his holo-screen. "This is ridiculous. All the research that went into perfecting the mind-body integration of pros-thetic tech, and we squandered it on this project, wasting time and energy, going through prisoner clips like you wouldn't believe, and still, exactly zero consistent results. Starting to think Ms. Anland's giv-en us an impossible task."

"With the right touch and proper application, any-thing is possible."

Kenton shrank back against the wall at that unmistakable voice. He knew her touch intimately, and shivers washed over him at the memory of her fingers tracing patterns on his skin with his own blood.

"None of you have an active enough imagination. All the boy needs is a push, don't you, darling?" she said, addressing the last words to Kenton. "When's Shadow's next match?"

"T-ten minutes, but 742's not ready for a fighter of his calibre!" the tech stammered, rushing to clear a path for the Torturer to step through.

"Make him ready. I've a special guest with me today. The High Consul wanted to observe the proceedings"—she paused, drawing out the tension caused by her mere presence—"personally."

She turned to Kenton, gesturing for him to come forward. Mental irons held him in place until being overridden by the suggestion of what she'd do to him if he failed to comply. Trembling, Kenton stepped off the treadmill and approached her.

"See how well I've trained him, Cousin?" she said to a man just coming into the room. "His acquiescence is simply delightful, isn't it?"

She took Kenton's face in her hands, eyes narrowing in a cruel smile at the flinch he couldn't suppress.

"See how he shakes like a leaf? But he knows better than to pull away. You'll manifest those—what was that quaint name the techs tell me you came up with? Slyrs?—for me in the Tomb, won't you, darling?"

She stroked his cheek gently, and Kenton's skin

crawled. The touch of her burned where it lingered against each exposed inch of his flesh. She was still looking at him expectantly, her grip on his chin turning painful as her nails dug deep enough to draw blood.

"I don't, I, I—"

"Won't you?"

"Y-yes, ma'am."

The Torturer let go of Kenton and stepped aside so that the man who'd followed her into the room could observe him clearly.

"742 looks better than the last time I saw him," the High Consul remarked. "Hopefully this session won't end with a termination attempt."

The words sounded so cold and unfeeling, as if the cousins discussed a machine and not a person. Kenton raised his eyes from the floor to get a glimpse of the man who talked so cavalierly about the lengths to which his cousin's torment had driven him.

The High Consul was tall, darkly handsome, and impeccably dressed. He held himself like a soldier, and Kenton almost expected him to have a sol in his hands. He wondered why for a moment, and then as the High Consul caught Kenton looking at him, the man smiled, in a horribly familiar way.

"Rolv Anland. I don't think we've been formally introduced. You certainly were quite the thorn in our sides, but now you'll be the greatest asset the Consul's ever had, and we'll finally be able to finish the work we began almost a decade ago."

Kenton nearly crumpled to the floor in shock as he

at last identified why the High Consul's easy manner struck such a chord of wrongness inside him.

The last time he'd seen that face, he'd been holding a broken string of pearls.

It was clear the man didn't recognise him, didn't place him as the little boy he'd once taunted before murdering his baby sister right in front of him. For so long, Kenton had thought him just some nameless, faceless soldier; but the man was in fact the High Consul of Skytown. He hadn't just carried out the attack against Kenton's family—he'd ordered it.

This man—and his cousin—had destroyed Kenton's life twice over, and if he didn't stop them, they'd happily do so a third time. Every atom in Kenton's body strained for him to lunge at Consul Rolv, to beat him until he would rise no more, and in the back of his mind, Kenton felt a stab of shame at the bloodlust that rose so easily in him.

Fear and a stirring of wisdom held him back: the knowledge of what the Torturer could do to him and the fact that it was not yet time. Kenton resolved that the man would be brought to justice for his crimes—his inhumanities—but today was not that day.

Today he had a match to win in the Tomb.

"Test me all you want; I'll never fight against my people for you," Kenton said softly. As long as he looked at Consul Rolv and not the sadist next to him, he could stand his ground. "Not even if she commands it. I'll die first; you know I will."

"You insolent—" the Torturer began, but the High

Consul caught his cousin by the crook of her elbow, ushering her away.

"Weren't you just saying we need to have an expansive imagination? I'm sure under your tender mercies he'll come around. Let's depart. It wouldn't do for the High Consul to be late to a state-arranged Tomb visit, would it?"

He swept out of the room, his cousin following, but not before levelling a look at Kenton that promised a private session with her whether or not he came away victorious from the upcoming fight.

"What insanity compelled you to provoke her?" the lead whitecoat spat, whirling on Kenton. "Her playing with you will set us back days—weeks even, and that's if you survive your match with Shadow to begin with." He set down his holoscreen and began to jab at the controls to shut down the monitoring equipment for the day.

Kenton said nothing, focusing every thought and impulse to keep his breathing under control, to not let the anxiety dashing around inside of him show on his face. But despite his dislike of the Tomb, the prospect of sparring against someone who promised to be a more challenging opponent than the vyss'ngryr intrigued Kenton, and he found himself not entirely unwillingly following the whitecoats as they hurried him down the hall and up a set of stairs to the Tomb's antechamber-slash-prep room.

"There 'e is!"

Kenton recognised the voice as Brett's, and when he looked to the announcers' booth he noticed Brett and Matt had been joined by a pretty woman who introduced herself as Jolene. Kenton wondered if they'd be as excited to intern at the Tomb if they knew at least half its participants fought under duress, only putting on a show because She would tear them to pieces otherwise.

Kenton didn't dwell on the thoughts for long, bracing himself as opening remarks were made, and the gate lifted to reveal a hooded figure holding a bo staff whom the sportscasters dramatically announced as, "the ever elusive, always mysterious, Shadow."

Shadow sprang at Kenton immediately. Kenton ducked low, rolled out of the way and snapped the quirn in his hand out to full length.

The full-face mask Shadow wore forced Kenton to anticipate his movements through body language alone, and the long robes Shadow wore made even that irritatingly difficult. The flowing fabric didn't in the slightest impede Shadow's graceful feints and parries, and every calculated blow he made pushed Kenton farther and farther across the Tomb.

Kenton ducked and spun, parried and struck, not yet ready to unleash the frix groaning in the sinews of his muscles.

Shadow moved like his namesake, slipping over rocks and boulders, contracting just out of Kenton's reach, then stretching impossibly long and landing multiple hits that Kenton struggled to counter, let alone return. Shadow fought at a completely different level than the Skytown soldiers, and Kenton started to smile, a genuine thing he couldn't hold back at the first real challenge he'd had since his initial bout in the Tomb. Shadow's unexpected moves forced him to give ground as fast as he gained it, and Kenton's blood started to thrum in his veins, the frix singing to him, pleading to be set free.

A quick glance up at the stands confirmed that the High Consul and his cousin were indeed in attendance at the match, and she raised one perfectly manicured eyebrow upon catching Kenton looking. Disappointing her would only bring pain, and it would be so easy to let the frix flow through him, his compliance saving him from a trip back to that blood-soaked room. But they couldn't be allowed to know he could summon the sparking energy on command, so Kenton gritted his teeth, his smile turning false, and turned his attention back to Shadow and the sandy floor of the Tomb.

Kenton held himself motionless, and the next time Shadow slipped past, whipped out with his quirn, catching hold of the hooded fighter when he twisted out of the way, tumbling them both to the ground. Shadow writhed beneath Kenton, but his legs had been tangled in his robes, and Kenton wrestled him into a chokehold.

"Yield," he rasped, breathing hard from the dual effort of keeping Shadow pinned and his slyrs battened down. "Yield, and I'll release you before you lose consciousness."

Kenton waited for the frantic tapping on his person that would signify the concession of the match. It never came. Still, Kenton held on, despite the fact that

Shadow stopped struggling once Kenton increased pressure on the man's throat.

The lack of movement had to be a ruse. If Kenton fell for it, he'd find himself face-down in the dirt with an arm around his neck. The consequences of losing with Her watching would be . . . disagreeable.

Out of the corner of his eye, Kenton saw the High Consul stand, most likely to call the match, and relief rushed through him.

That was when Shadow surged upright, heaving Kenton off him with strength beyond what Kenton had been prepared for. The quirn went flying from his hand, and Kenton rolled head over heels across the uneven ground before slamming into the base of a nearby tree. He jumped to his feet and reached for his weapon, stopping short when Shadow's robes detached and fell away as Shadow—

Changed.

Heavy robes billowed in the air like the flags of a rescuing army come suddenly over the hills at daybreak. Gloves split at their seams, claws bursting through the thick leather, arms lengthening, legs drawing up. The mask fell away, revealing white and black patterning surrounding snow-shadow blue eyes as a huge mass of sinew and teeth seemed to blot out the lights of the deathly silent arena.

The burning scent of crackling electricity slammed Kenton's awareness back into him, as somehow, his arms flew up into an "X," the white-blue intensity of raw, agonising frix throwing the battleground of the Tomb into stark relief.

The crowd stood as one, their shock at the unexpected transformation and Kenton's instinctive reaction a dull roar at the edges of Kenton's hearing.

"Tribe Anshi," Kenton breathed in S'hinoian. A slight twitch of Shadow's ear was the only indication the lithe klia'an resembling a snow leopard had heard him. "The scouts reported—no one survived."

Shadow padded around him, deftly stepping over his torn clothes, remnants of which hung from his belt and wristlets he still wore.

Kenton turned as Shadow continued to circle him, one half rotation bringing the High Consul into his line of sight. The man was still standing, an undecipherable look on his face. Soldiers to the left and right of him had hands on their sols, casting nervous glances between the impassive face of the High Consul and the improbable scene on the Tomb floor.

Shadow bunched his muscles to spring forward and growled low, a rumble that vibrated through Kenton's bones and prompted a round of excited jabbering from the three young sportscasters about what the snarling and bared fangs meant for Kenton's immediate future.

Kenton didn't have to guess; he understood every word. He parried when Shadow sprang at him, but not with lethal intent, just enough to keep up the ruse that he was battling for his life against the Tomb's top fighter—who had turned out to have more secrets than anyone knew, if he understood Matt, Brett, and Jolene correctly.

Shadow growled at him in terse battle speech,

slipping guttural s'hinioan between thrusts and feints.

"Half a decade of fights, and the one person who's forced me to reveal myself in all that time somehow knows my language? 'W' might just be right about you, Stormsurge. Speak with 626. He'll fill you in on our plans to destroy the corruption rotting Skytown from the inside out."

"The prisoner whitecoat? He's mixed up in . . . whatever this is? And who's 'W'?"

That was a question Kenton himself had been asked by the Torturer during those endless nights of suffering. He'd never in his life heard of "W" before coming to Skytown, despite his bold claims to the contrary the day he'd finally given up.

Shadow sprang at Kenton and pinned his arms to the floor where his slyrs wouldn't do much good unless Kenton flooded them with dangerous amounts of frix. He began to let the current build, wincing at the painful tingling while he waited for the answer, no longer afraid, only curious, thrillingly curious.

"The leader of the Cabal, and someone, I think, who has a vested interest in meeting you."

"Me?" Kenton mouthed, but Shadow didn't answer him, darting back as if sensing the rising levels of frix Kenton held ready to unleash.

"Attack," Shadow growled. "Come at me like you intend to kill me, and I'll show you something."

Kenton struck at the klia'an, nerves alight with frix and not a little excitement.

Shadow danced and ducked backward, drawing

them both towards the wall—an odd move for an experienced fighter. Kenton followed him regardless, taking the bait and hurling his forearm at Shadow.

The energy shield missed as Shadow spun away at the last possible instant, and Kenton's right slyr smashed through the plaster of the wall instead, catching onto the electricity running through the walls and snaring him tight. The fallen quirn was just by his foot, and he struggled towards it, managing to kick it into his free hand as Shadow prepared to pounce, lashing his tail to the delight of the screaming onlookers.

Kenton bashed at the plaster above and below his trapped arm, wincing at the stabbing jolts each hit produced. Somehow the frix in his veins kept him from being electrocuted, but he could feel the skin on his hands begin to blister as the sheer force of the current in the Tomb's walls coursed reckless through him, sticking him in place. He struck harder, throwing a desperate glance Shadow's way.

The klia'an wasn't really going to assault him when Kenton couldn't fight back, was he? Not after his clipped talk of seeking out 626 for answers. The look in Shadow's blue eyes showed only violence, driving Kenton to bash the cracking plaster with everything he had left, disregarding the awkward angle and wrenching his shoulder away from the wall as he poured every last bit of his frix into the current entangling him.

The Tomb went dark.

Kenton stumbled at the sudden loss of contact,

falling to his knees in a shower of sparks that was the only light in the blackened arena. Clips in the stands began to flicker with tiny pinpricks that illuminated the frightened faces of their owners, and Kenton heard angry shouting, a cry of pain, and then whirring as the Tomb's backup generators kicked in, casting the disturbed sands of the arena in an eerie green-yellow.

The sickly glow disclosed a truth Kenton had suspected from the moment the lights blew—no, from before, when Shadow had intentionally lured him to the wall, a suicidal move from a tactical standpoint.

The klia'an had disappeared.

Kenton kept his face towards the ground where the camera couldn't see him and let a small smile turn up the corners of his mouth. For the first time since the slyrs had been forcibly inserted, they were quiet where they hummed below his skin, having retracted the moment Kenton had jerked free of the current—hot, but not burning.

He'd thought himself alone, forced to keep himself tightly under control lest his captors suss out the truth and use him to create an army in his image, but Kenton no longer battled the frix, his thoughts reaching some form of peace for the first time since he'd been captured. He had allies. Who or whatever the Cabal was, they seemed aligned with his goal of stopping Consul Rolv and his insidious plans.

Kenton allowed himself one last smile and stood, tilting his head in defiance at the High Consul and his cousin. They'd wanted a show—they'd gotten one.

17

Laine opened his eyes to the unwelcome sight of his uncle standing over him.

"Gordon, what?"

Hadn't he just been in the middle of a lifeless forest on his way to Smoketown? Laine felt around, expecting the unforgiving wood of the tree in which he'd fallen asleep, but soft grass met his fingers—the grass of the field he'd ugly cried in until he'd thought his heart would burst.

"Get up, kid," his uncle said, a worn look on his face. "It's late. Let's go home. The hospital will call when it's time to collect Alanna's things."

Laine pushed himself off the ground, rubbing at his eyes and regretting it when dirt blurred his vision. "Weren't, weren't you going to ship me off to Earth?"

"I wish. Do you think I grow endless credits in my lab? Interstellar travel ain't cheap. Took all I had plus your parents' life savings to get y'all here in the first place. And what do I have to show for it? A traitor brother, a dead sister-in-law, and a lazy, dumb kid who can't stop asking the most idiotic questions."

He yanked Laine the rest of the way up and prodded him into a shuffling walk. "If I could afford t'fly you back t'Earth, you'd be there faster'n a lokian can shift its skin. But I can't, not right now, so looks like we're stuck together for the time bein'."

Laine stumbled alongside Gordon, each halting step confusing him that much further. This couldn't be reality. He hadn't . . . fallen asleep in the middle of that frix-ravaged field and dreamt up his escape from Ethaba and everything that followed, had he?

Laine pinched himself, slapped his face, and tugged his hair, drawing bemused looks from Gordon. A sharp sting of pain accompanied each action, and Laine let his hands drop to his sides as he struggled to accept the possibility that he was not, in fact, dreaming. But Shannon Beth and Jenna and the commander had seemed so real. Bo too, with his caustic attitude and dry, biting humour. It seemed unlikely he'd imagined all that, but in either reality there remained one constant. Mom was dead.

The call came early the next afternoon, and Laine hurried to the hospital, greeted by none other than Peter.

"You brought this on yourself, y'know?" the nurse said, lighting up in blatant disregard of the "no smoking" sign at the entrance.

Laine tried to go around him, but Peter moved to block his path, blowing smoke in Laine's face.

"If you hadn't tried to be a hero she could have died a dignified death, but no, you had to meddle. Because of you, her last moments were agony."

That's not true! Laine tried to yell, but the words stuck in his throat, and he shrank back from Peter's looming presence. Ethaba General suddenly seemed much larger, while the door Peter blocked was too small for Laine to fit through, but somehow he managed, shoving the nurse aside and blinking at the harsh lighting flooding the sterile space.

An unsettling quiet pervaded the never-ending halls and corridors of the hospital, and Laine kept losing his bearings as he wandered the maze leading to patient storage.

"This isn't right; this isn't right," he muttered as he yanked the door open, only to be met with rows upon rows of carefully labelled boxes stacked floor to ceiling. "I'm losing it."

There would be no finding Mom's things in the thousands of containers that stretched endlessly into the distance, far beyond the edges of the room. Laine shook his head—annoyed the staff hadn't set Mom's things aside for him—and picked up the first box, trying to read the neat script printed on its label. The text was indecipherable however, and Laine threw it down in disgust. The plastic container popped open when it hit the floor, spilling out its contents—but none of them were Mom's things.

Despair crept over Laine as he looked again at the never-ending rows. He'd have to sort through every single box to have any hope of finding anything.

He gritted his teeth and began the thankless task, losing time as piles of dead people's belongings rose up around him. But no matter how many boxes he opened, another always followed, and he hadn't come any closer to finding Mom's necklace.

The door opened, light eking into the dark room.

Laine hadn't even noticed how dim it had grown, but suddenly he could see clearly, and he ripped the lid off the box in his hands, gasping when he saw the necklace within. Other items sat beside the beaded jewellery: Mom's clip, her wedding ring, and a lock of her hair.

He touched the soft, ebony strands gently before lifting the lock out and pressing it to his cheek. He breathed deeply, but couldn't detect even a hint of Mom's flowery scent, and tears stung his eyes at the loss. He jerked around when the door creaked and opened further, and the box slipped from his hands, everything in it tumbling to the ground.

There, bathed in the soft glow from the hall without, stood Mom.

How?

It didn't matter.

Laine rushed towards her, choking back a cry, and she opened her arms to him. She hugged him tight the moment he reached her, swirling waves of black tresses floating around them like protective wings.

"I saw you d-die," he sobbed, unable to keep his emotions in check. "I saw—" he shuddered and buried his face in her neck, squeezing her close.

"My beautiful boy," she said, stepping back, one hand caressing his tear-stained cheeks. Then she kissed his forehead, like he was six again, and it was just the two of them against the whole wide world. "I know it hurts. You're scared and angry, and you've been betrayed by those who should have looked out for you."

"What are you saying?" Laine began, but Mom silenced him with two soft fingers on his lips. A tingle started in his gut, sweeping over him and setting his already rigid throat on fire. Despite how he clutched at her, Mom seemed to be just beyond the bounds of what he could feel, shimmering as her face grew soft around the edges.

"My darling Laine. I will always be with you. The anguish you feel now? It will not consume you. I forbid it."

She gently detangled herself from his grasp and bent to retrieve her necklace from the floor. Laine could do little else but tremble, eyes streaming so much he could barely see Mom as she settled the heavy, hand-beaded chain around his neck.

"Remember, Laine," she said, her voice soft, so soft, as the room dissolved away, the world dwindling to just him and her, "always remember; you are more than this moment in time."

The words echoed as she faded, darkness closing in like she'd never been there at all, and Laine fell to his knees, fingers grasping at empty air as the necklace burned so hot the beads seared into his skin.

He sat up, gasping, unable to breathe, the sharp smell of the forest thick in his nostrils after the fogged over, scentless haze he'd been wandering through. Bo was furiously hissing at him to keep quiet, but Laine ignored him, staring at his arms, and then quickly scrubbing his face dry. Bits of sharp sticks fell from his body as he did so—the pricks of pain he'd felt when he'd pinched himself in the dream.

He'd been so stupid, to think for even a moment, that any part of it had been reality. Gordon hadn't been entirely horrible to him, Peter had been uncharacteristically rude, and Mom—Laine pressed the heels of his hands to his eyes as they started stinging again. Mom had looked so beautiful, exactly as he remembered her from before. Even with his eyes wide open, taking in the early morning light across the forest floor, he could see her.

Laine flexed his empty fingers, before bringing his left hand to the necklace clasped around his throat. He could still feel the phantom touch where Mom had placed it on him.

"Miss you," he whispered, allowing tears to well up just a little before he blinked them back.

"Since you're awake, let's go. I don't wanna risk running into an ambush."

"So little faith in the commander's diversion?" Laine said, arching an eyebrow as he followed Bo to the ground.

The lokian shrugged, digging around in his pack for some dried meat, which he chewed while he answered. "When they don't find us in New Little Rock or on the main road, chances are our pursuers'll hole up outside Smoketown somewhere and wait for us to come to them."

"Suddenly bypassing it and walking to the capital is sounding much more attractive," Laine said, rooting around in his own bag for the spicy anlo jerky Woodley had given him.

Bo scoffed. "The city's high enough that snow still coats the sides of Mount Lalethusl this time of year, and you wanna hike that? Don't be stupid. We go by vercycle or we freeze to death before we reach even halfway to Skytown."

"Point taken, but detouring to Smoketown—where we know everyone's looking for us—seems like a risky move."

"Now you wanna weigh pros and cons?" Bo spat and increased his pace, making Laine stumble as he hurried to catch up with him. "You're the one who invited yourself along on this trip."

"Shoulda left when I couldn't walk, if you didn't wanna deal with me pointing out the obvious."

Bo stopped short and turned on Laine, fangs extended, a curt snarl lacing his words.

"I would've been perfectly happy to leave you had we not gotten roped into blowing up a mountain. With all eyes on us, I need you, you idiot, because I can run faster than you. Your inevitable capture is my, what's the saying, window of opportunity. They want you alive, and so you become the bait, the decoy while I steal a transport and go on safe to Skytown."

The familiar feeling of betrayal burned in Laine's chest, setting his teeth on edge. "After everything we've been through, you'd break the trust between us that easily?"

The lokian flicked an ear. "We're even on favours. In fact you might actually owe me one. If saving Kenton means delivering you up to our pursuers, I'll do it a thousand times over."

"You piece of—!" Laine whipped out his lacrosse stick and went at Bo, who dodged and parried Laine's follow-up attack with his quirn.

"What are you gonna do?" Bo laughed and thumbed on his weapon, filling the air with the metallic smell of crackling frix. "Deliver yourself up to the bounty hunters chasing us?" He jammed his staff into the ground abruptly and swung himself around it, his booted feet catching Laine square across the jaw.

Laine snapped back, slamming against a tree, unable to gasp a breath. Shaking his head to clear it of the dizziness, he did what he should have done to begin with and jerked his sol out of its holster.

Bo's eyes went perfectly round before he narrowed them and brandished his quirn in front of him, sliding into a defensive stance.

"I suppose you could try to kill me and collect the bounty yourself, but I don't think that'll keep your uncle from getting rid of you."

Laine swore at Bo, but it didn't stop the jerk from being right. He was stuck with the selfish lokian until they got to Skytown or the soldiers caught up with them, whichever came first.

"Fine," he said tightly and holstered his sol, breathing a little easier when the crackle from Bo's quirn faded in response. "But don't for a second think I'm not ditching *you* to save my own skin if it comes to it."

Bo nodded. "If it comes to it. Guess we'd better get to Smoketown and those vercycles before anyone finds us."

He began walking again, faster than before, and Laine clenched his jaw but matched pace with the insufferable lokian.

The forest grew sparser the higher they climbed, pockets of brackish water beginning to waylay their progress, and Laine wrinkled his nose at the awful smell coming from a few of them, filled as they were with decaying plant matter. The thinning trees allowed Sól to beat down harshly on him, and soon his own body started to stink and attract clusters of the flying insects that swarmed the gross pools dotting the mountainside.

A telltale whine sounded near his ear, and he smacked the back of his neck hard before wiping yellow-green bug guts off his gloves onto the foliage nearby. It figured that for all its differences, Thorunn would share Earth's penchant for bloodthirsty pests.

"Don't touch that!" Bo hissed, slapping Laine's hand away from the glossy plants.

"I've got protection," Laine retorted but then noticed the residue of the leaf that clung to his gloves had started to eat away at the frix-proof material. "Ich, why didn't you warn me before I went and ruined my gloves?"

Bo rolled his eyes. "They're hardly ruined; pat them in the dirt. They'll be fine."

Laine rubbed his covered hands in the soil a few extra times to be safe; good thing he hadn't cut the tips off his gloves like Bo had. His hands were sweaty, and his jacket enveloped him like a steam bath, but suffering the heat was better than accidentally losing one of his hands to a toxic plant.

"Thanks," Laine said, his earlier irritation towards the lokian having cooled somewhat. It was simply too hot and he too tired to keep wasting energy on being mad, especially when he might have to run for his life at any given moment.

"I'm curious," Bo said as they trekked through the thinning underbrush. He swatted away a particularly inquisitive fly. "You're on this grand quest to get justice for your mother, but what about your father? Don't I recall you saying Gordon framed him?"

Laine puffed out a sigh. "Maybe. This situation with my dad . . . It's complicated. Dad always put his work before us, and he really wasn't around much when I was little. He kept promising he'd change, spend more time with us, and I always wanted to trust that this would really be it, the last time he'd disappear for weeks with no warning, too absorbed in a work project to remember he had a family . . ."

Laine couldn't believe he was opening up to Bo, of all people—especially after the lokian had expressly stated he didn't care what happened to Laine if they got caught, not when they were so close to Skytown and Kenton—but maybe the heat of the day had knocked something loose in his brain.

He shook his head, memories coming thick and fast. All the birthday parties Dad had missed, the anniversaries where Mom had looked at the ring on her finger and tried to hide her tears. Laine had been lumped in with the parentless kid group on every "bring-your-dad-to-school-day." Each time the pitying looks from his teachers and classmates had grown worse until Laine started skipping whenever the occasion rolled around.

"Moving here, that was supposed to be our fresh start, but I guess some stupid soil samples from tunnels that weren't even irradiated were more important than our family."

"Having been in those tunnels, at least you know he was right?" Bo offered between gulps of water from his canteen.

"Still doesn't change the fact that Dad chose to break the rules and chase his personal research over putting me and Mom first. Dad . . . I dunno. I feel like an idiot for really believing that this time would be different, y'know? So maybe Gordon set him up, I wouldn't put it past him, but it's not outside the realm of possibility for Dad's current problems to be his own fault."

"And if it turns out he was arrested on false charges?"

The notion seemed to summon a wave of dizziness, and Laine put a hand out to steady himself.

"I—why are you pushing for my dad's innocence so hard?"

"Because you at least still have a father. Don't you owe it to him to find out the truth before giving up on him?"

"I—" Laine had been living with the presumption of Dad's guilt for years, resenting him and his actions for just as long. "I don't know if I want to find out."

"You remind me of myself as a kid." Bo swatted another fly, ears flicking like signals at the irritating buzzing. "My whole identity after I lost my dad was wrapped up in hating humans, and I couldn't see past that to give Ken a chance at first. It was harder still, when I came to terms with his innocence to let go of my, uh, uh, animosity because it would mean letting go of the beliefs and worldview I'd been clinging to."

Bo chuckled, the sound not entirely pleasant. "As you can see, I ended up compromising. I can admit there's a couple good humans—Ken of course, the lieutenant, and Shannon Beth—while still seeing you and your uncle and pretty much everyone else as the callous, greedy savages you are."

"You forgot to add Andy and Yoon Ah to the list, but I'll give you the others. We wouldn't be on the run right now if some ungrateful New Little Rock townie hadn't snitched on us."

Bo smirked and shrugged, unfolding his hands in an "you see?" gesture.

"It really doesn't matter to me whether or not Jack Riven is one of the good ones, but if he is, maybe you need to find your own compromise. If not"—Bo shrugged again—"good riddance, right?"

"Right," Laine echoed. He struggled to swallow past the lump that had formed in his throat at all the conflicting thoughts going through his mind.

He'd seen the small steps Dad had been taking since they'd moved to Thorunn. Dad had eaten dinner with them each night. He'd gotten home on time every day and hung out with Mom and Gordon instead of staying late at work. He'd even fulfilled his promise of coming to Laine's lacrosse match. Sure, that had ended badly, but he had been there, all the way to the end.

Had he just been pretending to assuage his own regrets?

On the other hand, his uncle had kill—had done what he did, and maybe Dad's arrest had been a trial run, a test to see how much he could get away with. First he ruined someone's reputation, then he moved on to murder, and after that it wasn't much of a leap to imagine Gordon assisting in the destruction of the Hinnom Forest to get whatever it was he wanted, whether that was money, fame, or just having his inconvenient relatives gone from his place.

The truth was in Skytown, Laine supposed. The soldiers had come from there and so had the arrest documents, and there had to be some sort of trail, digital or otherwise, leading to the answers.

The world swam in front of Laine, and he stumbled, the sweat slicking his face seeming to triple in volume.

"I don't feel so good," he mumbled and took a knee, breathing hard to stop himself from throwing up.

"Laine?"

Was that concern he heard in the lokian's voice? Laine shook his head, causing the nausea to redouble. No, Bo was probably just worried about Laine potentially messing up his escape plans. Determined not to look weak in front of the furred jerk, Laine pulled himself to his feet and attempted to forge ahead.

He made it all of two steps before his legs gave out on him, and next he knew Bo was pressing something against his forehead.

"You're burning up; here." Bo pushed a bottle against Laine's mouth.

Laine brushed him away, then thought better of it and accepted the drink. The taste that washed over his tongue was sweet, refreshing despite the lukewarm temperature.

"Why did you get lytorade, and I only got water for our trip?" he grumbled after taking several big gulps. His head throbbed, each pulse driving a fresh spike of pain into the back of his skull. "Are we almost to Smoketown?"

"It's another two hours if we stick to the forest, maybe thirty minutes if we take the road."

Laine clenched his fists and stood again. "I can make it. I'm not, not lettin' you ditch me out in the open."

"I don't think you'll make it even an hour," Bo said, getting one of Laine's arms over his shoulders. "Something musta bit you."

Bo started walking, dragging them both towards the edge of the forest despite Laine's protests.

He couldn't resist, however, when his legs felt like gelatin. They'd been hurting already from the uncomfortable sleep and forced climb, but the sickness sweeping through him had stolen the last of his strength. Even breathing was a struggle, keeping his wheezing breaths quiet an impossible task.

"D'y'hear that?" Laine said a short while later. The words didn't want to come out properly, and he touched a hand to his sluggish jaw, almost missing the concerned look Bo shot him.

"It's all I've been able to hear for quite some time. You're just now picking up on it?"

Laine wiped his sweaty forehead, straining to make out the rumbling sound of machinery barely audible above the pounding between his ears.

"We'll ge' caugh'," he whispered, not wanting to leave the relative safety of the forest.

"Only other option is to stay here and die," Bo said, and pushed him forward through the last of the underbrush and out onto a rocky road, deserted except for a few lizards that skittered away at the sudden commotion. The bare, sheer face of Mount Lalethusl rose up on one side of the winding path, the end of which curved away sharply to reveal the welcome sight of Smoketown belching thick, black clouds from the valley beneath.

"Now we jus' gotta ge' down again, huh?" Laine said, letting go of Bo and sinking to his knees. "I can ma'e it. Just give me five minu—"

An abrupt convulsion seized Laine, and the lytorade he'd drunk earlier, the jerky that had been breakfast, and a whole lot of nasty-looking green bile spewed out of him so forcefully he almost choked on the burning chunks that scraped his throat raw.

"Well, well, well, lookee what we got here."

Laine jolted, the strange voice sending a spasm of

fear through throbbing limbs. He'd told Bo going out to the road would get them caught. Weakly, Laine lifted his head to peer through bleary eyes at the man he could in no way escape, not in his feverish condition.

A grizzled bounty hunter levelled a sol at him, smirking crookedly. A long length of rope hung at his hip, and a homemade camo jacket set atop multi-pocketed khakis completed the ensemble.

"Told the boys thatch'all had t'come by the path 'ventually. They wanted t'wait by the gates, but I weren't born yesterday. No one with a bounty high as yers would jus' stroll through the front entrance. Was I right, or was I right? Secure 'im, boys."

He gestured at two equally rough-looking men with patchy beards and dirt-stained skin before crouching down and leering in Laine's face. "The name's Lewis. Samuel Hezekiah 'Sureshot' Lewis, an' you, Laine Riven, have jus' made me a very rich man."

Laine tried to resist as the greasy men bound his wrists together, but his struggles could better be called trembles, and he cursed the miserable fever flushing his face bright red. He looked around to see if Bo fared better than he, but the lokian was nowhere in sight, and betrayal, bright and overwhelming, tingled through Laine's core. The selfish, good-for-nothing lokian really had left him at the first inkling of danger.

Samuel Hezekiah noticed his frantic gaze and laughed, an unpleasant sound that grated on Laine's already-fraught nerves.

"Yer little buddy took off soon as y'started pukin' yer guts out. Gettin' bit by a wolf squeeter's never no fun." The bounty hunter patted his sol lovingly. "Don't you worry. We'll catch the varmint soon enough. I ain't never had a lokian hide on my wall afore, but there's a first time fer everythin'."

Laine could picture it, Bo caught and killed like just another trophy. The lokian wasn't his friend by any stretch of imagination, but he didn't deserve to be butchered, mutilated, and put on display just for the crime of being born a native of Thorunn. Rage welled up in Laine, lending him a moment's strength, and he spat as forcefully as he could in Samuel Hezekiah's stubbled face.

The man chuckled and wiped the spit from his cheek before backhanding Laine so hard that for a second he was terrified the bounty hunter had broken his neck.

"Kids these days," Samuel Hezekiah said, rising to his feet. "No respect." He motioned for his men to stand Laine up and started swaggering down the road.

Laine gagged again, vision spinning from how violently Samuel Hezekiah had struck him. The constant pulsating in his head increased, his brain battering at his skull until Laine feared grey matter would start oozing through his nose and ears. He managed several halting steps in the direction the men steered him, but the world soon fell sideways, and he lost consciousness amidst yells and the sound of rushing boots.

When he came to, he found himself strapped to a tree on the edge of a clearing overlooking the outskirts of Smoketown.

"Here's as good a place as any t'make camp 'til we catch that furred varmint," Samuel Hezekiah was saying. He trundled over when he noticed Laine had regained consciousness, and Laine held his breath to avoid smelling the stink that exuded from the bounty hunter with each new word.

"Laine, Laine, Laine. The boy with two bounties. Pleases me mightily t'see yer finally back with us. Lucky fer you we got a medic on the team. Be a cryin' shame if'n y'died 'fore we could collect—last I checked, yer pretty little face, is worth"—the man ran the back of one dirty finger across Laine's cheek—"one hundred an' fifty thousand credits. An' climbin'. But I'll net double that if I catch yer friend."

Samuel Hezekiah's grin vanished, transforming his demeanour. He'd been playfully threatening before, but the look that darkened his features made Laine stop breathing, convinced the man would crack his skull open if he so much as blinked.

"Make no mistake. I will kill that worthless waste of good air." Samuel Hezekiah patted Laine once more before he straightened, put a hand on the sol at his hip, and whistled, a sharp, jarring sound that caught the attention of everyone at the camp.

"Grab yer sols, ladies an' gents. We're goin' a-lokian huntin'."

"To think, we'd about given up on 742."

High Consul Anland flicked through the large holoscreen displaying the data collected from Kenton's bout with Shadow—who was now enemy number one, if the nervous gossip circulating in hushed whispers among the whitecoats was to be believed.

Kenton strained to hear what the man was saying over the customary murmur of the room while doing his level best to appear engrossed in the post-battle checkup he'd been subjected to.

"Now 'Stormsurge' is a darling of the people. In high demand, and the advance sales from his next few matches will keep the Hexagon flush until second frix."

"He's still useless for the expansion efforts if we can't unlock how those energy shields work," Torturer Anland sneered.

"Patience, Cousin. The rest of the Consul will be suitably pleased with these results. Today's match shows that the first event was not a singular one. You were right. He did just need the right motivation to manifest."

"It's not sustainable."

The High Consul and his cousin both turned in the

direction of the whitecoat who had spoken.

Kenton's pulse jumped when he saw it was 626. He still hadn't gotten a moment alone with the man to discuss what Shadow had told him. If Torturer Anland decided 626 needed punishing for speaking out of turn, he might lose his chance altogether.

"Humans—we're nothing if not adaptable. You keep throwing him into fights hoping the implants will activate, pushing him harder and harder each time? In the end he'll burn out."

Consul Rolv grabbed Torturer Anland's wrist before she could backhand 626 in the face.

"Hear the man out before you decide his opinion is worthless." He nodded at 626 to continue.

"Put 742 in a low-stress environment. Don't force combat upon him. Let him rest and recover without constantly anticipating a fight."

"You suggest allowing him to slough off his trauma, to undo my cousin's ministrations?"

The almost completely black of Torturer Anland's eyes showed what she thought of that opinion, and Kenton flinched back without conscious thought when her pacing brought her closer to him, remembering vividly the time she'd sliced open his back and drawn out his ribs one by one.

"626 has a point, High Consul," the lead whitecoat said, rubbing a hand over his stubbled chin. He'd been looking at his personal holoscreen, a darkening expression on his face. "No disrespect, ma'am, but you've broken him a little too much. Look at him. He can't even be in the same room as you without trembling."

Kenton hadn't realised he'd been doing so. He stopped, fisting his hands and digging his fingers into his palms to keep from starting again.

"Try it your way then," Torturer Anland said, hooking her arm through her cousin's as they prepared to leave. "But the instant we've gotten what we want, I'm stripping out those implants with my own hands."

"That doesn't make me keen to succeed," Kenton said, the words tumbling into the open before he could quite hold them back, feeling like he might vomit all the while.

Faster than he or anyone could react, Torturer Anland squeezed something in her hand. Kenton fell to the floor, gasping, the frix inside him sluggish as his blood struggled to respond to the cardiac event the woman had triggered.

"And now you've probably set their work—and ours—back months." High Consul Rolv snatched the controller out of his cousin's hands, releasing Kenton.

"I won't suffer disrespect," Torturer Anland rejoined, her furious expression turning an otherwise beautiful face into something grotesque.

"I promise, after our scientists have finished their undertaking, you can play with him to the fullest extent of your heart's desire." The High Consul patted Torturer Anland's arm in a consoling manner. "But we must let them do their work if we want our army." He nodded to the lead whitecoat. "Another time."

The two left while Kenton picked himself off the ground. His chest still felt like a full-grown anlo had sat on him, but it had been worth it to provoke the Torturer into losing control, and any setback he could effect against the Consul's war plans was a victory in of itself.

"I want Ms. Anland kept away from 742 from now on." The lead whitecoat switched off his clip as he spoke and gestured for the other non-prisoner white-coats to do the same. He gathered them to himself, keeping his voice low, and Kenton strained to hear the murmured conversation.

"Get that memo to everyone in the Hexagon. We can't exactly deny her a direct request, but we can 'lose' her communiques, or let them sit unopened while we discuss matters with the rest of the Consul."

"Ms. Anland won't forget that big a slight," one of the whitecoats said, a note of objection in her voice.

"Then we'd better make sure to keep in High Consul Rolv's good graces, yes?"

The others murmured their assent, and the lead whitecoat reactivated his clip, gesturing for 626 to come forward.

"Take 742 to one of the unoccupied executive prisoner suites. We're beginning our new approach immediately."

"Any belongings to fetch from your cell?" 626 asked, slipping Kenton's hands through a pair of cuffs.

"I don't even have a blanket," Kenton replied, testing the restraints. A simple exertion of will and he could force enough frix through them to snap them off, but such an action in a room full of so many hostile people would be counterproductive to the reprieve he'd apparently been granted.

626's lips twisted in disapproval. "It's not right," he said, ushering Kenton through the door. "Even if you've done half of what they say, you should still be treated more humanely than this. You're what, eighteen, nineteen?"

"Seventeen this year," Kenton supplied, then wished he hadn't at the dismay that prompted.

"Seven—you can't be older than my son! By Earth's laws—"

"This is Thorunn," Kenton reminded him, walking a little behind 626 as the man directed him through another door, and then down a corridor Kenton hadn't previously been permitted to enter. Annie's sweet little face flashed into his mind, and he clenched his fists against the pain the memory brought, against the fact that the man responsible for her death had stood not a metre from him, and he hadn't been able to do a thing about it.

"Something about this planet strips us humans of our decency."

626 shook his head. "Or maybe we never had any to begin with."

"Your actions today disprove that. And . . ." Kenton stopped walking and put a hand on 626's ear, letting the tiniest spark of frix brush against the delicate electronics of the prisoner clip. "Shadow told me I could trust you."

626 leapt back as if burned, one hand flying to his ear, which had gone red. Kenton wondered if it tingled as much as his fingertips did.

"Y-you can't!" The scientist's eyes went round, and he shook his head over and over, as if to dislodge the words Kenton had spoken. "Cameras are every-where, watching us all the time, listening to everything. Three weeks ago one of my, colleagues, for lack of a better term, joked at breakfast about wanting Ms. Anland to step on him. He keeled over during dinner that evening."

"The frix they put in me can make electronics act strangely," Kenton said, trying to reassure 626, though it didn't do much to combat the sweat bead-ing at the man's hairline, ready to trickle down his rapidly paling face. "They can't hear anything we're talking about."

"They can still see us—move before we look suspi-cious! Shadow had a device that allowed us to talk freely, but he always kept it on him, and I doubt I'll be seeing him again anytime soon. If I get hold of a jammer, then we can speak, but not before.

"You have to understand." 626 turned down an-other hall and tapped something into his holoscreen. The door in front of them slid open, revealing a small, nicely furnished apartment. "My family . . . If I step out of line, the powers that be here at the Hexagon will make even your torture look like a stroll along the beach in comparison."

Kenton nodded, trying not to let his disappoint-ment show as he stepped into his new cell.

626 removed his cuffs, pleading with his eyes for Kenton not to make a stir. He wouldn't, if he could help it. No matter what 626 had done to warrant his imprisonment, the man's family didn't deserve whatever terrors Torturer Anland would dream up if 626 caused too much trouble—trouble Kenton could prevent by keeping his head down and his interactions with the man suspicion free.

The door slid shut, leaving Kenton alone.

He wandered around his new surroundings, noting the doorless bathroom, combined kitchenette and living room, and the shoebox of a bedroom, also with no door. A couple of the sheets from the bed would take care of that.

Kenton's fingers trailed over the plush sofa in the middle of the apartment, revelling in the way the soft material sank under his fingers before plopping himself onto the inviting cushions. He let his legs hang off the arm of the sofa, flinging his own arm over his eyes.

After weeks of torture, experiments, fighting, and testing, he finally had a moment's peace, time to himself in a comfortable room. He had friends—or at least allies, and though Kenton wouldn't have put it past the High Consul to have planted 626 to win his trust, it didn't seem likely that Consul Rolv would have allowed Shadow to move so freely within the Hexagon had he known the man was a klia'an—and the sole surviving member of the tribe he'd ordered eradicated so long ago.

A small spark of hope fluttered in Kenton's chest.

He'd felt the initial stirrings of it after his first terrify-ing match in the Tomb, and it grew stronger every time he recalled Shadow's approving assessment of him, or the way 626 had risked the Torturer's wrath to advocate for Kenton. His current situation, the vel-vety cushions under his fingers, the bowl of fruit he could spy on the table—it was all due to him, the man who was terrified of stepping out of line for fear of what Torturer Anland would do to his family. The man who'd apparently involved himself in a move-ment dedicated to systematically destroying Skytown's corruption in spite of that. 626 was an en-igma Kenton couldn't quite figure out.

His stomach growled, and he eyed the fruit he'd spotted earlier. He plucked himself off the sofa and selected an étot from the plain blue bowl. The silvery skinned fruit—glittering like the snow its trees thrived in—felt cool in his hands despite the warmth of the room. Grief filled Kenton as he thought of Tribe Anshi and how so many orchards must have fallen to the wayside once the High Consul had fin-ished his monstrous work. Kenton had thought him-self alone, but Shadow truly had had no one, for near a decade.

Kenton's grip tightened on the étot, the juice run-ning sticky through his fingers. He raised the fruit to his mouth and took a bite. He almost wept at the on-slaught of taste that flooded his mouth.

Everything for days had tasted like ash, and ela-tion so strongly filled him at being able to indulge in the watery sweetness of the étot that he paid little attention to the juice dribbling down his chin. He sank to his knees, heedless of the cameras mounted on the walls, tears pricking his eyes. Madness, to be reduced to so pitiful a state over the sour-sweet tang, but Kenton had feared never regaining his lost sense and let the heady feeling consume him, savouring it as long as possible, even knowing that more étot sat in the bowl on the low table.

He ate a few more of the apple-sized fruits, leaving one for later, before moving to examine the door. He had to know what new prison he'd been thrust into, and what means he had of fighting back against his captors. A glowing palm scanner sat next to the entrance, and Kenton reached for it. The scanner brightened, warm to the touch, and with a *schnik* the door receded on each side from the middle.

Kenton stared so long at the open space that the panels slid shut, blocking his view of the corridor beyond, and he almost cracked the scanner's screen in his haste to open the panels again. The broad, inviting space beyond couldn't be real. It had to be a trick. Yet he'd walked down that hall with 626, and nothing had changed from how he remembered it.

The next time the door started to close, Kenton stuck his arm between the smooth metal and stepped through.

Nothing happened, no reprimand, no twinge of pain from his artificial heart, and Kenton cracked open eyes he didn't know he'd squeezed shut. What a sight he must look to anyone watching, like a klia'an kit venturing outside the den on its very first excursion. Bolstered by the sweetness lingering on his tongue, Kenton set out down the strangely empty winding hallway. Given the late hour, he wondered if the other prisoners on his floor were taking their dinners in their rooms—or if they even had access beyond them like he did.

The entranceway halfway down the hall reminded Kenton of the one that led to the Tomb. Another palm scanner sat next to it, and the ostentatious door opened just as easily to his touch. Bewildered, he stepped through and found himself in a whole new world.

An eclectic mix of people swarmed about the massive, six-sided room he'd entered, and Kenton's eyes were drawn to the only stationary object, a large credit exchange module that sat dead centre. He watched as the machine dispensed everything from food and clothing to books, toiletries and medical supplies. Kenton skirted the edges of the hub before heading to the module, noting which doors opened for him and other people sporting prisoner clips, and which ones appeared restricted to military personnel and whitecoats only.

Kenton avoided the on-duty soldiers and kept his head down as he approached the module, wondering how he would pay to access the food his stomach grumbled for. He could be excused then, for nearly colliding with the dark-skinned cadet who stepped directly in his path, looking at her friend and not her surroundings as she gesticulated wildly to her companion with one hand, a loaded plate of food balanced precariously in the other.

"Hey! Watch where you're—" Her jaw dropped, and Kenton recognised her as the blue-haired trainee he'd sparred with during the first phase of the white-coats' testing.

"Stormsurge!" her friend whispered almost reverently, very nearly dropping her plate.

Kenton allowed himself half a smile at the nickname his adoring public had invented. He'd take it over "742" any day, and the meaning of it was close enough to "Oso Frix" that hearing it brought him a small measure of comfort in the strange and awful place that was the Hexagon.

"Cadet Michaels," Kenton said, reading her name off her grey and white fatigues. "Good to see you again." He held back a laugh at the face she was making, lips pulled in, eyes wide as Thorunn's moons.

"Welcome to the Cirruca," she said, once she'd regained her composure, though her companion still appeared rather star-struck, her dish dangerously close to sliding out of her hands. "Wouldn't have thought someone of your fame would be down for slumming it with us common folk."

"I only found out about this place today. I'm curious to discover how the food tastes."

"Your match with Shadow! I forgot—here." Michaels broke a piece of bread in half and offered it to Kenton, elbowing her friend to do the same.

"Once you've managed to grab a bite, would you maybe"—Michaels bit her bottom lip before pointing to the far side of the Cirruca—"do you wanna spar?"

"Why not right now?" Kenton offered, noting that an onite wristlet encircled Michaels' left forearm. Sparring would provide the perfect cover for him to break and take it, so he could devise a jammer.

Michaels' eyes lit up, and she shoved her plate into her friend's already full hands, ignoring any and all sputtered grievances. She tugged on Kenton's arm, leading him towards the padded ring not dissimilar to the one in the labs. Overshirts came off first, then shoes, and Michaels deactivated her sol, handing it to the blank faced soldier who waved them past.

Kenton tested the springy, dark grey-mats with his bare feet, bouncing a little as Michaels went through warm-up stretches. He tried to ignore the gathering crowd, whispers of excitement rippling through the onlookers as more and more people realised Storm-surge had graced them with his presence.

How many of them knew he was a prisoner, he wondered, how fewer still would have been informed he was the Outpost Terrorist? The cheers wouldn't be half so vigorous if the whole truth of it had been circulated, the Consul's penchant for keeping secrets a boon in such a crowded place.

"Standard sparring rules?" Kenton asked as he adjusted his stance. Another laugh threatened to escape him when he saw that Michaels' red-haired friend had finished her plate of food and started on the cadet's, a petty act born of annoyance.

"Works for me," Michaels replied, blissfully unaware of the rapid disappearance of her supper. She counted down with Kenton—three, two, one—and the match was on.

Michaels rushed at Kenton, and he met her halfway, throwing his leg out in what he intended to be a sweeping kick to tumble her, but Michaels dove forward, propelling herself into a roll that put her behind Kenton, and he swung around just in time to block her follow-up punch.

"You've been training."

Michaels grinned, a bright thing that made her features sparkle.

"Would've been silly to bother you about a match otherwise." She sprang forward again, careful to pair her speed with solid footwork and evasive moves that made the most of her slight build. She'd made remarkable progress in just ten days, making Kenton intensely curious about Skytown's military training regime.

They fought through a medley of different forms and styles, Kenton favouring close contact and forearm strikes, and Michaels, kicks and jabs. A few times the blue-haired cadet darted in closer than Kenton expected, and he discovered the hard way that "standard sparring rules" at the Hexagon allowed for blows below the belt.

But despite the leaps Michaels had made in her training, Kenton still had years of experience that outweighed her growing skill, only allowing her to match him until the opportunity presented itself for him to grab a fistful of her wristlet in a move that appeared natural to anyone watching. The string of polished stones came apart like an icicle shattering, the pieces scattering over the spongy floor of the training mat.

Michaels' moment of shock over seeing her jewellery destroyed was all the advantage Kenton needed to tackle her to the ground, keeping her pinned while using her struggling body to disguise the fact that he was stuffing as many broken pieces of onite as he could into his pockets.

"Alright, alright, let me up," Michaels panted after a few moments of ineffective wriggling. "I yield—get your sweaty body off me."

Kenton rolled away and held out his hand. "Sorry about—" He gestured at her wrist.

"S'my own fault. I should have given it to Ashlyn. Good match though. I seriously need you to teach me all those weird moves you pulled."

She shook Kenton's hand and took several large gulps from a canteen she'd set by the edge of the ring before offering it to him. Kenton sniffed it and tried a cautious sip, wrinkling his nose at the slightly too-sweet flavour.

"'S good for you," Michaels said, laughing at the face he made. "Lytorade contains seven essential nutrients an athlete's body needs. Refuel, rehydrate, and re-energise, with lytorade." She sounded suspiciously like a commercial, and Kenton smothered a chuckle.

Michaels mock-punched him.

"No point in hiding it. I know your secret now. The mighty Stormsurge has a weakness for bad jokes that aren't even funny. Proves you're human like the rest of us and not a high-tech robot like some people"—she jerked a thumb at Ashlyn, who waved through a mouthful of stolen food—"have been theorising."

Kenton chuckled. First 626 and then Cadet Michaels. For all its awfulness, the Hexagon had a few decent people. And he'd gotten his hands on some onite. If things kept improving at such an alarming rate, he might even dare to nurture the hope sitting like a seed inside his heart.

"You caught me; I'm a real boy today."

That sent Michaels into peals of laughter, a lilting, pleasant sound that came to an abrupt end with a massive snort, which had her clapping her hands over her mouth. Her aborted jerk towards the outside of the ring in response was oddly charming, and Kenton felt the third smile in as many minutes tug at the corners of his mouth. Michaels collected herself despite the flush that darkened her cheeks at Ashlyn's good-natured heckling and raised her voice over the din of the dispersing crowd.

"Same time tomorrow?"

Kenton nodded and retrieved his shirt before setting out to explore the rest of the Cirruca.

A path cleared for him as he wended his way towards the credit exchange module. The stares from the other cadets and non-military personnel seemed a mix of adoring and jealous. A few of the higher-ranked soldiers eyed him warily, obviously aware of his identity as more than the crowd favourite "Storm-surge." Much as Kenton hated the idea of the men and women of Skytown blindly following the Consul's orders, their dedication to keeping his secret whilst he walked freely among them was something he didn't mind benefiting from.

Undisguised interest shone on the whitecoats' faces. A few of them had their holoscreens out, busily tapping away, and Kenton could just imagine what their reports sounded like: *Subject 742 used his newfound freedom to seek out a fight of his own accord. The new treatment is working. Manifestation is close!* Or something along those lines. They might have given him a larger maze, but they never intended to set him truly free.

The weight of all the strange eyes ate at Kenton, agitating the frix inside him in a way that sparring with Michaels hadn't. He felt eight years old again, six months freshly orphaned and still struggling to find his place in Tribe Osinan. The Innah had stopped the harshest words, but she couldn't stem the looks, and Kenton had thought he'd be flattened by the curious, sympathetic—and sometimes hateful—gazes directed his way. But Seri hadn't been afraid of him—wanting to play all day, every day—and bit by bit he'd grown more secure, so that even if the stares lingered, he didn't pay them any mind.

Kenton straightened his shoulders. If Cadet Michaels would keep treating him with kind words and a smile, he could ignore what anyone else in the Cirruca thought of him.

He reached the credit exchange module undisturbed and upon placing his hand on the scanner, discovered he had quite a few credits to his name, due to his fights in the Tomb. Enough numbers scrolled across the screen to keep him fed and in new clothes for a week, but right next to the positive green plus blinked an astronomically negative number labelled "debt." Kenton doubted they'd modified the system just for him, so likely everyone else at the Hexagon had a similar set-up, whether they were prisoners, trainees, or employees. He rather suspected the other Skytown residents would split their earned credits between food and debts, paying off a little at a time.

Kenton didn't bother wasting any credits on his debt, instead opting for a large tray of food and two books. The worn covers reminded him of the well-loved books he'd used to refresh his English in the basement of the house that once belonged to his family. Kenton ran his finger along the stained pages. One contained a history of Julius Caesar, the other a novelisation of the first season of *Task Force: Mars*. Not particularly gripping reading material but they were thick enough to suit his purposes.

He selected the *Task Force: Mars* novel and tucked it into his clothes before leaving his food to investigate the bathrooms on the far side of the Cirruca. If he was to start subverting the High Consul's plans, he first had to be able to find a means of roaming freely about the building—as freely as he could with his captors watching his every move.

To Kenton's delight, 626's warning about cameras being everywhere didn't extend to the toilets. He mentally thanked whatever high-ranking official must have caused a fuss at having his privacy intruded on, and slipped into a stall. The rows of urinals meant all the men inside kept their eyes fixed on the wall in front of them while doing their business and therefore didn't take note of who exactly had just occupied the stall in the far corner of the room that smelled so strongly not even artificial fresheners could neutralise it.

Kenton rolled the toilet paper and coughed a few times, waiting until the chatter died down and unlacing his boots in the meantime. The moment the bathroom went silent, he placed them at the foot of the toilet and climbed to the top of the stalls. When he poked at the large ceiling tiles, they shifted slightly. Kenton's heart jumped, and he pushed harder. At any moment, a soldier or a whitecoat or even the custodian could walk through the grimy door, and there'd be no easy explanation for why he was obviously attempting an escape.

Using the wall for purchase, Kenton put all his strength into shoving the tile ajar and hauled himself through the slim opening that appeared. The bathroom door swished open, and Kenton yanked up one dangling leg, hissing at the scrape he garnered from the tile's corrugated edge.

He stopped breathing. The odds of the new arrival noting the displaced tile in the back corner were low, but the longer Kenton left the gap uncovered, the more those odds increased. He mentally counted, reaching twenty before he heard a familiar trickling sound. Hoping the occupant had drunk a fair amount, Kenton grasped the edges of the tile and eased it back into place, wincing at the dust and bits of plaster that insisted on filtering down with each minute movement.

At last the light from below winked out, and Kenton was safe—for just under a half hour at least. More than that and someone might get suspicious that the boots he'd left behind hadn't moved in all that time.

He brought his wrists and elbows together, tapping his forearms twice, and a brilliant blue lit the crawl space between floors. "Permanent night-light" probably wasn't a use his captors had envisioned for the implants, but it was yet another function he'd be keeping from them as long as he could. The blue glow revealed a cramped, cobwebbed space not even tall enough for him to crouch in. The sides stretched away into darkness, thick support beams intersecting it every few metres, and Kenton tore away a piece of his undershirt, tying it to the beam nearest the reset ceiling tile.

He set off in the direction of the labs after orienting himself, careful to spread his weight evenly over the flimsiest of the tiles and resting here and there on the slabs of concrete marking the walls between the rooms beneath. He wound a few more scraps of cloth around subsequent beams as he went.

When Kenton arrived at another large section of ceiling panels he pushed aside heavy layers of insulated wiring, ignoring the pull of the flowing current, and set his fingers in the edges, careful to dim the frix glowing through his forearms before he attempted to ease up the tiling. The seals around the edges resisted him, and he let frix pool in his fingertips, biting his lip at the burning. But it did the trick, melting the caulking and loosening the tiles. Light peeped up through the few inches Kenton had managed to dislodge the ceiling panels, and he peered through the crack.

He didn't recognise the room, but a table just the right height for him to drop onto sat beneath him. The only problem was the three whitecoats milling about.

Kenton pulled back and reached out to the thickly bundled wiring. Too little frix and nothing would happen, too much and he could fry the whole system like he had back in the Tomb. That wouldn't go unnoticed, and they'd discover his abscondence from the Cirruca sooner rather than later. But he needed to get the onite he'd filched to 626 and fashion a jammer if he wanted to talk to the man without the watchful eyes of the Hexagon spying on their every move. Kenton pushed a pulsing thread of frix into the wires and scrambled back to the gap.

The door to the room beneath opened, and a whitecoat poked his head in.

"Leena, could you come next door a second? Our lights are acting up."

"Again? How are you drawing so much power? Jackson, come on."

She exited the lab, followed by an intern who looked about Kenton's age, which left the third whitecoat by himself, but the man was so engrossed in the test he was conducting that he never turned around, not even when Kenton slithered through the hole he'd created, landed with a soft thump on the steel table, and popped the large tile back into place with an audible click.

Kenton shook his head. The self absorption of the whitecoats had reached staggering levels, so it didn't surprise him when the man didn't bother casting a curious glance his way, and Kenton simply strolled out of the room, dusting off his hair as he went.

His luck ran out the instant he stepped into the hall beyond.

"742? You're not expected here right now."

"626, he wanted to see me," Kenton said, hoping the tall man didn't notice his socked feet. His cheeks went hot at the prospect of being found out so soon. "To collect data. I've been in a fight; the video should have been forwarded to the team."

"I thought you'd been suspended from all that for your mental health?"

Kenton shrugged, unable to swallow back the anxiety tingling along his teeth. "A cadet cornered me wishing to spar, and I didn't want to find out what would happen if I said no."

Kenton tucked his hands into his armpits, projecting the appearance of a nervous, agitated teen. Not hard to do, the way he was feeling. His ploy worked, the whitecoat waving him past and muttering about reviewing the footage and recommending disciplinary action for the cadet. He pointed out a room labelled *4-36-A* when Kenton quietly asked how he might find 626 and swept off down the hall, still grumbling to himself, one finger pressed to his clip.

The room was a few doors down, not far from a set of stairs marked *Hexagon Security Personnel Only* situated next to a lift flashing the words *Level Four.* Kenton filed away the information, set his hand in the palm scanner, and stepped through once the doors slid open.

"I'm here for my checkup," he announced, and the four whitecoats in the room whirled around, 626's eyes going wide at the unexpected intrusion.

He recovered quickly, striding over to Kenton and making his voice falsely cheery.

"About your jammed elbow? I got the memo, take a seat."

626 didn't wait for any kind of response from Kenton or his fellow scientists, instead pulling him over to the far corner of the room, where large sets of expensive-looking machinery hid them partially from view.

"The heck're you doing here?" 626 mouthed while rolling up Kenton's sleeve. He tapped on his clip light, pretending to check his elbow.

Kenton couldn't help but be impressed by the way 626 kept his head down, not allowing the camera inside his clip to catch any of Kenton's answer. He released some energy from his frix into the air anyway, disrupting the audio feed with white noise even if the camera didn't stop recording.

"If I give you onite, can you build a jammer?"

"Three months ago I'd've said no—I'm a botanist, for crying out loud, not a biologist, or whatever the heck this is they've got me doing. But ever since being here, meeting Shadow and getting involved with the Cabal, I've learned so many things. I can fix you up a crude but fully functional jammer in about ten minutes; if you assist me, we can get two out in that time. Just keep doing whatever you're doing to block the signals 'til then."

Under the cover of treating Kenton—who happily showed off his very real bruises from his match with cadet Michaels whenever one of the other whitecoats came too close—626 fashioned two small jammers. Kenton tucked his into his pants and gave the book he'd brought with him to 626, who laughed at the badly designed, flamboyant cover.

"Hah, *Task Force: Mars*! My wife was always trying to get me to watch it. Maybe it'll be easier to digest in written form."

"If you can make sense of the pages once we've cut the middle out," Kenton responded, and the man's smile slipped off his face.

"I hate that they've done this to you. Turned a kid into an experiment. If you're aligning yourself with our cause, I'm sure there's an explanation behind your purported actions as the Outpost Terrorist. The documents I've managed to sneak a peek at—nothing quite adds together, and I'm not inclined to trust the government that arrested me on trumped up charges."

626 slotted his jammer into the space he'd hol-

lowed out with a scalpel and patted the book's fanciful front.

"The charge you imbued should last around twenty-four hours. I'll try and arrange to see you before then, but for now, better hurry back before you're missed."

Kenton pulled on his boots and flushed three times, then once more, before emerging from the stall doubled over and holding his stomach. He was given a wide berth as he stumbled out of the bathrooms and feigned a limp back to his table, where his half-eaten food still sat. He'd almost reached the solitary plate of vegetables and some unidentifiable meat when Cadet Michaels stormed up to him, mad as a nest of killer bees.

"How could you?" she gritted out, features screwed up into a snarl. "You said yes. I didn't coerce you into anything!"

Kenton backed up a few steps, wary of her clenched fists that looked ready to fly at him.

"I don't care if you're some big hotshot. You don't get to willingly spar with me, and then get me in trouble for it."

Michaels blinked back tears, and Kenton took advantage of the moment to grab her wrist with one hand—hitting the palm scanner on the wall behind him with the other—and dragged her into the hallway beyond, hoping the cacophony in the Cirruca would disguise her shriek of surprise. It wouldn't do to make a scene and have the guards search him.

He'd certainly have his new freedoms stripped away if they found the bit of onite and metal shoved into his clothes.

"Michaels, please," he started, pushing her into a corner that blocked the hallway camera's view of them. Just in case, he sent a gentle shock of frix into the jammer nestled in his back pocket. "I'm sorry. I was somewhere I wasn't supposed to be, and I couldn't think of much else to explain myself."

Cadet Michaels furrowed her brow, still furious but confused by Kenton's words. He hurried to spill the rest of his thoughts before she stopped humouring him.

"I like you, Michaels. You've shown me decency many of the others have not. It was wrong of me to cause you trouble. How can I make amends?"

"But. You're Stormsurge."

"I'm also a prisoner," Kenton admitted. His heart sank at the shocked look Michaels failed to hide. "There's places here at the Hexagon I'm supposed to keep away from, and . . . this is the first day I've been allowed to wander so freely; my curiosity got the best of me. I panicked when I got caught. Please, forgive me?"

Michaels said nothing for several long moments, only jerking out of Kenton's hold, and he tucked his hands behind his back, ashamed he'd gripped her wrists so hard. He couldn't tell if the twisting feeling in his gut was from the hunger he hadn't yet satisfied or from apprehension.

"You'll owe me a favour," Michaels said finally,

crossing her arms. "With that joke of a credits repayment system, favours are the only currency that really matter around here."

"Anything that's in my power to grant."

"You're offering an awful lot for what they'll write up as a minor infraction on my record."

"It's as I said; I truly didn't mean to cause you suffering."

"Oh, oh you were thinking I'd get sent to Her?" A laugh startled out of Michaels, an incredulous look on her face. "I'm a soldier. She's not allowed to touch us."

Michaels reached out and thumbed the frix scarring just visible at the base of Kenton's neck. Her hand was cool, her touch gentle, and Kenton shivered at the first human contact in weeks that wasn't violent or testing related.

"Did she do this to you?"

"She certainly tried," Kenton whispered. He covered Michaels' hand with his own, relishing the touch even through her gloves.

"You'll owe me answers as well," Michaels said, pulling back from Kenton again, but slowly, the hurt and anger in her eyes dissipating. "And a few more sparring sessions once I come up with an explanation for this mess and get proper clearance to continue."

"Tomorrow evening?"

"We'll see. I'm still a lot mad at you."

"Thank you."

Michaels shrugged and walked back to the Cirruca, Kenton following several paces behind. He waited outside the door until his stomach started growling again, and then went in, found his plate, and put an end to the grumbling ache without further interruptions.

Kenton's life fell into a routine after that. He'd meet with 626 in the mornings for testing and sneak around the Hexagon during the day, learning its blind spots and secret spaces and liberating important documents to be passed on to the Cabal. It was exhausting, constantly having to pretend to work with the whitecoats while subverting them at every turn, but Kenton thought of the information they'd tortured out of him—how he'd placed everyone he loved in harm's way—and he kept pushing on, undermining the High Consul's plans one purloined data package at a time.

In the evenings he sparred with Cadet Michaels. She'd allowed him the use of her first name, Lachelle, once she'd accepted his contrition, and sometimes her friend Ashlyn and the other trainees joined them for a match or two. Kenton saw them using the moves he taught them with an ever increasing frequency, and every day the smiles that greeted him upon his arrival in the Cirruca rose the slightest bit.

"I only managed to recover one file today," he said under his breath to 626 during yet another round of testing. His arm stung from the needle that had been drawing his blood.

626 replied just as softly—while the jammers blocked out the audio and interfered with the camer-

as, they still had to be mindful of the whitecoats scurrying about the lab.

"You're helping more than you know. We're only missing a few key pieces of evidence at this point."

"I know the best course of action is to wait, and I realise they'll stop my heart permanently if I try anything, but every time Consul Rolv walks in here, all I can see is the sol he held against my baby sister's head, and it gets harder and harder to hold myself back. I hate what this place has turned me into."

"I promise, what the Cabal has planned, you'll get your justice."

"When?" Kenton said, catching 626's gaze and holding it. He didn't flinch even as a second needle pierced his skin and drew a vial's worth of blood.

"Before I came here," Kenton continued, "I didn't have a name for the evil that ripped my family away from me. Now I do. It's tangible. It parades in front of me, taunting me. The nightmares grow worse, and I fear only Consul Rolv's death will end them.

"I don't want to lose myself, and yet I fear I must. My friends, my family, everyone I have left will be slaughtered if that man has his way. But if . . ." Kenton paused and swallowed. His voice dropped even lower. "If I kill the High Consul, I don't think I can ever go home again."

626 withdrew the needle and dabbed at the sore spot, his hands warm and comforting against Kenton's bare skin.

"It won't come to that."

It was bold of 626 to make that promise, but

Kenton nodded anyway, struck by the earnestness in the man's eyes.

"In fact, a group of junior interns is coming to the Hexagon tomorrow, in advance of the symposium happening later this week. Word is, "W" will be undercover, and it'll end in a shocking way. Your freedom might come sooner than you think."

The edges of 626's eyes crinkled in a smile, which Kenton half-heartedly returned, wishing he didn't feel so sick. No matter what the Cabal could effect, his sleep would remain troubled and his heart restless until the threat to his people had been eliminated. If only that didn't mean abandoning the principles his father had instilled in him, that he'd striven so hard to adhere to throughout the entire mess he'd found himself in.

"A hollow freedom, if my soul dies through the gaining of it."

"You might feel differently when you're looking at the ashes of this place."

Kenton pictured it, the six-sided, five-storey structure of glass and steel reduced to splinters and shards and rubble. The image brought a certain measure of satisfaction.

"Time will tell."

626 readjusted his glasses, which had slipped down his face, and started resetting his workstation.

"That it will—by the way, my contact wanted to know, what's your name? All anyone knows you as is "742," or "Stormsurge." I can't imagine you're particularly fond of either, and I'm sorry I didn't think to ask before."

"I don't mind "Stormsurge," actually. It reminds me of the klia'an name I earned when I acquired these." Kenton gestured to the lightning-patterned scars covering his right arm. "But I do prefer the name my father gave me. It's Kenton, Kenton Wishings."

626 raised an eyebrow. "Curiouser and curiouser." He held out his hand for Kenton to shake, a quick glance over his shoulder assuring him that the other whitecoats—hunched over their petri dishes and holoscreens—weren't paying any attention to them.

"Nice to meet you, Kenton."

Kenton thrilled at hearing his name for the first time in over a month. He might have given it up to Torturer Anland during those awful days after his arrival, but she'd never bothered with it, and the whitecoats used the number he'd been assigned with a disturbing amount of glee.

626's outstretched hand, Kenton's name on his lips, the genuine smile on his face—Kenton felt real again. He hadn't dredged up that feeling even during his fights in the Tomb. He'd been frightened, yes, but still only the Consul's personal experiment, not treated as a person with his own thoughts and emotions.

Kenton glanced around the room himself. The whitecoats' absolute faith in the Hexagon's constant surveillance showed in their complete lack of suspicion about what he and 626 were up to in the corner. While no one was looking, he clasped 626's hand, eager to hear the man's name and return the favour of speaking it aloud, reclaiming a little bit of the humanity the Hexagon had stolen from them.

"I'm Jack. Jack Riven."

19

Laine still couldn't believe Bo had ditched him.

Well actually, he could. They both knew the bounty specified only one of them needed to be captured alive, and a single lokian against two dozen seasoned bounty hunters wasn't great odds. Heck, Bo had explicitly told him that he would split at the first sign of danger, so Laine's hurt was somewhat unjustified. But it didn't change the fact that he had left.

They'd gotten so far, and then what? Thrown away their shot at finishing their missions all because Laine had come down with a stupid fever? With a vercycle, Smoketown to Skytown was a laughable distance. They could have made it there in a day or less, never mind how ill Laine had been, and never encountered the bounty hunters.

It wasn't fair. The betrayal, no matter how expected—and really, he should have known better, given his history of being let down—still stung, stung like the burning flesh on his neck beneath the bandages.

The stinging abruptly multiplied tenfold, and Laine turned bleary eyes on the hoary-haired man who'd appeared at his side and started peeling off the pus-soaked layers. He attacked the skin below next, and Laine screamed, the feeling like sizzling acid being poured directly into his veins.

"Stop!" he moaned, the word tearing out of his throat like the sinews and muscles the quack stripped away. But no amount of thrashing dislodged the man, Laine's limbs restrained too tightly to free him from the clutches of the sadist masquerading as a medic.

"Thought you'd sedated him," a voice drawled in the silence between his screams.

"The anti-venom for the fenrir virus don't play nice with anaesthetic, but I gotsta cut out the last of the infection 'fore I can use the nano-diffuser again."

"Eerie, hearin'im shriek like that."

"Always feels worse in the moment. But it's a sight better than dyin' after losin' yer fingers an' toes all at once."

Laine passed out.

The sun seared directly overhead when he came to once more. The pain that radiated from his neck into his shoulder had faded to a dull throb, but his stiff muscles resisted his efforts to turn his head left or right.

The bounty hunters had taken his jacket, backpack, and weapons. The stack they'd made of his belongings on the opposite side of the camp near several vercycles tormented Laine with how close it sat. When he got himself free, they'd sorely regret the callous way they treated him.

The crunch of boots on loose stone alerted him to someone's presence.

"Did you really murder your ma an' blow up the Kansor Mountains?"

"What?" Laine stared in open-mouthed confusion at the newcomer, a sandy-haired man who reminded him of Dustin, but lankier, a few years older, and with twice the freckles.

"Guess murder's a bit of an exaggeration, but it is what the details of Doctor Riven's postin' strongly implied."

"He couldn't be happy with framing only his brother, could he?" Laine shook his head, hissing through clenched teeth at the resulting spike of pain. "My uncle's the worst person I've ever met, and I used to run with the Orquídeas."

"You must have done *somethin'* to warrant"—the bounty hunter paused and tapped his clip—"a hundred an' sixty thousand credits, wow."

"It's not just anyone who can say they blew up a mountain and walked away, so I won't deny that, but Gordon—my uncle—he's the one who m-murdered my mom."

Laine clenched his fists, wishing they were free so he could punch something. He hated the way his voice cracked whenever he talked about what had happened.

"And now he's pinning it on me? I did everything I could to save her. Everything."

"Includin' partnerin' with a lokian, I gather."

"The disloyal jerk's friend promised me he could cure Bowman's and—"

"That there proves your story's more full'a holes than a fishin' net," the bounty hunter interrupted, scoffing a little. "Ain't no cure to Bowman's."

"There most definitely is, and my mom would have recovered if Gordon hadn't interfered."

"You think, if there were some magical elixir floating around, that I would have just sat by an' watched each of my five elder brothers die, one by one? You think I'd be here, workin' for the old man 'stead of back with my folks doin' everythin' I could to make sure Jeb don't suffer the way they did? I can't go through that again, I just can't. Then you sit here, spouting some lie about a cure?"

The bounty hunter was almost shouting, his voice close to breaking. But beneath the hurt, beneath the acidic words he spat out, Laine detected an undercurrent of hope. He pushed on that opening.

"I swear, on my dead mother, recovery from Bowman's is possible. After she took the cure, Mom, her pain vanished. She didn't grimace when she smiled. I wasn't afraid that holding her hand would crush it. I can give you the cure."

The man drew back, his face full of suspicion. "Oh, I know for sure this is a trick."

Laine would have spread his arms wide if he hadn't been bound to the tree. He tried to make his eyes project sincerity instead.

"If someone you love is dying, don't you owe it to them to try everything?"

"Of course; I have!"

"In my jacket. There's ten, nine vials of a serum made from kitterstone. It'll work, I promise."

The bounty hunter folded his arms. His narrowed eyes said he didn't trust Laine, but the almost imperceptible cock of his head showed that Laine's words were swaying him, just the littlest bit.

"I'm to entrust my ten-year-old brother's life into your hands because?"

"He'll die otherwise," Laine said bluntly. "I know it. You know it. If you help me, I'll tell you how to administer the serum."

"An' when it don't work, I'm out a job, my reputation, an' my last survivin' sibling, all 'cause I foolishly listened to a kid who's got a one hundred an' sixty—make that sixty-five—thousand credit bounty on his head. My family needs that money. We're still in the hole from the medical bills an' the funerals."

"I shouldn't have to say it," Laine rejoined. The burning on his neck had started up again, and he panted against the pain, wishing for a little water to cool his aching head. "But if you walk away, if you refuse this chance to save your little brother, well, you'll still have your job, your reputation—you'll even have a share of those hundreds of thousands of credits."

Laine looked the man in the eyes, seeing his determination wavering, the spark of hope that Laine's words had lit fanning higher, bit by incremental bit.

"You'll have all that, but not your brother. And in the days after he's gone, taken in, in the most horrific manner, you'll hate yourself for not grabbing onto the last chance offered you."

The bounty hunter swore, and Laine allowed himself a hidden smile. He'd cracked him. And really, the vials were sitting useless in his jacket, still hidden there from when he'd tried to save Mom, before the end—he might as well bargain them for something.

The man slashed through the ropes binding Laine to the tree and yanked him up. The force of it hurt, and Laine jerked away, unable to keep himself from hitting the ground with his hands still cuffed behind him.

"Look, kid, do y'wanna pee or not?" The bounty hunter raised his voice so it carried through the small camp. "I can let you sit here in urine-soaked pants if you so desire."

Humiliation flushed through Laine that that was the cover they were using, but he had to go along with it if he wanted the man's help. He stumbled along behind him, nearly falling a few more times, but kept his feet until they reached the parked ver-cycles where Laine's belongings were stacked.

"Be quick about it."

The bounty hunter began to rifle through the pile as Laine whistled over the sound of absolutely noth-ing happening. The ruse worked, no one looked their way, and after a few minutes, Laine's jacket dangled in front of his face.

"The vials?"

"Inside, left breast pocket, the pocket inside that."

"These the ones?"

Laine nodded when the glass-encased, dark red li-quid came into view. The bounty hunter tipped the serum this way and that, watching it glisten in the sunlight.

"Jeb takes this, he'll live?"

"How far along is he?"

"Been diagnosed 'bout a month, hospitalised within the last two weeks."

"He'll make a full recovery then."

Kenton's lithe frame sprang to mind. He'd said the disease had afflicted him as well, and yet he showed no trace of it, no deformed bones or trouble walking. Bo might be utterly untrustworthy, but Kenton hadn't displayed any signs of guile the weeks he'd spent in Ethaba. He'd never lied to Laine, even when it would have been in his best interests.

"How does it work?"

Laine told him, Kenton's instructions burned into his mind, and made suggestions as to how to alter the strength of the dose for a child.

The bounty hunter looked at the vials like they were made of gold—no as if they contained water, and he'd been parched for days. Then he tied Laine to the nearest tree, stood and walked away.

"Hey!" Laine called, shocked and struggling ineffectually against the newly secured bonds. "What about our deal?"

"You don't go through what I have an' come out stupid. I go back to Smoketown while leavin' you with Old Sureshot, they might label me a coward for skippin' out, but I won't have the stigma of traitor attached to the name of Asher Shyer. If this don't work—" Asher shook his head. "I can't do that to Ma an' Pa. Might as well dig their graves myself."

He continued walking. He didn't turn back.

Afternoon faded into dusk, dusk into early evening, Frey throwing dappled shadows across the boulder-strewn clearing. Its twin was almost completely dark, Freja's pitted face wreathed in a waxing shade.

After Asher left, Laine had wriggled and wriggled and managed to work himself free. The bounty hunter hadn't left the knots looser on purpose, but it appeared his worry over his kid brother had made him careless. Guilt pricked Laine over the advantage he'd gained out of Asher's desperation, but the bounty hunter had the vials now—he wouldn't be too upset once Jeb was up and running around once more. Laine's immediate focus had to be on getting away before Samuel Hezekiah returned.

Light from the evening patrol flashed through the camp, and Laine pressed himself back against the tree, holding his breath until darkness again shrouded him. He lunged for his travel kit. The large knife inside made quick work of the bindings at his wrists and Laine shrugged on his pack, along with his discarded jacket, before darting back into the shadows. He waited the few minutes it took for the patrol to pass by before he crept towards the three vercycles glinting in the light thrown by the camp's central fire.

The middle transport caught Laine's attention, all bold reds and blues with large, stylised eagle feathers etched down the side. Running his fingers along the underside of its dashboard revealed a concealed panel, and when he depressed it, a tool compartment clicked open, fully stocked and containing everything

Laine needed to override the remote start and shutoff. He grabbed a screwdriver, pried up a section of metal under the dash, and played havoc with the wiring and contacts inside.

"Push to start," he muttered, pleased with his work.

It was a testament to how off-kilter the fenrir virus had rendered Laine that he heard nothing, no heavy breathing, no tramp of boots, nor the telltale whine of a sol charging before a blow knocked him away from the vercycle and sent him sprawling into the dirt. Laine spat pebbles and dust out of his mouth and twisted away from a second hit, but a kick caught him across the ribs, stabbing the air out of him.

"MaryAnne!" a gruff voice yelled. "Ain't Sam needs him alive?"

The woman, taller than Laine, and a good thirty pounds heavier by the looks of it, stomped on Laine's leg, and he yelped at the pain that shot through his still-recovering knee. Curling into a ball didn't lessen the impact of the assault, especially not when Mary-Anne sported steel-toed boots.

"Even he can't argue that this piece of scum deserves a good ole fashioned concussion for messin' with my vercycle."

MaryAnne continued kicking Laine, and he pulled his hands away from the vicious blows, trying to angle his pack towards her. But his head still rang with the hits she landed, encouraged all the more by the cheers from the bounty hunters who'd stayed behind to mind the camp and had nothing better to do than watch a grown woman beat a sick teenager.

"Fetch some rope!"

Fear shot through Laine. If they trussed him up again, he'd lose his last chance at escape. The eagle-feather vercycle sat tantalisingly nearby. If he could just get to it—it would mean leaving his lacrosse stick behind, and Laine wasn't prepared for the spasm of hurt accompanying that thought—but all he needed to do was climb on and start the thing.

MaryAnne paused in her attack on Laine's person to grab the rope someone passed up, and Laine scrambled away, willing his shaky legs to stand. MaryAnne's patrol partner laughed and grabbed Laine's arm, the grip painful even through the jacket he'd shrugged on.

"Ah, ah, ah, I ain't letting one hundred an' ninety-seven thousand credits slip through my fingers. Hold still, boy."

Laine twisted, almost wrenching his shoulder in his frantic attempts to get away from the man, but like MaryAnne, the bounty hunter was bigger and stronger than him and drew him back against his husky frame, pinning Laine's arms between them and rendering his kicks useless.

He couldn't plead, couldn't appeal to their pitiful excuses for humanity. Their bloodlust wouldn't be slaked until they'd killed Bo. He'd wasted his last card with Asher, and he couldn't hope to offer them anything better than the ever-increasing reward.

Gordon didn't have that kind of money, so likely Skytown would win the bid for his head. Not the way he'd wanted to get to the city, trussed up like a common criminal. He'd done nothing, absolutely nothing wrong since being on Thorunn.

So Laine fought, no matter how ineffective his writhing and scrabbling.

MaryAnne came closer with the rope, and the man holding him squeezed tighter, one arm coming up across his throat and making Laine light-headed. MaryAnne seized his abused arms—a smirk spread across her leathery face at his feeble resistance—and started winding the coarse rope around his wrists.

Laine swallowed back the sobs that begged an escape from his throat. This was how it ended. He'd made his final stand, and he'd failed. Failed with freedom close enough that he'd held it in his hands for one glorious moment.

An unearthly shriek cut through the jeering bounty hunters, shocking them into silence, into inaction. They seemed almost—paralysed.

"That'll be Old Sureshot baggin' himself that lokian," MaryAnne said, once colour returned to her face. The trembling of her hands travelled through the rope connecting her to Laine, and she looked as shaken as he felt.

The agony of that scream had lit fire along his bones. It made him forget how to think, how to breathe, and he felt shame flush through him upon realising he could have used the moment of stillness to wrench himself free of his captors—they hadn't knotted the binding yet. Instead, his pants were embarrassingly wet, and he stood like a dummy in the arms of the most unfeeling people on the wretched planet.

"What are you waitin' for?" The man holding Laine gestured at the rope in MaryAnne's shaking fingers. "Let's get the brat tied up an' secured where we can see 'im if he tries another escape attempt."

MaryAnne grabbed at Laine, but her hands fell away as that awful, ear-splitting sound rent the unnatural quiet of the night yet again.

Every muscle in Laine's body locked up, chills dancing through his arms, legs, across his face.

Danger.

Danger.

Danger.

He knew it in his bones—no, in the very marrow of his bones. He would die here this night. That scream could mean nothing else.

MaryAnne's swarthy face went white, and she stared somewhere beyond Laine with terrified eyes. Laine strained not to look, but the bounty hunter holding him forcibly turned him around before his grip went slack. The others surrounding him started to gibber at the last sight Laine could possibly have expected.

There, clinging from the sheer rock face on the opposite side of the camp, was Bo.

He was as Laine had never seen him, amber eyes glowing in the light thrown by the fire, eyes set in a face no longer resembling a human one, luminous, haunting eyes punctuated by gleaming fangs half the size of Laine's head and the slow, controlled whipping back and forth of the dark tail attached to an equally dark-furred, sleek body.

Panther, thought Laine wildly, his hysteric mind grasping at dimly remembered mythologies and histories Mom had impressed upon him in what seemed another lifetime. *Mishipeshu.* That was the closest he could come to describing the wraith-like appearance that wreathed Bo. "Lokian" suddenly seemed too limiting a descriptor. *He's turned savage. He'll kill us all.*

Even as Laine watched, numb limbs still freezing him within his captors' clutches, Bo's lithe feline form flickered in and out of existence, padding to the ground and stalking slowly, deliberately through the deep shadows.

He advanced on the frozen bounty hunters, a noiseless shade, reaching the centre of the camp before MaryAnne gathered the wherewithal to jerk her sol into the air and fire. The others startled into action and followed her example.

Their undoing was thinking they dealt with an animal.

Bo sprang unflinchingly forward, towards the thoughtlessly discarded fuel containers the bounty hunters had used to light the crackling flames. Their sols were still blasting when he flung the canisters into the hungry campfire, and the air around the small blaze ignited, engulfing the entire centre of the camp within mere tenths of a moment. The white-hot flames snatched at everything in their path—tents, supplies, and even the very rocks beneath the feet of the horror-stricken bounty hunters.

Faster than all that, Bo appeared at Laine's side, pushing through the fleeing mass of men and women all rushing to grab their belongings before the fire completely consumed them.

Laine gagged at the smell of burning flesh, winced at the screams of those who'd strayed too close to the inferno and been trapped inside the unsparing, unforgiving, blistering heat.

MaryAnne and her companions rushed to save their friends, and Laine hurriedly shook off the rope wound about his wrists and stuffed it into his pack, pressing a hand to his aching head as his former captors forgot all about him in their panic. Their shock would only last so long however; he and Bo had to leave before the bounty hunters recovered their senses.

Every line in the lokian's body was tense, muscles rippling under his glossy fur. He tipped his head towards the vercycles and vocalised at Laine, something that sounded like, *Any good?*

Laine nodded and swung himself once more onto MaryAnne's vercycle, patting the seat behind him where Bo could sit.

The lokian hissed, a look of trepidation crossing his features, but he leapt onto it at Laine's insistence, claws digging into the leather covering. It was just as well they'd be leaving before MaryAnne could see the damage to her beloved vercycle. She wouldn't stop at a mere beating if she caught them again.

"Gotta get my crosse," Laine yelled over the

screaming, "but I can't do that and drive this thing—grab it for me when I fly by?"

Bo yowled—*Not your errand boy*—but stuck out his neck and snagged the fallen stick as they started to move, picking up speed.

Laine circled back around once, using the sol-cannon mounted on the vercycle's front to shoot out the remaining transports' engines. No one would be following them on the smoking wrecks he left behind.

The vercycle wobbled at the tight turns he took as he flashed through the smoke and confusion, trying to get away from the *zuet-zuet* of solfire that dogged them, MaryAnne having finally noticed that the boy she'd forgotten about had succeeded in his second attempt at thievery.

"Sam!" she hollered, pointing an accusing finger with one hand and firing with the other, too far away to catch them on foot. But the men emerging from the forest weren't so distant or impeded by a lack of reliable transports. Laine's breath stuck in his throat when he saw just how many bounty hunters roared out from the trees, crashing through the underbrush, sols and sol-canons firing.

"Hold on!" Laine screamed at Bo. He ducked and dove and threw them into a roll that nearly took off his head he came so close to the ground. A blast of solfire ate through his jacket, the hot flash of it searing his skin.

Bo yelped.

My ear! it sounded like and then, *Not the path. Up the mountain.*

"It's too exposed," Laine protested, hunching low over the speeding vercycle. "We'll fall!"

Wouldn't suggest if no plan. Go!

Laine understood Bo's intentions just in time to swing the vercycle towards the mountain towering over them and pull his hood tight over his head, affording him the barest protection against the shriek that froze him in his seat. He tried to turn his head to see how closely Samuel Hezekiah's men pursued them, but the terrifying sound emanating from Bo locked his hands to the handles, setting them on a collision course with the many large rocks jutting up throughout the camp.

Laine tried again to break free of the torpor encasing him, but though the night air cut sharply at his face, and droplets of sweat prickled down his neck, he couldn't jerk his body free of the rigidity Bo's chilling scream had effected. At least the bounty hunters had been stricken by the same affliction, and their solfire petered out. Laine caught a glimpse of one man's glassy stare as he and Bo sped by. Their eyes met, the only parts of their bodies they could still control and hatred warred with fright in the man's pupils, constricted into tiny dots from the awful thrill of Bo's inescapable thrall and the terrible brightness of the dying explosion that went on and on and on.

Bo's claws swiped the back of Laine's neck, forcing him from his stupor, and he angled the vercycle at the sheer rock face of Mount Lalethusl just in time to avoid smashing into a massive boulder marking the outskirts of the camp, which was uncontainably on fire. The bounty hunters closest to catching him didn't fare so well, and Laine hunched lower over the vercycle at the crunch of glass and the whine of steel that drowned out the screams.

Somehow he managed to wrangle his nerveless fingers into aligning the vercycle vertically with the mountain, and they shot up, Laine tucking his feet into the footholds so Thorunn's heavy gravity didn't drag him out of his seat. Wind scraped his face, an unpleasantness that could have been avoided if he'd thought to tell Bo to grab the helmets on the ground as well. But he'd make do. He'd jumped from a mountain with less chance of survival.

The camp dwindled away below them, Samuel Hezekiah and his men following after their paralysis melted, loosing blasts that shattered parts of the mountain above and showered dust into Laine's un-protected face.

"Rear canons!" he managed to spit at Bo through a choking cough. MaryAnne's powerful vercycle was nothing like Gordon's Blackline. His uncle's transport was all sleek lines, designed for speed, not power, and it certainly didn't have the front and rear sol-can-ons the modified military machine beneath him did.

He heard Bo's shots connect, the bounty hunters shouting curses at them, and Laine strained to look over his shoulder at the men who dropped off one by one. Curiously enough, even those Bo missed started to peel away, retreating to the burning camp, the lights along their vercycles winking out.

Chased me all day. Must recharge or fall, Bo vocalised, sounding insufferably smug even through the inhuman tones blurred by the rushing wind.

A grin seized Laine's face, though solfire still dogged them. He aimed for a curve high in the mountain that would hide them from view, and before long the sounds of the camp faded into nothingness, snow appearing on the ground as they approached the peak.

When he was sure it was safe, Laine levelled out the vercycle and continued at a less madcap pace, heart still thrilling with the narrowness of their escape. He twisted in his seat to congratulate the utterly mad, yet fantastically brilliant lokian and almost crashed them into the rock face at the unwelcome and unsettling sight of Bo limply sprawled across the back of the vercycle.

He didn't appear to be breathing.

The rapidly cooling air drew a blanket of frost around them, and Bo's sweat-slicked fur crystallised right before Laine's eyes.

"Bo!"

He didn't respond, watery eyes open a crack. His nose looked dry, too dry, but Skytown was still too far for them to risk resting for a spell. The bounty hunters might get fresh transports from Smoketown and catch them again before the night was out. Besides, Bo's bulk would make getting him back onto the vercycle difficult if they stopped and then had to leave in a hurry. Bo could still slip off if he completely lost consciousness and his claws retracted.

Laine slowed even more—setting them to cruise—and dug in his pack for the rope he'd stuffed on top. Somehow Bo had managed to keep his lacrosse stick between his fangs throughout their reckless escape, and Laine extricated it as best he could before binding Bo to the vercycle.

"Just until we find a safe place to rest, okay?"

A twitch from Bo was all the response Laine received, and he picked up speed, his heart, which had never resumed a normal rhythm, starting to hammer rapidly again. He pressed a button and flicked through the holograph that projected the nav system. At their current pace, they'd reach the outskirts of Skytown in under thirty minutes. Laine increased their speed; Bo might not make it twenty.

The chill air bit at Laine, his jacket not much good against the winter weather that characterised the mountain's peak. Each breath was like drawing in fire, and Laine kept coughing, a chesty thing that threatened to rip his lungs in half.

However bad he felt, it had to be worse for Bo, who shivered despite his thick coat, laboured snuffles issuing from his mouth and nose. He'd led Samuel Hezekiah and his men on a merry chase up and down the mountain for a full day. Had he even stopped to rest, to eat, to gulp down a single mouthful of water?

Laine turned to check on Bo again. Other than the shallow rise and fall of his chest, he'd gone unnaturally still.

Skytown loomed in the distance, a speck of dark

against the white slopes of Mount Lalethusl. The nav display showed them being under ten minutes from the city gates. The energy gauge blinked a five-minute warning. The stupid thing would have lasted another two hours if not for the cold, and without a charging station the vercycle would be dead until daybreak—still a long ways off.

"C'mon, baby," Laine said in a coaxing tone, running his hand along the frost-streaked panel. "Bo came back for us. We can go a little farther for him. Please?"

They limped along a few minutes more, but the deepening cold forced them to a stop sooner than Laine would have liked. If the power had lasted a little longer, they'd have been in front of the city gates. How he would have explained Bo's presence to the guards, Laine didn't know, but they'd have at least been in range of shelter and possibly medical assistance. Now they faced a fifteen-minute trudge through the snow—double that if Laine couldn't get Bo to walk on his own.

Powered down, the vercycle sat useless in the snow, a hunk of steel and machinery too heavy for Laine to drag out of sight and conceal among the sparse, spruce-like trees laden with a silvery fruit that made Laine's stomach pinch. The bounty hunters would certainly find the vercycle when they inevitably gave pursuit, and each minute he wasted closed the gap between them and him and Bo.

Laine shook the lokian, shouted at him, but Bo remained still, a listless lump in his arms. Desperate and out of options, Laine unstrapped Bo's quirn from his back and fiddled with it until it lit up, casting an eerie blue over the shadowed snow. He pressed the weapon into Bo's flank and sent a jolt along it.

Bo came awake in a spitting mass of teeth and claws, one swiping paw catching Laine in the side and forcing him to drop the quirn, where it melted the snow around it. Bo scream-vocalised a few curses before taking in the blood spilling out beneath Laine's fingers and the stark landscape so very different to the one they'd left halfway down the mountain.

"Y'weren't wakin' up," Laine offered weakly, the pain and cold slurring his words as he continued to press his hands to his torso. "We're close, but I can't carry you."

Bo huffed and nudged over his pack.

Once Laine had patched himself up with the rolls of gauze and tape within, they began the walk towards the city's walls, keeping to the shadows to disguise their approach. The snow piled up in odd configurations, and Bo steered Laine towards a mound that rose strangely out of the snow. The lokian's paws folded underneath him once they reached the shape, unable to limp another step.

He's got the right idea, Laine thought, wanting to collapse to the ground himself. Unnatural warmth already seeped into his bones however, and he knew if he stopped moving he'd freeze to death. Bo had led them to the mound for a reason, and Laine jabbed at it with his crosse, surprised when the snow dropped off in clumps to reveal a metal door inset with unfamiliar glyphs.

The old onite mines, Bo vocalised when Laine turned an inquisitive look on him. *What your people murdered Tribe Anshi for.*

With that bit of disturbing information, Bo's eyes rolled back, and he slumped forward, passing out a second time.

Laine pulled at the stiff handle, but it didn't budge. He battered at it a few times with his lacrosse stick, but the dark-grey door refused to yield, stuck fast either from the cold or because a lock on the inside held it shut.

"C'mon!" Laine yelled, beating on the door with his fists. "Open."

Bo couldn't have led him to a dead-end, not when they'd both die if they didn't get into the mine. Someone had to be on the other side.

"Please. Please." He tried not to think of the last time he'd begged for something, shutting his eyes tight against the memory of a suffocating hospital room and the waking nightmare that had followed. He couldn't endure that again, not when they were so close. Not when a single metal door was the only thing barring their entry into the city atop the mountain.

"Please, my friend is dying. He risked his life to come back for me. He's good. He doesn't deserve to die. Please. I can't, can't lose anyone else."

No answer came, and Laine slid down to sit in the slushy drifts next to Bo. He ran his gloved fingers through the lokian's snow-laden fur.

"End of the road, huh? Sucks we made it this far and didn't get to rescue Kenton. Least we had some good times along the way."

Laine banged on the door one last time. Or thought he did, but his arm was so stiff he might have imagined it. Ice froze his jaw shut, rendering him unable to keep calling for help. The tears that escaped his wind-reddened eyes crystallised before they could run down his cheeks, and defeated, Laine laid his head against Bo's sleek hide and gave himself up to the cold.

———————————— ● ————————————

". . . in shock, where's my assisting nurse?"

"Wait 'til Lis sees this! A forest klia'an and a human, together?"

". . . soaked to the bone . . . any later and they wouldn't've made it."

He was warm, so warm, and then cold, and strange hands were touching him. Loud clanging drowned out what snatches of conversation he could hear, the reverberations settling in his bones.

"Stop," he rasped. "Lanae's whiskers, make it stop."

A hand touched his shoulder, the slight pressure of fingertips on his fur like hot coals, and an unwilling snarl tore loose from Bo's throat.

"'S jus' me. I see you've shifted back."

Bo blinked rapidly, and Laine's face blurred into view. He sat on a metal chair next to the bed Bo could feel beneath him, a blanket thrown over his shoulders and a steaming mug of something sweet-smelling in his hands.

"I'd offer you some, but Shadow said this stuff's toxic to klia'ans." Laine lifted one shoulder in an apologetic half-shrug.

"Shadow?"

"Says I haven't earned his real name yet, that nobody outside of 'W' has earned that right, though she seemed okay with telling me her real name. It's Lis, by the way."

"That's not . . . Where are we? Did the bounty hunters—?"

Laine laughed, but it wasn't an unkind sound—more incredulous than anything else.

"Those good-for-nothings could walk right up to the door and bang on it all they like—though they won't, Shadow saw to covering our tracks—there's no way they'll get in here."

Laine shifted in his seat, taking a long gulp of the beverage he held, apparently scalding from the way he yelped and then fanned his tongue, letting it loll out of his mouth like a kit on a sweltering 'tween frix evening.

The clanging persisted, unignorable, each low note setting Bo's fur on end. He hadn't thought the old mining tunnels still in operation, had thought they'd be a safe place to hole up until he'd figured out where Ken was and how to set about rescuing him. The active machinery spoke to a far more prominent use of the shafts and attached drilling stations.

"And here is?" Bo asked through gritted teeth. He worked his claws in and out of the blankets covering his hands in time to the rhythmic grinding of the gears. It was that or fiddle with the IV lines disappearing into his arms, and as weak and tired as he still felt, he'd rather not risk bursting the tubing if the contents within were keeping him in stable condition.

"Last place I ever thought we'd be. Deep below Skytown of course, but you knew that. It's *who* we're with that's the crazy part. Remember that terrorist group Woodley thought we ran with at first?"

"I don't think there was a day they weren't on the news," Bo replied, pretty sure what Laine was getting at,. wishing he'd hurry up and say it already. "I don't suppose you're about to tell me they're just misunderstood."

Laine's face quirked into a half smile, and he indicated the mug in his hands and then the room at large. "Hard to argue with them after they patched us up and gave us free food. Not being tied up's pretty nice too."

Footsteps sounded in the corridor beyond, and Bo struggled to pull himself to a sitting position. No matter Laine's easy trust of the people who'd saved them, it wouldn't do to appear fragile in front of the men and women of the Cabal.

The industrial grey door opened, revealing a long hall lit by ceiling-high rows of lights set in the walls, and a young girl walked in, followed by two uniformed people with sols strapped to them. Despite her youthful appearance—accented by curly hair styled into braided rows with brightly coloured hair ties and bobbles—she walked with an air of authority, a serious look in her dark, pretty eyes. Given their location and the security surrounding her, she had to be "W." The leader of the Cabal.

A shiver ran through Bo at that, imagining what sorts of atrocities she had endured to become a leader, so young, of the most notorious terrorist group on Thorunn.

A fourth person stood shoulder to shoulder with the dark-skinned girl—or would have, had he not towered over her. Bo stared at the odd combination, not entirely sure he wasn't hallucinating. The robed figure was a klia'an, and from the lost tribe at that, his white fur with its distinct black splotches so different from the black, brown, and honey dappled colouring of Tribe Osinan.

The group swept forward, the two Bo assumed to be guards standing at attention whilst the others pulled up chairs next to Laine, putting themselves between the blanket wrapped teen and Bo.

"I take it you're to thank for our rescue?" Bo rasped, suddenly horribly aware of his dry throat. "W"—Lis, Laine had called her—motioned, and one of the guards presented a water bottle to Bo, which he drained almost halfway before registering the gentle amusement in the newcomers' eyes. So much for his plan not to appear weakened.

"You're to thank for your rescue, really. Shadow here ran into unexpected trouble the other day, and we've been extra careful who we let inside our walls.

When we saw you two half frozen to death on our doorstep—"

"I cautioned her that it might be a trap," Shadow cut in, "but Lis has an uncanny way of telling the truth of things."

"I was right, wasn't, I?" Lis' smile encompassed her whole face, familiar in a way Bo couldn't quite pinpoint. "I've learned a bit from Laine here. I'm hoping you can tell me more."

The smile stayed firmly on her face, genuine, but layered atop some deeper agenda. Despite the klia'an at her side and Laine's baffling acceptance of them, Bo hesitated. Lis was human, and it would take much more than the apparent friendship between her and the Anshian klia'an to persuade Bo to let his guard down. And yet for all his misgivings, a familiar feeling persisted, nagging at him. He felt like he should know the girl, like he'd seen her somewhere before.

"Have you lived in Skytown *all* your life?" The question blurted out before Bo could help himself and something like fear startled through Lis' eyes.

No, not fear, trepidation; Bo could see hope laced through the worry. The reaction was minute and fleeting, Lis composing herself and visibly relaxing, determined to pretend Bo's query hadn't rattled her.

"Five years I've been at this, and no one but Shadow's ever asked something so similar in just that tone of voice. Tell you what"—Lis rose from her seat and withdrew a small holoscreen—"read through what Medic Hulda documented about your condition, and then you're free to come and go around here as you wish."

"But I didn't answer anything?"

"What you asked—how you asked it, you've more than confirmed what I've been hearing from my man on the inside."

"Which is?"

Lis shook her head and gestured for Shadow to join her as she turned to leave. "Our secrets can't be compromised any further. Not even for you. Not yet. But welcome to the Cabal. You're among friends here."

Lis smiled again, the seriousness that had never quite left her eyes returning full force. The lilting cadence of her voice wrapped comfortingly around Bo, like an old friend, prompting within him a burning curiosity. She'd neatly sidestepped his questions as well, admirable, but not something he'd have expected of a girl who looked like she'd just entered a human high school. It begged investigation that someone her age led such an organised and focused group of individuals.

After she and her entourage exited the room he said as much to Laine, who shrugged and slurped noisily at his still steaming drink.

"The Cabal members I've met so far are kinda a tight lipped bunch, but from what I've managed to gather, Shadow's from that tribe you said had been destroyed. Story goes he almost got himself killed looking for revenge, but Lis ran into him while exploring the mines one winter and convinced him there was a better way. So really it's the two of them running this joint—but Lis apparently knows some secrets the Consul would kill her for if they knew. That's what makes her the leader. Makes her 'W'."

Laine laughed, a wistful expression crossing his face. "Yoon Ah's gonna be so jealous I've met 'W'."

"They have a lot in common," Bo remarked and turned the holoscreen over in his lap to avoid the medic's diagnosis a little longer. He could feel something was different; he didn't need to know straightaway if he truly was stuck in one form for the rest of his life. "Both around the same age, both sticking their noses in places other people—dangerous people—don't want them."

"Me and Andy keep telling Yoon Ah to be careful with her investigations, but she's . . ."

"Stubborn as all get out?" Bo offered, smirking at Laine's long-suffering eye roll.

"I was gonna say persistent. If she gets caught—"

"You think they'd send her here?"

"Lis is certain they won't spare her, so they definitely wouldn't give Yoon Ah a pass. Course, they captured Kenton, and you know how we've been hunted."

Bo clenched his jaw at the memories. His sore limbs still protested the insane amount of non-stop running he'd been forced into while staying one step ahead of the bounty hunters outside of Smoketown.

"We haven't even been here a day," Laine continued, "and I've heard things about the illegal torture and hush-hush experimentation going on in this town that you wouldn't believe. Or maybe you would, knowing you."

"You're the one who's been denying what your government did to Ken's family."

Laine tapped the side of his mug. "I dunno. I've been wilfully blind, I guess. The tears and bloodshed which built the country where I lived on Earth—I suppose I wanted to believe humanity could be better here. The Consul used your people to cover their crimes, and I fell for it. After all my talk of not trusting adults. Stupid."

"It's good thing a teenager leads the rebellion, then."

Laine chuckled, but a distant look remained in his eyes, and Bo returned his attention to the holoscreen in his lap, flipping it rightside up. He sucked in a gasp at the information on the brightly glowing display.

"Good news?"

"I . . . I can shift!"

"That ain't news." Laine's eyebrows knit together in confusion.

"Is when assuming s'hinoian form could trigger—what's the phrase?—complications leading to death."

At Laine's sharp inhale, Bo explained the circumstances surrounding his injury and resulting disability, enjoying how Laine's eyes grew wide at the realisation of what Bo had risked in exchange for the ability to immobilise the bounty hunters during their reckless escape.

"Course, it says here there are limitations; I can't go crazy with shifting, but I really thought last time would be the last time, which would have sucked 'cause I'd been saving it for something special. But now . . ."

With care Bo could spend time in either of his forms. He could have his life back—partially, the underlying damage could never be undone, and he'd collapse if he pushed himself too hard too fast—but the large lettering spelling out the medic's positive prognosis on the holoscreen was more than he'd dared to hope for. He wondered how Ken fared at the hands of his captors. If they'd discovered his weak heart and used it against him.

Bo grit his teeth at the thought and began to climb out of the bed, snarling at Laine to find him fresh clothes when he asked what Bo was attempting.

"Against a multitude of odds, we made it to Skytown. Let's do what we came here to do."

20

The cold air shocked Bo in its intensity, so fresh and crisp he could taste the snow drifts piled up along the streets. He shivered despite the thick garments layered over his fur, drawing his hood tight around his face, both to block out the chill and to disguise the fact that he was klia'an. He and Laine were still wanted men after all. But if Shadow, the last of Tribe Anshi, had been able to hide in plain sight amongst the humans of Skytown since the murder of his people, then he and Laine could surely slip undetected through the unwitting citizens of the frostbitten city.

"Let them go," Shadow had said earlier that morning, content to stand in the doorway watching Laine and Bo tugging on boots and gloves. "Even if the children that pass for soldiers around here do manage to nab them, they won't think to connect them to the Cabal."

"They've seen my face," Lis had pointed out. "They know I'm 'W'."

"And how many dozens of teen girls are nicknamed Lis in Skytown? We do use this version of your name for a reason. You've refrained from saying anything truly incriminating in front of them, and all that aside, things are too far set in motion to be stopped by their possible capture and interrogation. By the time Lynn Anland finished with them, we'd already be closing the noose about her neck and those of her compatriots."

"Nice to know we're so highly valued," Laine had muttered, prompting a laugh from the two Cabal leaders.

"When faced with the monumental task of dismantling the corrupt and oppressive system responsible for the deaths of thousands, you'd be conflicted about possible wrenches in your plans too. That being said, do try not to get caught. We'd rather not have to rescue you two on top of everything else."

And now here they were, traipsing through slush to find answers Bo hadn't been comfortable asking from the Cabal. He ought to trust them in some measure, given that they'd treated him and Laine with nothing but kindness, but if Lis wouldn't share her plans, neither would he.

Laine's hand on Bo's shoulder broke him from his musings.

"*O'Tafferty's,*" Laine said, pointing across the street. "Bars are always good places to get info."

With what money, Bo didn't know, but the thought of food reminded him he hadn't eaten since getting the IVs out, so he followed Laine across the snow-trampled road. The dimly lit interior was a welcome relief from the biting cold of Skytown. The warmth did nothing to disguise the stink of smoke and unwashed bodies however, and Bo fought back the urge to start grooming himself, plopping down beside

Laine at a corner booth not too far from the doors.

A waitress came along a little while later with water and chips. Laine paid her with tokens he'd filched from the tip jar when the bartender had been distracted snapping at several patrons who'd gotten too rowdy for the gloomy establishment. When Bo had raised an eyebrow at the theft, Laine had just shrugged and pointed out that half the staff was also drinking and slacking off on the side.

In short, they'd managed to pick the seediest pub in Skytown on their first try, complete with a battered holoscreen hung in the corner, the cracked display distorting the colours of the broadcast, something about a scientific symposium happening the next day. Captions scrolled up the screen, a necessity given the discordant music drowning out the muttered conversations happening throughout *O'Tafferty's.*

"You really think we'll get intel here?" Bo questioned, stirring his drink with the little wooden spoon that had accompanied the yellow liquid.

"Sure as heck ain't gonna find Kenton at the grocery store."

"Of course, but *here?*" Bo indicated the sickly sweet haze that sat in the air, the couple patrons drooling on tables, and a furtive-looking teen about their own age whose awkward attempts at talking to the waitresses must have been the result of some idiotic dare. "We should at least have tried that hexy place Shadow was talking to you-know-who about."

"Must be nice to see another klia'an after so long." Laine crunched on a handful of chips, offering the bag to Bo.

"From all the five minutes I saw of him, I guess. He's a bit paranoid, but who wouldn't be, being the last of his kind and all."

"Can you not be depressing for just one day?" Laine said, mouth turning down at the side.

Bo shrugged and nibbled at the chips, instantly regretting it when fire started to burn his tongue. Why humans willingly subjected themselves to such torture he couldn't for the life of him fathom.

"I'll outshine Lanae and Lanaekim on a cloudless night when we find Ken," he retorted, trying to ignore the tingling inflaming his mouth. "After we're done here, we should investigate that hexon, hextant—"

"Hexagon?"

Bo snapped his fingers. "That's it. From the way Shadow talked, the place sounded important. We should have tried there first and not this—what's the word—dubious establishment."

"No, I mean—look, on the holoscreen, the Hexagon."

Bo twisted around and saw that the images on the broadcast had changed to show a pretty blonde lady standing in front of thick metal doors set in a towering building of concrete and steel. The ticker running at the bottom of the holoscreen read, "Free admission to Hexagon tomorrow for the first Annual Thorunn Energy and Development Symposium. This event to be streamed across all channels."

"Oh no, how will people get their daily fix of *Task*

Force: Mars," Laine said in a mocking tone.

"Sucks, don't it?" their waitress said from their left, and Bo startled, ducking his head to hide his face.

"Not a big fan of the show myself, but I'm pressed about missin' the reruns from the Tomb." At Laine's confused look she elaborated, "You must be new in town—we got an extra channel here at the top of the mountain. Most people watch it, as our only other choices are the farce of the news and endless marathons of bad cop shows. Here."

She set down the tray of food they'd ordered—Laine reaching for his plate as soon as it touched the stained tabletop—and tapped her clip, changing the channel before Laine or Bo could protest. "You'll love it even if this footage is from some of the early matches."

The waitress kept yammering on in the background, but Bo didn't hear a word of it.

The captions read "Stormsurge," but even wreathed in crackling blue-white frix, Bo knew the face of the figure savagely and methodically overwhelming a vyss'ngryr on the holoscreen.

Ken.

He'd found him.

"Ya gotta wonder, if the Tomb's pulling fighters of that calibre, why the army ain't snapped him up. Someone with his abilities woulda come in real handy 'gainst the Outpost Terrorist."

Laine choked on the mouthful of food he'd been inhaling, hacking and spluttering and prompting the waitress to leave to grab a cup of water from the bar.

"Seems you were right." Laine coughed again, thumping his chest to help clear his throat. "The Hexagon it is."

Bo jumped up from his seat, earning a quizzical look from Laine.

"You're not going now? Didn't you read the news strip? Tomorrow we can just walk in, no invites required."

"I can't wait that long, not knowing Ken's there and I can do something about it."

"Rushing in early with no plan's not gonna solve anything. I don't even have my crosse with me."

Bo stared at the human. Who was he, and what had he done with the reckless, impulsive Laine Riven?

"We . . . can at least scout around," he said, sinking back into his seat. "Plan an escape route or several from the building."

He watched Laine tear his empty chip packet into tiny little pieces while the footage from the Hexagon flashed through several different fights, some in a large underground arena against wild animals and trained fighters, and some in smaller, more intimate settings, but all with crowds of cheering onlookers.

Seeing Ken alive and reasonably well was a balm to wounds Bo didn't realise had been hurting so deeply. He could breathe again, after drowning in fear and worry.

"What about you?" Bo asked after the waitress had come and gone again, leaving them with only their drinks. "Think the Hexagon holds the answers you're seeking?"

"With any luck. All those scientists—I'm betting somebody somewhere can point me in the right direction. The trick will be not letting on that I have a personal stake in uncovering all of the esteemed Doctor Riven's secrets."

Laine said the name like he was chewing on something tough and bitter, squeezing the cup in his hand so tightly the wood began to crack.

"You could say it's for research—didn't Lis say her cover's an internship?"

"That could work." Laine nodded and wiped his mouth with the scratchy paper napkins before rising, leaving some of his stolen credit tokens on the table for the unwittingly helpful waitress.

The Hexagon wasn't hard to find, situated at the far end of town and built into the mountainside. Bo marvelled at the sheer enormity of the structure—it looked like it could fit the entirety of Tribe Osinan twice over with room to spare. The tall double doors—comparable in width to Ethaba's gates—admitted and discharged a steady stream of people. Each entrant, however, paused to pull off a glove and place a hand on a wall-mounted palm scanner before gaining access. Soldiers stood on each side of the door, motionless but watching the bustle keenly.

Bo and Laine split off into another section of the crowd jostling its way towards a smaller, less guarded entryway. The crush of people thronging about them comprised reporters and their bright-eyed assistants, and Laine put his pilfering skills to work once more, lifting a couple of passes that he and Bo showed at the side door. They were waved through, their press badges apparently enough not to warrant the other security measures.

Once inside they detached themselves from the news crews and wandered down a brightly lit hall-way the opposite direction from the signs reading *Toilets* and *Visitors' Centre*.

"The Tomb, this way," Laine said, reading from a square plaque on the wall. Bo studied it as well, an excuse to conceal his face from the harried-looking scientists rushing by. "That doesn't sound ominous at all."

"Sounds like a lead," Bo replied and started in the indicated direction.

Laine jumped in front of him. "Dude, scouting only, remember?"

Bo pushed past him into the corridor. Laine could follow or not as he wished. He knew what they'd agreed on, but if there was even a chance he could get Ken out of the oppressive building before the day's end, he had to see it through.

Laine scowled and rolled his eyes but accompan-ied Bo through the maze-like winding halls that led them deeper and deeper into the Hexagon. Bo com-mitted the paths they took to memory the best he could, grateful for the numerous signs pointing the way. They went down and up, across a small bridge, down a flight of stairs, then up again.

"I feel like we're literally going in circles," Laine said, pulling a small bottle of lytorade from his jacket. "We've been here, like, an hour, and we still haven't found this place yet."

It hadn't been that long, but Bo's aching legs were inclined to agree with Laine. After almost freezing to death, even a good night's sleep hadn't restored him to full health. But he had to keep going. He could rest once Ken was safe.

"Stop that," he snapped at Laine, who'd stashed his drink and started to mindlessly fidget with the plastic-encased name tag dangling at the end of his ill-gotten lanyard.

Laine sulked and ceased for all of two minutes before his fingers started twirling the tag again.

Spin. Flash. Spin. Flash. Spin.

Bo growled before he could repress the instinct, a scathing diatribe about to leave his lips when they turned the corner and were confronted by a large set of double doors, an automated ticket stand on one side, and an assortment of flashy concessions on the other. A thick rope hung between two rings on either side of the doors, barring further progress. When Bo raised his eyes to the bold lettering proclaiming the place *The Tomb* he caught sight of a blinking camera, which would surely set off an alarm if they attempted to force the doors.

"Well, when you can't go through the front . . ." Laine said and pushed Bo over to a narrow door set off to the side and signposted as *AV Room Authorised Personnel Only.*

"This looks promising." Laine fiddled with the locks a moment, and then steel panels slid back, granting them access to a narrow flight of stairs with a narrow door at the top that opened easily.

Bo blinked as his eyes adjusted to the lowered lighting in the room they'd entered. It was stacked high to their left and right with rows of devices that held recordings. A large three-panelled window directly in front of them looked out into the darkened Tomb, and computers were shoved into every inch of free space.

The room wasn't empty either, the three young adults huddled over a bank of holoscreens spotting him and Laine before they could make their retreat.

"Yo, you lost?"

"D-depends on your definition of lost," Laine said. "We're interns with, ah, Thorunn Crystal Broadcast News Network, um, and this is our first time in Skytown, and we just really wanted to see the Tomb."

Laine's voice grew stronger as he cobbled together a halfway decent cover story, and Bo tamped down on a purr of approval.

"We found it obviously, but we must've taken the long way, and we have no idea how to get back in time to stop our bosses from yelling at us."

"I feel you, bro," the man said, offering his hand. "We've been stuck in here prepping for the symposium for the last few days. They're expecting us to do all the work. All of it! If we weren't communication and journalism majors, we'd be failing so hard right now. I'm Matt by the way, and this's Brett and

Jolene."

"Don't you 'ave maps of the place downloaded to your clips?" Brett suddenly asked, scrutinising them carefully.

"Like he said, we're not strictly supposed to be here." Bo kept his head ducked as he spoke. The low lighting wouldn't highlight his features, but his eyes would catch the glow from the monitors if he wasn't careful. "We kinda, left our clips behind to dodge unwanted calls."

Brett nodded—a cheerfully long-suffering expression settling into place—and dug around in the drawer of a nearby desk.

"I get that. That's one thing I don't like about this place. They're always spyin' on ya."

"Oh, come off it," Jolene said. She hadn't stopped typing even with the unexpected intrusion. "You know the footage gets erased every third day."

"That's what they tell you," Matt muttered with a sing-song lilt, returning to adjusting the lighting and sound settings at his holo-display.

Brett let out a loud, "Aha!" and produced a crumpled scrap of paper. "Knew we 'ad this old thing around 'ere." He pressed the blue-tinted map into Laine's hands. "Should get y'back to wherever you've gotta be."

"You're a life saver, really, thanks!"

Bo rolled his eyes at the overly sincere gushing from Laine, but the wide-eyed fumbling bit seemed to charm the stressed students, their tiredness making them overlook Bo and Laine's entirely suspicious and flimsy explanations. Bo pulled Laine through the door before Jolene could tear her eyes away from the screen in front of her and catalogue anything amiss.

A bitten off exclamation from Laine made Bo stiffen.

"Look," Laine said, thrusting the paper in his face. "This isn't just a map—it's blueprints."

Bo snatched the paper from Laine, nearly tearing it in his haste, and perused it quickly.

"It's incomplete." He shoved the map back at Laine, not bothering to hide his disappointment.

"Did you see the date?"

Bo scanned the sheet again, and his eyes widened. "If they still have this, from back then—"

Laine nodded, carefully tucking the paper into his jacket.

"Odds are good somewhere they'll have the hard-copy records Lis mentioned she's looking for."

"That's good news, I guess, but a map with only two out of three, possibly four, levels listed still doesn't help me find Ken. We need a way to access the Tomb floor."

"I think Shadow can help us with that."

Bo hummed in agreement, and they started walking back the way they'd come, Consulting the map occasionally whenever the long, twisting hallways intersected, splitting off into confusing directions.

"There's a corridor marked here that'll take us directly out the back," Laine said, running a finger over the blueprints' faded lines.

"Lead on." Any path that kept them away from

the humans of Skytown was fine by Bo.

The door they found didn't budge at first, and Bo thought with distaste that they'd have to double back and duck past the scientists and news crews after all, but a few minutes of wrestling with the wood and steel yielded results. They left the door open a crack, in case the other end proved twice as stubborn.

Laine kept one hand on Bo's sleeve as they hurried through the unlit corridor, and sneezes tickled the back of Bo's throat, the dust his booted feet swirled up so thick it obscured what little his sensitive eyes could discern.

Bo lowered the hood on his jacket, using his whiskers and ears to guide them through the darkness, and kept his mouth firmly closed, breathing but little as they brushed through the layers of cobwebs left by tiny spinners. He tried to ignore the way Laine's hand tightened on his arm whenever one of the many-legged creatures skittered over their exposed faces.

The hallway they entered at the passage's end was wide and brightly lit. The sudden contrast caused spots to dance in Bo's vision, and distracted, he failed to immediately notice the rather alarming situation he and Laine had stumbled into.

Five armoured soldiers aimed glowing sols at them, and so unexpected was the sight that for a moment Bo thought the abrupt brightness had induced a hallucination. The sensation didn't abate upon seeing the wavy fire-red and curly sunset-blue shocks of hair respectively adorning the two lead soldiers.

Only idiots wanting to be gira'an snacks went out of their way to sport such bright colours so far from the Hinnom Forest. There was a reason Shadow's people's coats blended so effortlessly with the snowy mountainside after all. But if the humans wanted to court death, that was no business of his—not like the humming sols that promised severe burns and possible losses of limbs if discharged.

Bo slid his eyes over to Laine, whose jaw muscles bulged visibly from how hard he grit his teeth. A minute shift in Laine's stance was Bo's only warning before the teen threw himself to the side, drawing his own sol and firing as he went, dropping into a roll that put him behind a stack of cloth-draped equipment on the other side of the small squadron.

Bo took advantage of the confusion to dart back behind the door, wrenching it almost closed, and loosed a few shots of his own through the gap.

"Turn yourselves over," the blue-haired woman called out, "and we promise to—"

Solfire drowned out the rest of her words, but what did it matter what she said? Until the day being born a lokian was no longer a crime in Skytown, Bo would rather go down fighting than trust a merciless soldier's honeyed words.

Round after round of solfire echoed in Bo's ears until an abrupt silence blanketed the corridor, followed by muttered curses, the sols having run out of charges.

"Dang it, Michaels," one of the male soldiers said, his voice carrying in the forced hush. "You said this was gonna be easy. A milk run, practically."

"I was the one pushing to get us equipped with T-500's, remember? Sergeant Álvero refused to authorise their release."

"Well, yeah, because those sols pack a kick, Lachelle," the red-haired girl said. "He doesn't want to have to fix us up if something goes bad."

"What do you call this?"

Bo peeked out from behind the door. The soldiers—trainees really, they could hardly be older than him or Laine and were missing the decorative pins and lapels Jenna and New Little Rock's commander had sported—crouched throughout the corridor, some huddled together behind covered stacks of equipment like Laine, others wedged into the space between the walls and extruding pillars.

They all stared at each other.

"To heck with it," Lachelle Michaels said and leapt from her hiding spot towards Laine, probably gambling that his sol was just as depleted as hers.

"Oh, come on," Bo growled and sprang after her, tackling her to the ground before she reached halfway to Laine.

Lachelle Michaels writhed under his weight, twisting and kicking at him to free herself, managing to land a blow on Bo's head. She took advantage of his momentary dizziness and struck at him again before rolling to her feet, staying low to aim a sweeping kick that should have knocked Bo flat to the ground.

He jerked back before her intended blow could land, nearly tripping himself out of shock.

"How do you know that move?" he demanded, countering her jabs as she came at him furiously, pushing him farther and farther, almost into the wall.

Her mouth dropped open, her precise movements faltering upon hearing him speak her language. The split second of surprise was all Bo needed to lunge forward and get her jugular between his jaws, freezing everybody in the hall.

Everyone except for Laine, who sauntered over and plucked Bo's quirn from his back, thumbing it on.

"Nobody move!" he yelled, brandishing the weapon at Lachelle Michaels. "Or she gets it."

Thank you, Laine. Super helpful. It's not like I have the situation under control or anything, Bo thought and clamped down a little harder—not quite enough to make the woman bleed. She stayed tree-still but gasped out instructions to her comrades.

"You outnumber them. Finish it."

"Nuh-uh," Bo growled, giving her a little shake, his eyes darting warningly over to her friends. "You tell me how you knew those moves. That kick. That way of using your, your front of your arms to block and strike."

Lachelle Michaels' fellow soldiers watched without so much as twitching towards them, ashen-faced, lips pressed into tight lines. They did have the advantage of numbers, but the dark-skinned woman with her neck enclosed about by Bo's fangs was obviously more important to them than attempting a victory. Very new trainees, Bo guessed. Even the Igis

Chosen had left him and Ken behind as ordered.

Bo was the idiot who hadn't followed them to the forest, had ditched the smoking vercycle outside of Ethaba to get revenge on Laine, and had ended up in Skytown because he too had a friend he couldn't abandon. He knew how the humans felt and could use it against them.

"Tell me," he snarled again, rather enjoying the wide-eyed looks of fear and the way the hands inching up to their clips shot down again. "How do you know how Ken fights? Have you faced him? Tortured him for your own sick amusement?"

"I would never—I don't even know anyone named Ken!"

"Liar. There's footage of him everywhere, frix sparking out of him like he's the being you humans named this planet after."

"You mean Stormsurge? His name's Ken? Then"—Bo felt the constricting of Lachelle Michael's throat as she swallowed—"you're his lokian best friend."

Bo almost released her at those words, going very still himself.

"I think that's a given?" Laine said, turning the power up higher. Bo didn't stop him. If Laine wanted to burn through his gloves and give himself blisters, that was his prerogative. "How many other klia'ans would willingly bust into this stupid place to try and rescue the Outpost Terrorist?"

Sharp gasps went up from the Hexagon trainees—all except Lachelle Michaels. Apparently her friends hadn't been aware of that little fact, though she knew somehow.

Bo took a chance and let go of Lachelle Michaels. He retrieved his quirn from Laine and levelled it at her. "One more time. How do you know Ken, or Stormsurge, or whatever the heck you wanna call him, and how do you know about me?"

Lachelle Michaels rubbed her bruised neck. "We're sparring partners. Friends, I like to think."

She made some sort of gesture, and her friends tapped off their clips, coming closer, but staying at what Bo guessed they assumed was a safe distance. He smirked. He wasn't going to be the one to tell them how electricity worked.

Lachelle Michaels sat, raising her hands in a show of surrender.

"Stormsurge—Ken, I guess." A slight smile crept over her face as she said his name. "He's been teaching me moves during our matches, and we talk when we hang out in the rec lounge in between. The things he says—my mom always told me to be wary of blindly following the chain of command, and since meeting him, I keep questioning the things I see and hear. I mean, I did before, but when Storm, uh, Ken told me his secret and he was totally different than they'd been telling us, I started keeping my eyes open more."

"Hang on, Lachelle," the red-haired girl broke in, "you can't actually be entertaining the ramblings of a lokian? They're the worst kind of tricksters!"

"And you know this how?"

"Well, Shadow—"

"Was in disguise else the Consul would have killed him, we've been over this. You met Shadow many times—I met Shadow—did he ever hurt us? Have we ever witnessed anything to make us believe the stories we've been told, been *told*? With evidence consisting only of sketchy photos and heavily redacted records?"

"I think the tragedy of the Apollo XXII colony speaks for itself," one of the other soldiers said.

Lachelle Michaels shook her head. "Again, all we have are pictures of a ghost town and High Consul Rolv's word. Ken's been telling me a different story. One I wasn't sure he could prove either, but the fact that this lokian is standing in front of me is making me seriously consider if he has the right of things."

She rose to her feet but left her weapon on the ground, motioning for her friends to gather around her, and then collected their clips. Outrage clouded the trainees' faces when Lachelle Michaels tossed the devices to Bo and Laine, but she silenced them with a look.

"Everything gets recorded here. Luckily, the hall cameras were damaged in the firefight, but I'd rather explain our clips going dark because you used some sort of jamming device on us instead of having a gap in footage we can't account for."

The storminess began to clear from the soldiers' faces as they understood. They'd be in quite a bit of trouble regardless, but better to let their superiors think their clips had been taken from them than that they'd willingly entertained the enemy. After all, the last image on the clips would show Bo threatening Lachelle Michaels with lethal amounts of frix. And whether or not they agreed with Michaels, they'd have to keep quiet and repeat her version of events if they didn't want to end up facing the torturer lady Lis had mentioned.

"I assume you've all been tased before?" Bo asked, and the soldiers grimaced. Bo turned down his quirn until he had to strain to hear the humming. "This'll hurt less than that."

The soldiers gulped, as well they should. They had no control over the situation. Their sols had run out of charges, and Lachelle Michaels had stopped them from calling for backup. It would look better for whatever story they'd spin to whoever found them if their uniforms had scorch marks.

Stepping forward, the woman drew herself up straight and met Bo's gaze without flinching.

"Outpost Terrorist or not, Ken's the best person I've ever met, and if you'd risk death to find him, then I put myself in your hands."

Lachelle Michaels took a deep breath and lay on the floor, directing the others to do the same.

"Laine here can tell you," Bo said, ushering Laine past him as they both started to move closer to the exit they'd seen on the map. "I hate most humans. But I can find some measure of respect for you if you'll keep Ken safe 'til I come fetch him."

He pressed his thumb into his quirn, and frix streamed out, jolting the soldiers lying prone on the floor and leaving them dazed but unhurt as he and

Laine slipped out into Skytown.

———— • ————

"Lachelle?"

She jumped, hitting her elbow on the desk next to her bed as Kenton climbed up through the floor.

"What, why, how—?" Her eyes darted to the camera in the corner, and Kenton held up his palm, showing the small, black jammer tucked behind his thumb.

"We're safe to talk. You said it was urgent?"

"I didn't mean for you to come to me and Ashlyn's room! And certainly not through . . . the floor?"

The look on her face asked a thousand questions, and Kenton chuckled a little at the way her brows knit together.

"I'll explain after your thing." He took a seat in the single chair and motioned for her to continue, glancing around the room while Lachelle collected her thoughts. It wasn't much bigger than his own living space, though the bunkbed and cabinets shoved against one of the drab beige walls made them seem to crowd in closely.

Lachelle sank back down on the bottom bunk and grabbed an energy bar from the desk. She tossed it to Kenton before opening a bottle of lytorade for herself.

"You hear about the commotion earlier?"

"Only that all fights at the Tomb are suspended pending further notice. Can't say I hate the reprieve."

Kenton grinned and pushed his hair out of his face. He wondered if Lachelle's roommate could lend him a hair tie or two to keep it from falling into his eyes so much.

"It was because of intruders. Nothing serious, just some TCBNN interns who got lost. Or so was thought until they headed for an old, unused part of the Hexagon instead of going back to the news crews who are setting up for tomorrow. Still, my superiors didn't think much of it, so they sent me and Ashlyn and a couple of the guys to deal with them."

Lachelle's voice cracked a little, and she took a few sips of her lytorade. Her other hand massaged her throat, drawing Kenton's attention to the fresh bruises there. To the bite marks.

He was out of his chair and at her side in an instant, searching her eyes for permission before reaching out to brush his fingertips against the purpling dark skin.

"Lachelle!" he breathed, his own neck aching with sympathy pain.

"Courtesy of a lokian—klia'an you'd term it, I guess."

"Shadow—but he wouldn't. Returning here, after everything. It'd be—" He broke off, searching for the right words. "Ill-advised."

Lachelle started to shake her head, then winced and shrugged instead.

"Wasn't him, 'less he decided to dye his fur black and sport gold contacts to hide his blue eyes."

Kenton sucked in a breath. The features she described were unique to Tribe Osinan, that particular colouring not very common within the tribe at that. Lachelle saw his wide-eyed look and squeezed his hand.

"He didn't give his name. But he knew you. And he gave me yours. Ken."

"Kenton," he whispered, hardly trusting himself to speak lest the tears constricting his voice should burst free. He'd cried enough in this awful place. "Kenton Wishings."

Lachelle repeated his full name, and the sound of it in her pretty, lilting tones was enough to release the flow he'd been desperately stymieing. In all of the Hexagon, only Jack used his given name. To the others he was just a number or some prizefighter of unknown origin. To hear his name—his pet name at that—on someone else's lips was simultaneous relief and torture. Bo was supposed to be safe in the Hinnom Forest, not risking almost certain death chasing him to Skytown.

Lachelle squeezed Kenton's hand again.

"We let them go. We kind of had to, but we didn't tell anyone what really happened. I like your name."

Kenton smiled through glassy eyes, lifting their joined hands to wipe away the wetness from his face.

"As do I. My birth mother picked it out. Her second and last gift to me. I have three mothers, did you know?"

Lachelle cocked her head, indulging his rather transparent changing of the subject.

"Yes. The woman my father met during his university years—who, I gather, wanted a career more than a family—and my sister's mother, who all my earliest and fondest memories are of. She was beautiful, Lachelle. Dark skin like yours. Darker maybe, and jewels shone against it like stars in the night. She always wore the most vividly coloured headscarves, and she sang to me and Annie every day, even when times were hard.

"Umama would take us to the beach to build sandcastles or on safari to see the lions and the cave paintings left behind by her ancestors. Pa always fretted that something wild would get us, though he was the first in the colony to extend a hand in friendship to the klia'ans the first year we lived here. I miss them."

Kenton dropped his head onto Lachelle's shoulder as she put a comforting arm around him.

"After the soldiers came, when Tribe Osinan took me in, the Innah—our village leader—upended her life to look after me in addition to her own daughter. I can't but call her 'Mother' after that."

"Oh, Ken. I can't imagine. I'm glad though. That your friend walked away safe from our encounter. That I didn't cause you more heartache today."

Kenton squeezed Lachelle's hand at her thoughtful words, a warm feeling settling in his chest as he sat up and looked at her earnestly.

"I still owe you that favour, don't I? Given this morning's events . . . I think it's time you knew everything 626 and I have been up to."

Lachelle's eyes went wide. "Ken. What do you mean, what you've been up to?"

"Lachelle!" a bubbly voice called, and Lachelle went rigid under Kenton's hands.

"You have to hide," she said. Her eyes darted around the room. The bottom bunk was too small for Kenton to fit beneath, and the room didn't have a closet.

Kenton shook his head. "There's no time—do you trust Ashlyn?"

"Since we were six and she didn't tell my mom who'd actually eaten the last cookie. But—"

Ashlyn clattered into the room, chattering excitedly. She stopped short upon seeing Kenton and Lachelle—still sitting quite close, he realised. He blushed at the incredulous look spreading across Ashlyn's face.

"Lachelle!" She exclaimed, her voice sounding slightly strangled. "You should have told me you had . . . company."

"It's not like that," Lachelle hurried to explain, her cheeks darkening as well. "Remember what those intruders said about Ken earlier?"

"That he's the Outpost Terrorist." Ashlyn walked over to the desk and swung herself onto it. "Kinda hard to forget. But you seem to trust him, so I figure there's a good explanation. Like he was framed, or something."

Kenton's lips quirked up. "That wouldn't be out of the ordinary for this place. But no. I did the things they accuse me of. Being imprisoned here—it's probably no more than I deserve."

"Then why? You do know the crazy amount of damage you caused, how much you set back any advances we'd making on bettering life for people on

Thorunn?"

"That was the point," Kenton admitted. "I had to stop your people from destroying mine. Even a little delay would help us prepare our defences."

"Don't you think it's odd, Ashlyn?" Lachelle said and reached across the small space to clasp her friend's hand. "That despite the fact that there's no imminent threat to anyone living on Thorunn, we keep building and building our military? Our forces are more than large enough to deal with the Cabal—if we could just catch them. And"—she shot an apologetic glance at Kenton—"we've handled the situation with the Outpost Terrorist. So why do we still have enough troops to conquer a small nation?"

Ashlyn's free hand went to her hair, nervously twisting the orange-red strands.

"You're right that it seems like overkill. But Thorunn's dangerous. Between the TK-97s, and the rheas maximus and the frix, we can hardly go two steps without having to fight our way out of this and that."

Lachelle waved a hand dismissively. "Propaganda, Ashlyn. We know how to deal with all those problems. Our hovercars can outrun most things, and we can build tunnels for the frix. Think. Why did we settle here, of all places on Thorunn?"

"The rest of the planet is covered by impenetrable lightning storms. It's frix season year-round. Uninhabitable."

"For humans," Kenton said. "In the Hinnom Forest—my home—the trees are impervious to frix.

Tribe Osinan uses the sap to frix-proof everything, and we live there without fear."

"Should you be telling us this?"

Kenton chuckled a little at the women's furrowed brows. "Torturer Anland extracted it all from me quite some time ago. I fear my efforts as the Outpost Terrorist were in vain, now that she—and the Consul by extension—have the knowledge they were seeking. But you understand my meaning, yes?"

Ashlyn nodded, her freckles standing out in stark contrast to her rapidly paling face. "With the ability to frix-proof anything, we could fly our ships to any place on Thorunn. We could settle anywhere." She paled further, going a sickly green. "And we have enough troops that if any lokians tried to resist us, we could wipe them all out."

She jumped off the table, fists clenched into tight balls, shaking with what Kenton could only assume was barely repressed fury. "Even if they were nothing but mindless beasts—and that can in no way be true, given Shadow, and your friend I met earlier today— that would be . . . unconscionably wrong!"

"And now you begin to understand how badly you've been lied to," Kenton said, the frix flowing through his veins pulsing with his excitement at the prospect of gaining two more certain allies.

If Torturer Anland or her cousin or anyone on the Consul discovered that the cutting edge, experimental frix implants they'd bequeathed him could be controlled at will—with no more than a thought—their army would be truly unstoppable. He half suspected the lack of this knowledge was one of the only things holding back a deadly onslaught which would leave humans as the reigning power on the planet.

But someday soon they'd test on another highly trained prisoner, one less motivated to keep the secret to his or herself. They'd have their army and the ability to move freely during frix season. And somehow, Kenton and Jack Riven and everyone willing to throw in their lot with the Cabal had to find a way to stop the Consul from slaughtering Bo and Seri and the Innah and everyone he cared about before it was too late. If Jack's intel was good, everything would come to a head in a day or so.

Kenton wasn't sure what they had planned, but he was suddenly very sure of what more he could do to assist.

"There is hope. We can fight back."

"How?" Ashlyn whispered. "How can we stop this? They know everything we do."

Lachelle smiled and squeezed Ashlyn's wrist. "Ken has a way around that. And I suspect there are others like Shadow, working from the inside against these plans, working to keep us from becoming unwitting murderers."

"Lachelle has the right of it," Kenton said. He reached out and gently clasped Ashlyn's other hand before looking from cadet to the other. He took a deep breath—there was no going back from the course of action he was about to suggest.

"How would you like to join the Cabal?"

21

A discordant shrilling jarred Laine from the depths of a comfortable slumber. Bleary-eyed, he stuck out his hand, banging it against unyielding metal shelves in his frantic casting around for the clip he'd been loaned. Priority number one was changing that heinous call tone—just as soon as he could shut it off. Finally, Laine's throbbing hand snagged the tiny device, and he blinked in surprise at the code streaming across the narrow digital display.

Laine had contacted Yoon Ah just after dinner with Shadow and the others—it was unlike her to call again so soon. The line might be secure, but she and Andy weren't fond of taking unnecessary risks. Whatever had prompted her to reach out so late had to be important. He scrubbed at his eyes and thumbed the accept button, sighing in relief once the shrilling muted.

"Hi, Laine," Yoon Ah said when the call connected. "I don't suppose there's a room with a wall-sized holoscreen in that secret bunker of yours?"

"Several." He got to his feet and motioned for Bo to come along. The commotion had woken him, and he glared at Laine through narrowed eyes, tufts of fur sticking up every which way.

"You okay?" Laine asked Yoon Ah. "You don't

sound so good."

"Just get the leaders of the Cabal on the line, please."

Laine wrinkled his brow at the request, but went to find Lis—who'd apparently begged off going home that evening under the guise of sleeping over at a friend's house. She sat in the drill station's modestly sized kitchen, surrounded by close to twenty members of the Cabal, all going over their plans for the day ahead.

She frowned when Laine and Bo stepped through the doors. "Aren't you two supposed to be keeping out of sight and away from trouble in your room?"

"Don't be mad." Laine cringed when Shadow crossed his arms, ears flattening. "But my friend in Ethaba—the one I mentioned who's been talking with some of your people and helped get us out of New Little Rock? Since being here, I've told her everything."

Laine skipped back when Shadow unfolded from his seat, fangs dropping in a snarl of barely repressed fury.

"I know, I know, this place is top secret or whatever. But Yoon Ah and Andy—that's her boyfriend, one of my good friends—I trust them with my life, and they'd never turn any of us in. They want to help, and Yoon Ah specifically needs to talk to you both. She's on the line right now."

Lis sighed but covered her face with the scarf draped about her shoulders and gestured for Laine to connect his clip to the holoscreen on the wall behind him. The image started out too blurry and shaky to make out much of anything at first, but slowly the eerie green lighting of Doctor Frenally's creepy basement lab came into view.

Yoon Ah blinked at the assembled members of the Cabal through bloodshot eyes, face blotchy like she'd been crying.

"I know it's late, too late to bother most decent folk," she whispered. She pressed the heels of her palms into her eyes, and Andy pulled her into him, a soothing hand rubbing up and down her arm.

"You'll have t'forgive us if we don't quite speak sense. It's been a long night, an' Yoon Ah's had . . . a bad experience. Best if we just show you."

He did something beyond the camera's scope, and then footage timestamped only a few hours prior filled the screen.

———————— ● ————————

"Andy, can you hear me? Testing. Hello?"

"Transmitting loud an' clear. Let it be known, I still don't like this plan you have of investigating the tunnels alone."

Yoon Ah shivered and rubbed her bare arms before pulling her backpack closer to ward against Ethaba's customary chill. She kept her voice low to avoid attracting the attention of the guards half-asleep at their posts.

"You don't need two strikes on your academic record."

"I don't mind about losing the captainship if it

means you'll be safe."

"I do. Dad can't make special allowances for you just because we're dating, and I'm not letting you throw away your chance at a Skytown scholarship. I'll be fine. I doubt I'll encounter anything more troublesome than a couple mangy skreets, and I've got Min Soo's sol with me."

"Regardless"—Andy's voice dropped to a tone she'd never heard before—"something goes wrong, I'll be there, an' I've an open line to emergency services, just in case."

Yoon Ah nodded and paused outside a moment to capture footage of her entrance to the tunnels before setting a hand on the levers and pulling. Laine hadn't been gone from Ethaba more than two months, but the red dust of the surrounding landscape had already resettled over the inset grate, obscuring all evidence of use. She mentally thanked his lokian friend for never resetting the locks that kept it shut from inside. The guards might have noticed her burning a hole through steel in the middle of the night.

A few hard yanks and the door swung open, metal against metal groaning obscenely loud in the still of night. Yoon Ah ducked into the shadows, glancing at the dark figures ostensibly watching the place, but though they twitched helmeted heads in her direction, they didn't see her, and the dappled moonlight concealed the slightly open door. She spared them one last look before peering into the gap and the dark void that lay before her.

"Let's see what's so important about this place that

they had to fake radiation signs to warn people away."

Yoon Ah slipped inside and pulled the grate almost shut, crouching so as not to bang her head on the low ceiling. The tiny sliver she'd left open shouldn't be noticed until sunrise, and she'd be gone long before then. She tapped on her clip light to reveal thick layers of dust, disturbed in one area by a few sets of prints—Bo's and Laine's, she guessed—leading under the gates.

Yoon Ah turned and headed in the opposite direction, deeper into the tunnels, passing rows and rows of sealed entrances. The ground sloped, and the walls inched taller until she could walk fully upright, but she progressed slowly, stopping to investigate each door. She didn't bother with the locks, not when she had the portable, industrial-grade laser cutter she'd borrowed from shop class. Dad really needed to stop leaving his keys on the kitchen table.

Six doors, then seven, and she hadn't found anything to explain the half-hearted security and warning signs posted outside, her Geiger counter still showing it was safe to proceed. Each room sat empty, nothing but silt and dirt filling them. Odd depressions and jutting earthen shelves suggested they'd been safe houses once upon a time, before the Apollo XXII colony had learned to build moderately frixproof structures, but anything of value or use had long since been cleared away.

"It's weird though, that they'd take the time to seal up these doors if they'd planned to abandon them?"

"Could be they're filled with poisonous gases? New Little Rock has issues with that," Andy mused.

"My readings are all clear. Nothing down here except slightly too alkaline soil."

Andy hummed noncommittally, the soft press of his typing a comforting sound in Yoon Ah's ear. She wondered what he thought of the map his computer was generating from the footage she streamed back to him.

She kept walking, door after door revealing the same non-story, her boots tramping along the packed dirt beneath her. Her footsteps were the only sound in the dim, snaking corridor, and when even that got to be too loud she shifted to walk tiptoe, ignoring how the stiff leather pinched.

The passageway ended abruptly, and Yoon Ah almost ran into the wall, letting out a squeak she regretted when Andy's concerned voice came over the line.

"I'm okay. But there's nothing. No new doors or empty rooms."

"Maybe if y'go the way Laine did?"

"That only leads beyond the gates."

"Still, Laine left in a hurry—could be he missed seeing some things on his way out."

"I'll backtrack and check in a moment."

Yoon Ah blew out a sigh and grabbed a bottle of lytorade. She set the laser cutter on the ground to properly untwist the cap.

It clanged.

"Did you hear that?" she breathed.

Yoon Ah stopped trying to open the bottle,

dropped to one knee, and hurriedly brushed away the dirt beneath the heavy tool. Her fingers touched metal, so cold she thought it ice at first.

"Andy, there's a door here."

She grabbed the laser cutter again, turning it on, and the iron before her began to glow, the hot edges of the jagged circle she made peeling back and briefly illuminating the cramped space. The middle dropped away, and Yoon Ah counted three seconds before she heard a thump.

"That's deep—not going down there, are ya?"

Yoon Ah took a deep breath and squared her shoulders. "You know I have to."

"Really think y'should turn back. That might have been an old well shaft in the past, an' those can get nasty."

"I've got my gas mask, and I do see some hand-holds."

"Alright, love. Just, be safe?"

Yoon Ah nodded and unstrapped her backpack. No way was she getting stuck if the vertical shaft ended up narrower than anticipated. After tying back her electric-blue hair and securely adjusting the grey-green mask over her nose and mouth, she lay next to the hole and eased her legs over its edge until her left boot hit the first metal rung.

"Descent proper begins now."

She didn't move though, heart spasming against her chest. One step at a time and she wouldn't fall. She was safe, and Andy was on the line with her. She wasn't alone. Thinking it didn't stop her fingertips from tingling or the chill that laced the underground space from enveloping her. The lenses of the mask covering her face started to fog from her shallow breaths.

"You can do this," she muttered, voice low to keep Andy from overhearing.

Doctor Riven's arrest, Laine's flight from Ethaba, Doctor Frenally's secret—and abruptly terminated—stealth tech project, the dubious financial transactions she'd subsequently discovered while interning for Mrs. Frenally—everything led to the tunnels on the north side. The truth lay just below her feet.

If she could make them move.

She heard Andy inhale, presumably to check in with her, and Yoon Ah forced herself down the sturdy iron rungs, eyes fixed on the packed-earth wall keeping them in place.

One boot hit the metal that had fallen from the gaping hole above, and Yoon Ah looked up, straining to see how far she'd come through blurry plastic lenses. A judicious application of her shirt took care of the outer covering, and she closed her eyes, waiting for the insides to lose their vapour film.

When she opened her eyes again, she could see clearly. Too clearly and a scream tore itself from her throat, eliciting Andy's worried voice over-loud in her ear.

She couldn't make herself stop, not even to describe to Andy the nightmare she'd flung herself into.

They were all around her, to her left and right. Beneath her feet, and propped up against the walls. The air filtration system of the mask was the only thing keeping out the smell. Yoon Ah half-fancied she could taste it anyway.

"By Saint Ailbhe! Hang the captainship, I'm on my way!"

She could hear Andy still speaking, but his words were little more than jumbled sounds against the hitching groans dragging themselves from her throat. Yoon Ah squeezed her eyes shut again, as if that would block out the long-entombed secret surrounding her.

She hadn't gone looking for this. Not this.

After spending hours connecting with members of the Cabal over the edda-net and pouring over old news briefs, she'd known something wasn't quite right with the histories touted throughout Thorunn, but she'd never expected her investigation would lead her here. To the bottom of a formerly sealed well shaft, hidden under layers of dust and behind signs warning most rational people away. To stand amidst the truth of a lie so well maintained that the men outside probably didn't even know what they guarded.

Yoon Ah dared not move, not even to shift her weight lest the door section she stood atop should tilt and send her rolling into them. As long as she kept her eyes shut, she could pretend she was okay. Andy would reach her soon, and he was seeing the footage from her still-recording clip, so he'd be better prepared and wouldn't break down upon seeing what she'd gotten herself into. He could pull her up, and she wouldn't ever have to look at them again.

At the bodies.

At the half-decayed faces, and long strands of rotting hair. At the scratches on the wall from whomever of them had been thrown down still alive. At the bug-eaten clothes riddled with solfire burns. At the tiny rattle still clutched in an equally tiny hand.

Yoon Ah wished she could reach through her mask to wipe away the tears trickling thick and fast down her cheeks. Despite how tightly she squeezed her eyelids together, she couldn't stop seeing the images seared into her mind. She couldn't change the fact that in this moment, she was alone, deep underground, Andy still too far away.

She couldn't stop the sick reality that was her, standing in a grave.

———————— ● ————————

"Can't say I envy your friend, but at least everyone knows now what happened to the so-called 'lost colony'."

Laine glared at Bo. He'd had to excuse himself to the bathroom to be violently ill after seeing the transmitted footage. He couldn't fathom how much worse it must be for Yoon Ah.

"Have some sympathy, you jerk," he said, pressing a hand to his still-burbling stomach. "Hardly anyone deserves to stumble into something like that, and definitely not Yoon Ah."

"But it does mean the Cabal has undeniable, irrefutable, irrevocable proof to back up their claims when they, what's the expression? Blow the lid on the

Consul's whole operation."

"I'm never going to let you watch *Task Force: Mars* again."

Laine pulled on his gloves and checked that his boots were laced up before grabbing his jacket and lacrosse stick.

Any lingering doubts that klia'ans had been the cause of the colonists' demise had been eradicated. The weakly scratched messages on the walls told a horrifying story, and he imagined all of Thorunn would revolt once they knew the truth.

Lis herself had gone pale, as much as a dark-skinned girl could, before reminding everybody that events had already been set in motion and they would proceed as planned.

Shadow had mentioned something about handling the addition of the new footage and set himself up in a corner talking quietly to Andy and flicking through holoscreens while the members of the Cabal crowded into the kitchen had dispersed for the night, returning to their rooms to rest and prep for the day ahead.

But despite all their begging and pleading, Lis had refused to assign Laine and Bo a place in the Cabal's mission, telling them they'd already helped quite enough, somehow having heard about their altercation with the Hexagon cadets. They weren't forbidden from leaving the base, exactly, but Shadow had strongly implied it would be in their best interests if they sat on their thumbs in their rooms.

"Yeah, I'm not leaving Ken a second longer in the hands of those murderers," Bo growled, checking that his quirn was fully charged and stuffing the extra sols he'd "borrowed" into his jacket.

"My dad neither. Gordon must have known. He had to have."

A sudden throbbing in Laine's clenched fist alerted him to the fact that he'd punched it through the chair in front of him. The flimsy wooden structure wobbled and collapsed, taking Laine's pack with it. He fished the sturdy bag out of the wreckage, sucking at splinters and shaking his stinging hand to try and lesson the pain.

"They won't notice that at all." Bo gestured to the detached legs and cracked seat of the chair.

Laine stared at him with as much apathy as he could muster and threw a blanket over the heap. Bo's vexed look didn't change, causing Laine to roll his eyes before shoving the entire lot under the bed.

"Satisfied?"

Bo shrugged and headed for the door. Laine joined him, and they peered around it. Seeing no one in the hall, they eased through, their hurried footsteps muffled by the ever-present clanging of grinding machinery.

"You sure this is the way?" Laine asked, after the third turn that spilled into an empty corridor.

"No reason Shadow would have lied to me."

"I find it hard to believe that he and Lis—who we met all of seventy-two hours ago—would be dumb enough to trust us with their most closely guarded secrets."

"Shadow was careful not to mention the location

of the passage, just that it existed. A little bit of illicit time in their records room got me the rest." Bo tapped the clip he'd affixed to his ear, projecting the schematics of the base. "According to this, we're close."

"Hey!"

Laine looked away from the glowing blueprints and grimaced as he caught sight of a young man who'd been guarding the end of the hall.

"I'll say," Laine muttered and stepped aside as Bo drew his quirn, activated it, and fired before the confused Cabal member could get another word out. They propped the unconscious man up against the wall, using the brooms and crates stacked in the hall to make it appear that he stood upright.

The man's head flopped forward as soon as they'd finished, promptly ruining the illusion.

"Whatever, it'll buy us some time once they realise we're not in our room," Laine muttered and followed Bo past the unfortunate guy into the tunnel that would lead them straight to the Tomb.

"Did you happen to lift an extra jammer with those sols?" Laine asked as they pushed up a hidden cover and hauled themselves into the heart of the Hexagon. He'd seen the place from above through darkened windows, but it was odd to actually stand on the freshly raked gravel and sand.

"You think I woulda let you tag along otherwise?" Bo snorted, opening his hand to reveal a small, black object. "From what I overheard, we've about a full sun-cycle before these go dark. Course, Ken and I'll be long gone by then, but these should make us pretty much invisible, so no more running into that Lachelle Michaels woman and her friends in the meantime."

Bo flicked up his hood, hiding the yellow glow of his eyes, and Laine made quick work of the locks on the main door. The wood overlaid panels slid apart with a soft hiss, and they squeezed through the small opening into the dimly lit hall beyond.

"You've been quiet," Bo remarked as they walked at a brisk pace through the mostly deserted maze of doors and hallways the Hexagon boasted.

Each time they heard footsteps, they ducked into a shadowed alcove or other blind spot—of which there were plenty. Hexagon security relied too much on the cameras tucked into those out-of-the-way places, Laine realised. Too bad for them, he and Bo carried powerful, onite-based blocking devices.

"Just thinking through some things," Laine replied, peering into the windows of the next room they came to. He shook his head at Bo's questioning eyebrow. "Another lab."

Bo twitched like he wanted to lash out with his tail but settled for hissing through his fangs instead. They'd been traversing the halls since five in the morning, and it was nearing half past. None of the rooms they'd found had revealed prison cells or living spaces, and Bo grew more and more agitated, popping his claws in and out and growling softly.

Any other time and Laine would have grinned at

the klia'an's restless ticks, but after Andy and Yoon Ah's late-night call, his mind kept tumbling over the implications of their discovery. Bo and Kenton had been telling the truth. The Consul—or at the very least, one or two members of the twelve—had slaughtered the first inhabitants of Ethaba and blamed the disappearance of the Apollo XXII colony on Tribe Osinan, fuelling the deep-seated mistrust of the klia'an people.

How could the soldiers from that day live with what they'd done, going so far as to stage an empty town and film it to be touted as fact? A sick feeling settled in Laine's gut when he remembered the fascinated glee with which Doctor Grennal had gone over the subject in history class. Had he known of the awful truth buried beneath everyone's feet? The truth Dad had nearly discovered and for it been framed and locked away. He was somewhere in the Hexagon too, among the endless labs, circular hallways, and sets of stairs.

Laine didn't know what he'd say when he saw him again—if Gordon hadn't arranged for Dad to have an accident of some sort, since he clearly had a knack for engineering those.

Bo's hand on Laine's arm jostled him out of his thoughts.

"Cadet dorms," Bo read from a small mounted plaque. "Don't think that's the direction we want."

"Definitely not the way to avoid that Michaels lady," Laine agreed.

They turned down another white-walled corridor.

It ended in a stairway opening into a three way intersection. Yet more signs hung on the wall directly in front of them, pointing the ways to the elevators and bathrooms respectively.

Bo threw an arm across Laine's chest before he could step down into the brightly lit space.

Laine gritted back his instinctive retort about the excessive force Bo had applied and cocked his head, straining to hear what Bo's sensitive ears had picked up. It wasn't fair that the klia'an could still hear twice as well as him even with his hood up. They both retreated up the stairs, crouching low to peer into the hall as the unmistakable sound of rapid footsteps drew closer.

Laine eased his borrowed sol out of its holster. They'd be fine if whoever it was just kept walking.

Please keep walking. Don't come this way.

Bo's quirn hummed next to Laine, the tip of it glowing blue where it peeked out of Bo's jacket. Laine stayed absolutely silent, his eyes darting to Bo's, and they shared a look of determination before flicking their gazes to the hall once more, where the men had approached close enough that Laine could make out snatches of their conversation. One of the speakers caught Laine's attention. He knew that voice.

"Of course, there's still the matter of that loose end."

"I thought that's what you were paying Old Sureshot and his ilk for?"

"They lost him, can you believe it? Apparently a good-for-nothing lokian paralysed them and stole him away—not that I was actually going to follow through with the payment."

"Not much parts you from your credits, that's true. Wouldn't happen to be the same lokian that tricked your nephew into letting it stay in your basement, would it?"

"I should have called that in when I first found out about it, my reputation be damned."

"Now, now, Riven, it's that good reputation that let you get away with defamation and murder."

"Not completely reassuring when my brother's spawn still isn't stashed off-world where he can't make a fuss."

I'm right here.

Bo grabbed the front of Laine's jacket. "No," he mouthed. "They're going past. Focus."

"Glad your concerns won't stop you from presenting at the symposium."

"My work in the Hinnom Forest is going to change the future of Thorunn forever. What's an accusation of foul play in the face of global expansion?"

"What indeed? And we have the other Doctor Riven to thank, for unwittingly funding your research."

"My brother never was any good at keeping track of his finances, and when the lovely Mrs. Riven started asking questions, well. You know how that ended."

Gordon chuckled as he clapped a hand on his colleague's shoulder, talking about his role in Mom's death as if discussing a subject as mundane as taking out the trash. That's what he thought of them as, garbage, to be used and discarded as if they were only puppets in Gordon's sick personal show. They wouldn't have even moved to Thorunn if it wasn't for him cajoling Dad with offers of a better life. He'd taken advantage of them from the beginning, stealing their money, Dad's good name—stealing Mom.

Laine wrenched himself out of Bo's grip, adrenaline matching his strength to the other teen's, earning himself a torn jacket sleeve for his troubles.

"What was that?"

The fading footsteps faltered just as Laine tumbled down the stairs and sprawled into the hallway. He jumped to his feet, ignoring the spike of pain that shot through his right ankle, and pointed his sol at the stunned face of the treacherous, backstabbing, lying charlatan masquerading as family.

Gordon's hand shot out, and he hit something on the wall to his right, eyes narrowing as a smirk spread across his face.

The sudden harsh lighting that washed over the hall in time to a blaring alarm painted the man in sweeping shades of red, deepening the cruel smile he directed at Laine.

"You lose," he mouthed and twisted to avoid the shots Laine loosed from his sol, the blasts tearing chunks out of the wall behind him. He threw Laine a two-fingered salute, then dragged his colleague through a door Laine hadn't noticed before, slamming it shut before either he or Bo could reach him, and no amount of pounding on the door forced it to budge.

"Look what you did!" Bo hissed, almost spitting in Laine's face as he shoved him up against the wall, knocking the breath out of Laine when his shoulders hit the hard concrete. The sol dropped from his hand.

"He killed my mother!" Laine screamed back, kicking at Bo despite the pain and grabbing at the klia'an's shoulders. He didn't have claws, but fingers dug into muscle still hurt. "He doesn't get to keep breathing when she's not."

"I'm all for burning this whole place to the ground, and your uncle with it, but I can't. find. Ken. like this!" Bo shook Laine with each word before gesturing at the flashing lights and the constant shrilling of the Hexagon's alarm system.

"Even if you could get through that door, you're not making it far on that ankle."

Laine looked down, trying to comprehend what Bo was blathering on about. The haze of fury flooding his vision with red even between the flashes interfered with his sight, but he didn't need to see his leg to feel the slow-blistering agony that started in his toes and crept up his skin.

"Can you fix it?" he gasped, slumping forward into Bo, the abused limb refusing to support him further.

"Ken had our regen-rig when he was captured."

Laine swore and struck the wall, yelping at the resulting crunch that seared hot up his shin as he twisted wrong.

Bo retrieved Laine's fallen sol, looped his left arm over his shoulder, and set off at a fast clip towards the elevator at the end of the hall, dragging Laine more than anything.

"My map shows a medical wing two levels down. Might be a nano-diffuser there."

Laine nodded, pain wiring his jaw shut.

"I should just ditch you," Bo muttered, the words barely filtering through the scarlet rush in Laine's ears. "I hate that after everything we've been through, I actually care what happens to you. Idiot."

"You'll have, my undying loyalty." Laine struggled to push the words out through gritted teeth, tears streaming unwilling from his eyes. Each step jostled his possibly broken ankle further, but Bo—the sadist—took no notice, concerned only with getting them away from the screaming alarm.

"I can't do this," Laine sobbed as Bo hit the down button next to the closed elevator. A particularly vicious ache stabbed through him, a dull pressure that started in his heel and radiated through each of the tiny bones in his foot, spreading up into his thigh where it felt like a vice had been clamped on. The tension kept ratcheting up, threatening to pop his knee off.

At least it wasn't his left knee this time, but how it felt . . . His initiation with the Orquídeas had included being locked inside a frigid meat locker until his lips had turned blue, and he'd bitten his tongue from the uncontrollable chattering of his teeth. Not even the hazy California sun had been enough to warm him up again, and it had resulted in his second trip to the emergency room that summer.

Every moment of that agonising memory found a home in his knee.

"My leg's gonna"—he patted at Bo—"gonna fall off. My leg."

"Shut up," Bo hissed. He stabbed at the button again and pulled out his quirn. As soon as the door opened he loosed several frix bolts at the occupants, shoved Laine inside, and rolled the two bodies of the men he'd incapacitated into the hall.

"There's gonna be more where those came from. Lanae's whiskers. I can't express how much I despise that you've gotten under my skin. Here." He shoved two small objects in Laine's face. "I know you hate medicine, but you need something if we wanna exit this, this, metal box alive."

In too much pain to protest, Laine accepted the pills, gagging at the bitter taste before a mouthful of warm, too-sweet lytorade washed them down. Relief wasn't instant, but it was swift, and by the time the car came to a grumbling stop, Laine had the presence of mind to stand on his non-broken foot and brace himself against the wall, sol clutched firmly in one hand.

"Sorry I screwed up your search for Kenton," Laine said, just as the door slid open, a contingent of masked soldiers greeting them. Several well-placed shots took care of the armoured men and women, but Bo loosed a few more blasts of frix to be sure.

"No, no," he replied while waiting for Laine to hobble over the limp but still-breathing bodies. "I had absolutely planned for security to get called on us

and you to smash your foot within an hour of us being here."

He flashed Laine a closed-mouth smile that didn't
reach his eyes. "We are doing great at the moment."

"I deserved that," Laine muttered. Whoever said
sarcasm was lost in translation hadn't met Bo. Laine
was easing over the limp form of the last fallen soldier when a memory struck him. A memory of himself and Kenton waylaying an unsuspecting med student to take his place. A quick look around revealed
several locked doors labelled *Hexagon Level Five Storage and Maintenance.*

"Bo, wait—everyone's still searching for us. That
body armour might fit over our jackets."

The klia'an doubled back with an approving purr,
and soon they'd relieved the soldiers of their clips,
weapons, and relevant outerwear before stuffing their
unresisting forms into one of the maintenance rooms.
A bit of rope from the well-stocked shelves helped
bind the Hexagon soldiers' wrists together, and satisfied with a job well done, Laine limped away from
the resealed doors, Bo strolling along beside him, his
furred face covered completely by the near-black helmet he'd commandeered.

The walls on level five were darker, an almost depressing shade of grey marred by oddly whitewashed parts, as if someone had scrubbed too hard at
the wall when removing an undesirable stain and
they'd never bothered to repaint. The alarm still
blared happily away, but after a peek around the next
corner showed a mass of white-coated men and wo-

men going about their tasks as if deaf to the constant ringing, Bo and Laine straightened up, lengthened their stride and fell into step behind another group of soldiers patrolling the hall. They split off upon seeing a sign pointing the way to the medbay, but no one paid them any mind, likely used to seeing soldiers conducting their own private missions.

Three corridors later, and it was almost a game, Laine thrilling at how close he and Bo could get to the ambling scientists, so obsessed with the rapidly scrolling lines of data on their holoscreens that they hardly looked to see who'd bumped them. Laine had even been so bold as to swipe a palm-sized holoscreen from one of the whitecoats' back pockets.

"That's the place," he said as they reached the end of the next hall. A sign mounted above the jamb proclaimed the room ahead the *Hexagon Trial Laboratory*. To the right of the door sat another entrance set with thick steel bars, and when Laine glanced down it, he saw a dark corridor stretching almost to the other end of the Hexagon. Muffled cries and pleas drifted from the intersecting passages that spilled light into the hall at regular intervals.

"Ain't time for a shift change yet," one of the two guards on duty said to Laine as he and Bo approached the lab.

"I coulda sworn Ed weren't that shrimpy," the other said, her hand darting to her sol on instinct.

Bo dropped the guards while they hesitated, jumping out of the way as their bodies convulsed from the shock of the frix.

Laine hit the fire alarm set into the wall and helped Bo pull the unconscious soldiers clear of the door as it opened, discharging a stream of scientists clutching all manner of papers and equipment. Some of them had holoscreens clenched between their teeth as they struggled to wheel out bulky machines amidst dismayed utterances of "Not again," and "Bet there's no freakin' fire; I'm sick to death of all these stupid drills."

The doors started to slide shut, but Laine unslung his lacrosse stick and jammed it between the steel panels, ducking under it to get inside. The departing scientists hadn't bothered to switch off the lights on their way out, and Laine squinted at the harsh brightness that filled the room.

"Nano-diffuser's there," Bo said, pointing it out. The machine was stationary, bolted to the floor with thick steel plates and screws, and twice as large as Ethaba General's model.

"I'll get you settled, then I'm searching those cells."

Laine nodded, biting back a groan as pain started to overwhelm him again. He scrambled into the machine and stripped off his boots and pants, unable to decide whether the cool surface under his ankle was bliss or fresh torment.

"Set it to full," he demanded and stuffed his pants leg into his mouth for something to bite into. He could have asked Bo for another pill, but the memory of losing consciousness on the roof of Ethaba High held him back. Bo looked at him, shrugged, and did as Laine asked, stepping back warily as the nano-diffuser whirred to life.

Laine didn't pass out.

He wished he had.

The world fell sideways, throwing him dizzyingly through empty space, increasing the frantic pounding of his heart the longer reality tilted away from him. A fire raged, consuming him, the flesh melting from his bones as he was burned alive.

Laine's stomach convulsed and twisted in its attempt to flee his body, spewing choking bile up his scream-torn throat. And just when the flames ebbed and the dark receded enough for him to see the box of death he'd willingly climbed into, the machine sliced into his foot, prompting an inhuman shriek to burst from him as layer after layer peeled away until only bloody bone remained.

A slight pressure at his elbow brought him back to reality, and he realised that Bo held his hand. The soft, leather-like material, which faded into ticklish fur, brought Laine an immeasurable amount of comfort, and he squeezed back, clinging onto the contact as the pain spiked and ebbed.

"Thought you went to find Kenton?" he slurred out, the bitten through mess of his pants leg falling from his mouth.

"I checked every cell. This isn't the level he's on, and I doubt he's up top where your Consul plays at being a government. Didn't see anyone who might be your dad either."

"Level four, then?"

"It's always the last place you look."

Laine climbed out of the nano-diffuser, retrieved his crosse, and the two of them wound their way back to the elevators—which curiously only ran between levels three and five—Laine's foot quite recovered and able to take his full weight once more. It still felt a bit tender but given that Laine had tortured it through weeks' worth of healing in minutes, he wasn't about to complain. If anything, the niggling twinges served to remind him of what an idiot he'd been, both that morning and since the moment he'd arrived on Thorunn.

From the very beginning he'd let Gordon get the better of him, not taking him seriously, and for it, his uncle had destroyed his life.

Mom had wanted him to start over, but he'd let his hurt over the sudden move stoke his anger towards Dad, and when he hadn't risen to the bait, Laine had needled Gordon. Who'd let him, pretending to turn a blind eye to his antics, all the while plotting and scheming to rid himself of his brother's family as soon as possible after stealing their life's savings to fund his research. He seemed to be planning a little light genocide to boot, if Laine properly understood what he and Bo had overheard.

The man had had the gall to laugh while discussing Mom's death, that miserable moment in time which had Laine walking around half a person, gutted so deep nothing filled that void, not the near-death adventures he'd had on the Cerado, nor the barbed exchanges he'd had with Bo, or even the thrill of escaping Samuel Hezekiah and stumbling into the heart of a government-labelled terrorist group.

Firing his sol at Gordon in the hallway had been the closest to alive Laine had come in weeks. He wished that scared him more than it did—Bo had probably been right to try and hold him back. But he could keep himself in check until they found Kenton. Once he and Bo had been reunited, Laine's part in Bo's journey would be over, and he planned to find Gordon and introduce him to a nice, dark corridor.

Sorry, Mom. I'm stuck in this moment in time. I can't be whole again until he isn't.

"This has to be it." Bo pointed to a nondescript door, as boringly grey as the others lining the hallway, all indistinguishable but for the numbers flashing above their frames.

Laine's head spun from looking at the telescoping rows, and he focused instead on the entrance in front of them, wondering what the 742 displayed on the tiny holoscreen meant.

Bo rapped hard on the door. "Official business, open up!"

There was no answer at first, and after waiting a few moments, Bo raised his hand to knock again, but stopped when the panels separated and slid apart with a soft *snick.*

Laine hurried inside after Bo. The small apartment was neat and tidy and less sparse than he would have expected of a prisoner's. A quick scan revealed it to be empty as well.

"Maybe the bedroom?" Laine pointed to the sheet hanging from the doorframe on the other side of what passed for the living room.

"Perhaps. I can't hear anything with this stupid helmet on, let me—"

Six feet of lean muscle and controlled force dropped onto Laine, tumbling him to the ground and rolling him onto his back. Whatever Bo had been saying was lost as a familiar voice growled in his ear,

"Takes a special kind of fool to think the soldiers around here actually knock before barging in."

Kenton looked . . . extraordinarily healthy for a prisoner, his shoulder-length blond hair falling silkily in Laine's masked face, corded muscles bulging with the effort he exerted to keep Laine pinned. "I don't know how you acquired those uniforms, but I'm not giving any interviews, and that's final."

"Don't you see my quirn?" Bo asked, voice squeaking as he struggled to release the strap keeping his face hidden. "It's me!"

Laine managed to free an arm and popped off his own helmet.

"Hi!" He couldn't help laughing at how round Kenton's eyes went, at how his mouth dropped into a small "o" of shock. "Not who you were expecting with the rescue party, huh?"

Kenton shook his head and released Laine, allowing him to sit up and dust himself off.

"Lachelle said she'd seen you, but I didn't . . ." He reached a trembling hand towards Bo. "You're in front of me. You're truly here."

Bo bounded forward, brushing Laine aside, and crushed Kenton in a fierce hug.

"Yeah, I'm here."

"And sounding very human, no wonder I didn't recognise your voice."

A sound like a motor starting filled the room, prompting Laine to draw his sol before he realised the loud vibrating emanated from Bo, his happy purring louder than Laine had ever heard it as he and Kenton muttered to each other in Klia'an and Bo tugged and pulled at his friend, checking him over in between hugs and forehead nuzzles.

"But why are you here, Laine?" Kenton said, switching back to his oddly accented English.

"Tell you later. We gotta get."

The ever-present alarm was muted in Kenton's room, its incessant blaring fading to background noise, but the military comm line Laine and Bo had been listening in on since relieving the level five soldiers of their gear warned of several patrols coming their way, fast. The soldiers had doubtless found the hapless guards they'd left trussed up and missing their clothes, clips, and weapons. He and Bo couldn't pretend to be slightly-out-of-place trainees much longer, and Kenton's depressingly small living space wouldn't hide them for any meaningful length of time.

Kenton's smile faded, and he stepped away from Bo, causing the klia'an's mane to puff up at the odd response.

"I can't go with you."

"Yes, you can, Ken," Bo said, tilting his head to the side. He looked as confused as Laine felt. The guy had been a prisoner for weeks, forced to fight crazy battles, and probably illegally tortured—if the whispers going round at the Cabal's base held any truth to them. He should be jumping at the opportunity to escape. "There's a secret tunnel in the Tomb that'll take us right outta here."

Kenton placed a hand over his chest. He closed his eyes, as if the words he clearly didn't want to say physically pained him.

"They tore out my heart, Bo, ripped it out and put . . . a beatkeeper of plastic and metal in its place. It has a wide-range remote trigger linked to a master kill switch that operates on a frequency onite won't block. If they miss me for more than a few hours, She'll shut me down. I can't leave the building. Not now."

Bo opened and closed his mouth, at a loss for words.

"Does everybody have one of those in them?" Laine asked haltingly, and Kenton looked at him with a half smile.

"Just me. You should have no trouble rescuing—"

"You're giving up?" Bo cut in. "Just like that, after everything, while I'm standing here telling you there's a way out? A way back home?"

He drew his jacketed forearm across his face, but it did little to hide the clumped, damp fur under his eyes.

Kenton gripped his friend firmly by the shoulders.

"Never!"

He lowered his voice and angled Bo away from the wall, where, Laine suddenly noticed, a small camera blinked unobtrusively at them. "There is a plan. After it's set in motion then I can attempt destroying the device keeping me contained."

"Or you could tell me where to find it," Bo demanded. "And we end this."

Just then, Laine's clip crackled to life.

"First set of intruders spotted, all units converge at 742's quarters. Repeat, converge at inner hallway three, central control has eyes on the targets."

Kenton didn't hesitate and thrust Bo and Laine out of his room despite their protests, calling out instructions before shutting the door in their faces.

Laine refastened his helmet, trying not to scream at the abrupt end to their failed retrieval mission. They would have to come back later and try again after Lis had enacted whatever scheme the Cabal had planned.

"Did he say . . . to go through the walls?"

"I don't think he's well." Bo turned and sprinted down the hall towards the bend that would take them back to the elevators, and from there, to the Tomb. "This place, it's hurt him beyond what I could've imagined."

"Guess it's down to you and me now, for better or worse."

"Is that an admission of friendship?"

Laine grinned, the words coming easily despite his harsh panting as they ran. "Can't see as I owe you anything less, all the times you've saved me."

"You up for figuring out a new way to rescue Ken?"

"Soon as we get a moment to breathe."

The alarm, never having stopped, clamoured louder than before, drowning out the rush of their booted feet and the intermittent crackles in Laine's ear. Before they could gain the corridor that loomed ahead to their right, armoured soldiers appeared, their freshly charged sols glowing with reds and blues and greens. Each man and woman also carried a riot shield, tall enough to duck behind.

Laine spun on his heel and headed the other way, but more heavily armed Hexagon personnel flooded in from the end of the hall, cutting off his and Bo's last escape route.

Laine swore and retreated to stand side-by-side with Bo, drawing another sol and ignoring the slight sting through his gloves as he charged it up too fast. For all the good it would do. He and Bo had been firing rather indiscriminately since he'd surprised Gordon into activating the alarm, barrelling through any soldiers or unfortunate scientists impeding their path.

Laine had only a few charges left between his sols; presumably Bo's situation was the same. Laine's only hope was that last he'd checked, the bounties on his head still said "capture" not "kill." That wouldn't help Bo much, but Laine had worked with less before.

He shoved the klia'an behind him and fired, unleashing chaos.

22

Up against the wall was a terrible defensive position, but Laine covered Bo from in front, the human giving as good as he got, a sol in each hand keeping away the bulk of the enemy solfire. Bo had managed to jam his helmet back on, which at least protected him from stunning headshots.

The Hexagon soldiers had ducked behind their shields, firing above and around them, and though Bo's quirn could send frix travelling along the ground and under the makeshift barricades, it only dropped the front row at most, the soldiers behind them springing instantly into place, far more of them than Bo had charges left. The sol he held grew heavier by the minute, the hard shell of its grip moulding itself into his hand. He kept squeezing, kept picking off the wall of approaching soldiers, his weapons fusing into him, becoming one with his body as he loosed shot after desperate shot, relying on their opponents' reluctance to fire lethally at Laine to keep him safe.

Envy swept through Bo at the actual shields the squadron carried, more effective than body armour for deflecting solfire. If only he could snatch one up from the fallen soldiers, he could wield his quirn as a staff and preserve its remaining energy.

The *zuet-zuet* of solfire, the wailing of the

unending alarm, the thumps of bodies falling to hard concrete—it all blended together in an indistinguishable cacophony. Bo lost sense of time as he aimed precisely, making each bolt of frix count. Twice he switched out the sol in his hands, delaying, but not preventing, the moment he'd been dreading.

Laine went rigid in front of him, out of charges, just as Bo's quirn sputtered, the blue glow fading. He dug his thumb into his sol's trigger, but that too, produced only empty hissing, and he had no more fresh weapons tucked into his jacket. Bo shrank back against the wall. He couldn't die with Ken just on the other side of the door he could still glimpse from the corner of his eye. He couldn't see how he and Laine could outmanoeuvre the endless stream of Hexagon soldiers either.

Something fell onto him—Laine—he realised numbly. The human clutched at him, covering him with his body, fingers digging in tightly when grasping hands attempted to pry him off. Bo clawed at the solid floor beneath them, anchoring them to the ground.

"Anyone got a sedative?" he heard someone yell after initial attempts to part them proved futile, and Bo's stomach twisted, nauseous with the realisation that they would drug Laine and drag his unconscious body off Bo, and then end it, two to the head, that easy.

"Pass this to Conners," a second voice said, and booted feet thudded towards them. Bo curled his fingers around his quirn. Maybe he could take the soldier by surprise and hold him hostage like he had Lachelle Michaels.

Whoever it was tripped and fell halfway to Bo and Laine, what little Bo could see of his feet tangled in dark mesh netting.

"Ain't you heard? It's impolite to steal a man's kill."

"Samuel Hezekiah," Laine muttered, twisting away from Bo enough to allow him to see the bounty hunter striding down the hall, trailed by the rest of his crew. A middle-aged woman with an unpleasant smile on her weathered face held a large netting gun, its bulk resting comfortably in her hands.

"You can't be here," the Hexagon squadron leader barked. "This is official Hexagon business; leave now or face arrest."

Samuel Hezekiah hooked one thumb into his belt, his sol resting against his right shoulder, glowing with a ready charge.

"Arrest? You know who I am, boy?"

"Certainly, which is why, sir, we're giving you a chance to stand down instead of taking you into custody immediately."

Bo pushed Laine off him and flicked his eyes towards the limp bodies that hadn't yet been revived by their comrades. All the soldiers had turned to confront the new threat, standing between them and Samuel Hezekiah, ready to fire if the bounty hunters stepped any closer. Their distracted state allowed Bo and Laine to scoot subtly backwards until they hit what Bo had been jealously coveting the whole desperate fight: a riot shield next to a fallen cadet.

"Custody?"

"Yes, sir, as I've stated, this is official Hexagon business. Apologies for any financial loss you might suffer, but that's something you'll have to take up with the Consul."

Samuel Hezekiah considered the man's words for a long moment, in which Bo and Laine inched even farther away from the standoff, discreetly rifling through the shallowly breathing bodies for fresh weapons behind the relative safety of their newly acquired shield. Something hard flashed in the bounty hunter's eyes. He lowered his sol and shot the Hexagon soldier in the gut, sneering at the man's scream as he collapsed.

"This ain't about money no more. A man's got his pride."

The other soldiers closed ranks around their fallen leader, one of them jumping forward to tend the wound, the others shooting with abandon at the bounty hunters, who had no compunctions about hoisting up the unconscious bodies of those Bo and Laine had downed earlier and using them as live shields.

"Sam!" the woman with the netting gun called, pointing out Laine and Bo in the gap created by the rushing soldiers. "They're gettin' away!"

"Confound it all," Samuel Hezekiah said, and cursed. "Nasir, grenades!"

"Oh, no you don't," Laine said and whipped his crosse off his back, darting out in front of their riot shield just as three small, black objects came hurtling their way. He caught the first two in a jerking lunge and snagged the third with a wrenching twist of his spine Bo had only thought possible by klia'ans.

Unaffected by the injury-inducing move, Laine spun with the momentum and launched the grenades back at the soldiers and bounty hunters faster than either party could react. The deadly missiles exploded on impact, blowing massive chunks out of the walls and sending everyone in the corridor flying, concrete dust and flash bomb smoke instantly obscuring visibility.

Bo abandoned the shield, grabbed Laine, and fled.

———————— ● ————————

An earth-shaking boom rippled through Kenton's room, throwing him from his agitated pacing to his knees. His door unsealed, and he unsteadily picked himself up, looking curiously at the open entrance.

A quick peek through it showed the closest doors to his sliding apart as well, their occupants similarly curious and showing their faces at the unexpected noise and happenings. Likely all the cells had unlocked with the force of the explosion, but Kenton couldn't make out much beyond the smoke-choked area. He drew up his short-sleeved shirt to cover his nose and mouth, eyes watering as he took in the bloody diorama directly before him.

Groaning Hexagon soldiers rolled limply on the ground, reaching for crackling sols blown out of twitching fingers. The men and women who didn't wear the navy-blue and grey uniforms hadn't fared any better, head wounds bleeding profusely, arms and legs at odd angles. One man sat with arms wrapped around knees drawn up to his chest, rocking back and forth and staring at the wall.

In minutes, a medical team led by a man Kenton recognised as Álvero appeared, with reinforcements who cuffed the people in dusty, brown jackets, stripping away their weapons and wrestling the lesserly injured of the intruders to their feet, pleading with a tall, burly man to comply, promising that their sentences wouldn't be so harsh if "you will just co-operate, Mr. Lewis, please."

Kenton searched the faces of all the men on the stretchers and those being led away, hands secured behind their backs.

Laine and Bo were not among them, and he fell to his knees in relief. The countless moments of terror Kenton had endured since reaching the Hexagon had paled in comparison to the moment he'd heard the shooting begin.

He'd leapt up, arms close to sparking with barely restrained energy—and immediately started convulsing, his captors doubtless taking cruel delight at both causing and watching his inability to assist his best friend. He'd thought he was going to have to listen to Bo die, right on the other side of the wall, after all Kenton had sacrificed to keep him safe. But somehow Bo and Laine had escaped and, if they were smart, had headed for the exit.

He withdrew into his room when Álvero approached, the memory of his heart constricting mere moments before stopping him from braving the chaos without. The medic flashed a small jammer at him.

"Despite everything, the symposium is proceeding as planned, so, so are we." He winked at Kenton, another ally at the most unexpected of times, and Kenton wondered what had prompted the man to align himself against his employers. Maybe Lachelle's covert recruitment had extended beyond her own squad members. "Find 626, I'll cover for you here."

Kenton raised his eyebrows, and Álvero nodded, then gestured down the hall with a quick cock of his head. "She never voiced her suspicions, but we've all had them. There *is* some resemblance, to be sure."

He ran back to his team before Kenton could ask what he meant, leaving him to pull on his boots and what training gear he was allowed in his room before setting off in the opposite direction, heading for the lab Jack frequented.

The place was empty when he arrived, the light still on and papers strewn untidily across the desk as if the botanist had left in a hurry. Kenton had expected to find him and the other whitecoats preparing for the presentations many of them had been openly boasting would change the future of Thorunn forever. They must have come up with something fantastically better than unstable, frix-charged soldiers to be so enthusiastic.

The ruckus in Kenton's hallway shouldn't have reached the labs, so it was odd that no one occupied the apparatus-littered room. He investigated the other labs, discovering that none of them were in use either. A messily scrawled checklist pinned to a cork notice board caught Kenton's attention, and he mentally struck himself.

The symposium.

That was it. They'd all been called away already. A quick glance at the clock showed it to be early yet—they would start in an hour, presumably plenty of time for the still-patrolling soldiers to contain the disturbance that Laine and Bo and the other intruders had caused.

Jack wouldn't be among the presentees—ostensibly prevented from sitting in the main conference hall courtesy of his prisoner clip, but actually because he'd planned to slip away to the Tomb, the only room in the Hexagon spanning two levels. Whoever designed the place ought to have a stern talking to for failing to account for such an obvious security flaw—but that made it the perfect meeting spot for the members of the Cabal posing as junior scientists who were supposed to slip in amongst the legitimate interns on level two.

Kenton sighed. The crawl through the walls and ceilings to get up to level three wouldn't be pleasant, but he had to return to the narrow spaces with their layered masses of circuitry if he wanted to reach the Tomb without chancing an encounter with anyone who might have forgotten their research and rushed back to retrieve it before his or her presentation. He ran a hand through his hair and pulled himself back into the ceiling, making sure he reset each disturbed tile before setting off on the uncomfortable crawl.

Kenton took a deep breath before entering the antechamber-slash-prep room of the Tomb. He'd never been there of his own free will before, not even during all his spying. Something about threading frix into the scanner and being granted access felt momentous, like a terrifying yet wonderful thing was about to happen. Maybe Torturer Anland waited on the other side, eager to kill him slow for overstepping his bounds and he was picking up on that cruel anticipation. Nevertheless, he gained nothing by staying back, and if he were to die, at least he could do it knowing Bo had escaped yet again.

He took a breath and crossed the threshold. No one appeared to stop him, so he continued walking, trying to quell the hope budding beneath his breast. If the Cabal succeeded today—if the Consul forgot to terminate him in the confusion—he'd be free. Free to go home, free to pursue High Consul Rolv and demand justice for Umama and Pa and Annie, and free to finally rest, no longer plagued by the nightmares of a past he couldn't erase.

The main entrance to the Tomb slid open with a little more coaxing from his frix, and Kenton slipped inside the dimly lit space.

Two figures moved about in the shadowed sports booth that hung over the arena. Kenton wished he had some liana vines to climb, but there were enough handholds on the battle-pitted walls that he could scramble up to the box with a running jump. He kept to the darker areas of the quiet space as he executed the manoeuvre, booted feet propelling him noiselessly upwards.

His fingers had just latched onto the ledge jutting out from under the booth's double-panelled glass windows when the doors on the opposite side of the Tomb burst open, and a very dishevelled Laine and Bo came tumbling in, almost colliding with each other as they raced to the middle of the room.

"What the heck, you guys!?" a girl's frustrated voice called, stopping the two in their tracks, and they turned, cringing in a very guilty manner when they caught sight of the speaker, who'd popped open the window to Kenton's left.

He almost laughed at the fact that neither the girl—who must have been the contact from the Cabal—nor the two on the ground had spotted him yet, dangling quite high above the unforgiving floor of the Tomb.

That didn't last long, and Bo started shouting in Klia'an, ripping off his helmet and pointing an accusing finger at Kenton.

"You said you couldn't go with us! The way out's right there!"

The girl in the booth flung a rope ladder out of the open window and clambered down, followed by Jack, who did a double take and almost fell upon seeing Kenton's precarious hold on the ledge. He reached out an arm, and Kenton accepted, pulling himself onto the sturdy ladder, which felt more metallic than textile under his fingers, explaining how easily it held each person's weight.

"Do you have *any* idea how badly you could have compromised the mission? All the work Shadow and I have done over the last few years, the last decade?" the girl said, marching up to Laine and Bo, while fiddling with a holoscreen that she aimed at the doors, the white coat she wore swirling out behind her. It contrasted well with her dark skin, and a chord of familiarity struck Kenton hard upon seeing her braided hair.

"It's fortunate the Consul is so bent on the complete conquest of Thorunn that they're going ahead with their plans despite the, the, absolute baldashery you two have managed."

"Pride makes fools of us all in the end," Jack agreed, hurrying to catch up with her.

Laine started when the man spoke and wrenched off his helmet with shaking fingers. He tapped on his clip's light.

"D-Dad?" he stuttered, and Jack went whiter than freshly bleached bones.

"Kid? What—how? Does your mother know you're here?"

Laine's face crumpled.

"Laine, son, what's wrong?"

Laine raised an unsteady hand to his neck and clutched at something beneath his clothes.

"Mom. She, she—the night they took you away she collapsed. Bowman's."

Jack shook his head as Laine's words sank in. Laine withdrew his hand from his jacket. In his palm sat a pretty beaded necklace, one Kenton re-membered Alanna wearing before her emergency surgery.

"But, the cure," Kenton said, stepping into the light Laine's clip cast.

"Gordon found out—or rather, he knew the whole time, that's what got you arrested, by the way. But uh, he, uh."

Jack moved towards Laine, who flinched back, every line in his body tense, eyes darting to the door, then to his father, then back again. He seemed to be fighting a battle with his body, as if part of him des-perately wanted to reach out and hold on to Jack but another part of him throbbed with a desperate desire to flee. He looked miserable, his eyes starting to turn glassy with tears.

"Dad, he stole all our money, framed you to cover up a decade old massacre, and, and . . ."

Laine couldn't get the words out, and a shudder ran through Kenton at the implication of the truth grief prevented him from speaking.

"Your traitor brother murdered your wife in cold blood," Bo said bluntly, and Kenton darted forward to grab Jack when he reeled backwards at his best friend's indelicate breaking of such unwelcome news.

The girl from the Cabal laid a hand on Jack's arm.

"I'm so sorry. I didn't know you were the other Doctor Riven. It's all true. Your brother's in league with the Consul's inner circle, and the list of crimes and cover-ups we've traced back to him is horribly extensive." She gave Jack's arm a slight squeeze. "I know it's no comfort at all, but we will see him brought to justice before the day is out. They'll all be brought to account for the things they've done."

Jack didn't respond, openly weeping. Laine stood awkwardly to the side, twitching towards his father like he wanted to comfort him somehow but had been separated too long to know how to initiate the contact.

Kenton put his arms around Jack instead. The scientist had often told him in wistful tones how much he longed to reconcile with his estranged son. Kenton didn't think either of them had imagined they would meet again like this, with the devastating fact of Alanna's death between them. Kenton mourned her too, recalling the fragile smile of the beautiful woman. She'd been nothing but kind to him, even after learning his secret. Her being gone, it was wrong, very terribly wrong.

"I must apologise, I know this is an awful time—"

"Ya think, Lis?" Bo interrupted.

The way he pronounced the girl's name made Kenton snap his head up to study her face—she looked about fourteen or fifteen, and her eyes, there was something about her eyes he couldn't look away from.

She stared back just as intensely, unperturbed by Bo's sarcastic interjection.

"Before we go any further, I need to know. Kenton. Ken. Do you remember me?" She suddenly looked very young, those hauntingly familiar eyes round and imploring.

Kenton didn't respond. He couldn't speak, couldn't even breathe as memory after memory flooded him, confusing jumbles of images pulled from his nightmares that contradicted the hope blossoming into a bright fire within his chest.

The girl reached forward and brushed the tips of his fingers with hers, as if only allowed that little bit of contact.

"Kenton," she said again, ignoring the others staring at her like she'd lost her mind. "Brother. It's me."

His heart stopped.

And restarted, pulsing painfully against his ribcage, his hand closing around hers in a crushing grip.

"Annie?" he whispered, tears starting to blur his vision. He could see it now. She'd changed quite a bit since age six, but those beautiful eyes were the same, and she had Pa's chin.

"Wait, I thought your name was Lis?" Laine asked.

"Annalise." The words fell unbidden from Kenton's lips. "For our great-grandmother."

"Oh, Ken!" Annie reached across Jack and embraced Kenton properly. All of them were crying uncontrollably. "When the news first broke about the Outpost Terrorist, I started to dare to hope. And then when they captured you and showed that footage from the Tomb on TCBNN, I thought I would die. But I didn't, I didn't really believe it 'til now."

Kenton couldn't believe it himself. His little sister was alive? The same sweet Annie he saw blown to bits in his nightmares? The Innah had searched as long as she could before the soldiers returned to dispose of the bodies, but neither she nor any others of Tribe Osinan had found any other survivors.

"How?"

She shook her head, wiping her face dry with her billowy white coat. "We've wasted enough time as it is." A loud banging from the Tomb doors punctuated her words.

"I initiated a lockdown after those two arrived, but that won't hold forever. We have to get this broadcast out. The symposium's due to begin any minute."

Annie tapped rapidly at her holoscreen, presumably sending messages to her compatriots, then gestured for them all to hurry back to the announcement booth. Once they'd gained the relative safety of the small box filled with audio and visual equipment, she turned serious eyes on Kenton.

"I didn't choose this place simply because it was a convenient place for 626, pardon, Doctor Riven, and I to meet."

Jack went over to the holoscreens displaying running lines of code.

"I suggested this to 'W' or is it Annie, now?"

"Either's fine," she said, equally busy at another machine. "Code names won't mean much after today."

"Annie it is." Jack dipped his chin in acknowledgement. He still blinked back tears, a muscle twitching in his clenched jaw. "I suggested this place because I've learned it's the most powerful broadcasting station in Skytown—in all of Thorunn to be precise. There won't be a screen in any city, any outpost town that won't receive the Cabal's message."

"This will explain everything," Annie said. "We tell the truth and watch it spin out from there." Her finger hovered over the key that would start whatever havoc she was about to unleash.

"Everyone ready? Dismantling the system in three, two . . ."

23

"**N**ow back to you, Alicia."

"Thanks, Mark. It's been over four hours since insider sources alleged that the Hexagon went into lockdown sometime in the early morning. High Consul Rolv continues to deny anything might be seriously wrong and has confirmed the symposium will continue as planned. No further details have been given, and our crew inside the Hexagon is having a hard time transmitting any visuals back to us."

"That's right, all we have is the live audio from David in the main conference room. Dave, y'there?"

". . . Yes, thanks, Scott. We've been told we can't run video until the presentations start. You'll notice me whispering 'cause I'm trying not to let on that I'm recording anything at all."

"And we appreciate your discretion. We're doing our best to boost your audio here at the station."

"Thanks, Alicia. It's hard to remain unperturbed with the palpable air of tension lingering over the room. Sources tell me alarms have been heard on the lower, restricted levels, most audible near the entrance to the Tomb. Initial inquiries returned answers about a routine drill, but when we sent an intern to fetch some equipment from our hovertrucks, we discovered that in fact, we'd been placed on lock-down, no one in or out of the Hexagon until further notice."

"And how long do y'anticipate that'll last for, Dave?"

"Hard to say for sure, Scott, but there's been rumours swirling of containment efforts for a deadly gas leak."

"Shouldn't everyone have been evacuated in that case?"

"Certainly, if the rumours hold any merit, but you know how quickly false info spreads when people start panicking. Shoot. Someone's coming this way—I'm going to have to cut this short."

"Of course. Stay safe and report in when you can."

". . . Thanks, Alicia, talk soon."

"That was David Sharid, reporting live from inside the Hexagon. Now back to our on-the-ground correspondent. Mark, your team reported a disturbance outside the building not long ago?"

". . . That's right, Alicia, several eyewitnesses alleged seeing the infamous Samuel 'Sureshot' Hezekiah Lewis arguing with the guards before forcibly gaining entry to the Hexagon. We've sent a couple journalists to corroborate the reports, and we should know more details shortly."

"Understood. We'll sit tight until then. Thanks, Mark."

". . . My pleasure."

Trish popped her gum loudly and grabbed a fresh

rag to continue wiping down the bar at *O'Tafferty's.*

"Those news cats are really milkin' this new development for all it's worth, huh?"

"It's more interesting than reporting on the setup for whatever dry presentations those pompous scientists are trying to cram down our throats."

The comment was offered by her co-worker and the owner of the bar, Stephanos Dimopoulos. It would be great if he remembered to bring in a bottle of bleach once in a while, but if he couldn't be bothered to spend the bare minimum on maintaining his establishment, Trish didn't care to waste her own measly credits on shining up the place.

"Tell me about it. Did they really have to hijack all the channels?" Her fingers caught on a piece of tacky gum, and Trish grimaced. Working at *O'Tafferty's* paid the bills, but it wasn't the life she'd imagined for herself when she'd left Earth.

"The Tomb play-by-plays will cycle back around in the rerun circuit soon enough."

"I know. But the season finale of *Task Force: Mars* airs today," Trish said, taking her frustration out on a particularly crusted section of bar. "And I'm gonna miss it, just like I do *every* single time it comes back around. I'm either dyin' of a fever, workin' a double, or runnin' to Smoketown to make sure my folks haven't expired yet. I don't even like the stupid show, but everyone else on this storm-riddled planet has seen the season nine finale except me, and it's gettin' real tiresome to be left outta the loop."

"'Science is the Future of Thorunn,' don't you

know?" Stephanos quoted, busy with putting away the remainder of last night's dishes, freshly dried. "The discoveries made over the last few months will change Thorunn as we know it, so don't forget to switch on your holoscreens nine a.m. sharp, February fifth."

"And to make doubly sure we wouldn't miss it, they turn on everyone's sets anyway. Times like these, those conspiracies put out by the, what's it called, the cable?" Trish snapped her fingers. "The Cabal, that's it. They start not to sound so crazy after all."

"Least I can still mute the darn thing," Stephanos said and reached for his clip.

"Hold it." Trish stopped him with a sudsy hand. "Somethin's happenin'."

The view cut from the news station to an ostentatiously panelled room that had to be where the vaunted presentations would be delivered. A large holoscreen took centre stage on the wall behind a thick podium. The camera panned around the room, showing a large number of seated attendees, before focusing on the thin man who stepped up to a microphone and spoke in a reedy voice, welcoming everyone present and those watching at home, mostly repeating the same drivel that had been running on the news ticker all week.

Despite herself, Trish watched. It was either that or try to wrangle old Drunkface MacAllister into paying for his long-abandoned drinks from the night prior, and the way the man snored—slumped over a table in the corner—she much preferred watching television to that unenviable task.

"And now, what you've all been waiting for—some of us much longer than others, heh—our first lecturer of the day, the esteemed Doctor Gordon Gray Riven, here to present his body of work entitled, *Frix and You*, subtitled, *The Indispensable Hinnom Tree: Practical Applications both Personal and Global*."

The moderator droned on for a few minutes more, listing the doctor's accolades and the short list of his published works, and then the man himself stepped up to the podium, a self-satisfied grin on his face at the applause that rippled through the room. He pulled out a pair of glasses and cleared his throat.

"What an honour to stand before you all today."

He sounded just as stuck up as the others, and Trish prepared herself for another disappointingly boring shift counting the cracks in the ceiling and tolerating Stephanos' slothful approach to work.

"What I present to you all has indeed been a long time in the making, set back by malicious interference on many, many fronts, but my team and I refuse to learn the meaning of the word failure, so I am pleased to say . . ."

Trish stopped paying attention and reached for her own clip to mute the insufferable droning. Her hand stuttered halfway to her ear when the screen behind the scientist went black.

Static filled the Hexagon monitor, and gasps from those in the conference room filtered through *O'Tafferty's* holoscreen speakers as the image of a young girl faded into view. Then the same thing happened to the holoscreen in the bar itself, cutting off the surprised exclamations from the TCBNN anchors.

Stephanos jerked forward. "What the—!?"

"Shh!" Trish snapped her damp rag at him as the teenager solidified on the bar's screen. "This might actually be worth watchin'."

The girl began to speak, and Trish dropped onto a stool to listen, all half-hearted attempts at cleaning tossed aside.

"Some of you might know me as Lissa Mambane, the newest chemistry intern here at the Hexagon. Others call me Lis, and still more know me as 'W,' the leader, founder, and driving force behind the Cabal— not at all a terrorist organisation as the High Consul and the rest would have you believe."

Trish sucked in a breath. That little girl was the leader of the notorious Cabal? The group whose bounties were valued at two hundred million credits each? She had a pair of steel ones, publicly announcing her identity, that was for sure.

"I am all, and none of these people. My name, my true name, is Annalise Victoria Owami Wishings. I was kidnapped as a little girl after the murder of my parents during the Apollo XXII Massacre, an event orchestrated and carried out by our own ruling Consul members, who specifically and meticulously created and perpetrated a false narrative that protected them from Earth's retribution and unjustly shifted blame onto the innocent native inhabitants of this planet.

"I am here today to expose each deceit, each un-truth, every single lie; to demand justice for High Consul Rolv's crimes, and to halt in its tracks the ma-licious, systematic planning of a second, far more ex-pansive genocide, which will not leave a single per-son on this planet unaffected."

Trish stared, speechless, at the screen. All around her, the few frostbitten patrons who'd started shuff-ling in for breakfast did the same, expressions of shock and disbelief scrawled over their faces. No one ate or spoke or drank, too enthralled by the pictures and dates and text—the damning text—filling the screen as a voiceover continued the narration, unfold-ing the brief of what Annalise had mentioned one ugly, sordid point at a time.

<hr>

Annie is alive!

The thought reverberated around Kenton's mind —lighting up every dulled spark, every darkened synapse—and threw him into a state of incoherent disarray, unable to reconcile the fact of her solid in his arms with the death scene he'd relived night after night for years.

She's alive!

The shock of that terrible day must have warped his memory, seeding his night terrors with the worst possible scenarios his grief could supply. The Innah had found nobody else living when she'd stolen back after seeing Kenton safe to the Hinnom Forest, ce-menting his fragmented recollection of what had happened and leading him to believe himself truly alone.

Annie, sweet little Annie was alive.

She had to be at least a little annoyed with the way Kenton couldn't stop touching her, trying to convince himself she wasn't a vivid hallucination, and he wasn't still convulsing on the floor in his room.

From the moment she'd switched from the live feed to a pre-recorded video, he'd taken her in his arms and hadn't let go. He kept running his fingers across her hands, turning her palms over and feeling the softness there, wondering at her colourful nails and resting his thumb over the pulse point of her wrist, her lifeblood a steady thrum under her skin.

"You're alive," Kenton kept muttering. He pressed kisses into her braided hair and inhaled its sweet coconut-like scent.

Annie had explained that Jack had recorded her live opening and tagged it onto the footage that followed, the whole fifty-minute video set to play in a continuous loop for the next forty-eight hours, broadcasting to all of Thorunn in exactly the way the Consul had meant the symposium to. Annie had had an outro already pre-recorded, meant to air while she rejoined Shadow, freed the prisoners, and escaped the Hexagon, but in light of Kenton being alive and confirmed to be her brother, she'd wanted to wait and add a more complete closing statement.

Kenton didn't care what she wanted to say or do, as long as she permitted him to stay with her for whatever time he had left. It hurt, knowing that at any moment Torturer Anland could press a button and forever separate him and Annie. He kept stroking her hair and squeezing her close, hoping fervently that the High Consul and his cousin would hold back on his termination until the end of Annie's broadcast.

His death might even fuel her fire that much further. Consul Rolv had personally destroyed their family, and whatever Annie had planned with the Cabal would likely pale in comparison to what she might unleash in the wake of Kenton's passing. He just hoped it wouldn't hurt her too much. Wouldn't break her.

He closed his eyes and rested his chin on her head, trying to smile through the lump in his throat and listening intently as Annie's message continued to play, no detail left out of her explanation.

She'd been snatched away from Consul Rolv by a young South African soldier who'd seen in the frightened little girl the perfect solution to his childless marriage. He'd argued Annie was too young to remember the destruction and carnage they'd wrought on Ethaba, and the High Consul—feeling magnanimous after his victory—had agreed, the whole of his forces retreating when the creatures Annie termed "rheas maximus" had approached the city, drawn by the scent of blood.

Kenton supposed that was when the Innah had risked her life to pull him from the ashes of their burning home.

The soldiers had returned later and disposed of

the half-eaten bodies, sealing them inside Ethaba's tunnels and marking the area unsafe. They would have gone on to destroy the Hinnom Forest, but their ongoing conflict with Tribe Anshi—who had struck one final, desperate blow to reclaim Mount Lalethusl while the military was off slaughtering innocents—had forced them back to Skytown. By the time they'd dealt with the insurgence in a bitter conflict that decimated the Consul's forces and exterminated all but one of the Anshians, second frix had started, preventing them from returning to Ethaba and continuing their murderous work.

In the meantime, Earth had started asking questions the Consul found very uncomfortable to answer and so had changed their tactics, deceiving the remaining and later settlers of Thorunn into believing the klia'an people—colloquially termed lokians—had murdered the Apollo XXII colonists, hoping that with everyone's minds poisoned against the natives of Thorunn they could rebuild their military forces to full strength and finally seize the coveted resources of the Hinnom Forest.

When they made their move this time, there would be no opposition, no one to stand against them and speak for the klia'an people as Kenton and Annie's father had done.

Kenton hugged Annie closer as he contemplated the information. He'd had some inkling of the enormity behind the reasons Consul Rolv had taken their parents from them, but he hadn't realised the extent of the man's crimes. So hateful had the people of

Thorunn become towards klia'ans that simply exposing the truth of that awful night wasn't enough.

And Annie had known it. She'd lived with the mind-breaking secret of their parents' murder for years, pretending she didn't remember, all the while digging into all the other terrible things Rolv Anland and the eleven additional members of the Consul had done and covered up over the years.

The video laid out each of those things, highlighting the atrocities the governing members of Thorunn had committed against the people they were supposed to protect.

Kenton heard Laine and Jack gasp when Gordon Riven's name came up in the latter half of the broadcast, the betrayal he'd carried out against his own family written starkly in undeniable black and white on the holoscreen.

He imagined similar exclamations were being choked out across Thorunn, in every home, every shopfront, every school, as lists of names scrolled by, names of people the Consul had imprisoned, experimented on, and discarded after they'd died screaming in agony. Annie had clips of that too, and Kenton had to look away, remembering all too well the hot slice of a surgeon's scalpel.

Shadow joined them at one point—having entered through the hidden tunnel in the Tomb—and nodded in acknowledgement at the siblings, his quirn and a glowing sol held loose in each hand.

The video drew to a close, and Annie gently detangled herself from Kenton's grip, sparing only a single glance for the buckling Tomb doors. The loud banging of the soldiers on the other side hadn't ceased, and from the way the noise had become measured and solid, Kenton suspected they'd fetched battering rams.

Annie gestured for the others to stand out of frame, all except Kenton, whom she pulled to her side, and when the footage stopped rolling, briefly explained their relationship and his identity as both the Outpost Terrorist and the Tomb favourite Stormsurge, highlighting the Consul's further lies and hypocrisy regarding him.

The banging grew louder, joined by a firm pounding on the door of the sportscaster box and punctuated by the ever-present wail of the alarm Bo and Laine had set off. The clash of sounds heightened the tension that had settled over the room, lending solemnity and urgency to Annie's closing words.

"Even now, the Consul is mobilising their most loyal soldiers to eliminate any dissenters—which will be most of you, having seen what you've seen. Beyond that, they would cut you down just for knowing the truth. Slaughter you, easy as breathing; happily, mercilessly. High Consul Rolv has turned on his own people before, and he'll do it again.

"Will you let that happen? Will you let them come into your homes, your children's schools, your places of work, and let them strike you and your loved ones down? Will you let them blame your deaths on the guiltless Iokian people when Earth asks what happened?

"Or will you stand and fight?"

Annie's voice, already firm to begin with, grew stronger, her conviction bolstering her words, lighting them with an unquenchable fire.

"Fight for the truth. Fight for your lives and the lives of those dearest to you. Fight to stop the unjust debts that cripple our economy and force our people into servitude. Fight to stop the appalling torture of those imprisoned for slights real or imagined. Fight to avenge the wrongful, needless deaths of the nearly one hundred eighty men, women, and children of the Apollo XXII colony. Fight for the future of Thorunn.

"Fight to be free."

Annie cut the broadcast.

Kenton waited while she and Jack fiddled with the recording, making sure it couldn't be tampered with or erased after the military team still pounding on the Tomb's doors broke through. He imagined that every man, woman, and child on Thorunn had set down their toys, pencils, gardening spades, and dishrags—cast down their clips even, horrified by the extent to which their government had spied on them—and had picked up their sols, ready to defend themselves against the corrupt soldiers coming for them.

There would be a revolution; Annie's revelations left no other choice.

The Tomb doors crashed to the ground as they surrendered at last to the battering rams, the noise almost drowning out the similarly besieged announcement booth doors bursting simultaneously from their frame in a great groaning of wood and steel. Billowing smoke filled the staircase beyond, and sols appeared in Jack's and Laine's hands.

Bo gripped his quirn between his gloved fists. It appeared to have lost its charge, but Kenton could remedy that problem.

Shadow sprang to Annie's side, offering her a sol, and a smile stole over Kenton's face.

"You won't need that. They think fear controls me."

He took a deep breath.

"It doesn't."

Blue enveloped him, the familiar rush of white-hot frix crackling in his ears, enough to drown out the surrounding clamour. Lightning burst through him, forming his slyrs and standing his hair on end. He revelled in the tiny sparks that danced along his arms and fingers, at the surge of power singing in exultant joy at finally being set free.

He sent a spark through Jack's prisoner clip, destroying it harmlessly, before reaching a frix-wreathed hand towards Bo, taking his quirn from him and smiling at his friend's stunned look when he returned the weapon glowing and ready to best the men and women about to enter the room.

The smoke started to dissipate, and the soldiers began to charge but jerked to a halt when Kenton stepped forward, the haze of blue energy that surrounded him humming in a menacing, almost sentient manner.

"St-Stormsurge?" the lead soldier stuttered, the steady grip he had on his weapon faltering at the unexpected sight.

The slyr in Kenton's right hand dissolved into a writhing ball of frix. He raised his other arm to shield himself and aimed the mass of crackling electricity at the soldiers.

"My quarrel is not with you," he said calmly. The frix distorted his voice, making it sound louder and multilayered, and he couldn't help the flush of pleasure that ran through him as the Hexagon military drew a collective breath at his commanding tone and imposing presence. "Walk away."

The soldiers looked at each other, seemingly ready to heed Kenton's words. But their moment of hesitation was followed by a wince from the team leader, whose hand shot to his ear, eyes widening then narrowing as he listened to whatever orders had been relayed to him.

Kenton barely had time to countermand the subsequent bursts of solfire, loosing the frix curled in his palm with unerring accuracy.

Bo, Shadow, and Laine sprang into action as well, adding their own solfire to the fray, and together the four of them pushed their attackers down the stairs and out into the hall, treading carefully to avoid fallen bodies.

Kenton bit back his mixed feelings at seeing the corpses Shadow left behind. He always wanted to avoid bloodshed if he could help it, but the Anshian klia'an had no such compunctions, and Kenton supposed he might have felt much the same had he been older during the Ethaba massacre.

They moved forward as a unit—Jack and Annie keeping to the back—and fanned out once they reached the bottom of the steps. Kenton was careful to keep in front of Annie so he could deflect any stray solfire. A quick glance over his shoulder showed him that Bo had given Annie his body armour, and gratitude swelled within Kenton's heart at his best friend's selfless actions.

An endless stream of armed men and women came their way, but Kenton lashed out with arcing laces of frix that swept his opponents from their feet before they could close in and deal out real damage.

Bo stayed at his side, shocking any daring soldiers who managed to dart under the frix, his fangs and glowing eyes on constant display. He couldn't unleash a paralysing scream without shifting to s'hinoian form, but his continuous growling was almost deterrent enough, every single cadet, lieutenant, major, or captain freezing in their tracks when they saw him.

Shadow stayed shifted to klia'an form as well, taking advantage of the greater dexterity to aim deadly blasts of solfire at the oncomers. The hall quickly piled up with bodies and riot shields, discarded sols lying inches from where they'd spilled out of their owners' bleeding hands.

There must have been a terrible odour, but the only scent that stung Kenton's nostrils was the iron-rich smell of the shredded ions he alone could see. Frix burned along his bones like a ravenous fire, seeking out targets with little conscious effort on his part. He'd been suppressing the near-immeasurable energy for so long that it felt like flying—no, like hunting in the Hinnom Forest—no, like drowning, a sensation so indescribable that nothing he'd ever experienced came close to truly defining the tingles rushing through his body, erupting in a popping shower of sizzling sparks over and over and over again.

And that moment, caught up in the euphoric elation coursing through him, was when he saw Her.

She swept towards their little group like a dark spectre, marching through the bedraggled ranks of soldiers who parted for her before she could reach them, ceasing their fire as soon as she passed.

Kenton's breath caught in his chest, the frix in his hands suddenly burning him painfully. Annie, Shadow, Bo, Laine, and Jack—they couldn't return the way they'd come. If it wasn't already, the announcement room would soon be swarming with the soldiers who'd battered down the doors of the Tomb, cutting off that escape. Kenton had counted on himself and his allies fighting their way to the level two public entrances, where the rest of Annie's resistance awaited them. His frix would have been able to undo any electronic locking mechanisms barring their way, and beyond that, they had Laine, who'd proven handy with doors.

All of that was about to become impossible. A single press of the master kill switch Kenton could see clutched in the Torturer's hand, and he'd be immobilised, rendered helpless and useless. The tears that rolled unchecked down his cheeks steamed away as soon as they touched the frix crawling across his face, concealing the signs of his internal distress.

"Annie, Bo," he called, his throat tightening at the prospect of being once again separated from the two people, above all others, whom he'd die for. He'd hoped he'd have more time. The scant hours he'd spent with them during the broadcast and the ensuing firefight weren't enough. He didn't want Annie's last memory of her big brother to be him writhing on the floor, reduced to a puppet for a woman who delighted in treating people as less than human.

"You must take the others and go."

"Not a chance," Annie replied, edging closer to him. "I'm not leaving you so quickly after finding you again."

Kenton winced. She wouldn't have a choice. He caught Bo's eye, his friend's expression pinched, mouth set in a hard line. He knew why Kenton wanted them to leave, and the burden of explaining to Annie would fall on him, after. Yet he also refused to forsake Kenton, and he took courage from knowing he wouldn't be alone, at the end.

The solfire ceased as Torturer Anland trod over the groaning bodies of her own soldiers to reach Kenton. Each side watched, anxious to see what would happen. Kenton wouldn't have put it past the fatigued soldiers to attempt shooting her in the back if the fear of retribution, swift and brutal, hadn't been drilled into them.

Shadow growled a warning, but even he held himself in check, knowing the Torturer wouldn't have approached so brazenly if she had no means of protecting herself.

When she was but an arm's length away, Kenton saw it, an energy shield like the one that had covered the outpost town nearest to Ethaba. A protective radius extended out to the four guards on either side of the woman, originating from a device hung jewellery-like around her neck. Somehow they'd figured out how to harness enough power to radically miniaturise shielding technology, though Kenton doubted they'd been able to make more than a few copies.

He was abruptly thankful he'd determined early on to thwart the scientists' attempts to make him manifest his frix. Had they known the technology was controllable and implanted it into their army, each soldier could have been his or her own battery for the shields. Able to harness lightning itself, they'd have been unstoppable.

Torturer Anland smirked at him.

"You thought you could actually accomplish something by hiding your control of your abilities. Need I remind you from whence they came? What the Consul bestowed it can also withdraw."

"Haven't you taken enough?" Kenton asked, the frix that layered his voice masking the exhaustion lacing his words.

"Never." The sneering grin that twisted the red slash of her mouth pulled tighter, warping her sharply beautiful face into something monstrous.

"I could have reduced you to nothing from the safety of my dear cousin's panic room. But I yearn to see the terror in your eyes when I unmake you for the last time."

She curled her fingers into a fist and squeezed.

"Don't look," Kenton gasped, drawing on every ounce of his strength to magnetise his feet to the floor, to keep himself standing in defiance of the jerking, unhurried death she bequeathed to him.

And then—

Nothing

Kenton did indeed stay rooted in place, the bright blue frix doing its job of anchoring him to the ground. But despite Torturer Anland's fingers going white from how hard she clenched the trigger, his artificial heart still pulsed beneath his ribs, steady, unwavering.

The vicious smile on Torturer Anland's face morphed into a frown of confusion. She pressed her fingers more tightly into her palm, blood seeping out from beneath her nails, and still Kenton stood, frix leaping up and across his legs, arms, chest. He could see his electrified eyes reflected in her hateful ones. She opened her palm and slammed her other hand into the device, but to no avail, and the panic that had been beating in Kenton's heart slipped away, transferred into his tormentor.

"You tell me right now how you tampered with this!" she screamed at him, coming as close as her shield allowed.

"Surely you haven't forgotten?" Kenton said. Peace probably wasn't the feeling she expected of him, but he couldn't deny the absolute state of calm he'd entered upon understanding just why the kill switch hadn't worked. "You gave me these powers."

She'd never tried using the device on any of the other occasions he'd manifested the frix. After all, he'd always performed for them in the arena, their perfect dancing automaton. She wasn't to know his frix would block the signal when onite wouldn't.

He hadn't known either—not until just then—or he might have staged a breakout much sooner.

Kenton shot forward and grabbed her, his frix-enclosed fist punching through her barrier and catching on her wrist. He brought up his left hand and smashed the device at her neck, destroying the energy shield. The guards jumped to fend him off, but a frix shockwave exploded from him, bouncing them back to the walls.

Kenton struck the trigger from Torturer Anland's hand and sent a surge of energy through it. The kill switch popped in a shower of sparks on its way to the floor, and Kenton crushed what was left under his boots.

The Torturer scrabbled at him, trying to dig her nails into his skin, but the frix twisting about his face rebuffed her, the resulting screams of frustration and agony darkly pleasing to Kenton. Her soldiers stayed where he'd thrown them, staring at something behind him.

He turned, holding the struggling woman in one hand, to see a rush of uniformed persons flooding the already-packed hallway.

Annie's face split into a wide grin and even Shadow relaxed a little, his ears perking up when he saw the new arrivals. Reinforcements from the Cabal had made it, just in time.

The Hexagon soldiers who'd finally climbed up from the Tomb and made their way onto the scene halted upon seeing the guerrilla forces. None of them looked too unhappy that Kenton had wrestled the most hated person in Skytown into submission.

He formed a dagger of frix and held it to the Torturer's throat, where it burned her, though he hadn't pressed it deeply enough to draw blood. For so long the woman had embodied every single awful thing that had happened to Kenton since entering Skytown, and applying just a little pressure would rid him of her forever. The thought was frighteningly intoxicating, and for all his resolve to never kill if he could help it, Kenton wondered if Thorunn wouldn't be better off without the sadistic Torturer Anland.

"You can't keep that up forever." Her hands scrabbled at Kenton's unyielding grip, each breath coming in a rattling wheeze. "My cousin has an identical remote trigger. The instant your frix reserves run dry, it'll be the end of you."

Her tone was ice cold, not jeering, not taunting, simply matter of fact, stating something irrefutably true. The desire to stab her and be done with it surged powerfully in Kenton, and he thrust her away before he could give in to the base urge.

She stumbled, not expecting the sudden release. Her guards had already been manhandled off the floor and restrained by the Cabal forces that continued to surround them, and none of the other

Hexagon soldiers lifted a hand to defend her despite the orders she spat at them.

Kenton saw the moment Torturer Anland realised none would help her, that not a single one of the men and women who'd followed her would leap to her aid. Their anticipation and relief at being freed from fear of a slow, agonising death if they crossed her was writ clearly across their faces.

One of Annie's people approached Torturer Anland with a sol in one hand and cuffs in the other, and her eyes went wide before narrowing as she launched herself at Kenton, fingers outspread.

"Stop!" Kenton cried in alarm, and several shots issued from a nearby sol, but his panicked yell did nothing to deter the woman. He tried to twist out of the way, but stumbled over debris, going down hard as she fell atop him, her nails piercing through the thin layer of frix that danced over his skin, digging like claws into the exposed flesh of his arms to get to the implants beneath.

"Release me, for your own good, please!" he pleaded, struggling to sit up, but the High Consul's cousin merely grinned at him, the skin on her pale face starting to bubble and blister, the full force of Kenton's frix draining from him into her jerking body.

"I can't. I, I *won't*." She spat the words through a mouthful of blood, still smiling that awful smile.

"Please, please, let go," Kenton begged again, trying to lower the frix searing along his bones to levels that would allow him to dislodge her. He was going to be sick from the smell of her burning skin and hair.

Torturer Anland shook her head, digging her nails deeper, tearing Kenton's blood from him yet again and touching deep within.

"There's that desperation I've been craving." She laughed, the sound horribly distorted by the crackling frix that consumed her. She opened her mouth to say something else but uttered no words, only a scream that crawled along every inch of Kenton's body, vibrating in harmony with the frix destroying the woman from the inside out.

Kenton did everything he could to shake her off, but each of her arms was clasped about each of his, forcing a circuit that fed and fed itself, weakening him and killing her. Kenton willed the frix to dissipate, hoping to break the flow of electricity and release them, but to his horror and despair discovered the frix had escaped his control, using his body as both a power source and a conduit, gorging itself upon the Torturer, a hungry energy that would not be satisfied until it had devoured the sadistic Lynn Anland.

One of the Cabal members sprang forward, presumably to separate them, but Shadow caught the lad by the shoulder and forced him back. "Touch her, and you'll be caught by the current. Not the way you want to die."

And dying she was.

Kenton could only watch, unable to close his eyes as the frix he could no longer tame flared brighter and brighter inside the Torturer, melting her flesh from her bones, the boiling mass of it sliding slick and pulpy over his hands and dripping unevenly onto the floor. Underneath the static buzz of the sparking frix, Kenton could hear the sound of her clothes and skin sizzling and popping, strips flaying away like fatty, frying anlo.

He couldn't speak, couldn't bring himself to move, couldn't lift their joined arms to wipe away the tears stinging his eyes. All those nights that she'd cut him open, beat him, deprived him of food and water and sleep—he'd wished for peace, for the pain to end, for her to leave him alone and vanish somewhere where she couldn't hurt him again. But not like this, never like this. If he could let go, he would, he would in a heartbeat.

Kenton strained and strained and suddenly felt something snap, the current connecting them melting away.

But it was too late.

Her heart no longer beat inside her sunken chest. What was left of her body had swelled to a grotesque size, and before Kenton could dig the charred remnants of her nails out of his skin, her one remaining eye burst from her half-exposed skull, spraying into his face over the distant rush of someone screaming.

It wasn't until Laine pulled him from the floor that Kenton realised he'd been emitting the wrenching wail. He clamped his mouth shut and twisted away, not wanting to catch the other teen up and destroy him as well. Laine brandished his covered hands.

"Frix-proof gloves, remember? Anyway, I think that was a defensive mechanism that instinctively kicked in when she grabbed you. I don't think for one second you'd react to me and Bo or Annie the same way."

"Better not to test fate," Kenton said, shying away from Laine's helping hands. He tried not to be sick over the burbling remains of Torturer Anland at his feet. The last nauseating image he'd seen of her warped face would stay with him a long, long time. But the ordeal was over, his struggle against her done.

And they had to keep fighting. The High Consul was not yet defeated.

"I trust you have this situation under control?" Annie said to one of the women pointing a sol at the meekly surrendering Hexagon forces, many of whom had lost the contents of their stomachs at the scene that had played out before them. Kenton wondered how she could sound so calm amidst so much carnage.

"Yes, ma'am. Outside is chaos, but more and more soldiers are turning to our side, and the civilians have stepped up in a big way. Might be another few hours 'til we have everything fully in hand, but the tide's turned in our favour, and we'll be able to proclaim victory before the day is out."

"Good. Shadow, Cabal Team Four, you're with me. We're going to find the High Consul and end this." She took a spare sol from another of her soldiers and primed it. Shadow moved to her side, his ears pinned back, a low growl rumbling from him.

Kenton followed them down the hall, hating that his baby sister marched into the heart of danger. But

Rolv Anland still led the Consul, could yet kill Kenton with the press of a button should he fail to maintain the energy sparking through him. The strain of it weighed on him after the last horrible ordeal inflicted by Lynn Anland. He'd never expended himself so much so long before. The frix would abandon him—and soon. They had to get to the High Consul's panic room before then.

"Lis?"

A young man rushed towards them, skidded to a stop and doubled over, hands on his knees while he fought to regain his breath. He didn't appear much older than Annie herself and wore similar clothes, a classmate perhaps, which explained his easy familiarity.

"No one could reach you on your clip. Interference of some sort." He swallowed and panted, forcing out the words between gasps. "We have to get out. The High Consul locked himself up top and rigged the whole place to blow. We have thirty, maybe thirty-five minutes, tops."

Annie swore, and Kenton cringed at the ugly words.

"This is preferable, right?" he asked. "If the Hexagon is destroyed, his kill switch will be as well."

Annie shook her head, a grimace settling onto her face. She kept walking towards the stairs.

"Shadow got a peek at that panic room when he was still undercover here. There's no time to go into specifics, but it's built to withstand an explosive force three times as massive as that created by bringing this place down."

Bile rose in Kenton's throat, the roiling of his stomach accentuated by the ropes of frix that seethed inside him.

"We . . . have to go there."

"I have to go there," Annie said, stopping once she reached a door marked *Authorised Personnel Only.*

"Not alone," Shadow snarled, hefting his quirn between his hands. "This is my fight too."

"I know," Annie said. She reached out and squeezed his forearm. "But the rest of you—Laine, Doctor Riven—you shouldn't be here."

"We won't abandon you at the final hour," the man leading Cabal Team Four said. The other fighters nodded in agreement.

Jack stepped forward and shook Annie's hand. "It's been an honour."

"Dad!" Laine protested, but Jack put a hand on his shoulder.

"My first responsibility is to keep you safe. I've failed at that 'til now. Let the Cabal deal with this, and let's go home."

Laine opened his mouth, then shut it, and pulled Bo into a one-armed hug.

"Stay safe."

"Won't singe a whisker."

———————— ● ————————

Once the last few Cabal members had disappeared up the stairs, Laine turned to his father.

"We're not going back to Ethaba, are we?"

"If there's one thing I do know about my brother, it's that he hates feeling trapped. He'd never hole up in a metal box, no matter how safe it was."

Laine shuddered, disgusted that his time in the claustrophobic Kansor cave network had lent him something in common with his uncle.

"The Hexagon garages then."

"If he came on his Blackline, that's where he'd have headed."

"Probably too much to hope he's still there, right?"

"The odds might just fall in our favour," Dad said as he hurried down the hall and headed into a corridor that Laine and Bo had traversed once upon a time. "Gordon would never leave his research behind. By the time he's fetched it all, bypassed the lockdown, and gotten to his vercycle, we might just catch up with him."

"And that's something you two share in common," Laine muttered. Not quietly enough, however, as Dad frowned at him.

"I'm not a huge fan of vercycles, you know that."

"No, your stupid research," Laine said, gritting his teeth to try and keep his anger in check. "You just had to chase it, no matter the consequences."

"Because nothing Gordon said added up. Our tests kept coming back with contradictory results. Laine, I had to find out what my research was being used for. We came to Thorunn to start over, not get sucked into covering up murder and facilitating genocide."

Laine jumped in front of Dad and whirled around,

stabbing a finger at him.

"It doesn't matter how noble your intentions were. Facts are, you couldn't leave well enough alone and got yourself locked up when we needed you most. If the soldiers hadn't arrested you that night, you'd have been there when Mom collapsed."

Dad's eyes squinched together, and he stuffed his fist into his mouth. He looked like he was physically in pain. Good. He deserved to feel some of the hurt he'd caused over the years.

"Maybe Gordon wouldn't have been so bold if you'd been there for us. Maybe she wouldn't have died." Laine pulled aside his jacket collar, revealing Mom's necklace. "Gordon was going to ship me off to Earth without even letting me attend her funeral, and this is all I have left of her!" He tucked the intricately beaded jewellery back beneath his shirt, its weight the coldest comfort.

"Over and over again you abandoned us, always saying you'd change, but you never have! Your work always takes centre stage, and has it ever, *ever* brought us happiness?"

"I tried, Laine, I tried!" Dad was halfway to shouting, sobs catching in his throat. "You rejected all my attempts to reconcile with you after that year."

"Because I thought you weren't real! That whole year I never saw you—"

"We were penniless, I had to work four, sometimes five jobs just to keep the lights on—"

"I know. Mom explained it to me enough. But I was seven. I only saw you in pictures."

Laine's voice rose to fever pitch, dropping as he screamed at his father, the years of hurt and frustration pouring out uncontrollably. "I thought you had died! That the you that returned wasn't real. None of your apologies ever hit home because a dead man offered them to me. And then you stopped trying and threw yourself into your work, abandoning me again, just when I was starting to accept that maybe, just maybe, you were who you claimed to be."

"Laine—" Dad reached towards him, his eyes red and wet, his face once more like that of a stranger's, framed as it was by the unfamiliar beard speckled with bits of grey.

Laine spun on his heel and took off towards the door marked *Hexagon Hover Garage*. "Let's just find Gordon," he called over his shoulder, not wanting to hear his father's weak defence of his actions.

The garage was mostly empty, only a few TCBNN vehicles still hovering over wide charging stations. Laine caught the flash of a vercycle and shoved Dad out of the way as Gordon's Blackline almost ran them over.

Laine drew his sol and fired, hitting the back of the sleek vehicle. It sputtered, dropping dangerously close to the ground, but still cleared the doors and flashed into the snowy streets beyond, trailing large clouds of smoke. Laine fired again, his shots finding their target for all that Gordon zigged and zagged, the blasts catching the Blackline broadside and sending the vercycle spinning into a snowbank.

Laine raced to the wreckage, slipping in the sooty

slush lining the ground outside the Hexagon. Dad helped him to his feet, but the delay allowed Gordon to grab one of his bags, abandon the once-beautiful machine, and dart down an alley before they could catch him.

Laine kicked at the Blackline before chasing after Gordon. The man had obviously been to Skytown many times before, scrambling over fences, dashing through narrow gaps between houses, and ducking across streets full of angry citizens in his rush to escape. Finally, he threw himself under a military-styled hovercar and came up unharmed on the other end. He gestured wildly at the occupants of the transport, and it turned its sol-cannons on Laine and Dad, forcing them to take cover behind a set of dumpsters.

"Where'd you learn to handle a sol like that?" Dad asked, breathless, his chest heaving.

"Was good on Earth, got better the night of Mom's collapse helping defend Ethaba from Kenton and Bo. Been carrying one off and on since."

"Laine," Dad said, tears starting down his face once more, and Laine knew instantly that he wanted to resume the conversation they'd been having inside the Hexagon.

Why couldn't he just let the subject drop? Laine had no desire to rehash the grievances of the past. But the Hexagon vehicle was still firing, and it seemed Dad was determined to get his piece out while they waited for an opportunity to move again.

"I didn't know. I'm so very sorry. I can't tell you how much I wish I'd thrown away my pride and let your mother's family help us sooner. Believe me, there is nothing I regret more than abandoning you and making you feel unwanted, and I have spent every single moment since working to ensure I never put us in a situation like that ever again."

"We're in a terrible situation now, aren't we? And Mom ain't here to accept your apologies so easily."

"I know. Oh, Laine, I know. Nothing I can do can ever make it right. I can only beg your forgiveness, though I don't deserve it."

The hovercar stopped firing, seemingly satisfied with their inaction, and Laine peeked around the dented dumpsters. A set of revolutionaries had caught the soldiers' attentions, and they flew away to deal with them, leaving Laine and Dad to unfold themselves from their temporary refuge.

Gordon had eluded them so far, but without his prized vercycle they still had a chance at catching him. They bobbed and weaved across the street to where they'd last seen him, all the while ducking stray solfire and jumping out of the way of duels and brawls, the whole of Skytown having turned into a warzone after Annie's broadcast.

Laine dug in his pack for a spare shirt and tore it in half, offering one side to his father. He tied the rest around his face to protect against the smoke and cold. Dad stared at the fluttering cloth as if he couldn't believe Laine had handed him something without being commanded, then secured it behind his ears.

The muddied snow obscured any and all footprints, so Laine headed for the city walls. Unless Gordon knew about the secret tunnels in the mountain-side, he'd have headed to the gates, as far away from the epicentre of the impending Hexagon explosion as he could manage. Dozens of people also streamed to-wards the walls, fleeing the thick fighting that charac-terised the city streets and impeding Laine's progress.

"When," he started, jogging alongside Dad past a row of smoking houses. "When was it that you stopped caring about me?"

Dad lost his footing, and it was Laine's turn to help him up, unwanted sympathy nudging him at the sight of the man's skinned knee and wet pants, the thin material not at all suited for Skytown's winter weather.

"I never stopped caring, Laine. But I've been selfish, didn't express my love when you needed it most. Your mother . . ." He sighed and brushed dirty snow out of his hair. "Alanna, maybe she was too quick to accept my contrition—and I too grateful to have her absolution that I didn't try hard enough with you."

But he had tried, and Laine had pushed him away, happy to live in a world where he never accepted Dad's attempts to set things right, because—when he really thought about it—if he forgave the man he only opened himself up to be hurt again. Holding Dad at arm's length kept him safe.

Or so Laine had thought. Really, he'd wasted all the years they could have had together in some twis-ted attempt at punishing his father for all the hurt he'd felt. Clinging to his anger, his resentment—it hadn't brought him anything beyond fleeting moments of satisfaction. Had Laine ever been happy, hating Dad all that time? Had he ever been free from bitterness?

"I see him!" Dad's yell broke through Laine's thoughts.

He squinted against the morning glare, catching sight of the familiar bag slung across a fleeing figure's shoulder. He wasn't far, and Laine ran with everything he had in him, closing the gap before Gordon could slip away again.

His uncle turned, drew his sol, and fired, the shot tearing Laine's sol from his hand. A second blast hit Laine in the chest, wringing an agonised cry from Dad, too far behind to stop his brother from killing his son.

Laine staggered, the solfire eating clean through his body armour and jacket at so close a range. But the searing beam never reached his flesh, and though he dropped to one knee, he didn't fall.

Mom's necklace had frustrated Gordon's lethal shot.

Laine closed his eyes and touched the now fused lump of metal and beading. Mom was gone, and yet, she was still with him, still watching out for him despite everything. And the man responsible for taking her from Laine stood mere feet away.

Laine opened his eyes, pulled out his lacrosse stick, and rushed Gordon.

He reached his uncle before the man could pass through the city gates and swung out with his crosse, bowling him to the ground. Laine whipped the metal staff again, forcing Gordon to stay down, beating the man's hands until they bled, dark red running in steaming rivulets down his face. It was smart of Gordon to protect his head, even if it earned him broken fingers, but Laine hadn't caught his mother's murderer to be thwarted by some bits of mangled flesh. He drove his lacrosse stick at the man's groin, bringing it up for a death blow when Gordon's hands instinctively shot to the tender area.

His stick jerked to a stop at the top of its arc.

"No!" Dad yelled, an anger on his face that Laine had never provoked in him before, both hands gripping the crosse-cum-cudgel. "I will not let him turn you into a murderer. I may have failed you in everything else, but in this I shall not."

"He deserves it," Laine protested, trying to yank his lacrosse stick out of Dad's firm grasp.

"My job is to protect you, even from yourself, and I won't let you do this thing. Furthermore, as my brother, Gordon is my responsibility, not yours."

"How can the little brother be his elder's keeper?" Gordon said. He spat a mouthful of blood through a wet chuckle.

"He must," Dad said. He refused to relinquish his grip, and Laine gave up the fight, darkly curious to see what Dad would do. "When his own flesh and blood has behaved as shamefully and abominably as you. You had me arrested and imprisoned on charges you falsified and submitted yourself. You sat by and watched while Lynn Anland tortured children and other innocents under her cousin's command. You just tried to kill my son!

"But above all else, you stole Alanna from us. Without guilt, without it ever weighing on your conscience even once, and all over money. You murdered her. My heart. The light of my eyes."

Dad gestured with Laine's crosse. "Get up. Start walking."

"You can't mean . . ." Gordon stared at the war-torn streets he'd almost escaped.

Less and less people emerged from the swirling smoke. Solfire of all types punctuated the dark mass with bright flashes, a mix of tiny bursts from personal hand pieces and massive concussive blasts from military-grade weapons. Laine cringed at the screams and crack of crumbling plaster that followed the loudest sounds.

"I mean."

"Jackie, c'mon. You've had your fun. If we linger here, we'll all get tagged by stray fire."

"I shouldn't, but I'm giving you a chance. You make it to a transport, you get to live."

Gordon pulled himself to his knees, and then to his feet, something in Dad's face convincing him that trying to find an abandoned vercycle was his only shot at salvation.

Dad cuffed Gordon over the head when he didn't move right away.

"I'm walking, I'm walking!"

"Good. Now run." Dad grabbed Gordon's discarded sol and started firing.

Gordon yelped and sprang forward, narrowly avoiding the bloodied people fleeing all around him, their torn clothes fluttering behind them as they sought the safety to be found beyond Skytown's gates. When he'd gone too far to turn back, Dad let his hand drop, a hard stare etched onto his face.

Laine stepped closer to him, a little in awe of the fury his father had displayed. He tried not to jump when Dad clapped an arm around his shoulder, squeezing the top of it a little as they watched Gordon run full tilt at an abandoned vercycle. Once he reached the machine, he pumped a fist in victory, stood the smoking vehicle up, and swung a leg over it.

He turned to sneer at them, and a stray bolt of solfire caught him in the back of the head. Gordon toppled off the seat and crumpled to the ground like a wet piece of paper, the vercycle falling atop him as more shots zipped through the air.

"Am I insane for wanting to run out there, into that, and check that he's really dead?" Laine asked. He touched his hand to his throat again. Mom's mangled necklace was still warm despite the frigid air, and he missed her so much his whole body ached with it.

His family was smaller again by one, but it didn't feel much different. Didn't bring Mom back. Gordon's limp body in the debris-filled slush couldn't begin to make her loss feel even slightly okay.

"We should stop thinking about him." Dad's voice cracked just a little as he gestured to the Hexagon still standing at the far end of the smoke-wreathed city. "Our friends need us."

Laine spared a last, lingering look at Gordon's crushed corpse—what little he could see of it under the pitted metal—then grabbed his sol and ran after Dad towards the doomed building.

"This won't ever be fast enough," Laine muttered, their pounding feet carrying them too slowly towards the Hexagon. They had to keep twisting out of the way of sizzling sol blasts, and Dad's thin-soled shoes had nearly come apart at the seams. Any further abuse and he'd be running barefoot in the bloodstained snow.

"There." Laine pointed to a still-locked garage. The windows of the adjacent apartment were dark, and his deft hands made quick work of the minimal security. Dad pulled a face but refrained from commenting on Laine's breaking-and-entering skills. A single vercycle hovered on one side of the messy garage, humming and ready to fly.

The double-seated transport dipped as they clambered on, but held their weight without crashing to the ground.

"Dad?" Laine said after he'd secured the shiny black helmet that had been hanging from the hand grips. He revved the vercycle, pointing it towards the imposing silhouette of the Hexagon. "What you did for me back there, with Gordon?"

He touched the crosse restrapped to his back, grateful that the bloodied staff hadn't become a murder weapon. If he'd carried out his initial plans, he'd never have been able to step onto a lacrosse pitch without thinking of the moment he'd used his stick to end a life.

"You've never, I mean, that was . . ."

Laine squeezed the grips tightly in his gloved hands. He hadn't expected Dad to get between him and his bloodlust, hadn't expected to feel so relieved that his hands weren't the ones to bring an end to his treacherous uncle. Dad had protected him, saved him from doing something irredeemable, and though it didn't erase the years of hurt, it did prove his sincerity. And now, salvaging what small chance they had of being a family—a broken, grief-stricken family, but a family nonetheless—the means of it lay in Laine's hands, if only he could speak the words.

They burned at him, frightening in how much he realised he meant them. Uttering them—it was the hardest thing he'd ever make himself do, and it didn't change the awful happenings of the last few months, but it could finally set him on the path Mom had wanted for him. He would speak his heart. He would make things right, for himself, and to honour her.

"Dad. For everything that's happened in the past until now—" Laine's voice cracked, but he kept going, knowing if he stopped before heading into the middle of an active war zone that he might not have another chance.

"I'm sorry. And I forgive you."

Dad inhaled sharply, but a large boom cut off his reply, spurring them into action. They shot out of the garage towards the smoking Hexagon, where a dwindling number of Skytown forces still fired upon civilians, Cabal members, and turncoats alike.

Laine bumped the vercycle up to rooftop level to avoid the solfire that crisscrossed the streets, mentally apologising for the gardens ripped apart by the vercycle's propulsion engines as they zoomed atop the neatly maintained spaces, flashing around steel supports and between decorative concrete pillars.

"Close your eyes!" Laine shouted when they came upon a glass-encased porch too quickly for him to veer upward and over. They burst through the first and second set of windows in a rush of tinkling glass.

The vercycle started wobbling after that, inching closer and closer to the ground no matter how desperately Laine pointed its nose towards the flurrying sky.

"It's gonna blow!" he yelled and gave up the battle, setting the damaged vehicle down and dragging Dad off it. Laine shielded him when the explosion tossed them into the building opposite.

"They're not supposed to do that, the regulations—"

Dad's sleeve had completely torn through, and Laine grabbed the tattered ruins of his spare shirt and wound it around Dad's arm, ignoring his yelps of pain. He had glass shards embedded there as well, but they'd have to pull them out later. All that mattered was getting to the Hexagon and helping where they could before the groaning building buckled fully.

"We're way past worrying about regulations, don't

you think?"

Dad flashed a wry smile at him and squared his shoulders. They took off running again and quickly reached the offensive line formed by the combined members of the Cabal and the defected soldiers.

"We heard a bang, but the Hexagon's still standing?" Laine asked, tearing off his helmet. The cold air was a welcome relief on his sweat-drenched face.

"Seems only half the explosives went off. We can't get through to Lis, but she and Cabal Team Four must have done something to stymie the worst of the damage."

"The High Consul never does anything without a contingency plan," Dad said, his eyebrows knitting together in worry.

"That's what we're afraid of. We need to get back in there and get Lis out. She's our leader, but she's a fourteen-year-old kid too. I can't leave this place with her death on my conscience, not before exhausting every option to try and save her."

"How can we help?"

The man shook his head. "'Less y'can convince the rest of the Hexagon soldiers to join our side, there's not much you or anyone can do. They keep shooting our vercycles out of the air, and no one can get closer than this without taking a blast to the head."

"But that's—" Dad's eyes were wide, and he bit at his fingers, distress turning his skin ashen. "The Hexagon's implosion will destroy those soldiers too."

"And us, if we're not clear before the rest of the detonation kicks in. I've ordered my men to hold their positions as long as we can, but we're running out of time."

"There!" Laine said, pointing to the wrecked roof. About a dozen figures had appeared, Kenton immediately identifiable by the sparking frix crackling around him. Was it Laine's imagination or did the other teen seem almost spent, the frix bubbling weakly as he and several others raced after the retreating figures of a tall man and several armed guards?

"Well, I'll be," the Cabal member said, lowering his sol in disbelief. "They must've breached the panic room."

Consul Rolv stayed one step ahead of Kenton and Bo and Annie, stopping just as he reached the edge of the roof and turning to confront his pursuers. Kenton and his companions pulled up short.

Nobody loosed any blasts or rushed the Consul, and Laine realised with a stomach-swooping drop that everyone on Kenton's side had run out of charges. The only thing that sheltered them from the deadly fire of High Consul Rolv's bodyguards was Kenton's frix. If Shadow or Bo or Annie jumped from behind the protective wall, they'd be instantly shot down, but by the way the frix had started to sputter and fade, they might not even remain safe until the building exploded—at which point they'd all be dead.

"There's really nothing we can do?" Laine shouted.

As if summoned directly by his feelings of helplessness and frustration, a dark shadow appeared in the falling snow beyond the ill-fated structure, which swayed and wobbled, ready to collapse at any moment.

No.

That was the High Consul's plan. The contingency Dad had mentioned. Laine rushed over to a discarded vercycle and examined it in case the Cabal had missed something and the twisted heap of metal could somehow be coaxed into flying. But the machine was beyond saving, even for him, and Laine slammed his fist into its dented side. Bo and Kenton and Annie—they would all die while Consul Rolv was flown safely away.

It wasn't fair. It shouldn't end like that, not after everything those three had gone through to find each other.

"Need a ride?" a familiar voice called, and Laine jerked his head up to see Asher Shyer speeding towards him, a grin spread wide on his frostbitten face. "Hop on!"

Laine did so without thinking, and they shot towards the Hexagon, looping around and under and twisting this way and that to avoid the barrage of solfire that came their way.

"I thought you were in Smoketown?"

"Sure was. Your cure worked, Laine. Jeb's gettin' better. Ma can't stop cryin', an' even Pa's crackin' the rare smile, though he worries the effects are only temp'ry. When I saw that news broadcast, I knew you'd be in the thick of it somehow, so afore it finished, I grabbed my vercycle an' pushed it to speeds no man should aim for to git here."

Asher went into another roll, and Laine clutched at him as they spun in dizzying circles, caught in the middle of the blasting solfire.

"Drat, can't shake 'em."

Another contingent of Hexagon soldiers appeared out of the smoke and snow, each piloting military-grade vercycles, their humming shields repelling the deadly shots from below. Laine stared in shocked wonder as four vercycles broke off and surrounded them, protecting him and Asher from the blasts they'd been madly dodging.

The lead vercyclist flipped up her helmet's visor to reveal the pretty features of Lachelle Michaels, who gestured at the slowly amassing vercycles behind her. They had to number at least thirty and set to work dispatching the Hexagon's ground forces.

"We're done taking orders from a system that would have had us commit genocide. I'm counting on you two to blow that retrieval craft out of the sky. Ashlyn and the others will clear the way, and I'm going to rescue Ken."

Laine grinned at her and drew his sol. Despite the size of the hulking transport approaching the Hexagon through the smoke and smog, despite the fact that the crumbling building might burst apart and engulf them all without notice, a brash confidence filled him.

"What are we waiting for? Let's go save our friends."

——————— • ———————

Standing atop a battered, burning building that might drop from underneath him at any moment while sheltering behind the exhausted frame of his traumatised best friend was most definitely not where Bo had ever imagined he'd end up on that fateful day in the Hinnom Forest when they'd overheard Laine's uncle casually plotting Tribe Osinan's destruction.

The Cabal members who'd accompanied him and Ken had dwindled to a fraction of their initial number, some caught in the traps littered along the way to the High Consul's panic room, others falling to enemy solfire. Consul Rolv wasn't much better off, his forces reduced to a mere six guards after a number of well-placed shots from Shadow. Though the fighting they'd endured had been stressful and upsetting, Bo had savoured the dread that had overtaken the High Consul when Ken had breached the doors of the panic room and forced the man to flee.

Consul Rolv had led them on a frantic chase through the winding corridors and hallways of the Hexagon's upper levels, darting through sterile meeting rooms and cramped office spaces in an attempt to lose them or at least slow their pursuit. He'd failed of course, getting only as far as the edge of the Hexagon's roof, he and his men protected solely by a shield similar to the one his cousin had wielded. Bo was glad she'd died.

Ken also had a barrier up, blocking the barrage of

solfire barrelling their way, the soldiers at Consul Rolv's side having seemingly endless charges. Ken's whole body trembled with the effort it took to keep standing, to keep drawing on what little reserves of frix he had left. They hadn't managed to get close enough to the human to snatch the kill switch from him, the man having set off the first of the explosions that would bring down the building the instant Ken had reached to burn through his shields.

Ken's chest heaved as he fought to breathe through the strain. If he kept expending frix on the shield that kept them all safe, he'd run dry in minutes. But saving himself would mean exposing them to danger, and Bo had been Ken's friend long enough to know he'd never do that. He'd rather die first, and it was grossly unfair that Ken had to choose between keeping himself or his sister and best friend alive.

Without warning, the crackling wall of frix in front of Bo fell away, and Ken dropped to his knees. White-blue sparks still jumped around him, his energy not completely exhausted, but when Bo reached for him, his skin was clammy despite the falling snow that sizzled and turned to steam when it touched him. Ken winced at each delicate flake, clenching his jaw until the muscles in it bulged.

When Bo realised the High Consul's men had stopped firing—their sols having run out of charges at long last—he sprang towards the man, but a sudden rumbling pitched him forward as the building shifted, sending everyone sprawling.

Consul Rolv recovered quickly, standing with a little help from one of his men. He held up two small devices.

"Call off your cat, 742, unless you wish your friends to die."

Kenton exchanged glances with Annie, and they both gestured for everyone to stand down.

"Now, you're going to let me fly away from here. Any of you attempts to stop me . . ." He mimed pressing the button in his hand, opening his other to mimic the building exploding.

"He's bluffing, Ken. He wouldn't blow the building before he escaped." As Annie spoke, a dark mass appeared through the smoke surrounding the Hexagon.

Bo's stomach turned over at the sight. Rescue had come, but not for them. The High Consul would flee the wreckage of Skytown and condemn them to die the instant he'd flown beyond the blast radius. Ken placed his right hand on Bo's shoulder and hauled himself up.

"Annie's right. He won't detonate the remaining charges now that salvation draws near." He patted Bo and walked towards the man, grim determination in his eyes. He covered a quarter of the distance and then halfway, the Hexagon soldiers closing rank around Consul Rolv as Ken approached.

He didn't run, the frix that swirled in weak eddies around him flickering with each halting step. He would have just enough energy to destroy the shield that still protected the High Consul but nothing after that, and the man knew it as surely as Bo did.

Annie and Shadow started after Ken, and Bo hurried to follow. If they were close enough when Ken destroyed the shield they might be able to wrestle the deadly triggers from the man before he could activate them. It probably wouldn't work, given that the High Consul and his men still outnumbered their forces, but Bo wasn't about to let him blow them up or murder Ken right in front of him without at least trying to prevent the inevitable end.

"Alright!" Consul Rolv said, lifting his hands again to display the two near-identical devices he held in each. "I'll broker a deal. Your life for mine."

He presented his open palm to Ken, the shiny black trigger sitting invitingly behind loosely curled fingers.

"How foolish would I be, to selfishly preserve myself when you still hold the means of all our destruction?"

The High Consul's face twisted into a sneer, and he withdrew his hand, tapping his gloved fingers against the second device. "Clever boy. Take the other instead, then. It's on a timer. Two minutes, and we all fall."

Before Ken could object, Consul Rolv bent and slid the detonator through the shield. He backed up a few more steps as the looming shadow behind him grew. The snow fell in thicker and thicker sheets, making it hard to see just how close the transport was.

They had to stop the High Consul before he could escape with the trigger that would kill Ken. Bo picked up his pace, confident that if the sneering human hadn't blown them all to bits yet, he certainly wouldn't while deliverance hovered so close. Bo walked, then ran, then sprang at the closest guard. He grappled with him as the others did the same, leaving Ken alone to face the man who'd murdered his family.

From the corner of his eye, Bo saw Ken reach the small device and pick it up, turning it over in his hands and trying to decide the best way to dismantle it without igniting the remaining charges that would topple the building. When he took a deep breath and closed his eyes, Bo's heart dropped. He knew what that look meant.

Ken had determined that the only way to render the trigger impotent without inadvertently activating it was to destroy it using the last dregs of his frix. Doing so would mean his immediate death at the hands of the High Consul, but it would save them all. And Kenton Oso Frix had a bad habit of sacrificing himself when weighing his life against another's.

"No!" Bo snarled, his yowl catching everyone's attention. He swiped at the soldier beneath him and knocked the man's head against the snow-slick concrete until he went limp, trying to untangle himself and get to Ken before it was too late.

Annie glanced at him and caught onto what Bo was looking at, terror transforming her face when she obviously made the same connection he had. With a strength Bo didn't know school-age human children possessed, she threw off the soldier she'd been battling and flung herself at Ken.

"Don't do it! We'll find another way!"

How could they, when their enemy had set the detonator on a countdown of which less than a minute remained?

"My life for yours, for all of yours—" Ken shook his head, the radiant smile gracing his face making him look ethereal, as if he were a being of stardust and space itself. "How could I choose otherwise?"

He sent a burst of frix into the device, and it came to pieces in his hands to the sound of Annie's aborted shriek. The soldiers Shadow and the others had managed to pin stopped struggling, eager to see their leader snuff Ken out.

Consul Rolv raised his fist into the air, his lips quirked up in a mockery of delight.

Ken dropped to one knee, his frix dying in a cascading shower of sparks until the glow faded, the air around him suddenly very dull. "I knew you wouldn't let me go, no matter what you promised," he said.

Annie clung to him and buried her head in his chest, weeping. He stroked her braids with a gentle hand, hugging her to him.

Bo walked up to the siblings and put an arm around them both. The man who was about to callously take Ken away from them forever smirked from the safety of his shield. With Ken's frix depleted, they had no way to get to him, to disarm or thwart him. They couldn't save Ken.

A giant hovercar emerged out of the smoke and

snow in a great belching of its propulsion systems, blowing slush into their faces.

"It's been lovely," Consul Rolv said, stepping to the very edge of the roof. "I'm so going to enjoy watching you die."

The door of the transport slid open, but before the man could leap into it, the hovercar lurched—struck by solfire—and he pulled back, eyes wide, searching for the source of the blasts. He wasn't given another chance to jump onto the vehicle.

A roaring vercycle shot out from behind it and flipped over, firing its mounted sol-canons. The vessel dropped from the sky, dashing the High Consul's plans of retreat and finally breaking the man's implacable expression, fury contorting his face as he stabbed at the button in his hand.

"You're that eager for your own destruction? Then let us all perish in this wretched place."

Bo clutched at Ken, but his friend kept his feet, and his breathing, harsh as it was, stayed even. The building started to shake, its rumbling throwing them off balance, and when Bo next looked at Consul Rolv's narrowed eyes, he realised what the man had done. He'd tossed Ken the master kill switch for his mechanical heart, pretending it was the detonator but holding onto the Hexagon's blast trigger the entire time. He'd just been buying time for the hovercar to reach him—but the new arrivals had disrupted his plans when they'd taken the massive aircraft out of commission.

The vercycle with its glowing sol-canons circled

back around, and its second rider yanked off his helmet. Laine locked eyes with Bo, his face a mixture of worry and relief.

"If you wanna live, jump, and jump now!"

Bo sprang forward, dragging Annie and Kenton with him. He hadn't heard it before, too focused on the prospect of losing his best friend, but the appearance of Laine and the other man who looked suspiciously like a bounty hunter alerted him to a fair number of vercycles shooting their way. A quick glance at Shadow confirmed that he'd also picked up on the humming, his ears flicking forward as he ran, trailed by the remaining Cabal members who probably thought Bo crazy but had enough faith in their leadership to follow Shadow and Annie without question.

The ground jolted beneath him as he ran, Ken and Annie on his left, Consul Rolv forgotten in their haste to gain the edge of the Hexagon's roof. Cracks split the concrete under his feet, and Bo leapt sideways over the rapidly disintegrating stone, pushing Ken in front of him, forcing him to keep running. They'd almost reached the edge when Annie stumbled in one of the gaps and rolled in front of Bo, jagged pieces of concrete ripping through her body armour.

"I got her!" Bo yelled. "Keep going!"

Ken didn't hesitate, throwing himself off the Hexagon the next instant, and without waiting for Annie to recover her breath, Bo caught her up and hurled her after her brother. He launched himself off the crumbling roof moments later, flinging out his arms and legs as he hurtled through the air.

Bo fell for a long moment, and just when the thought flashed through his mind that he'd made a terrible mistake in trusting Laine, he hit something solid that punched the breath out of him. His chest ached where doubtless he'd displaced a rib, and the vercycle he'd smacked into wobbled concerningly. Through snow-bleary eyes he could just about make out similar scenes all around him, sleek grey and white vercycles emblazoned with the Hexagon insignia—a black "H" inside a six-sided, light-blue polygon—zipping through the haze and snatching Kenton, Annie, Shadow, and the surviving members of Cabal Team Four from the air.

They didn't catch anyone else before speeding away.

The Hexagon exploded, fiery and cataclysmic. Plumes of smoke billowed out, thick bars of molten steel shooting into the air and crashing to the ground below. If the Hexagon soldiers still on the roof were screaming, Bo couldn't hear it over the screeching of metal and groaning of wood and stone, as each level collapsed one by one, the weight of the Hexagon forcing its battered body deep into a cavernous hole that greedily swallowed the walls, columns, supports, and even the foundations. Bo hoped the inferno that engulfed the wreckage would last for days, battling intermittent snowfall to scorch the land around it until nothing but cinders, rubble, and ruin remained of the cursed place.

He twisted in his seat to watch it all, hanging on

for dear life as the initial blast tossed all the vercycles forward, sending quite a few of the lightweight transports spinning through the air, reminding Bo of his and Laine's terrifying descent from the Kansor Mountains. But unlike that harrowing experience, his current means of escape had thrusters its pilot used to correct their heading and increase their velocity as they desperately sought to escape the blazing building retching ash and smoke. The heat of it blew Bo's fur back, and he shielded his face so as not to break his promise to Laine about his whiskers.

The smoke didn't clear for a long, long time, the journey away from the explosion's epicentre seeming to stretch on for an age, and Bo came close to fainting, having inhaled dangerous amounts of the toxic smog swirling through the air, but finally they touched down on the outskirts of Skytown.

Everyone was coughing, bruises and soot mottling their faces and clothes, but they were all alive. Lachelle Michaels lifted a drooping Ken off her vercycle and laid him on the ground before pulling a portable ventilator out of her pack and attaching a mask to Ken's pale face.

Bo nodded his thanks at the rider who'd caught him as she removed her helmet—showing herself to be Lachelle Michaels' redheaded friend—and made his way on unsteady legs towards Ken, wondering that they'd survived.

They'd won. They'd won, and everyone had escaped from the rooftop with their lives. Everyone on their side at least. Consul Rolv hadn't made it off the

Hexagon as far as Bo had been able to tell—doubt-less, Annie would send some of her people to confirm it once the fires died down.

But that wasn't Bo's concern at that moment. He pushed his way through the crowd gathered around the settling vercycles and knelt beside Ken, catching his hand in a firm grasp as Ken cracked open puffy eyes. He struggled to breathe and fought against the machine pumping clean oxygen into him before see-ing Bo properly and calming.

The sun broke through the clouds at that moment and shone on Ken's face, his matted, snow laden hair glistening in the mid-morning light. He tried a few times to speak before regaining control of his voice. Annie came up and held his other hand in the mean-time, brushing tiny flakes away from his cheeks. He stared at her and then Bo with wide eyes, the blue of them reflecting the bright sky above.

"I don't remember . . . after I jumped. Is this . . . Did we make it?"

Bo's grin of savage joy was answer enough.

CODA

Five years. Laine still couldn't quite wrap his head around it.

From Ethaba High dropout to lauded Smoketown College graduate. He'd returned to school after the excitement across Thorunn had started to die down, thrown himself into his studies, and made it into higher education on a lacrosse scholarship. He'd gotten quite a shock that first day when his new roommate had turned out to be Bo.

He probably should have expected it, given how tirelessly Annie and Shadow had worked after the fall of the Consul to restore order to a post-Hexagon Thorunn. The members of the Consul who'd survived had been rounded up and justice meted upon them and others elected to fill the twelve empty seats the traitors had left behind.

Shadow headed the new Free Thorunn Consul now, surrounded by the most capable men and women from across Thorunn, including Commander Woodley—who'd promoted Jenna to her old rank before leaving New Little Rock—and a few klia'ans from Tribe Osinan. Bo's attendance at the college was a natural outcome of the work the new Consul had done to improve human-klia'an relations, and he hadn't been the only klia'an to live on campus—though he had been the first.

Their five years at school together had resulted in some . . . tumultuous times, but Laine couldn't imagine it any other way, and tomorrow they were to embark upon the first joint human-klia'an expedition to explore and map the lands beyond the mountains, an endeavour made possible by a marriage of human and klia'an tech and financed by the *Alanna Jane Riven Foundation*. Hopefully they wouldn't run into any of the bounty hunters who'd managed to escape from Skytown and might still hold a grudge.

Yoon Ah—her appetite for investigation somehow whetted instead of extinguished by her awful ordeal in Ethaba's tunnels so long ago—had convinced her advisor to let her join the undertaking and have it count for a semester's worth of college credits towards her degree in field forensics.

Andy was understandably worried but supportive, having gone on to work in the ESReC after high school—coordinating his efforts with the Free Thorunn Consul—and coaching lacrosse on the side. Principal Kim had been very generous to Andy and had taken him in after his parents had been arrested and tried for their part in the whole messy affair.

The baby rheas maximus they'd found so long ago had been still clinging to life, but barely, when former Cabal members had carted Doctor Frenally away, and it had been requisitioned immediately by the rheas maximus research team in New Little Rock. The tenacious bird had eventually recovered and lived a happy life far away from the depressing prison of Doctor Frenally's nefarious lab. Though the scientist and his wife had been changed people after their release, Andy never moved back in with them, instead electing to start planning a future with Yoon Ah, to which Principal Kim had happily given his blessing.

As Laine stood on stage and waited for his turn at the microphone—the tube that didn't yet hold his diploma smooth in his hands—he caught sight of Dad in the crowd. He lifted one hand in a subtle wave, which Dad acknowledged with a small grin and a dip of his head.

Learning to live without Mom had almost broken them, but the path to forgiveness and healing that Laine had discovered in the middle of the worst year of his life had seen them through the dark times. Laine's hand went to his throat, a habit of his when thinking about Mom. Her necklace—painstakingly repaired and restored—rested there, his constant companion through every hardship. Its slight weight made tears sting his eyes, but he couldn't imagine going a day without wearing the bright beads she'd carefully chosen and crafted once upon a time on the banks of the Pamunkey River.

I've got so much to show you, Mom, Laine thought, shuffling forward once his name was called. *I know, somehow, you can see this.*

After the commencement ceremony, he planned to go home long enough to hang his cap and gown at her grave—a simple headstone set underneath an arch of trailing liphiz blossoms. Peter had helped erect the memorial and been understanding and gracious when Laine had profusely apologised for how he'd treated the nurse.

Ethaba held many painful memories, and Laine was more than ready to leave them all behind for what promised to be one crazy year. If he and Bo had managed to hack it through the Thorunn wilderness with two sols, a quirn, a lacrosse stick, and the barest semblance of a plan, they could certainly do it again with a properly outfitted and equipped team—which also included Dustin, who'd done his best to help Laine catch up after returning to Ethaba High in the middle of his junior year. Suffice to say, Laine had seen Dustin in a different and far more appreciative light since.

Laine shuffled through the notes on his clip for the hundredth time and stepped up to the podium.

"I'm supposed to give some sort of inspiring speech," he said. "To encourage you all to go out there and make the most of your lives. I could go on about my accomplishments, but I know you're sick of seeing my face and ready to never hear the name Laine Riven again."

A titter ran through the crowd, and some of Laine's college friends let out loud whoops and amiably heckled him at that. He waited until the laughter died down, his expression turning serious.

"Instead, I want to talk about who inspires me. Who never gave up, who never hesitated to throw themselves into peril to save others. I want to share a story I've never told before about the heroes of

Thorunn." He paused and winked at Bo, who rolled his eyes and tugged his graduation cap down to cover his face when their classmates predictably turned to look at him. "About my friends, Bo of Tribe Osinan and Kenton 'Oso Frix' Wishings."

———————————— ● ————————————

It always seemed to be the middle of the night when the half-formed images and memories swirling around Kenton's mind woke him. He sat up and rubbed at weary eyes, knowing he wouldn't be able to quiet his thoughts enough to lie back down for a little while. The spinner-floss curtains shifted, allowing his next-door neighbour to enter on bare feet. He'd expected Seri, but Lachelle—who'd been sharing his adopted sister's room during her ambassadorial visit—entered instead, a borrowed spinner-floss robe draped about her.

"Bad dreams?"

"Always."

Lachelle laid one soft, warm hand on his arm and rubbed it in a soothing manner.

"Why don't we go visit the memorial?"

Kenton nodded and slipped out of his hammock before pulling on his boots and fetching his quirn.

"Want I should wake Annie?"

Kenton shook his head. "She's got a big day tomorrow, what with Laine coming back to Ethaba and all. Just wish he hadn't poached my best friend from me."

Lachelle laughed, the light lilting sound prompting a chuckle of his own.

"You ever wish you were going with them?" she asked after they'd climbed onto Kenton's blue and white vercycle. They left the thickly clustered hinnom trees and headed to the Apollo XXII commemoration site set halfway between the forest and Ethaba.

"I've had enough excitement to last me several lifetimes." Kenton put his hand on his chest, where his artificial heart still pulsed steadily. "I'm not going to waste this second chance with Annie. But what about you? Still no regrets about taking the position of official liaison between humans and klia'ans, the ones this side of the sea at least?"

"Someone had to, since you wouldn't. Besides, it gives me an excuse to visit my favourite person."

Joy stole bright into Kenton's heart at Lachelle's words, and he couldn't quite hold back his grin. He was still smiling when they reached the modest cemetery constructed in memory of his parents and the other Apollo XXII colonists, their bodies finally laid to rest in a quiet place far removed from the scene of their deaths.

"Umama, Pa." Kenton knelt before their memorial markers and traced the inscriptions he and Annie had engraved in the square stones.

"It's been almost twenty years, but your dream of a peaceful and united Thorunn is coming to fruition at last. I only wish you could be here to see it."

Lachelle knelt next to him and laid her head on his shoulder, rubbing comforting circles on his back. They stayed like that until daybreak, whereupon

Lachelle stood and helped Kenton to his feet.

He trailed his hands over the stones one last time.

"May you sleep in peace," he whispered.

Then he and Lachelle started back towards the forest that would forever be Kenton's home, disappearing into the early morning mists as the sun began to rise.

GLOSSARY

Anlo — A pack animal that roams the Cerado. Has features in common with buffalo and triceratops.

Bowman's Disease (Raxilsish) — A terminal illness with no known origin. Symptom include: tiredness, fever (in children), headaches, easy bruising, dehydration. Slowly liquefies a patient's bones until their body collapses.

Cabal — A resistance group formed to oppose the Consul.

Cerado — Thorunn's Serengeti. Based loosely off the nonfictional Brazilian Cerrado.

Chishish Tree — A type of tree that grows in the Hinnom forest. Its wood is extremely sturdy and is often used in place of metal by klia'ans.

Chsaa-rhee (Rheas Maximus) — Giant pterodactyl-like animals. Intelligent and savage.

Clips — All-purpose communication devices worn on the ear. They have a small digital display but can project a much larger holographic screen.

Crosse — A shorter, alternate way to say "lacrosse stick."

Edda-net — Thorunn's intranet.

ESReC — Ethaba Scientific Research Centre.

Ethaba — A town between the spaceport and the Hinnom Forest.

Étot — A silvery fruit similar in taste to an Asian pear. Thrives in very cold temperatures.

Fenrir Virus — Carried by and contracted from giant, furry mosquito-like insects colloquially termed "wolf 'squeeters." Causes fever and vomiting, and attacks the body in a manner not unlike leprosy, eating away at extremities if not immediately treated. Named after the giant wolf that bit off Tyr's hand in Norse mythology.

Frey and Freja — Thorunn's twin moons.

Frix — Specifically the static-acidic drops that fall with the rainstorms during first and second frix, but widely used as a catch-all term for any type of electricity on Thorunn.

Gira'an — A large, flightless bird, similar to a Roc, that lives on the slopes of Mount Lalethusl. Mostly inactive during winter.

Hexagon — The most important building in Skytown. Six-sided, it houses the government, the Tomb, prisoners, labs, and the military.

Hinnom Trees — The sap of these trees can negate frix's destructive properties when properly processed. Skytown is willing to do anything to acquire this resource.

Holoscreen — Any holographic screen. Can be on a tablet or projected into the air.

Igis — A gauntlet marking passage into adulthood.

Innah — The title of Tribe Osinan's clan leader.

Kansor Mountains — A mountain range overlooking New Little Rock. Home to a large chsaa-rhee roost.

Kitterstone — A crystalline red stone that is a vital component of the klia'an cure to Bowman's disease.

Klia'an — Native name of the shifter people of Thorunn. Also the name of their language and their humanoid form.

Lanae — Klia'an name for one of Thorunn's twin moons. Also used as a mild expletive.

Lanaekim — Klia'an name for Thorunn's other moon. Also a princess in Klia'an myth.

Likshish — An animal similar to a rock Hyrax.

Liphiz Blossoms — A type of flower found in the Hinnom Forest that is used to aid healing.

Lokians — The human term for klia'ans. Sourced from the trickster god of Norse mythology.

Lytorade — An electrolyte-based sports drink that is popular on Thorunn.

Mishipeshu — A Native American mythological panther.

Mount Lalethusl — The mountain atop which Skytown was built.

Nano-diffuser — A medical machine for advanced healing. Human tech.

Narprolepscene — A very powerful opioid-based drug. Its use is banned on Earth and is severely restricted on Thorunn. The only medicine proven to be effective against the intense pain Bowman's disease causes.

Onite — A mineral used as a gold substitute both in jewellery and electronics.

Orquídeas — A street gang Laine was mixed up in back on Earth.

Osteomalacia and Hypophosphatasia — Two degenerative bone diseases.

Pamunkey — A Native American tribe from the state of Virginia. Also a river.

P'rraa — Klia'an word for "father."

Quirn — A bo staff-like weapon that stores and releases frix. Can be rigid or collapsible.

Regen-rig — A medical machine for advanced healing. Klia'an tech.

S'hinoian — Klia'an feloid form. Also the name of the language spoken when in that form.

Skreet — A scavenger reptilian-type animal.

Slyr — A special klia'an shield reserved for young klia'ans who perform exceptionally well during Igis.

Sól — Thorunn's sun.

Sol — A solar powered laser gun similar to a phaser.

Sol-cannon — A very large, powerful sol.

Solfire — The discharge from a sol or sol-cannon. Power ranges from stunning to lethal.

Spinners — Giant spiders that live in the Hinnom Forest. Their silk is used by klia'ans to create a variety of cloths and many types of garments.

Task Force: Mars — An old procedural cop show set on Mars that runs on repeat on one of Thorunn's limited selection of entertainment channels.

TCBNN — Thorunn Crystal Broadcast News Network.

The Tomb — An underground stadium similar in look and function to the Colosseum.

Tribe Anshi — An (almost) extinct klia'an tribe that lived on Mount Lalethusl. They mined onite from within the mountain and tended the étot orchards that grew on its slopes.

Tribe Osinan — A klia'an tribe living in the Hinnom Forest.

Umama — South African word for "mother."

Vana'byss — A type of amphibious reptilian creature with vanishing abilities.

Vercycle — A floating motorcycle; the primary form of transport on Thorunn.

Vyss'ngryr — A large, velociraptor-like animal with an almost impenetrable hide.

ESTHER T. JONES has been writing stories in her head since she was five. She loves wandering the wilds of rural America—where she's dreamed up many a story. When not writing, Jones can be found gardening, playing flute and piano, and designing costumes centered around her novels.

At present Jones is working on several stand-alone young adult novels as well as a multi-book series set in a distant and mysterious era.

———— • ————

Find @etjwrites on www.etjwrites.com, instagram,
or twitter for updates on new books and appearances.
Your thoughtful review is much appreciated.